George Oliver

The History of the City of Exeter

George Oliver

The History of the City of Exeter

Reprint of the original, first published in 1861.

1st Edition 2022 | ISBN: 978-3-37505-757-2

Verlag (Publisher): Salzwasser Verlag GmbH, Zeilweg 44, 60439 Frankfurt, Deutschland
Vertretungsberechtigt (Authorized to represent): E. Roepke, Zeilweg 44, 60439 Frankfurt, Deutschland
Druck (Print): Books on Demand GmbH, In de Tarpen 42, 22848 Norderstedt, Deutschland

THE HISTORY

OF THE

CITY OF EXETER.

a

THE HISTORY

OF THE

CITY OF EXETER.

BY THE

REV. GEORGE OLIVER, D.D.

WITH A SHORT MEMOIR OF THE AUTHOR,

AND

AN APPENDIX OF DOCUMENTS AND ILLUSTRATIONS.

EXETER:

WILLIAM ROBERTS, BROADGATE.

LONDON: LONGMAN, GREEN, LONGMAN, AND ROBERTS.

1861.

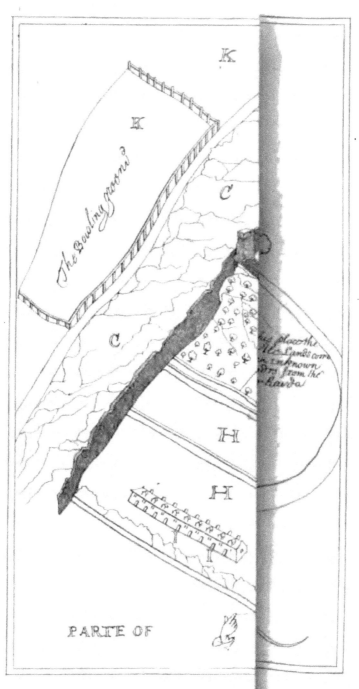

A. The old draw-bridge over the ditch.
B. The Assizes & Sessions house built about 1624.
C. The outer ditch of the Castle
D. The inner Castle ditch converted into Gardens.
E. A Garden.

CONTENTS.

Page

PREFATORY NOTICE AND MEMOIR OF THE AUTHOR xi

CHAPTER I.

Exeter under the Britons and Romans 1

CHAPTER II.

The fruits and effects of Christianity on the Pagan Britons — Their consentient faith with the Christian churches of the Continent — The subjugation of our island by the Saxons, Jutes, and Angles — The happy conversion of these new settlers to the Catholic Church .. 4

CHAPTER III.

Exeter besieged by Penda, King of Mercia, in 633, but effectually relieved by the British King, Cadwalinus. Submits to the sovereigns of Wessex 12

CHAPTER IV.

Exeter besieged by Sweyn, King of Denmark — Its gallant and successful resistance — Infamous policy of King Ethelred — Sweyn returns to invest the city, which, through the treason of its Governor, falls into his hands on the 19th of August, 1003, and is demolished — Canute, the son of Sweyn, succeeds to the sovereignty of England .. 18

CHAPTER V.

The influence of religion on the heart and government of Canute — His special favour to Exeter — The restoration of the Saxon line in the person of Edward the Confessor — Prosperity of this city, and the removal of the See to it from Crediton 22

CHAPTER VI.

Harold, son of Earl Godwin and brother of Queen Editha, assumes the reins of Government, with the good will of the nation, but loses the crown with his life at the battle of Hastings — William, Duke of Normandy, is declared King of England — Exeter, opposed to his sovereignty, submits after a siege of eighteen days — To overawe the spirit of insurrection, the citadel or castle is rebuilt — The Domesday — Foundation by the Conqueror of St. Nicholas's Benedictine Priory — The King's death at Rouen — Strange event at his funeral in St. Stephen's Church at Caën 29

vi CONTENTS.

CHAPTER VII.

Page

Henry I. befriends Exeter — Bishop William Warelwast rebuilds its cathedral — The prevalence of Simony in the middle ages — The fatal shipwreck of the heir to the Crown — Charter of King Stephen — Siege of Exeter — Accession of King Henry II.   35

CHAPTER VIII.

Bright prospects of Henry Plantagenet at his accession — State of the contest on the rights of the Church between the King and the Primate, Thomas à Becket — The conduct of our townsman, Bishop Bartholomew, in that controversy   44

CHAPTER IX.

Reigns of Richard Cœur de Lion and John — The Crusades, the Interdict, and the subjugation to Papal Domination — Queen Berengaria — Extraordinary floods in England   49

CHAPTER X.

Henry III. succeeds to the English crown, and grants to his brother Richard the Earldom of Cornwall, to which he attaches the city of Exeter with its castle — This new Earl elected King of the Romans — The history of Exeter Bridge   54

CHAPTER XI.

Accession of Edward I. — The first Prince of Wales — Character of the King — Death of the Lord-Paramount — Privileges of the City — Question of the murder of Walter de Lechlade — Parliament held in Exeter — The King's grant of a new Seal to the City — Great Diocesan Council of Exeter   61

CHAPTER XII.

Accession of Edward II.—Recall of Piers Gaveston — Edward the Black Prince Lord-Paramount — Captivity of John, King of France — The Black Pestilence; its disastrous effects on Exeter — Bishop Grandisson. His recognition of the distinction between the ecclesiastical and civil powers   71

CHAPTER XIII.

Reign of Richard II. — Exhausted exchequer — Insurrection against the capitation tax — Energy of the King — His subsequent misgovernment and deposition — Accession of Henry V. — John Wickliffe — The Lollards   75

CONTENTS.

vii

CHAPTER XIV.

Page

Henry VI. — His reception at Exeter — Civil war — Edward IV. assumes the crown — Visit to this city — Death of the King — Usurpation of Richard III. — Murder of the Princes in the Tower — The King killed at Bosworth Field — Perkin Warbeck repulsed at Exeter — His surrender at Taunton, and imprisonment in this city — Henry VII. at Exeter — Royal charters — Visit of Princess Catherine — Marriage with Prince Arthur, and subsequently with Henry VIII. — Progress of literature — Degeneracy of morals 79

CHAPTER XV.

Prosperous state of the nation at the accession of Henry VIII. — The woollen trade of Exeter — Extravagance of the King — Embarassed state of the exchequer — Appeal to parliament for pecuniary aid — Resistance to the proposal of a property-tax — Bridgeman the member for the city — Thomas Cromwell's influence with the King — Degradation of parliament — Oppressive taxation 90

CHAPTER XVI.

Accession of Edward VI. — Changes in the tenure of land — State of the poor — Prayer-book of King Edward VI. — Resistance to its introduction — Siege of Exeter — Loyalty and fidelity of its inhabitants — Death of the King — The Lady Jane Grey — Queen Mary — Her marriage with Philip of Spain — Royal letter to the citizens of Exeter — Age of religious persecution — Its inconsistency with the spirit of Christianity 96

CHAPTER XVII.

Elizabeth's persecution of the Catholics — Charters of the city confirmed — Loyalty of Exeter — Title of " Semper fidelis" conferred — Elizabeth's encouragement of commerce — First Act for the relief of the poor — Accession of James I. — His predilection for the Scotch — Parliamentary control over the Royal prerogative — Charles I. — Coronation repeated at Edinburgh — Plague of 1625 — Spread of disaffection — Intolerance towards the Catholics — Their adoption of the King's cause — Parliamentary party at Exeter — Capitulation to Prince Maurice — The Queen, a refugee at Exeter, gives birth to the Princess Henrietta — She embarks at Falmouth — Visit of the King to Exeter — The city surrenders to Fairfax — Puritan desecration of the churches — State prisoners and executions at Exeter — Barbary pirates on the west coast 105

CONTENTS.

CHAPTER XVIII.

Page

Protectorate of Cromwell — His son Richard proclaimed his successor — Death of Richard near Winchester — Connection of General Monk, the restorer of monarchy, with Exeter — Charles II. recalled by the new Parliament — Rejoicings at his proclamation in Exeter — Visit of the Grand Duke of Tuscany to the city — Stay of the King at Exeter on his route to London — Character of his reign — His demand for the surrender of civic charters .. .. ,. 130

CHAPTER XIX.

James II. — His character — Rebellion of the Duke of Argyle — Landing of Monmouth at Lyme Regis — His defeat at Sedgmoor and subsequent execution — Judge Jeffreys and the " Bloody Assize"— National discontent with James's rule — Birth of a prince royal — Landing of William Prince of Orange at Torbay — His reception at Exeter and progress to London ◆ Abdication of the King 139

CHAPTER XX.

The Revolution — Character of the reign of William III. — Former neglect of sanatory measures in Exeter — Provisions for lighting the city — Preservation of the peace — Supply of water — The Workhouse — Pictures contained in its Board-room 146

CHAPTER XXI.

Observations on some of the Churches in Exeter 153

CHAPTER XXII.

Devon and Exeter Hospital — Labours of Dr. Alured Clarke to secure its establishment—Opened January 1st, 1743—Portraits in the Boardroom — The County and City Prisons — Cemeteries — Avenues and approaches of the city — Bridge over the Exe — Markets — General advantages of the city — Extensive nature of the physical and moral improvements effected 161

CONTENTS. ix

PART II.

CHAPTER I.

HISTORY OF THE CASTLE OF EXETER 179

CHAPTER II.

THE ANCIENT PREBENDAL CHURCH within the Castle of Exeter 193

List of Prebendaries of Hayes 199
      ,,   ,,   Cutton 200
      ,,   ,,   Carswell 203
      ,,   ,,   Ashclist 204

CHAPTER III.

DESCRIPTION OF THE GUILDHALL 205
     Armorial Bearings 208
     Portraits 214
     City Swords and Cap of Maintenance 222
     City Seals 224

CHAPTER IV.

List of Mayors 226
     ,,   Recorders 235
     ,,   Sheriffs 237
     ,,   Town Clerks 241
     ,,   Chamberlains 242
     ,,   Swordbearers 243

CHAPTER V.

REPRESENTATIVES OF EXETER IN PARLIAMENT 245

CHAPTER VI.

HISTORY OF THE HAVEN OR CANAL OF EXETER 249

APPENDIX

OF

DOCUMENTS AND ILLUSTRATIONS.

Page

I.—Chronological Table of ACTS OF PARLIAMENT relating to the COUNTY and CITY of EXETER, and the DEVON and COUNTY PRISONS situated at Exeter 269

II.—Table showing the Date of Commencement of the CATHEDRAL and PAROCHIAL REGISTERS of EXETER and its suburbs.. .. 277

III.—Chronological Table of CHARTERS of the CITY of EXETER.. .. 278
CHARTER OF KING CHARLES I. to the City of Exeter 289

IV.—COURT ROLLS and ACCOUNT ROLLS of EXETER 305
Abstract of the Roll of the Curia Civitatis 26, 27 Ed. III. .. 312
Abstract of the Compotus Civitatis 42, 43 Ed. III. 319

V.—Extracts from the EXETER DOMESDAY relating to the City .. 323
Observations on the Extracts 325

PREFATORY NOTICE

AND

MEMOIR OF THE AUTHOR.

THE Author of the 'Lives of the Bishops of Exeter' did not long survive the publication of that work. He left behind him, in a state fit for publication, a Civil History of the City of Exeter; but had, unfortunately, made very little progress in preparing any documentary Appendix of the nature of that which has given great value to the ecclesiastical portion of his History.

It is with a view to supply this deficiency (at least to some small extent), as well as to correct any oversight that might occur in the text itself, that the writer of this notice has undertaken to assist in carrying the present work through the press.

The late lamented Author enjoyed the confidence both of the Municipal and the Ecclesiastical authorities of this city, and might doubtless have obtained access to the important and valuable records of the city as easily as to the registry of the diocese; but it is to be regretted that he availed himself only very partially of this facility in respect of the former class of documents. Hence the rise and progress, the fate and fortunes, of the municipal organization and internal history of Exeter must await the researches of some future historian. Meantime the present work is cer-

PREFATORY NOTICE.

tainly in every respect superior to the History published by the Author in 1821, especially in the second part, which has been wholly recast, and contains much valuable information.

The writer of this prefatory notice does not profess to coincide entirely with all the views of the learned Author. He leaves them, untouched, to the critical judgment of the reader; but he can bear testimony, from personal knowledge, to the great diligence, candour, and love of truth which distinguished him, and the readiness with which he was wont to impart the stores of his extensive local researches and his tenacious memory for the benefit of his numerous friends, and even of those who had no other passport to his assistance than their desire of information or the gratification of literary curiosity. On more than one occasion Dr. Oliver had the good fortune to render important aid in the conduct of genealogical and judicial inquiries.

Of his printed works, those which are best known, and on which his literary character must mainly depend, are his Parochial Antiquities of the Diocese, of which part only has been yet published; his 'Lives of the Bishops of Exeter;' and, above all, his 'Monasticon of the Diocese of Exeter,' which must ever be regarded as a repertory of information, for which Dugdale's well known work, even in its latest and most enlarged form, will be searched in vain. For this purpose, the registers and records of the cathedral were opened to him by the liberality of the officers of the Bishop and Chapter; and by these, as well as by the friendly aid of Lord Arundel of Wardour, and of other gentlemen, whose family muniments were made

PREFATORY NOTICE.

accessible to him, or whose official or other sources of information were made available on his behalf, he was enabled very largely to extend the scanty collection of Dugdale so far as relates to the Western diocese. It is much to be wished that his parochial collections, many of which are still extant only in unavowed communications to local journals, may hereafter be published in a more permanent and methodical form.

Of Dr. Oliver's family and personal biography, it is believed that little was known in his lifetime even to his most intimate friends. On such topics he was not usually communicative. He was born of respectable parents; of whom his father was a native of Scotland and a Presbyterian, and his mother a native of Sligo and a Roman Catholic. She survived her husband many years, and had the charge and education of her four children. The Author, who was the eldest, was born at Newington, Surrey, on the 9th of February, 1781, and was educated at Sedgeley Park and Stonyhurst, where he is said to have acquitted himself with credit. In 1806, he was admitted to holy orders by Dr. Gibson, titular Bishop of Acanthus, and in the following year was appointed to the Exeter mission, where he arrived in October of that year. He was not, as some have supposed, a member of the "Society of Jesus."

From that time until his death in the month of March of the present year, he was continually resident, with few and short intervals, in this city, where he obtained the general respect and regard of his fellow citizens of all professions and conditions. In 1844, the degree of Doctor of Divinity was conferred on him by

PREFATORY NOTICE.

the late Pope Gregory XVI. He left an unmarried sister, his nearest surviving relative and one of his legatees, who is still living, but is unhappily afflicted with hopeless blindness.

Dr. Oliver was an earnest and honest adherent of the tenets of his own Church, and it would be idle to deny that his partialities are very perceptible in his narrative of political events so far as they are connected with the ecclesiastical or secular history of Exeter. But his private intercourse and literary correspondence were free from any tincture of asperity or intolerance.

The writer of this brief notice is glad to have this opportunity of recording the sentiments of esteem and respect with which he regarded him during an uninterrupted friendship of more than thirty years.

He wishes to repeat here, what is stated hereafter, that the reader must consider himself much indebted to the aid and assistance of the writer's friend, Mr. John Gidley, for supplying the materials for the documentary Appendix.

EDWARD SMIRKE.

August, 1861.

HISTORY

OF

THE CITY OF EXETER.

CHAPTER I.

Exeter under the Britons and Romans.

WITHOUT recurring to unauthenticated legends and traditions of Trojan founders and governors of Exeter, we may safely pronounce that its beautiful and commanding elevation—its rapid and navigable river, fed by so many tributary streams—the salubrity of its atmosphere, and the fertility of the surrounding country, must have invited and attracted the native Britons to establish a settlement here at a very early period. By them, as we learn from Asserius (de Rebus Gestis Aelfridi), it was called *Cairwich* [or *Caerisk*], the City of Waters.

The Romans, as their conquest of the island progressed in this direction, would naturally wish to profit by the same local advantages. Whether there is sufficient authority in the Chronicon of the Church of Exeter for the assertion that in the year 49 of the Christian æra, Vespasian, the Roman general, besieged this British city for eight days, when it was relieved by King Arviragus (by some supposed to be Caractacus), may be fairly questioned. " Anno dñi xlviiij. Vespasianus, cum exercitu Romano, civitatem Exoniensem octo diebus obsedit, et minimè prævaleret, Arvirago Rege civibus præstante auxilium." We have the authority of Eutropius, that the Emperor Claudius,

B

2

HISTORY OF EXETER.

the fifth Cæsar, sent Vespasian into Britain, where he fought thirty-two battles, and subjected two very powerful tribes, twenty towns, and the adjoining Isle of Wight to the Roman empire. That it gradually and eventually yielded submission to that persevering and belligerent nation, cannot admit of contradiction. A Roman encampment was formed in the very heart of our city; tesselated pavements have been discovered, even in our days, across the upper part of South Street, and in the inclosure on the North side of the Cathedral. Penates have been found near the old Broadgate; baths near the upper market; besides innumerable Roman coins,[1] ancient pottery, and several sepulchral urns. For the better protection of their conquest, a summer camp was also erected on Stoke Hill. Whilst subject to the Roman authorities, the arts of industry and civilization would be fostered; agriculture would be encouraged and rewarded; commercial enterprise would be promoted and patronized. In a poem quoted by Henry of Huntingdon, our city is described as famed for the exportation of metals, "Excestria clara metallis."

But empires, like individuals, have their limited periods of existence and prosperity. All must be subject to the common mutability of earthly things, and alike experience the vicissitudes of the times. Distracted with intestine divisions, invaded on every side by hosts

---

[1] Westcote, in his 'View of Devon,' completed in 1630, relates that "some eight years since two or three labourers making a dike to fence a plot of ground, a small way distant from the Castle of Exeter, where no dike was in former times, found certain bricks three feet deep in the earth, and under them a little pot of the same matter, wherein were divers pieces of Roman coins, both silver and gold. The youngest of time was Antoninus Pius. Thirty came to my hands, most of them of divers stamp, and fair. Somewhat nearer the Castle there was found in the garden a fair ring, in which was a beautiful stone set, and thereon engraved the true idea of Cleopatra, with the asp at her breast." Stukeley, in his 'Itinerary' (1724), mentions "two pecks of coins lately dug up near St. Martin's Church, and a great Roman pavement of white square stones behind the Guildhall." See Dean Milles' Report of Discoveries near Broadgate, in 1778, in vol. vi. of the Archæologia; also Shortt's Sylva Antiqua Iscana. Dr. Bennet has shown distinctly that our Isca was one of the Roman military stations in Britain.

ADVENT OF THE SAXONS.

of barbarians, the overgrown empire of Rome was tottering to its ruin, and hastening to complete its destiny :

"Suis et ipsa Roma viribus ruit."

By an unwise policy, her governors here, especially Maximus[2] (who had been proclaimed emperor by the troops, and, crossing over to Gaul, made Treves the seat of his empire), had drained the island of its warlike youth to fight the battles of the Eastern and the Western empires ; and the actual storming of Rome by the Goths compelled the Cæsars to withdraw the veteran[3] legions from Britain. The Saxon Chronicle says, that " in the year 418 the Romans collected all their hoards of treasure in the island, and some they hid in the ground" (no doubt with the hope of eventually returning to resume possession), " and some they carried with them into Gaul." To the same purpose Ethelwerd says " Scrobibus occultant thesaurum." Lib. 1, Chronic. The defenceless population of Britain lay then exposed to the merciless irruptions and depredations of the Picts and Scots. In their excess of misery the Britons are said to have supplicated their former masters to afford them adequate protection ; but in vain. Driven finally to despair, embroiled in civil discord, and suffering from famine and pestilence, their proud tyrant, as Gildas describes their sovereign Vortigern, with his infatuated council, sent an invitation to the two Saxon buccaneers Hengist and Horsa to become their auxiliaries. They readily accepted the offer, and, as the Saxon Chronicle relates, at first they slew or expelled those northern invaders ; but " in the sequel turned their arms against their employers, and destroyed them also by fire and the edge of the sword." Flushed with

---

[2] This perfidious tyrant, after reigning about five years, was defeated by Theodosius, and beheaded on the 28th of July, A.D. 388.

[3] It is generally believed that there were never more than four Roman legions in the island, besides auxiliaries, viz., the 2nd, called " Legio Augusta," the 9th, the 14th, subsequently relieved by the 6th, and the 20th, "Vicesima victrix."

4   HISTORY OF EXETER.

victory, these daring chieftains urged their countrymen,
the Jutes and Angles, to come and share their good
fortune and form settlements in the island. Reinforced
by these hosts of marauders, within a century and a
half the whole of the country, with the exception of
Wales, and, as Dr. Lingard observes (Hist. of England,
vol. i. p. 233), of the tract of land from the Land's
End to the River Exe, and one-half of Exeter, fell
under their domination. Their exterminating policy
.drove a considerable portion of the aborigines along
our western shores to the opposite maritime coast of
Armorica, which, from such colonization, obtained the
name of Britannia Minor, or Brittany. Bishop Grandisson in his Register, vol. i. fol. 27, A.D. 1328, adverts
to the identity of the languages of these colonists and
of Cornwall : "Minor Britannia, cujus linguâ ipsi utun-
tur Cornubici."

CHAPTER II.

The fruits and effects of Christianity on the Pagan Britons — Their consentient
faith with the Christian churches of the Continent — The subjugation of our
island by the Saxons, Jutes, and Angles — The happy conversion of these
new settlers to the Catholic Church.

CHRISTIANITY is the parent of innumerable blessings
to the human race. It softens and refines the manners,
imposes a curb on the passions, purifies and regulates
the affections, excludes selfish feelings, exerts a favourable influence on the useful and ornamental arts,
respects and honours and dignifies the female sex,
encourages the decencies, proprieties, and charities of
domestic and social life, and improves the condition
of every rank in the commonwealth. It teaches the
poor to be contented with their present lowly state, to
submit from conscientious principles to the constituted

INTRODUCTION OF CHRISTIANITY.

authorities, and to approve themselves as useful and exemplary members of the community; whilst it admonishes the great and the opulent to be meek and humble of heart—moving in the perpetual presence of the same Creator and future Judge; and to regard themselves, not so much as the proprietors of their wealth and superiority, as His trustees and stewards for the benefit of others—as the very almoners of the Deity for the relief, comfort, and protection of their less-favoured fellow creatures. The truth of these reflections is illustrated in the case of the Britons, the original population of this island. Their manners and social habits were barbarous and revolting in the extreme. Their Druidical worship was a melancholy compound of absurdity and of cruelty, tinctured, it seems, by a Pythagorean belief in the transmigration of souls. But when the light of Christian faith beamed on this benighted people, a marvellous change of ideas, habits, and manners succeeded amongst them.

In the investigation of this extraordinary revolution, the historian must ever bear in mind that his province is not to invent, but to relate events; that, whilst matters of opinion may admit of desultory or speculative essays, matters of fact must be delivered with great integrity and judgment. It is reasonable then to infer from the constant intercourse between Rome, the seat of empire, and Britain, that the knowledge of the Christian faith was introduced into this province in the earliest times; though, at this distant period, it is utterly impossible to ascertain the names of the first heralds of the Gospel. Gildas, the British monk, who wrote in 560, laments the absence in his time of all national records, adding that, if such had ever existed, they must have perished in hostile conflagrations, or been conveyed out of the country by exiled citizens,—" si qua fuerint, aut ignibus

HISTORY OF EXETER.

hostium exusta, aut civium exilii classe longius deportata, non compareant."[1]

St. Paul congratulates the Romans (i. 8) that "their faith was spoken of throughout the whole world." During the reign of the Emperor Claudius, Pomponia Græcina, a native of Britain and the wife of the proconsul Aulus Plautius, had embraced Christianity, or, as Tacitus describes her, was "superstitionis externæ rea." Claudia Rufina is mentioned as a Briton by Martial, and with her husband Pudens, the senator, is noticed by St. Paul (2 Tim. iv. 21).[2]

From the 'Ecclesiastical History of Britain,' composed by Bede upwards of a century after Gildas, we learn that Lucius, a tributary sovereign in the island to the Roman Emperors, sent a message to Pope Eleutherius (who filled the chair of St. Peter at Rome from the year 176 to 192), requesting that, through his means, he might be made a Christian—that he soon obtained the effect of his petition—that the Britons retained the faith so received inviolate in all its integrity, and practised the same without molestation until the reign of Diocletian, "sumptam fidem Britanni, usque in tempora Diocletiani principis, inviolatam integramque, quietâ in pace, servabant;" that during the ten years of persecution by that remorseless tyrant, Britain was ennobled by the martyrdom of Alban at Verulam, and of Aaron and Julius at Caerleon upon Usk. He adds in his Chronicon, what Gildas had stated before him, that they suffered in company with many other victims of both sexes, "cum aliis plurimis viris ac fœminis felici cruore damnavit persecutio." The same venerable historian pro-

---

[1] Every lover of historic truth would do well to consult Dr. Lingard's work on the Anglo-Saxon Church, and especially Note *a*, in the Appendix to vol. i.

[2] [See an ingenious essay on Claudia and Pudens, by the late Archdeacon of Cardigan.]

RECOGNITION OF THE PAPAL SUPREMACY.

ceeds to show that with the return of peaceful times, the faithful emerged from their hiding-places in the forests, deserts and caverns of the earth, rebuilt by degrees their temples, which had been levelled to the ground, and then openly celebrated divine worship.

The orthodoxy of our British ancestors, their consentient belief with the other Christian churches on the continent, is attested by their sending Eborius Bishop of York, Restitutus Bishop of London, and Adelfius Bishop of Lincoln, as their representatives in the Council of Arles, A.D. 314. Other prelates moreover were sent by them to the Council of Sardica in 347, as well as three to the Council of Rimini in 359, as we learn from Sulpicius Severus.

That the seven Bishops of Britain did not reject the Papal Supremacy, seems probable from the following facts:—1st, That St. Augustin, the envoy of Pope Gregory the Great, invited and importuned them to cooperate with him in preaching the Word of God to the Saxons; and 2nd, from their own confession, that his doctrine was true, "veram esse viam justitiæ quam prædicaret Augustinus" (Bedæ Hist. lib. ii. cap. 2). As to the question of the right time of keeping Easter, that could be solved only by astronomical observation. The errors of former computations had been corrected in every other part of the Church; but the sequestered Britons and Scots continued to employ the old cycles, and thus opposed themselves not merely to the custom of Rome, but also to the express decree of the General Council of Nice in the year 325. The whole subject is sensibly and dispassionately discussed by the late learned and Rev. John Whitaker,[3] Rector of Ruan Lanyhorn

---

[3] This great scholar was born at Manchester in 1736, and was buried in his church of Ruan Lanyhorn, 14th November, 1808, to which he had been instituted 23rd August, 1777, on the presentation of Corpus Christi College, Oxford.

HISTORY OF EXETER.

in- Cornwall, in his History of the Cathedral of Cornwall, vol. ii. p. 231.

"The great Council of Nice in 325 settled the dispute for ever in that decisive mode in which half of the disputes of man must be settled at all, by making the minority yield to the majority; and determining for Sunday next after the 14th day of the moon." He then shows that "the British Christians had not conformed to the sentiments of St. Polycarp, but did conform to the opinions of St. Anicetus, the Bishop of Rome; that the Britons derived their Christianity, with all their modes of Christian worship, immediately from their masters the Romans." And in a note, p. 234, he adds, "Dr. Borlase supposes the error of the Cornish to have been their refusing to acknowledge the Papal authority, when the very cycle for which the Cornish Britons contended was originally Roman itself; and when therefore the only contention could be for one cycle against another *equally Roman.* In writing upon these points, our authors," he continues, "are almost sure to show their Protestantism at the expense of their understandings." We might refer our readers to Wilkins' 'Councils,' vol. i. p. 8, where mention is made of a synod holden by St. David in 519, and his subsequent one at Victoria, when all the Welsh clergy attended and admitted the decrees as a standard, after receiving the sanction of the Roman Church, "Ecclesia Romana auctoritatem adhibente et confirmante."

But though there was a community of religious belief in the Roman and British Churches, yet owing in part to the inroads of Arianism and Pelagianism and to civil commotions, and to habits of incessant warfare with the Picts, Scots and Saxons, a woeful relaxation of discipline and morals was introduced; and the corruption, according to Gildas, prevailed almost uni-

ANGLO-SAXON SUBJUGATION.

versally. He informs us that about the middle of the sixth century the Britons were governed by no less than five distinct princes, viz., Constantine, Aurelius, Vortiporius, Cuneglass, and Maglocunus; all men of blood, polluted with iniquity, who seemed to set at defiance all laws human and divine. Amongst these profligate sovereigns, Constantine ruled over Damnonia, which comprised a considerable part of Devon and the whole of Cornwall. He upbraids him with his gross perversion of justice, with the violation of his most solemn promises at God's altar, with living in open adultery, discarding his lawful wife notwithstanding the prohibition of Christ, and of the Doctor of the Gentiles, "What God hath joined together, let no man separate" (Matt. xix. 6), and "Husbands, love your wives" (Ephes. v. 25). He conjures him no longer to prove himself the enemy of his own soul; nor expose himself to the avenging and unquenchable flames of hell; to return to Christ, who willeth not the death of the sinner, but that he be converted and live. He implores him to break asunder his bonds, and abandon his vicious courses, and return like the prodigal son (Luke xv.) to the tenderest of fathers, and he then will experience "how sweet is the Lord." The Welsh annals appear to testify to this king's reformation of manners before his death.

We have sufficiently referred to the consentient belief and doctrine of the British and Continental Churches, although in matters of *discipline* (which vary according to times and circumstances) there was not the same uniformity. From the Britons we may now pass to the Anglo-Saxons, who from mercenary auxiliaries, eventually became the lords and proprietors of the soil, and at one period established eight independent sovereigns, one of which was elected and designated *Brit-Walda*, or *Bryton-Walda*, *i. e.* the

Wielder of British power. The first Britwalda was *Ælla*, king of the South Saxons · or Sussex; the second was *Cealwin*, king of the West Saxons or Wessex; the third was *Ethelbert*, king of Kent; the fourth was *Raedwall*, king of the East Angles; the fifth *Edwin*, king of the Northumbrians; the sixth *Oswald*, who succeeded Edwin in his kingdom; the seventh *Oswio*, the brother of the said Oswald; and the eighth was *Egbert*, the king of the West Saxons. Originally the *Saxons* formed themselves into the three kingdoms of Sussex, Essex and Wessex: the *Angles* retained for their dominion Norfolk, Suffolk, Cambridge, and the Isle of Ely, but in process of time added to these, by conquest, the two kingdoms of *Bernicia* (which extended from the River Tees to the Firth of Forth) and of *Deira* (which comprehends the lands between the Tees and the Humber); and eventually merging these two kingdoms in that of *Northumbria*. The *Mercians* formed their kingdom out of the inland counties on either side of the Trent; whilst to the *Jutes*, from Jutland, were assigned the County of Kent and the Isle of Wight. Such partitions of territory amongst the conquerors perhaps facilitated the expulsion, or retirement, of the Britons from these respective allotments, but must have contributed to sow the seeds of jealousy and intestine discord; and thus prepare them also to succumb to the descents of daring and successful pirates. Unquestionably they served to alienate the Britons from co-operating with St. Augustin in the labour of converting these warlike races to Christianity, and thus to retard the progress of the all-civilizing Cross.

When Pope Gregory the Great in 596 had determined on the attempt to convert these kingdoms, he, · with this view, directed Augustin with about forty of his religious companions to proceed forthwith towards England. The enterprise was regarded on the Continent as appalling and dangerous. It was considered prudent by these foreign missionaries to sail for the Isle of Thanet, within the dominions of Ethelbert, King of Kent, whose authority extended to the south side of the Humber. He had married Bertha, a Christian daughter of Caribert, King of Paris, son of Clotaire I.; and her husband had guaranteed to her the free exercise of her religion, and had assigned to her the ancient British church of St. Martin, near Canterbury, where her chaplain, Luidhard, Bishop of Senlis, performed for her the divine services. On landing, Augustin despatched a messenger to the king, stating that in obedience to Pope Gregory they had travelled from Rome to bring to England the glad tidings of salvation. Ethelbert returned a gracious answer; desired them to remain where they were for the present; and issued orders for their being supplied with all necessaries. After a few days he visited the island and honoured them with an audience; thanked them for the benevolent zeal which had prompted them to undertake so fatiguing an expedition for his benefit and the welfare of his subjects; assured them of his protection, provided them with a residence in his capital, the city of Canterbury, with a liberal maintenance, and permitted them the use of the said Church of St. Martin, where they began to keep choir, and to celebrate masses, says Venerable Bede, and preach and baptize, until they obtained, after the Sovereign's conversion to the faith, a more ample licence to preach and to build and reconcile temples for the solemnization of religious rites (lib. i. c. 26). From this central focus, religion gradually extended her light and cheering influence. Both king and people were edified and charmed with the innocent and regular lives of the missionaries, with their disinterested and indefatigable zeal, their meek-

12   HISTORY OF EXETER.

ness, patience, and charity; they crowded to their
spiritual instructions, and when the king was publicly
baptized at Pentecost 597, his example was voluntarily
followed by many of his subjects; for he faithfully
adhered to the lessons he had received from his teachers
and guides, observes Venerable Bede, that he must
never *force* any one to embrace Christianity; for the
service of Christ must be free and spontaneous, and
never compulsory. Happy would it have been for mankind, if so just an estimate of the Deity's forbearance
and clemency—so sweet to all, and whose mercies are
above all His works (Ps. cxlv. 9), had been taught and
practised by all succeeding rulers; that legislators had
equally respected the weaknesses and prejudices of
their fellow creatures, and had never resorted to penal
laws or coercive restrictions on the sacred and inalienable rights of conscience.

CHAPTER III.

Exeter besieged by Penda, King of Mercia, in 633, but effectually relieved by
the British King, Cadwalinus. Submits to the sovereigns of Wessex.

If, in the silence of the Saxon Chronicle, we may
believe Matthew of Westminster in his ' Flores Historiarum,' we must state that about this time Exeter
was besieged by Penda, the powerful and ferocious
King of Mercia. He invested the city with a large
army, but was suddenly attacked, and made prisoner by
Cadwalinus King of the Britons; and, as the sequel
shows, redeemed his liberty, by entering into an offensive
and defensive treaty with his conqueror.[1] Yet before

---

[1] "Anno Gratiæ 634, Penda rex Mer- | onum venit Exoniam et obsidit. Rex
ciorum cum maxima multitudine Sax- | Britonum Cadwalinus celeriter Exo-

DOMINATION OF THE KINGS OF WESSEX.

the end of the 7th century the city succumbed to the dominion of the kings of Wessex; and under the mild, benevolent and firm government of *Ina*, the early legislator—who, after conquering the Welsh and Britons, placed them under the protection of equal laws, and of Egbert the friend of Charlemagne, who, as early as 809, had added Cornwall to his dominions [2]— Exeter must have felt comparative security, and have advanced in civilization. During the subsequent reigns of such sovereigns as Alfred, Athelstan, and Edgar, it must occasionally have been favoured and cheered by the royal presence. In the course of this chapter we shall lay before our readers what scanty details we have been able to glean of this period of our annals.

That Exeter had a monastery before the end of the 7th century is manifest from the life of *St. Winfrid* or *Boniface*,[3] consecrated Bishop on the 30th of November, 723, by Pope Gregory XI., and afterwards promoted to the Archbishopric of Mentz, and to this day regarded as the Apostle of Germany. This extraordinary man sprang from a good family in Crediton, and at an early age was sent for education to the monastery in this city, " in Exanchester, quod modo Exonia dicitur," then governed by the Abbot Wolphard, as we read in Bishop Grandisson's Legenda Sanctorum, ob. June 5, 755.

In the time of this Winfrid or Boniface there lived in or near this city Sidwella, eldest of the devout sisters Juthwara, Wilgitha and Gadwara, daughters of Benna, a noble Briton. At her father's death her cruel stepmother,

---

niam petivit, consertoque prælio, Penda de tali tumultu non promunitus, continuo captus est, et ejus exercitus dissipatus. At Penda cum aliam evadendi viam non habernt, Cadwalino fidelitatem juravit, et obsides de subjectione invenit," &c.—Flores Historiarum, p. 210, London ed. 1570.

[2] " Eam regionem, quæ Cornubia di-

citur, Egbertus subjugavit sibi et suo adjecit regno."—Matthew of Westminster, A.D. 809.

[3] Both before and after his consecration, he and others used these names indiscriminately.—See the Epistles in Dr. Giles's edition, Nos. 36, 41, 73, 91, &c.

14 HISTORY OF EXETER.

covetous of the fortune of Sidwella, which was considerable in the eastern suburbs of the city, engaged one of her servants, a reaper or mower (fœniseca), to dispatch her whilst employed in her devotions near a well in "Hedwell mede" at a short distance from the Parish church, which still bears her name. Unfortunately her Acts have perished since the destruction of the city by Sweyn. All that is said of her in the ancient Martyrology of this Cathedral is comprised in the following sentence:—"Augusti secunda die, in Britannia foras murum civitatis Exonie, Sancte Sativole Virginis et Martyris." The Church, subsequently erected in her honour and name, was believed to contain her tomb. In the catalogue of relics said to have been given to the said Monastery of Exeter by King Athelstan, we find a portion of the "Reliquiæ S. Sativolæ Virginis et Martyris." [4] But a dark cloud was gathering in the political horizon. The Danish and Northern sea-kings were in the habit of sailing forth early in the spring, seeking whom they might devour. They had paid a cursory visit to our defenceless coast as early as 787, but the decisive victory of Egbert at Hengston Hill in 835 had taught them caution for a time; till they reappeared with redoubled strength. Their approach spread dismay; for their progress was everywhere marked by carnage and conflagration.

We believe their first descent on Exeter itself was in the year 876. In the ensuing year a body of cavalry from Wareham in Dorsetshire proceeded to join their comrade freebooters in this city, and, though hotly pursued by King Alfred, they succeeded "in getting within the fortress, where they could not be come at,"

---

[4] There is reason to suppose that Prince Richard, the relative of St. Boniface, and his three children, Winebald, Willibald, and Walburga, so venerated for sanctity, were also natives of this neighbourhood.

as the Saxon Chronicle expresses it; nor did they leave their quarters until midwinter. During their stay, the monastery must have been sacked and demolished. In 894 these scourgers of God reappeared before the city and invested it; but Alfred hastened to the relief of the burgesses, and the Danes hurried back to their ships, and contented themselves with ravaging the coast. This sovereign, the founder of the British Navy, befriended Exeter; but he gave its revenue, with his royalties in Wessex and Cornwall, to his learned tutor and biographer Asserius, who tells us of his royal master's unexpected liberality — " ex improviso dedit mihi Exanceastre, cum omni parochia quæ ad se pertinebat in Saxonia et in Cornubia " (De Rebus Gestis Ælfridi Regis). After a reign of thirty years, this heroic sovereign died in 901. Mr. Sainthill, in the first volume of his 'Miscellanies,' has engraved a penny of this king struck at Exeter.

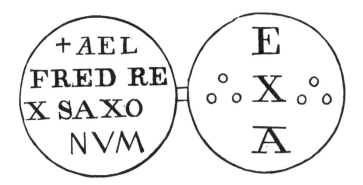

To Athelstan, who governed the realm from 925 until his lamented death on October 27, 941, Exeter must ever look up as her special benefactor. He frequently honoured her with his presence; he refounded her minster or monastery dedicated to SS. Mary and Peter, which eventually was transformed into a cathedral by Edward the Confessor; and he surrounded the

16   HISTORY OF EXETER.

city with regular fortifications, and built its castle. To
add to its rank and importance he gave it the privilege
of a double Mint. That diligent investigator, Mr.
Sainthill, has discovered a rare specimen coined here.
Instead of the king's bust, the obverse presents but a
simple cross. The circular legend proclaims him King
of the whole of Britain :

ÆDELSTAN REX TO. BRIT.

The reverse supplies the name of the Mintmaster,
perhaps one of the Reynold race :

RÆGENOLD MO. EXONIE CIV.

This true father of his country, after expelling the
disaffected Britons from Exeter, where they had theretofore enjoyed equal rights and privileges with the
Saxon inhabitants, and compelling them to retire beyond the Tamar, and after extending his conquests to
the Land's End, near which he founded the Sanctuary
or church of St. Burian,[1] spent Christmas here with
his nobles and court, and held a Witenagemote or
Parliament, when a body of laws was enacted, which
may be seen in Brompton's Chronicle, for the due
protection of property, the impartial administration
of justice, and the condign punishment of transgressors.
And here we may notice the strange assertion of
Hoker and Izaacke, that our city was formerly
called "Moncton, from the multitude of its monasteries, from the year 450 until the reign of King
Athelstan, who, in the year 932, first called it Exeter."
The charter to which they refer, if it be genuine (its
date, 670, is manifestly inaccurate and the names

---

[1] See his charter in the 'Monasticon Dioc. Exon.' p. 8.

ANGLO-SAXON BOUNDARIES.

of the witnesses belong to an antecedent period) can bear no such construction. For the king professes to grant to the Monastery of St. Mary and St. Peter, Prince of the Apostles, at *Exanceaster*, a manse called *Munecatun*; and then are distinctly specified the boundaries of this manse in the Saxon language. We believe the property lay along the *Sut Brook*,[5] which rises in the south-east part of St. Sidwell's parish and is fed by several springs and wells; but it is now in great measure covered over in Newtown, passes along the bottom of Paris Street and Holloway, and empties itself into the Exe below the quay. The late Mr. Kemble attached importance to the accuracy of the boundaries described in Anglo-Saxon charters, for they were obtained by actual perambulation; and he adds, that " Names unknown to the present owners of property remain sacred in the memory of the surrounding peasantry, and of the labourer that tills the soil. I have more than once walked, ridden, or rowed, as land and stream required, round the bounds of Anglo-Saxon estates, and have learnt with astonishment, that the names recorded in my charter were still used by the woodcutter or the shepherd of the neighbourhood." (Archæological Journal, No. 54, June, 1857). But let us resume our narrative.

Though Athelstan had refounded the monastery there, his premature death had left his work incomplete. During the Danish visitations and inroads, the religious members of such sanctuaries of piety and learning throughout the country had been massacred or dispersed: the minds of the population had become more disposed to the profession of arms

---

[5] So distinguished from North Brook; the source of which is near the higher hedge of Little Gratnor field, Stoke Hill. Passing down the valley through Polsloe (where it was sometimes called Mynchyn Lake), thence through East Wonford as Wonbroke, it crosses the road to Topsham, and finally discharges itself into the Exe below Northbrook House.

C

18   HISTORY OF EXETER.

than the uniform routine of the cloister; and it was reserved for the peaceful reign of *Edgar* to restore the ancient order of things. Accordingly we read in the Chronicle of Florence of Worcester, that, in the year 968, he obtained a colony of monks for Exeter and placed over them an exemplary Abbot, called Sideman, whose merits within five years later raised him to the dignity of bishop of Crediton. It is more than probable that our illustrious monarch honoured Exeter with his presence both before and after his marriage with Elfrida, the daughter of Ordgar, the Earl of Devon who was buried in this city in 971. In Mr. Sainthill's Miscellanies (vol. ii. page 152) is engraved a coin of King Edgar, which presents the peculiarity of an X (the designation of Exeter) both on the obverse and reverse. To the grief of the nation he was summoned away by death on October 27th, 975. Of him the Saxon poet sung, "There was no fleet so proud, no host so strong, as to seek food in England while this noble king swayed the sceptre. He reared up God's honour: he loved God's law: he preserved the people's peace. . . . . . . God was his helper; and kings and earls bowed to him and obeyed his will; and without battle he ruled all, as he pleased."

CHAPTER IV.

Exeter besieged by Sweyn, King of Denmark — Its gallant and successful resistance — Infamous policy of King Ethelred — Sweyn returns to invest the city, which, through the treason of its Governor, falls into his hands on the 19th of August, 1003, and is demolished — Canute, the son of Sweyn, succeeds to the sovereignty of England.

THE imbecile government of Ethelred, the son of Edgar, his inaptitude for business and love of pleasure, and the aversion of the nation towards his unnatural mother

SWEYN'S SIEGE OF THE CITY.

Elfrida, held out encouragement to the Northern pirates and freebooters to renew their predatory descents on Britain. Incapable of opposing effectual resistance, the king sought to bribe and purchase their forbearance from hostilities at any price; and perhaps his frequent subsidies may in some measure account for the immense amount of his coinage still preserved in the Royal Museum at Stockholm.[1] But these ferocious and covetous barbarians valued truces and treaties only so far as they suited present convenience. Under Swegen, or Sweyn, King of Denmark, their fleet appeared off Exmouth in 1001, and soon the flames of villages—the groans of their expiring victims—the shrieks of the fugitives—announced the rapid approach of the enemy towards Exeter. Its citizens relying on the strength of their fortifications, and conscious of the utter ruin that must await them if they fell into the invader's hands, determined to oppose a desperate resistance. He had calculated on taking the city by storm; but was wofully disappointed, and gallantly foiled in the attempt. A diversion was made in their favour by the combined forces of Devon, Somerset and Dorset, under the generals Cola and Eadsig. The battle was fought at Pinhoe near this city. On this occasion Pallig,[2] to whom Ethelred had proved a most generous benefactor, "contrary to all his plighted troth," says the Saxon Chronicle, deserted the king's cause, joined his Danish countrymen with a considerable force, and enabled Sweyn to obtain a decisive victory. The next morning, "after burning the villages of Pinhoe and Cliston, and many good villages which we are unable to name," he deemed it prudent to abandon Exeter and to re-embark his troops at Exmouth.

---

[1] See Mr. Sainthill's vol. ii. of Miscellanies, p. 137.

[2] This naturalized Northman met his tragical end in the general massacre of his countrymen late in the following year, in the presence of his Christian wife, Gunilda, and his children.

HISTORY OF EXETER.

Our infatuated sovereign, in the course of the year 1002, was alarmed by a report that the Danes, domiciled in England, were preparing "to bereave him of his life, and afterwards all his counsellors; and then to take possession of his kingdom without any gainsaying." Without further proof, he determined to sacrifice them all at once to his suspicious and short-sighted policy. On one and the same night—the feast of St. Brice, 13th November—great and small of either sex, " majores et minores utriusque sexus," says Florence, fell, the unsuspecting victims of the royal vengeance. We believe, however, that hoctide was not subsequently kept up in memory of this detestable massacre, but was instituted nearly half a century later in commemoration of the national joy at being rescued from Danish sovereignty, and at the glorious coronation of Edward the Confessor at Winchester, at the solemnity of Easter.[3]

As might be expected, this tragical expedient served but to exasperate the foes of England. Sweyn had been stung with disappointment at his unsuccessful attempt against Exeter; but on hearing of this unparalleled massacre of his countrymen, and of the brutal murder of his own sister, he vowed indignant revenge. In the course of the spring of 1003 he embarked with a powerful fleet and army; and in due time re-appeared before this city. The inhabitants might again have offered a successful resistance, the banner of England might have continued to wave in proud defiance on the castle, if the governor had 'not been a traitor. He was a Northman named Hugh, indebted for his position not to merit or talent, but to the preponderating influence of Queen Emma in the state councils. This perfidious man introduced the enemy on the 19th August,

---

[3] The festivity of hoctide was celebrated soon after the termination of the Easter holidays. [Its real origin is open to question.]

BETRAYAL BY HUGH THE GOVERNOR. 21

1003, as we learn from the Chronicon of the Church of Exeter. Never was calamity more signal—never destruction more summary. The brave inhabitants were immolated to the insatiate vengeance of the victor; the churches with their annexed libraries and archives were wantonly consumed in the flames,— "Ecclesiæ, in quibus numerosæ et priscæ Bibliothecæ continebantur, cum libris incensæ sunt" (Wm. Malmes. lib. ii. cap. 4):[4] the monuments of art were dashed to pieces; public and private property given to pillage; the fortifications utterly demolished, and the city reduced to a pile of ashes. To those inhabitants who survived the general onslaught, it may have been some consolation to witness the traitorous governor dragged off in chains by the enemy. (See Brompton, after Henry of Huntingdon, the Saxon Chronicle, Florentius, and Simeon of Durham.) The king, perceiving that affairs grew worse, proposed a truce, which was accepted on his paying 36,000l.; an enormous sum in those days. Never was England more humbled; never so prostrate at the feet of its vanquisher; and never was it doomed to be governed by such a despicable monarch. He died unpitied in London on 23rd April, 1016. Sweyn had died on 3rd February, two years before, and had appointed his son Canute to succeed him. Had Edmund Ironside, the spirited son of Etheldred, been permitted to live, his prowess might have achieved the independence of his country; but on 30th November, 1016, he also was snatched away by a sudden and violent death at Oxford, and Canute was proclaimed sole monarch of England without opposition.

---

[4] There was an old saying, and a true one, prevalent in those days, " that a monastery without a library was like a castle without an armoury."—Merryweather's Bibliomania, p. 50.

CHAPTER V.

The influence of religion on the heart and government of Canute — His special favour to Exeter — The restoration of the Saxon line in the person of Edward the Confessor — Prosperity of this city, and the removal of the See to it from Crediton.

CANUTE exhibited in his government a wonderful proof of the benign influence which the spirit of Christianity exercises over the human heart. He had been educated in a bad school, where rapine, perfidy, sacrilege, and murder were unblushingly taught and practised; but when he was once securely fixed on the throne, it was his study to expiate the cruel wrongs inflicted by his father and himself on his new subjects, and to ingratiate himself by acts of conciliation, by easing their burthens, by administering the laws with strict impartiality, by restoring church property and doing honour to religion in the persons of its ministers.[1] Exeter very soon experienced the benefit of his protection. He invited and encouraged the fugitives to return; he assisted in rebuilding its fortifications, and in the erection of houses and churches. In his charter, preserved in the Register of Bishop Bronescombe, fol. 111, and granted in the year 1019, he sets forth that he had been credibly informed by the " Dux " Dekelwerdus, that his officers in the province of Devon had imposed the yoke of vassalage on the estates appropriated to God's Church, to St. Mary and All Saints, which is in *Exencestre,* and that its monastery had been destroyed by the pagans and its royal charters consumed by fire. In virtue of his supreme authority in

---

[1] William of Malmesbury, lib. 2, c. xi., thus describes his system of government :—" Ingenti studio Anglos sibi conciliare; æquum illis jus cum Danis suis in consessu, in consilio, in prælio concedere. Monasteria per Angliam, suis et patris excursionibus partim fœdata, partim eruta, reparavit."

GOVERNMENT OF CANUTE. 23

the land, for his soul's welfare, and for the redemption
of his own transgressions, and to secure the blessing
of God upon his kingdom, he granted a charter to the
new Abbot Akelwoldus, and his present and future
brethren abiding in the said monastery, which would
put them in full possession of all their previous rights
and privileges. The royal signature is attested by the
Archbishops of Canterbury and York, five bishops, five
dukes, five abbots, and five officers; but in the copy
printed in vol. ii. of the Monasticon Anglicanum,
page 536, this number of witnesses is more than
doubled.

The course of his reign was signalised by deeds of
beneficence and charity. In the fifteenth year of his
government, 1031, he proceeded to Rome; and our
early historians take delight in commemorating his
liberality and piety. He was accompanied by Livingus,
the very discreet Abbot of Tavistock (whom he afterwards promoted to the united sees of Crediton and
St. Germans). The memorable letter which he
despatched by that favourite ecclesiastic to his English
subjects, fortunately preserved by William of Malmesbury and Florentius, is so graphic and interesting
that we make no apology for submitting it to our
readers.

"Canute, King of all England and Denmark and the Nor-
wegians and a part of the Swedes, to Egelnoth, the Metro-
politan, and to Alfric, Archbishop of York, and to all Bishops
and Prelates, and to all the nation of the English, as well
Nobles as Commoners, greeting. I signify to you that I lately
repaired to Rome to pray for the remission of my sins and the
safety of my realms and of the people subject to my authority.
Long since I had vowed to perform this pilgrimage, but had
hitherto been prevented by state affairs and other impediments.
But now I very humbly thank my Almighty God, who has
allowed me life to visit his Holy Apostles Peter and Paul, and
every sacred place within and without the city of Rome, and,
according to my wishes, to honour and venerate them in person.
And I have done so principally because I have learnt from wise

HISTORY OF EXETER.

men that St. Peter the Apostle received from the Lord the great power of binding and loosing, and that he was the key-keeper of the heavenly kingdom; and therefore I considered it highly profitable to seek his patronage with the Lord.

"Moreover be it known to you, that at the Easter solemnity there was a great concourse of nobility, with the Lord Pope John (XIX.) and the Emperor Conrad, and all the princes of the nations from Mount Garganus to the nearest sea; who gave me an honourable reception, and made me valuable presents, especially the Emperor, who bestowed various precious gifts of gold and silver vessels and rich mantles and robes. I availed myself then of the opportunity to represent to the Emperor and to our Lord the Pope, and to the assembled princes, the grievances of all my subjects, English and Danish, that they might be granted a more reasonable permission and safer protection in their journeys towards Rome, and freedom from detention in the way by so many obstacles, and from unjust taxation; and the Emperor acceded to my wishes, as also did King Rodolf,[2] who was the master of those barriers; and all those princes decreed that my men, as well merchants as pilgrims, should henceforth travel to and return from Rome in peace and lawful security, without any detention at barriers or demands of officers.

"I next complained to the Lord Pope and stated my great disapprobation of the large sums required of my archbishops, who, pursuant to custom, repaired to the Apostolic See to receive the pallium. A decree was consequently enacted that this was never to occur again. Whatever I solicited from the Lord Pope, and from the Emperor and King Rodolf, and the other princes through whose territories lies our passage to Rome, was most willingly conceded for the accommodation of my people, and the grant was confirmed by their oaths under the testimony of four archbishops and twenty bishops, and in the presence of a numberless multitude of dukes and nobles. Wherefore I render my heartfelt tribute of thanksgiving to Almighty God that I have successfully accomplished whatever I had desired and purposed, and that all my wishes are fully satisfied.

"Now let it be known to you all that I have humbly devoted my future life to the all-powerful God and to reform my conduct entirely, to govern my realms and subjects justly and piously; in all things to observe the strictest equity; and if heretofore, by the impetuosity of youth or negligence, I have acted wrongfully, I am prepared with God's help to make ample atonement. Therefore I entreat and command my council, to whom I have

---

[2] Rodolph III. (called by Ingulphus *Robert*) was the last king of Burgundy, and is stated to have conveyed his dominions to Henry III., king of the Romans, son of the Emperor Conrad.

CANUTE'S LETTER TO HIS SUBJECTS. 25

committed the charge of the government, that on no account, for fear of me, or to win the favour of any person in power, they consent to any injustice, or suffer it to spring up in any part of my dominion. Moreover I command all sheriffs and provosts of the realm, as they value my friendship or their own safety, that they abstain from doing an unjust act to any man, rich or poor; but to allow all persons, noble or ignoble, rich or poor, to possess their legal rights, and that no deviation from justice be connived at, either to favour the King, or to serve any powerful nobleman, or to increase the royal exchequer; for I need not money acquired by injustice and extortion.

" I wish you now to know that I am proceeding to Denmark, with the advice of my Danish council, to conclude a firm peace and treaty with those nations which had impotently desired to rob me of my crown and existence; but God destroyed their power. May He continue, in His mercy, to preserve us in integrity of life and honour, and to dissipate and bring to nought the power and strength of all our enemies! At the conclusion of peace with the neighbouring nations, and after settling the concerns of my eastern dominions, so that all apprehension of hostilities be removed, I purpose to embark for England in the course of the summer. But I have sent this letter as my precursor, that all my subjects may rejoice at my prosperity: for you are all aware that I have never spared myself any labour, neither will I, to promote the welfare of all my people.

" And now I command and conjure all my bishops and provosts, by the fidelity which they owe to God and to me, that before my return to England ye cause all debts owing to God, according to the ancient law, be discharged: viz. the plough-alms—the tithes of cattle born during the present year—the Peter's pence [3] due from towns and villages—the tithes of fruit in the middle of August—and the church-shot payable to the parish church at Martinmas. For these and similar dues, unpaid at my return, distress will be enforced according to law. Fare ye well."

This powerful and religious sovereign survived his return for several years, and died at Shaftesbury on 12th November, 1035. Many of his coins, struck in the Exeter Mint, are engraved in Mr. Sainthill's work before mentioned. To Canute's praise we must add that, as early as 1022, he had ordered the Laws of King

---

[3] Charlemagne, 200 years before, had established this payment in Gaul. See Pope Gregory VII.'s ninth letter.

26   HISTORY OF EXETER.

Edward the Elder, the son of Alfred, to be translated from the Saxon into Latin, and to be observed by all his subjects in Denmark and England, for their superior wisdom and equity—" propter earum æquitatem," writes Matthew of Westminster.

The unexpected death of King Harold, surnamed Harefoot, and King Hardicanute, within seven years, opened the way to the throne of England for Prince Edward, a lineal descendant of the old Saxon race of Cerdic, and the son of Etheldred by Emma. He was now at the mature age of forty, and had been severely trained in the school of adversity. Illustrious by birth, he was known to be more illustrious by his virtues, and therefore his accession was hailed with unbounded joy by the nation. His subjects, conceiving themselves to be emancipated from a foreign yoke, justly felt that now they had got the right man in the right place, and in the fittest conjuncture of affairs. " Quæ tunc, quæso erat Anglis omnibus lætitia, cum rediisse cernerent antiquam successionem et patriæ libertatem." [4] The goodness of his heart—his affability of manners—his moderate habits—his contentment with the patrimonial demesnes of the crown—his voluntary relinquishment of that odious impost called the Danegeld—his anxious study to relieve the public burthens—his incredible charities to the poor—and his bountiful gifts to churches and monasteries—made him the idol of his people; whilst the code of laws which he had digested from the varied local customs of his English, Danish, and Mercian subjects, and the enactments of preceding sovereigns (with such alterations and amendments as time and experience suggested to his wisdom), afforded sufficient protection for life and property, and made the people feel they had a constitution worth

---

[4] Words taken from the ancient Lesson read formerly in Festo S. Edwardi, 13th Oct., during the cathedral-service here.

REIGN OF EDWARD THE CONFESSOR.

defending. For a long period the laws and customs of "the good King Edward" continued to be household words in the mouths of our forefathers, who regarded his auspicious and peaceful reign as the era of England's prosperity. During his time we believe the parochial division of the kingdom was effected, and each inhabitant acquired the knowledge of his proper spiritual shepherd.

But if the country at large had cause for congratulation on possessing such a wise and benevolent sovereign, with what affectionate gratitude did Exeter regard him as her greatest benefactor? Under his auspices she grew into greatness. Her population rapidly increased. Her trade, internal and external, was flourishing. William of Malmesbury thus describes Exeter:—"Ubi omne abundat mercemonium, ut nihil frustra desideres, quod humano usui conducibile judices" ('De Gestis Pont. Angl.' p. 145). Being a well-fortified city, the King determined, with the approbation of the Pope Leo IX., to transfer the now united sees of Cornwall and Devon from the little village of Crediton, "a Cridiensi villula," to this important place. Leofric, who had filled the office of chaplain of the court, as well as of chancellor, and probably was well known to his Holiness, when, as Bruno, the latter governed with such high reputation the bishopric of Toul, had recently been nominated to the See of Crediton, and had felt the expediency of such removal. To do the prelate greater honour, the King, with his accomplished Queen Editha,[5] with both the archbishops, several bishops, and an immense concourse of the nobility and dignified clergy, graced

---

[5] William of Malmesbury describes her as "Fœmina, in cujus pectore omnium liberalium artium esset Gymnasium." Her encouraging condescension to Ingulphus, whilst a young scholar, afterwards the learned Abbot of Croy-land, is beautifully recorded in his history, page 62. Dying 5th April, 1075, she was buried near her husband at Westminster. We hope Miss A. Strickland will employ her talents in doing justice to such a queen.

28 HISTORY OF EXETER.

his translation with their presence. In the royal charter bearing date A.D. 1050, the king announces his having placed the endowment of the new bishopric of Exeter on the altar of St. Peter; that he then conducted the prelate by the right arm, whilst the queen supported the left arm, to instal him in the episcopal chair. (See Bishop Brantyngham's 'Reg.' vol. i. fol. 106.)[6] The 'Domesday' sets forth the munificent endowment by this pious monarch. How Exeter must have exulted at the contrast, of seeing a conventual church converted into a cathedral! and, instead of the services being performed by eight monks, to witness their celebration by a bishop, twenty-four canons, twenty-four vicars, fourteen choristers, besides a considerable number of clerks and officers! Under the fostering care of this first Bishop of Exeter, and his immediate successor Bishop Osborn, religion made such unprecedented progress, that we learn from the old missal of St. Martin's Church (dedicated on the 5th July, 1065), that in the following reign, the city could boast of its twenty-nine churches, to each of which William the Conqueror allowed the Provost of Exeter to pay a small annual sum from the public taxes,[7] at Easter and Martinmas.

We need not add that the death of this father of his country,—" honor et gloria Anglorum dum vixit, eorum ruina dum moritur," (Chron. de Mailros, 160), on 5th January, 1065-6, after a short illness, plunged the country into mourning. " Plangebatur amarissimè," says Simeon of Durham.

---

[6] [The genuineness of this charter has, however, been called in question.]

[7] " Infra xv dies post Pascha solvendi sunt xxix^d, xxix capellis per manus Prepositorum Exonie quos dedit Rex Willielmus de collectâ gabuli."

" Item, in Octabis Sci Martini solvendi sunt iterum per manum Prepositorum Exonie, ut supra, infra quindecim dies post Pascha." The silver penny of the time may have been equivalent to the present half-crown.

CHAPTER VI.

Harold, son of Earl Godwin and brother of Queen Editha, assumes the reins of Government, with the good will of the nation, but loses the crown with his life at the battle of Hastings — William, Duke of Normandy, is declared king of England — Exeter, opposed to his sovereignty, submits after a siege of eighteen days — To overawe the spirit of insurrection, tho citadel or castle is rebuilt — The Domesday — Foundation by the Conqueror of St. Nicholas's Benedictine Priory — The King's death at Rouen — Strange event at his funeral in St. Stephen's Church at Caën.

As an Anglo-Saxon burgh, Exeter possessed the advantage of municipal government. Domesday records that its burgesses had lands without the city amounting to twelve carucates, which paid no custom but to the city itself, and that it enjoyed the same privileges as London, York, and Winchester. Its chief officer was the Wic-reeve or Provost. He had to collect the King's revenue, and he exercised the same authority in the town as the sheriff did in the county of Devon. Both officers were appointed by the Crown.

Shortly before his death Edward had named the Queen's brother, Count Harold, as his successor to the throne, as a reward for his faithful services;[1] for, says the Saxon Chronicle, "to him was committed the realm who at all times had faithfully obeyed his rightful lord by words and deeds, and neglected nothing needful to the service of his sovereign King." On 6th January, at the conclusion of the Royal obsequies at Westminster, the crown was placed on the head of the new king, but he was not destined to wear it long. Unfortunately he had to oppose his own brother Tostig, the exiled Earl of Northumberland, who was leagued against him with

---

[1] This is corroborated by the admission of the partisans of his rival William. Ordericus says, "Ægrotus Princeps concessit Haraldo;" and William of Poitou, "Dono Edwardi, in ipsius fine." It is amusing to read in Abbe Feller's 'Dictionnaire Historique,' art. *William I.*, "St. Edouard, Roi d'Angleterre, l'appella au trône par son testament," when William himself acknowledged on his death-bed, he had no better right to England than what he had derived by the sword of conquest.

HISTORY OF EXETER.

the powerful King of Norway, and also William, Duke of Normandy,[2] who had long coveted the prize. The former opponents had scarcely been crushed at Stamford Bridge, on the Derwent in Yorkshire, in one of the bloodiest conflicts recorded in our annals, when he learnt that William had actually effected his landing at Pevensey on Michaelmas-day.[3] By a rapid movement he arrived with his army at Senlac, a place formerly so called, in the neighbourhood of Hastings; where, after achieving prodigies of valour in that memorable and decisive battle of 14th October, he fell mortally wounded; and with him perished for a time the hopes and liberties of England.

William, though victorious and crowned on the Christmas-day of the year 1066, was conscious that the heart of the nation was adverse to him. Naturally of an overbearing and headstrong character, presenting a striking contrast to the saintly Edward, the new sovereign showed that he preferred to be feared rather than loved by his subjects. Acting on the principle that all the lands in England were, by right of conquest, derived or holden mediately or immediately from himself,[4] he hastened to grasp the estates and property of Englishmen and to transfer them to his Norman barons and his foreign auxiliaries and adventurers; he depo-

---

[2] This extensive province, part of the ancient *Neustria*, derives its name from the Northmen, inhabitants of the peninsula of Jutland, the islands of the Baltic, and the shores of the Scandinavian continent, who perpetrated ravages throughout France during the ninth and tenth centuries. In 886 they advanced up to Paris and Sens, scattering devastation around them. King Charles, surnamed Le Simple, ceded to their chieftain Rollo, for a settlement erected into a duchy, this valuable territory, and further gave him in marriage his daughter Gisella, with Mans and Bretagne, about the year 912. Rollo received baptism, and took the name of Robert. William the Seventh duke in succes-

sion, and commonly called the Conqueror, was the illegitimate son of duke Robert, by Herleva. This concubine subsequently married Herluin, and had Robert, Earl of Mortain, and Odo, Bishop of Bayeux, who were thus uterine brothers of the Conqueror. In this province were the bishoprics of Rouen, Lisieux, Evreux, Seez, Bayeux, Coutances, and Avranches, so often occurring in the Domesday.

[3] He had crossed over in a ship called *Mora*, the gift of his wife Matilda. See note in Prevôst's edition of Ordericus Vitalis, vol. ii. p. 125.

[4] [This "principle" was adopted rather as a conventional legal maxim than as a fundamental fact.]

THE NORMAN CONQUEST.

pulated whole districts[b] to administer to his passion for hunting; he enacted the forest laws written in blood; he revived the odious Danegeld; he ordained that all legal proceedings in the Royal courts should be conducted in the Norman-French language instead of the vernacular tongue; he strove to force upon the parishes a foreign clergy; he required that all parties and companies should disperse, all fires and candles should be extinguished, between eight o'clock in the evening and four o'clock in the morning, at the tolling of the melancholy curfew, when Anglo-Saxons in solitary darkness might brood over their grievances. But let us confine our attention to Exeter.

Its citizens "wealthy and brave" (as Ordericus represents them, lib. iv. Eccl. Hist.) were animated with most deadly hatred against the Norman. A band of his mercenaries on board of a squadron of his fleet had been driven by a tempest into the port of Exeter, and had been treated with insult and inhumanity by the populace. The burgesses, sensible of their danger, made preparations for self-defence, improved their fortifications, and despatched emissaries to excite a similar spirit of resistance, which, as appears from the Domesday Survey, was specially successful at Lidford and Barnstaple. When William sent a message to this city that he required their oaths of fealty to his person and the admission of a garrison within their walls, they returned a peremptory refusal, but at the same time consented to pay him such dues and service as they had been in the habit of rendering to their native monarchs.

---

[b] To obtain sufficient extent for his new forest he demolished thirty-six parish churches, and without scruple sent adrift a large population attached to the soil. In so doing he had also a political motive, viz., to provide a place of refuge for his Norman adherents opposite their own coast, in the event of a general insurrection of the English. With this view he erected strong castles at convenient distances — at Christchurch, at Malwood, at Porchester, and at Sarum, and improved the fortifications of Winchester. But how fatal did this New Forest prove to his family!—to Richard his second son, to William his third son, and to his nephew Robert! See William of Malmesbury, lib. iii.

HISTORY OF EXETER.

William was little accustomed to submit to conditions dictated by his subjects. He raised a considerable force, of which a large portion was composed of Englishmen, and advanced with a determination to inflict summary vengeance on the audacious insurgents. At four miles' distance he was met by the magistrates, who implored his clemency and gave hostages for their fidelity. With 500 horse he approached one of the gates, and to his astonishment found it barricaded against him, and a crowd of combatants bidding him defiance from the walls. It was in vain that, to intimidate them, he ordered one of the hostages to be deprived of his eyes. The siege continued for eighteen days; nearly fifty houses, as we learn from the Domesday, were destroyed; in different assaults the besiegers sustained severe losses of men, but by the sudden falling of a portion of the walls a passage was opened to the enemy; the citizens at last submitted, but on more favourable conditions than could have been anticipated. Political expediency, joined to respect for valour, prompted William to be satisfied with their oath of allegiance and the admission of a garrison; but their lives, property, and immunities were secured, and the besieging army was removed from the vicinity of the gates to prevent all opportunity of plunder. This must have occurred in the winter of 1067. The King, after reducing Cornwall to submission, returned to Winchester to keep Easter. In the following spring Githa, the mother of the late King Harold, dreading the rapacity and brutality of the Normans, sought refuge within our walls, and succeeded eventually in escaping to Flanders with many of our inhabitants; " cum multis de civitate " (Simeon of Durham).

In 1069 the malcontents in Cornwall attempted to seduce our citizens from their allegiance to the Conqueror, and on their refusal to join them, proceeded

THE DOMESDAY BOOK.

to invest the place, but they were seasonably relieved by the King's lieutenants Fitzosborne, Earl of Hereford, a principal commander at the battle of Hastings, and Brian, son of the Earl of Bretagne.

Of all the king's despotic measures, the most revolting to the national taste and feeling was the inquisitorial survey, called Domesday, of every acre of land, and in some places of stock, within the conquered country. The Exchequer copy of the survey was commenced in 1083 and finished three years later. Amongst the muniments belonging to the chapter of this cathedral is a manuscript transcript of the original rolls or returns made by the Royal Commissioners for the counties of Devon, Cornwall, Dorset, Somerset, and Wilts, descending to the minutest details.[*] The population must indeed have been completely overawed, to swear evidence against their own interests; but he set at defiance public opinion, and maintained a large standing army to crush disaffection and opposition at its first appearance.

Truth, however, compels us to admit that if the spirit of the nation was humbled and broken, and if its own nobility had disappeared under the sword of conquest, or been impoverished, or exiled, or incarcerated, yet in the progress of time considerable improvement was apparent in the manners of society, in public security, and in the cultivation of the arts and sciences; for, at the period before us, the Normans ranked amongst the most civilized and polished people of Europe, their

---

[*] Our readers are aware that the Exchequer copy was printed at the expense of Government in 1783. Thirty years later the same authority decided on publishing the 'Exeter and Winton Domesdays,' the 'Boldon Book,' and the 'Inquisitio Eliensis;' and accordingly these valuable records issued from the press in 1816; but it was discovered that fol. 327 was then wanting in the original Exeter manuscript. About eleven years later, the present Sir Walter C. Trevelyan, Bart., in arranging some family papers, met with that missing folio, and lost no time in submitting it to our present respected Chapter Clerk, Ralph Barnes, Esq., who has restored it to its proper place. This folio has been printed in the same type as the rest of the vol. of the year 1816. [The reverend author pronounces too severe a judgment upon this celebrated survey.]

D

34   HISTORY OF EXETER.

clergy were better trained and disciplined, better informed and more efficient. They re-animated the torpid
state of religion in this country, and William of Malmesbury confesses that he saw churches and monasteries
arising in every direction in a new and superior style
of architecture, and that the wealthy nobility vied with
each other in founding costly monuments of their genius
and piety.

We learn from the Norman writers that the king
selected a commanding site within our walls for the
erection of a castle, and appointed Baldwin de Sap,
otherwise called de Molis, or de Brioniis, and sometimes de Exonia (from having made Exeter for a time
his principal residence here), to superintend the works,
and to establish a competent garrison. But this will
form the subject of a separate chapter·in Part II.[6]

In the Monasticon .of the Diocese of Exeter, we have
shown that the king was the original founder of St.
Nicholas' Benedictine Priory, a dependency of his
noble abbey of Battle. To this establishment he seems
to have granted Harold's fee in this city and vicinity.
At the suppression of this priory, the Crown sold this
fee, or St. Nicholas' fee, to the Mayor and Chamber
of Exeter, who, as long afterwards as the 8th April,
1560, resolved "that there shall be provided a seale of
purpose wherewith all copies made for any parcel of
that lande shall be sealed" (1st Act Book, page 184).

With all his accumulation of power and wealth,
William was not happy. Reflecting in his solitary
hours on the course of his eventful life, he felt that he
ruled over a justly discontented people impoverished
by his wrongs; that in his immoveable purpose he had
spread wide wasting misery and desolation over a flou-

---

[6] This officer, a kinsman of the
Conqueror, was rewarded with the
Manor and Barony of Oakhampton and | its castle, and the Shrievalty of Devon,
"in which county alone he was granted
159 lordships," as Relham has stated.

DEATH OF THE CONQUEROR.

rishing and beautiful country. His conscience now up-braided him with acts of cold-blooded oppression and multiplied wrongs, for each of which he was soon to render an account to Him who is no respecter of persons, and anticipated the calamities that were to be visited on his children. Death deprived him of everything at Rouen, on 9th September, 1087, and his corpse lay abandoned and disregarded, until by the charity of Herlouin it was conveyed to St. Stephen's church at Caen for interment. During the funeral service, after a sermon by the Bishop of Evreux, there stepped forth a burgess of the town, called Asselin, and loudly pro-tested against the corpse being buried there, calling the living God to witness that the ground was still his; that the late King robbed his father of it to build an abbey here, without making any compensation to him for it. "I now reclaim it by *Clameur de Haro*, and I forbid you to inter the body here." Henry, the king's youngest son, amidst the general consternation, now came forward and made the required payment. The service then went on, and the body was lowered into the ground in a stone coffin, and there lay until the grave was rifled in the civil wars in the year 1562.

CHAPTER VII.

Henry I. befriends Exeter — Bishop William Warelwast rebuilds its cathedral — The prevalence of Simony in the middle ages — The fatal shipwreck of the heir to the Crown — Charter of King Stephen — Siege of Exeter — Accession of King Henry II.

PASSING by the reign of the impious and voluptuous despot William Rufus, who was so suddenly bereaved of his crown and life by the visitation of God, we come to that of his youngest brother Henry. He had profited by a liberal education, and, though possessing the here-

D 2

HISTORY OF EXETER.

ditary duplicity and stubborn self-will of his family, he is said to have consulted the feelings of his English subjects by abrogating the curfew law, and by partially restoring the laws of Edward the Confessor. To this commercial and thriving city he granted a charter of freedom from all imposts and duties known by the name of *tolls* and *customs* in the other towns and cities of England—an important privilege in those days—and he attached a forfeiture of ten pounds to the act of disturbing our burgesses in the exercise of this their chartered right. He further granted them the fee-farm of their city for the yearly payment to the Crown of 39*l.* 1*s.* 6*d.* This sum he made over to his queen, Matilda, the daughter of Malcolm, King of Scotland, by his wife Margaret, sister of Edgar Atheling. With the consent of her husband Queen Matilda appropriated two-thirds of that pension in perpetuity to her foundation of the Priory of the Holy Trinity, London; the residue lapsed to the Crown on her death in 1118, and was increased by King Edward by his charter, dated Waltham Cross, 6th February, 1332. The memory of this benefactress to Exeter was held in special veneration by her citizens during the four ensuing centuries; and the Act Books of the Chamber show that, until 4th September, 1528, "the obit of Molde the good Queene" was duly maintained at the costs of the Mayor and Council.

Early in Henry's reign his kinsman William Warelwast, our diocesan, whose biography we have given in our Lives of the Bishops of Exeter, undertook to rebuild our cathedral. The Chronicon of the church simply specifies the year 1112, "anno MCXII primo fundata est Exoniensis ecclesia."

For the preceding half-century the emperors of Germany and the kings of France had exhibited to Christendom the unseemly and scandalous spectacle of retain-

REIGN OF HENRY I. 37

ing in their hands vacant abbeys and bishoprics until they could find pliant tools unfit for the office of pastor, or else purchasers at their own price and standard. The late king, William Rufus, in his lust of power and sacrilegious avarice, gloried in following their mercenary and disgraceful traffic, nor did his successor, notwithstanding the oath he had taken at his coronation to maintain "the laws of the Church," hesitate to walk in his brother's footsteps, to trample on the canons and violate the ancient legal immunities which the Church possessed in the reign of St. Edward the Confessor. To such innovations, to such *abuses*, as even Voltaire calls them in his 'Annales de l'Empire,' the Popes offered a vigorous opposition. They studiously laboured to eradicate simony and to point out the line of demarcation between the spiritual and temporal power. A compromise was accomplished before the death of our primate Anselm, but a formal concordat between the respective monarchs of Europe and the Holy See might have prevented those collisions of authority which too often disgrace the middle ages.

By his Queen Matilda, the king had only two children, William and Matilda. The former in his eighteenth year met with an untimely fate on 25th November, 1120, off Barfleur, on board the *White Ship*, bound for Southampton to join his father, who had sailed over on that morning; but they were never to meet again. All the passengers, in number nearly 300, were buried with the vessel in the waves, except one named Berold. This sad catastrophe at once determined Henry to venture on a second marriage, and on the 2nd of February next ensuing he took to wife Adelaide, the beautiful daughter of Geoffry, Duke of Louvain; but here his hopes of issue were disappointed, perhaps in punishment of his conjugal infidelities, for he had

HISTORY OF EXETER.

many illegitimate children. He had given his only daughter above-mentioned in marriage to the Emperor Henry V., when she was but twelve years of age; but after a union of eleven years[1] the Emperor died at Utrecht in 1125, when her father decided on recalling her, and matching her with Geoffry Plantagenet, a youth of sixteen, son of Fulco, Earl of Anjou and subsequently King of Jerusalem. By this stroke of policy he calculated on securing protection to his continental dominions, and on preventing his nephew Stephen de Blois from succeeding to his throne. But he was obliged to proceed with caution, for he anticipated that his Norman as well as English barons would be opposed to the novelty of a female reign. Late in 1126 he convoked an assemblage of the leading nobility and clergy in London, and proposed, in the event of his dying without male issue, that they would accept his daughter, the ex-empress, as heir-apparent to the throne. To this proposal they consented, and ratified their consent by a solemn oath; and none displayed more earnestness in the matter than his nephew Stephen. In the meanwhile the king was secretly negotiating the marriage, which according to Matthew of Westminster was performed 3rd April next ensuing. It proved a most unhappy union; for though it produced to him three grandsons, Henry, Geoffry, and William, the remainder of his days was embittered by the jarring contentions and final separation of their parents. He died, after a short illness, at St. Denys le Froment, near Rouen, at midnight, 1st December, 1135, æt. 72.[2]

---

[1] The fruit of this union was a daughter, Christina. See Laurence Patavel, vol. i. p. 101.

[2] Geoffry's life terminated on 7th Sept. 1150, æt. 41. His separated wife survived until 10th Sept. 1167, and was buried at Rouen; but part of her remains were deposited at Bec Abbey, and were discovered on 2nd March, 1684, and again in levelling the ground in 1846.

USURPATION OF STEPHEN.

The crown of England had been the object of Stephen's ambition, since the fatal shipwreck of his cousin Prince William. He had won the popular favour by his frankness of manner, easiness of access, liberality, and chivalry. Hastening to London, he was welcomed with acclamation and proceeded to Winchester, where he took possession of the immense treasures of the late sovereign, which he lavished amongst his partisans, and actually procured himself to be crowned at Westminster, on St. Stephen's day, 26th December, nearly a fortnight before the burial of the deceased monarch.[3] After assisting at the solemn obsequies of his uncle at Reading, the new king proceeded to Oxford, where he published to the world his celebrated charter of the liberties of the English church and of the national rights. We submit a translation from the original Latin charter in the possession of the Dean and Chapter of Exeter, to which is still attached a portion of the seal, representing the king seated on his throne :—"I Stephen, by the grace of God, and with the assent of the clergy and people elected King of the English, and consecrated as such by William, Archbishop of Canterbury and Legate of the Holy Roman Church, and confirmed by Innocent (II.) Pontiff of the Holy Roman See,[4] from my reverence and love of God do grant, that the Holy Church be free; and I confirm unto it due reverence, and I promise that I will neither do nor permit anything simoniacal in the Church and affairs ecclesiastical. I admit and confirm that the justice and power of ecclesiastical persons and

---

[3] According to Gervase, the corpse reached England on the 4th of January, where it was met by Stephen, and honourably conducted to Reading, for final interment in his presence. — See Wm. de Malmes.

[4] See the Bull of Pope Innocent II., in Richard of Hexham's Hist. de Rebus Gestis Stephani Regis. The Papal confirmation is simply grounded on Stephen's election, "communi voto et unanimi assensu tam procerum quam populi."

40   HISTORY OF EXETER.

all clerks, and the distribution of ecclesiastical favours,
be vested in the hand of the bishop. I decree and
grant that the dignities of the churches confirmed by
privileges and ancient custom remain inviolate. I
grant that all the possessions and tenures holden on the
day when King William my grandfather was living
and died, be free and quit of any re-claim of suitors.
But if the Church should hereafter challenge anything,
which it now has not, of what it held and possessed
before the death of the said king, that I reserve to my
favour and dispensation for recovery or investigation.
Moreover I confirm whatever has been granted to them
since the death of the said king by the munificence
of other sovereigns, or the donation of princes, by
the offerings or purchase, or any conveyance of the
faithful. I promise that I will maintain peace and
justice in all things, and to my utmost preserve their
rights. I reserve to myself the forests made and
maintained by my grandfather William, and my uncle
William; but all the additional forests made by King
Henry I restore and concede to the churches and the
realm. If any bishop or abbot, or other ecclesiastical
person shall, before his death, reasonably dispose of his
own property, or should have decided as to its disposal, I grant that it remain valid; but should he be
surprised by death, let the distribution thereof be made
for his soul's health at the discretion of his church.
And whilst the seats continue vacant by the death of
the proper pastor, I will commit them with all their
appurtenances to the hand and custody of clerks until
a pastor be canonically substituted. All exactions and
wrongs and misdemeanours improperly introduced,
whether by the sheriff or any other persons, I absolutely
extirpate. I will observe good laws and ancient and
just customs in murders and pleas and other causes, and

CHARTER OF KING STEPHEN. 41

I command and ordain their observance. All these things I grant and confirm, saving my royal and just dignity.

" WITNESSES — William, Archbishop of Canterbury.
Hugh, Archbishop of Rouen.
Henry, Bishop of Winchester.
Roger, Bishop of Sarum.
Alexander, Bishop of Lincoln.
Nigel, Bishop of Ely.
Everard, Bishop of Norwich.
Simon, Bishop of Worcester.
Bernard, Bishop of St. David's.
Owen, Bishop of Evreux.
Richard, Bishop of Avranches.
John, Bishop of Rochester.
Atheluf, Bishop of Carlisle.
Roger, the Chancellor.
Henry, the King's Nephew.
Robert, Earl of Gloucester.
William, Earl Warren.
Ralph, Earl of Chester.
Robert, Earl of Warwick.
Robert de Vere, ⎫
Milo of Gloucester, ⎬ Constables. ·
Briant, the Earl's son, ⎥
Robert de Oilly, ⎭
William Martin.
Hugh Bigot.
Humphry de Bohun.
Simon de Beauchamp, Steward of the Household.
William de Albini.
Eudo Martin, the Butler.
Robert de Ferrers.
William, the Proctor of Nottingham.
Simon de Saint Liz.
William de Albemarle.
Paganus Fitz-John.
Hamo de Sancto Claro.
Ilbert de Lacy.

" Given at Oxford in the year from our Lord's Incarnation 1136 to wit, the first year of my Reign."

42   HISTORY OF EXETER.

If the king had stood faithful to this engagement, he would have disarmed all serious opposition; the pretensions of the haughty ex-empress, who delayed landing in England until 30th September, 1136, would have vanished into air, and the sad calamity of a civil war would have been averted. But he soon violated his solemn promises, insomuch that even his own brother Henry, the influential Bishop of Winchester, discountenanced him. Exeter, "ever faithful," took the lead against the perjured monarch. The want of good faith—the disregard of plighted promises and solemn oaths—was lamentably characteristic of the middle ages.

In the preceding chapter we have alluded to Baldwin de Exonia. He had married Albreda, the Conqueror's niece; had received a grant of the signory and castle of Nehou in Normandy, and for his services in the successful invasion of England had been rewarded with 159 lordships in Devon alone. On his death, his eldest son Richard succeeded to his honours and estates; and according to Monsieur Greville (Anciens Châteaux du Département de la Manche, page 100), assumed the cognomen of De Ripàriis, Redvers, or Rivers. King Henry I. treated him with such favour and confidence that he created him Earl of Devon, and added to his extensive territory the manors of Tiverton and Plympton and the Isle of Wight. At his demise, his son Baldwin, with a grateful sense of the obligations of his family to the late sovereign, was the very first to raise the standard of loyalty in the cause of Matilda, the ex-empress.[5] With his family and retainers he fixed his headquarters in this *his* city and castle, "in Excestra oppido suo" (says Simeon of Durham). "Baldewinus de Redvers Excestram oppidum suum contra

---

[5] "Primus quidem omnium Baldewinus de Redvers caput suum levavit in Stephanum, firmato contra eum castello Exoniensi."—'Chronica Gervasii.'

regem firmavit " (Ricardus de Gestis R. Stephani); he strengthened the fortifications with the determination of suffering every extremity rather than consent to a surrender. Stephen hastened to invest the city, with an army composed of English and Flemish troops, and for three months pressed the siege with unabated vigour. The garrison and citizens opposed a gallant and skilful defence; but at length were compelled to capitulate for want of water. It might have been expected that this protracted resistance, which had cost the victor an immense expenditure, would have been visited with exemplary vengeance; but the historians on both sides agree that he exercised the most considerate clemency, and that he amply indemnified the clergy of this cathedral for the injuries inflicted during this lengthened siege. He seems to have contented himself with seizing the property and exiling the person of his prisoner Baldwin from England and Normandy, who nevertheless succeeded eventually in recovering his honours and estates.

The king, after a distracted and turbulent reign, after experiencing the vicissitudes, calamities, and horrors of civil war, and rendering the realm a prey to conflagration, rapine, and carnage, at length listened to the overtures of reconciliation, and entered into a solemn compact with Henry Fitz-Empress on November 7th, 1153 (for death had snatched away his own ambitious son Eustace about three months before); by which he at once adopted Henry for his son, and declared him to be his heir and successor to the crown in the event of his death. The earls and barons swore that if either of the parties violated this pacification, they would renounce him and support the cause of the unoffending rival. The king survived this happy event until October 25th of the following year; and

44   HISTORY OF EXETER.

Henry succeeded tranquilly to the throne, and was crowned with extraordinary pomp at Westminster on Sunday, December 19th, the same year (1154).[e]

CHAPTER VIII.

Bright prospects of Henry Plantagenet at his accession — State of the contest on the rights of the Church between the King and the Primate, Thomas à Becket — The conduct of our townsman, Bishop Bartholomew, in that controversy.

FEW sovereigns in our annals have ascended the vacant throne with more brilliant prospects than Henry Plantagenet. He was twenty-four years of age, brave and comely; his continental dominions had been greatly extended by the death of his father Geoffry, and by his own marriage with Eleanor, the daughter of William, Earl of Poitou and Duke of Aquitaine; he was already blessed with a son and heir, and with the prospect before him of a large family, so that there was little chance of a disputed succession. The clergy and barons had joyfully witnessed his solemn vow to govern the nation according to law, and protect his subjects in all their rights and privileges; and England congratulated herself that the golden age, the peaceful government of St. Edward the Confessor, was restored. To add to the general satisfaction, Cardinal Nicholas Breakspeare, a native of Langley in Hertfordshire, had just been elected for his superior merits to the Chair of St. Peter; who took the title of Adrian IV., and was the

---

[e] Amongst the 136 letters and charters that were in the Treasury of this Cathedral in Bishop Walter Bronescombe's time (1258-1280), were King Stephen's confirmation to William Warelwast, Bishop of Exeter, of the possessions of his see; his charter, granting 7l. 10s. to the Church of St. Peter "in manerio de Colinton cum hundredo;" and several grants to the See and members of the Chapter.

ACCESSION OF HENRY II.

first Englishman that had attained this chief dignity in the Christian world. So overjoyed was the king with his people at this event, that a special embassy was despatched to congratulate his Holiness on an elevation so honourable to himself and to his country. But in sober truth we may express our regret, that the pontiff, professing himself to be "the servant of the servants of God," and the vicar of Him who has proclaimed "My kingdom is *not* of this world" (John xviii. 36), should have deluded himself into the fancy, not merely of being an accepted umpire between contending suitors, but of inheriting the right of disposing of Ireland, a Christian country, in favour of the ambitious Henry. The Papal Bull may be seen in Ralph de Diceto's 'Historia,' p. 529. The miserable jurisprudence of the feudal ages admitted this abuse of power, as we witness in the cases of several Emperors of Germany; and we read with disgust, how readily rival princes, in the giddiness of senseless passion and ambition, sought and accepted such papal donations. Thank God, for the peace of mankind, such pretensions have long been exploded![1] For the best report of this

---

[1] How admirably is traced the line of demarcation between the civil power of the State, and the spiritual power of the Church, in the 'Declaration of the Catholic Bishops in Great Britain, A.D. 1828,' page 14!—

"The allegiance which Catholics hold to be due and are bound to pay to their sovereign and to the civil authority of the state, is perfect and undivided. They do not divide their allegiance between their sovereign and any other power on earth, whether temporal or ecclesiastical. They acknowledge in the sovereign, and in the constituted government of these realms, a supreme civil and temporal authority, which is entirely distinct from, and totally independent of, the spiritual and ecclesiastical authority of the Pope and of the Catholic Church. They declare that neither the Pope nor any other prelate or ecclesiastical person of the Roman Catholic Church has, in virtue of his spiritual or ecclesiastical character, *any right, directly or indirectly, to any civil or temporal jurisdiction, power, superiority, pre-eminence, or authority within this realm;* nor has any right to interfere, directly or indirectly, in the civil government of the United Kingdom, or any part thereof; nor to oppose in any manner the performance of the civil duties which are due to his Majesty, his heirs and successors, from all or any of his Majesty's subjects; nor to enforce the performance of any *spiritual* or *ecclesiastical* duty by any *civil* or *temporal* means. They hold themselves bound in conscience to obey the civil government of this realm in all things of a temporal and civil nature, notwithstanding any dispensation or order to the contrary had, or to be had, from the Pope, or any authority of the Church of Rome. " Hence

46 HISTORY OF EXETER.

discreditable transaction, we refer our readers to the fourth volume of Lanigan's Ecclesiastical History of Ireland. In the sequel, very many persons in this county and city adventured settlements in that distracted country.

Exeter is stated to have suffered very severely in the year 1161, as well as Canterbury, London, and Winchester, from conflagration (Angl. Sacra, vol. i. p. 300); and about this period the king issued his charter to his citizens of Exeter, which was attested by Bishop Bartholomew, Reginald Earl of Cornwall, and Thomas Becket his Chancellor, confirming all the right customs which they had possessed in the reign of his grandfather Henry I., as freely, honourably, and justly as the Barons of London, "Barones de London," —*i.e.* the leading members of the municipality, the aldermen and merchant-princes of the metropolis,— then held and enjoyed their liberties.

The king was naturally able, but self-willed, impatient of contradiction, very suspicious, furiously vindictive, and jealous of all power that did not emanate from, and centre in, himself. The venerable primate Theobald and the Chancellor above-mentioned retained some influence over him; and, distinctly foreseeing that a contest was coming on between the civil and ecclesiastical courts, addressed a letter to the King just before his death, which occurred on April 18th, 1161, recommending to him " the liberties of the Church," and cautioning him against the machinations and intrigues of its enemies. Whether such liberties ought to have been conceded to it by the State—

"Hence we declare, that by rendering obedience in *spiritual* matters to the Pope, Catholics do not withhold any portion of their allegiance to their king, and that their allegiance is entire and undivided; the *civil* power of the State, and the *spiritual* authority of the Catholic Church, being absolutely distinct, and being never intended by their Divine Author to interfere or clash with each other.

" ' Render unto Cæsar the things that are Cæsar's, and to God the things that are God's.' "

CIVIL AND ECCLESIASTICAL CONTEST. 47

whether they were expedient or not, as a counterpoise to the then undefined prerogative of the Crown— whether they served as a bulwark and breakwater against the tide of wanton despotism,—are questions with which the historian, as simply the relater of *facts*, has nothing to do. He is not called upon to justify or condemn the policy of Constantine the Great, of Theodosius, of Justinian, of Charlemagne, of our own Alfred, and Edward the Confessor, in conferring and confirming such immunities on their clerical subjects; but he has to beware of confounding ancient with modern times and opinions : he has merely to state the usages of the feudal ages, to ascertain if such were chartered liberties—part and parcel of the constitution and law of the country, and as such, sworn to be maintained by the sovereigns, at their respective coronations. If that can be proved, then the parties, lay or clerical, to whom privileges have been accorded, must be warranted to defend established rights by every legal means. Deny, then, this constitutional liberty of asserting and exercising self-defence ; and you are compelled to withhold your admiration of Cardinal Stephen Langton and the Barons of England for wringing Magna Charta from the hands of King John : we must cease from extolling the spirit which prompted the cry, " Nolumus leges Angliæ mutari ! " ; we should erase the names of the patriots who bled in the field or died on the scaffold, or who boldly stood forward to maintain their municipal or collegiate franchises. For if *they* be entitled to praise and honour, it is solely because they clung with desperate courage to what they believed *the law* gave them—because they gallantly appeared in the breach against supposed arbitrary encroachment.

During the contest between Henry II. and the Primate Thomas, the merits of which are so much discussed and variously represented by modern historians,

48   HISTORY OF EXETER.

we are therefore bound to transfer ourselves to me-
diæval times; to become, as it were, contemporaries
with the parties, without being influenced by actual
usages and opinions and the altered judicature of the
country. We should bear in mind, that the primate
had filled the office of chancellor with great credit, was
thoroughly acquainted with the king's character, and of
all men most competent to form a correct judgment
whether he had law, equity, and justice on his side.
Again it is undeniable, that the king himself subsequently renounced his innovations called *customs*, and
engaged never to exact them in future. (See Concilia,
vol. xxxii. page 392, Paris ed. A.D. 1644.) It is
contended by some of our writers, that Bartholomew,
the then learned and distinguished Bishop of Exeter,
took part against his primate. It is true that, in the
early stage of the contest, he sought, from his love of
peace, to moderate and reconcile differences; but these
writers ought not to have suppressed the fact that he
soon discovered his mistake,—that he offered the
primate to share in the exile he had chosen to give
place to wrath—and on being dissuaded from such a
step by this persecuted superior, he employed his interest and means at home, to serve him, notwithstanding the imminent danger of incurring the king's displeasure. (See Giraldus Cambrensis, Ralph de Diceto,
&c.) Bartholomew was selected by his fellow bishops
to pronounce the discourse at the reconciliation of the
cathedral-church of Canterbury on December 21st, 1172
(the Saint's natal day), which had been desecrated
by the barbarous murder of the primate nearly a
twelvemonth before. Our bishop was also the author
of a narrative of that tragic event, which, we suspect,
was used by Bishop John Grandisson, when he compiled those Lessons which were formerly read in our
cathedral on December 29th, and the octave day,

RICHARD I.—KING JOHN.

January 5th. Bishop Bartholomew was a stanch advocate of the liberties and interests of his see and its churches. We have printed his appeal to King Henry II. in favour of Colbroke, concluding thus:— "Humbly and devoutly, O illustrious King and dearest Lord! I have recourse to your dignity and wisdom, that for the love of God and reverence of the holy Apostles, Peter and Paul, and for the hope of an eternal recompense, you would graciously protect the rights and possessions of this church of Exeter, and preserve them harmless, entire, and inviolate."

CHAPTER IX.

Reigns of Richard Cœur de Lion and John — The Crusades, the Interdict, and the subjugation to Papal Domination — Queen Berengaria — Extraordinary floods in England.

KING HENRY II. closed a chequered life, embittered with domestic misery, at Chinon on July 6th, 1189, and was succeeded by his undutiful son Richard, who met his untimely fate within ten years later, when the throne was seized by his perfidious brother John. Neither of these princes, from their headstrong passions, produced much benefit to their subjects. Richard, though he dazzled the world by his deeds of chivalry, exhausted the resources of the country by his imprudence and extravagance.[1] His successor, by his tyranny and lust, entailed disgrace on himself and misery on his subjects.

During this period little is recorded of our city. Both

---

[1] To pay the king's ransom from captivity, England was drained of immense sums, which never returned for circulation. Towards this payment Exeter paid a large proportion. This may possibly account for the rarity of the coins of his reign, and that of his father. [But we know little about the medium for transmitting such payments abroad at this time.]

50 HISTORY OF EXETER.

Henry and his two succeeding sons had granted and confirmed its charters. King John[2] allowed it the privilege of annually choosing a representative of the Crown from amongst her burgesses or middle class; such chief magistrate to be dignified with the title of Mayor, as in Winchester, London, and Canterbury.* Our city, justly regarded as the metropolis of the west, the centre of commerce and the seat of letters, was now irradiated by three of its natives: Bartholomew, its Bishop; Baldwin, the Primate of Canterbury; and Joseph, the first Latin poet of his age. Of the first of these contemporaries we have elsewhere treated in our Lives of the Bishops of Exeter; on the other two we may have to enlarge in another place. But we may here observe that Joseph, in his Antiocheis,[3] sung the praises of Exeter in such glowing strains as to enrapture Leland, who informs us, in his interesting work, De Scriptoribus Britannicis, that he found a copy in Abingdon Abbey:— " Urbem Exoniæ tam exquisite, tam dextrè, tam denique magnificè vel ad æthera tollit, ut facile credas, Musas ipsas, cum profluente Helicone toto, vati ea concinenti, præsentis-

---

[2] King John was partial to this city, and to its Priory of St. Nicholas a special benefactor. The Close Rolls show that he and his Queen Isabella made some stay within its walls on their return from Poitou the last time, 1207. See 'Close Rolls,' fol. 433 b. May it not be on that occasion he assigned a mayor to the city?

[3] The learned T. Duffus Hardy, Esq., in his 'Description of the Close Rolls,' p. 179, relates that a French translation of the Antiocheis was borrowed, on the 17th of May, 1250, from the Master of the Knights Templar, London, by King Henry III. for the use of his Queen (Eleanor of Provence); and that, on the 5th of June following, the said king commanded an artist, viz., Edward of Westminster, to paint the " History (i. e. 'story') of Antioch " in the royal chamber within the Tower of London; and that eleven years before this he had ordered his royal uncle Richard's "Single Combat" to be painted in a chamber within Clarendon Palace.

Hoker, in his MS. History of Exeter, p. 237, says of this Joseph, that " he is believed to be a priest of our cathedral;" adding, "he was excellently well learned yn all good letters, but especially yn poetrie, and for his excellencie yn the Greeke and Latyn tounges he was sayde to excelle all others yn his tyme." But we must differ from Hoker, when he claims another illustrious scholar for a native, and for prior of the Benedictine Priory of St. Nicholas here, in the person of Alexander Neckham. The truth is, he was not connected with Exeter. He never was a member of the Benedictine Order, but followed the rule of St. Augustin, and dying abbot of their monastery of regular canons, at Cirencester, in 1217, was buried in Worcester Cathedral.

CRUSADES — INTERDICT — PAPAL SUBJECTION. 51

simas adfuisse." How unfortunate that he has not copied and perpetuated this description!

It may not be inappropriate here to allude to three subjects connected with this period :—1, the crusades; 2, the general interdict of the city and kingdom; 3, the inglorious vassalage attempted to be entailed on our beloved country by the pusillanimous King John, who dared to subject it to papal domination.

Our readers are aware that the crusades were expeditions undertaken by the Christian princes of Europe, partly to rescue the Holy Land from the possession of the infidels, and partly with a view of stemming the progress of those barbarians, who meditated the subjugation of the whole of Christendom. " Nam tua res agitur, paries cum proximus ardet."

The Turks and Saracens were then the sworn enemies of Christianity, and it has been justly observed (Quarterly Review, January 7th, 1814, page 460), that "as long as the maxim of the Turkish Government was perpetual war, it was undoubtedly the right and duty of Christians to combine for the expulsion or extirpation of their common enemy." It may also have proved good policy to make the enemy's country the seat of war ; for experience teaches, that men are more generally energetic when they act on the offensive than when they confine themselves to defensive operations. And it is very certain that the infidels were much disconcerted by these crusades — that they learnt to respect the valour of their assailants, and to entertain a wholesome fear themselves of it. If these expeditions eventually proved unsuccessful, we must take into consideration the want of concert amongst the Christian chieftains—the national jealousies of the heterogeneous masses—the absence of discipline, which is the life and soul of the military service—the insalubrity of the climate—the difficulty of obtaining regular reinforce-

HISTORY OF EXETER.

ments, accoutrements, and provisions—but especially the bad faith of the Greek emperors. Yet, notwithstanding the ultimate failure, it must be confessed that Europe derived considerable benefit by the introduction of useful knowledge, by improvements in navigation and commercial enterprise, and military science.

The interdict—that desperate remedy, never to be resorted to but with the utmost moderation and circumspection—was promulgated on the eve of the Feast of the Annunciation of Lady Day (March 24th) 1208, and continued in force until July 2nd, 1214. During this long interval, the churches of the land were closed, the bells were silent; no burials of the dead were permitted in consecrated ground, and then without any funeral service; marriages and churchings took place in the porches of the churches. On Sundays sermons were preached in the open air within the churchyard; the administration of baptism to infants, and of penance and communion to the dying, only could be allowed. This sudden plague of darkness filled the country with consternation, and undermined the cheerfulness of temperament hitherto so characteristic of the English people.

The faithless and profligate John, finding that a general disaffection to his government prevailed amongst his people, and that Pope Innocent III. had proceeded to depose him and release his subjects from their allegiance to him, and even to authorise the King of France to make a conquest of England, was abject enough to tender homage and fealty to papal domination, and to pay a yearly tribute of a thousand marks to be enabled to wear his crown. It is heart-cheering to witness the sterling patriotic spirit manifested by our ancient English historians, in condemnation of these unwarrantable pretensions of the pope, and of the despicable

QUEEN BERENGARIA.

cowardice of the monarch. Probably our noble country would have become a province of France, if the tyrant's unexpected death from chagrin had not let loose the indignation of the people against such usurpation. But whilst we reprobate the pope, with other modern writers of honest English hearts—such as Dr. Milner (History of Winchester, vol. i. 237) and Dr. Lingard (History of England, vol. ii.)—for pretending to dispose of a kingdom which was not his own to bestow, are we not equally bound to despise the *acceptors* of such unrighteous donations? Even John himself could hardly complain of such abuse, when he had invoked its exercise, to recover Normandy from the King of France.

In concluding this chapter we may notice the fact, that King Richard I. assigned this city of Exeter— "Civitatem Exoniæ"—as parcel of the large dowry[4] of his Queen Berengaria. He had married this accomplished princess, daughter of Sancho, King of Navarre, at Cyprus on May 12th, 1191. After the death of her lord, she fixed her residence at Mans, and there finished her days about the year 1230. She had compounded with John, her brother-in-law, for her dowry of 2000 marks, or 1333*l*. 6*s*. 8*d*., payable half-yearly; but his avarice made him meanly neglectful, insomuch that Pope Innocent III., by a letter dated January 21st, 1208, admonished him to consider how he tarnished his character and provoked Almighty God, the father, protector, and vindicator of the widow, by such dishonourable conduct. But, though he manifested some show of repentance and shame, yet at the period of his death, October 19th, 1216, her arrears amounted to no less than the sum of 4040*l*. We are

---

[4] The estates lay in Berks, Devon, Essex, Gloucestershire, Hants, Herefordshire, Lincolnshire, Northampton-shire, Oxfordshire, Somerset, Sussex, and Wilts.

54   HISTORY OF EXETER.

not satisfied, however, with Miss Strickland's statement
(Lives of the Queens of England, vol. i. page 323)
that the non-payment of the queen's arrears by that
" felon-king " was the *cause* of the interdict,[5] or that
she never had honoured England with her presence.

From Ralph de Diceto we collect, that, at the commencement of this inauspicious reign, our island was
visited with extraordinary floods, and that a calamity
so destructive of life and property was specially felt in
this city :—" Anno 1199 subita et improvisa aquarum
inundatio pluribus in locis per Angliam facta est;
unde plures homines submersi sunt et domus eversæ,
maximè apud Excestre."

CHAPTER X.

Henry III. succeeds to the English crown, and grants to his brother Richard the
Earldom of Cornwall, to which he attaches the city of Exeter with its castle
— This new Earl elected King of the Romans — The history of Exeter Bridge.

By the death of John, the crown devolved to his eldest
son Henry (III.), a child but nine years old. Fortunately he had faithful guardians, and the heart of the
nation was with him; so that, the cause of Louis of
France visibly declining, he judged it politic to withdraw from the kingdom. It appears, however, from
Henry's letter to Geoffry de Mariscis, Justiciary of
Ireland, dated " Exeter, February 12th (1218), the
second year of our reign," that the king had contracted
a heavy debt with the French prince to induce him
to " depart out of our realm, which at length the Lord

---

[5] Indeed this cannot be the case ; for
we have seen the Pope's letters addressed to the King, and dated 3 Nones
of Sept. 1207, 10 Sept. 1207, from Viterbo ; from the Lateran Palace, 12
Kal. Feb. 1208, 11 Sept. 1208, and 12

Sept. 1209.   The Commissioners appointed by his Holiness to urge the
King to do justice to the much injured
widow, were the Bishops of Ely and
Worcester.

PRINCE RICHARD GOVERNOR OF THE CITY.

hath marvellously and mercifully" accomplished. (See Hardy's Description of the Close Rolls, p. 156.) The youthful sovereign added much to his popularity by confirming the Great Charter on February 11th, 1224.[1]

During the contest between the Barons and John, the latter had manifested a partiality for foreigners, and had lavished his bounty upon them. As the son felt himself more securely seated on his throne, he began to withdraw his confidence also from the old nobility and tried friends, and to make himself the tool of foreigners and favourites. Amongst other ill-advised measures, he demanded the indiscriminate surrender of wards and castles; and he proceeded to deprive Robert de Courtenay of his hereditary right of Governor of the Royal Castle of Exeter, and after a short period created his own brother, Prince Richard, Earl of Poitou and Cornwall, granting, on August 10th, 1231, with a limitation to him and his heirs for ever, the city and the castle of Exeter as an appendage to the Earldom of Cornwall. Occasionally Prince Richard kept his court in this city, and is recorded to have behaved with condescension and liberality towards its burgesses. Enriched, as it is said, by his tin mines and ample dotation of lands, he freely spent his money in erecting his noble castle of Wallingford; and in founding the Cistercian Monastery of our Lady of *Hales* in Gloucestershire; and on November 9th, 1251, the date of its dedication, he sumptuously entertained there the king and his queen, thirteen bishops, most of the barons of England, and more than three hundred knights. Unfortunately he was dazzled with the offer of a crown by the Electors of Germany, and was installed "Romanorum Rex, semper Augustus," at Aix-

---

[1] The reader will do well to bear in mind the subsequent enactment, 45 Edward III. cap. 4—"If any statute be made contrary to the Great Charters, it shall be holden for none." [Such a prospective nullity would now be ineffectual, and has, in fact, never been regarded by any parliament at any time.]

56   HISTORY OF EXETER.

la-Chapelle,[2] on the Feast of Holy Innocents, December 28th, 1256. It was a dearly-purchased honour, and a severe drain on his revenues, compelling him often to return home to replenish his coffers. On the 7th of May, in the *third year of his reign*, he granted to the mayor, bailiffs, and citizens of Exeter and their heirs for ever, the fee-farm of Exeter for the ancient stipulated sum of 13*l.* 9*s.*, payable in even portions at Easter and Michaelmas, reserving to himself and his heirs the right of taxing this city, as often as the kings of England should impose a tax on their cities and boroughs. This charter was sealed " sigillo nostro regio."

The absence of our royal Lord-Paramount on the continent encouraged the discontented barons to break out into open sedition against the government of King Henry. They had indeed much cause of complaint, for the sovereign preferred strangers to his native subjects, was very exacting, unfaithful to his word, and little disposed to the improvement of his country. At first his brother Richard, a man of moderate views and more foresight, suggested to the king the expediency of attending to the correction of abuses; but, finding him bent on pursuing his evil courses in Church and State, he took part with Simon de Montfort, Earl of Leicester, who had married his sister Eleanor, and with the Earls of Gloucester and Hereford, in opposing his brother; though he could never be persuaded to join in invading the just rights and prerogatives of the Crown. Returning from Germany, he found his country embroiled in civil war. To the king he lent his best services, and with him was taken prisoner in the disastrous battle of Lewes on May 14th, 1264; but

---

[2] Dom Martino observes that the German emperors wore a triple crown —a silver one as kings of Germany, an iron one as kings of Lombardy, and a golden one as kings of Rome ; and that the kings of Germany were to be crowned at Aix-la-Chapelle, by the Archbishop of Cologne, assisted by the Archbishops of Mayence and Treves. See p. 203 and 207 ' De Antiquis Ecclesiæ Ritibus.'

REIGN OF HENRY III.

by the gallantry of Prince Edward, the heir apparent, who obtained the victory of Evesham on August 12th of the ensuing year, the royal cause was restored, and the tranquillity of the realm gradually re-established. Our Lord-Paramount was thus enabled to revisit his foreign dominions; but disappointments and domestic afflictions compelled him to return to England. Dying at Berkhampstead in Herts, in February, 1272, he was buried near his queen, Sanchia, and their second son, Henry, who had been brutally murdered in the church of Viterbo by his outlawed cousins, the Montforts, a twelvemonth before, and his English honours and estates descended to his surviving son, Prince Edward. The king enfeebled in body and mind expired at Westminster nine months after his royal brother, viz., November 16th, 1272.

During his long and eventful reign, our city had merited his favour and confidence by its stanch and inviolate fidelity. Twice at least he had confirmed its liberties and privileges; he had authorised its burgesses to raise the toll of murage for building and maintaining their city walls; and there is every probability that from the year 1265 they were empowered to elect their representatives in parliament. Perhaps no town suffered less during the baronial contests. Industry and commerce seem to have thriven, and two newly-founded religious communities—the Dominicans and Franciscans—were, after some opposition, established amongst us.

We cannot conclude this chapter without recording the munificent and invaluable service achieved by one of our citizens, Walter Gervase, or Gervys, " a notable man of God," as Hoker describes him. During the years 1231 and 1239 he discharged the office of mayor; and with the example before him of the considerate zeal and charity of Benezet, who had succeeded in

58 HISTORY OF EXETER.

1184 in throwing a stone bridge over the Rhone at Avignon, our Walter Gervys undertook a similar benevolent work for the benefit of Exeter. The transit of the river Exe by ferry had long been felt a source of inconvenience and risk, especially during inundations. The narrow wooden bridge for foot-passengers was often swept away by the rapidity of the current. By active and perseverant applications, far and near, to the humane, and by his own liberality, he accumulated, says Hoker (p. 242), nearly ten thousand pounds towards erecting a stone bridge of twelve arches. Our readers should bear in mind that the river Exe, which had long been the property of the city, from Checkston [3] at its mouth up to Exeter, was then navigable to this point, and that boats came up directly with the tides, laden with wines and other merchandise, to its quay. For the perpetual maintenance of this useful work—the piers of which rested on piles, while the stones of the foundations were cramped with iron and run with lead—Guardians of the bridge were appointed; and we find in fol. 63 of the Cartulary of St. John's Hospital, that the rental for its support (February 2nd, 1401), arising from tenements and gardens, amounted to 15l. 11s. 4d. This public benefactor died in 1259, and was *probably* buried in the Chantry Chapel of the blessed Virgin Mary, which he and his first wife Alice had founded [4] on the bridge nearly opposite St. Edmund's Church. He had indeed expressed a wish in his will [5] dated on the

---

[3] See the inquisition taken here on 29th August, 1290, before Malcolm Harlege. Isabella, the Countess of Devon, had, six years before, obstructed the navigation by the erection of the Topsham wear, commonly called, from her, Countess Wear.

[4] In a deed of our Chamber, dated 4th February, 1403, is their appointment of Thomas Locquiet, clark, to serve this chantry, then vacant, and

specially to pray and celebrate for the souls of Walter Gervey and Alice his wife, the founders of this chantry, and for the souls of their predecessors and successors, and also for the Mayor and Commonalty of Exeter, and for all benefactors to the said bridge. His salary was to be 4l., paid quarterly. Moreover, the said Thomas "in eadem cantariâ personaliter resideat."

[5] The will may be seen in Hoker's

THE BRIDGE OF EXETER.

Saturday in Easter week 1257 to be buried in the public cemetery of St. Peter's Cathedral near the remains of his father, Nicholas Gervys, and he gives his horse as a mortuary; but when the Chantry was taken down in July, 1833, the only skeleton found was that of a tall man, lying about eighteen inches below the surface, with the feet towards the door, the body lying in a direct line; and it was decently re-interred in the same site.[e]

Our learned town-clerk, John Gidley, Esq., has kindly called my attention to a passage in Hardy's Description of the Close Rolls, page 167 :— " Peter de Colechurch, the incumbent of St. Mary Colechurch, near Mercers' Hall, and the celebrated architect of the first London Bridge built with stone, is stated, in the Annals of Waverley, to have died in the year 1205 and to have been buried on the bridge. During the demolition of *that* bridge in 1832, the remains of a body were discovered in clearing away the chapel-pier, and were probably those of the said architect. This supposition is strengthened by the fact that the place in which they were found was under the lower floor of the chapel in an inclosure, built up in small courses of freestone."

From our episcopal registers we collect, that this original stone bridge over the Exe suffered much from inundations, and that the parochial chapel of Cowic, dedicated to St. Thomas Mart., at its western extremity, was, in consequence, utterly demolished, and that a new church, at a distance from the river and, as it were, in the centre of the parish, was provided. This was consecrated by Bishop Edmund Stafford on Tuesday,

---

large MS., fol. 303. One clause is curious, viz., an annual charge of five shillings on his estate, " ad susten- tationem lampadis continuè ardentis coram corpore Christi in Ecclesia S. Jacobi in civitate Exon, in parochia ubi primo accepi sacramentum."

[e] By his wife he left two daughters, one married to Sir William Speke, Knt., with a fortune, in land, of 20l. per annum; the other, wife to Sir John Fitz Geoffry, had an equal fortune. Walter's second wife was called Margaret.

60 HISTORY OF EXETER.

October 4th, 1412 (Reg. Stafford, vol. ii. fol. 287). In a subsequent flood, the bridge itself was threatened with destruction. In a memorial addressed by our Mayor, John Phillingford, in 1448, to Cardinal John Stafford, Archbishop of Canterbury, he represents that the damage cannot be repaired under a cost of two thousand pounds; that "the bridge was of the length or nearly, and of the same mason-work, as London Bridge, *except the housing upon it;*" and implores him to exert his influence with the executors of the will of Henry Beaufort, late Bishop of Winchester (ob. April 11th, 1447, proved in the Prerogative-court of Canterbury, September 11th, 1447), for the appropriation of a part of his alms-deeds to this good and necessary work. Our charitable Bishop Lacy, on February 2nd, 1448-9, granted an indulgence of forty days to all the faithful contributing to the building of a new belfry, *novi campanilis,* for the church of St. Edmund on the said bridge; and on June 15th following he encouraged them in the like manner to assist in the repairs, reconstruction, and maintenance of the bridge itself (Reg. vol. iii. fols. 307-317). Leland, in his Itinerary, assigns to the bridge fourteen arches. William of Worcester, who had seen it above eighty years before, gives it sixteen, and says its length was 400 feet. Mr. Jenkins, in p. 216 of his History of Exeter, 1806, gives thirteen only, " not two alike." [7]

The patronages of the parish-church of St. Edmund's as well as of St. Mary's Chantry, both coeval with the erection of the bridge, were vested in the Mayor and Chamber of this city. The first rector of St. Edmund's " super pontem Exon " is Vivian, admitted by Bishop Walter Bronescombe, on August 25th, 1265, " ad presentationem majoris et civium civitatis Exoniæ ve-

---

[7] [The discrepancy is explained by the probable conversion of small arches into larger ones.]

ACCESSION OF EDWARD I.   61

rorum patronorum" (Register, fol. 33). But a chapel
dedicated to St. Edmund had previously existed in the
vicinity, as the deed of Peter de Palerna alone sufficiently demonstrates.

Hoker, in his MS. History, records that "about the
end of November, 1539, *one of the mydle arches of Exebridge fell down, and was now buylded* by Edward
Bridgeman, then Warden of Exebridge, for which he
bought great store of stones at St. Nicholas' late
dissolved; and then the prophecie was fulfilled, which
was, as it was then saide, the ryver of Exe should run
under St. Nicholas Church." We suspect the cut stone
now serving for a curb-stone at the east corner of
Gandy Street, and evidently the shaft of an ancient
cross, was amongst the débris of this purchase. When
this bridge was demolished in 1778, the late William
Nation, Esq., bought this remarkable shaft for one
guinea, and fixed it against the corner of his house,
where it still remains undisturbed.

CHAPTER XI.

Accession of Edward I. — The first Prince of Wales — Character of the King —
Death of the Lord - Paramount — Privileges of the City — Question of the
murder of Walter de Lechlade — Parliament held in Exeter — The king's
grant of a new Seal to the City — Great Diocesan Council of Exeter.

HENRY III. died on 16th November, 1272, during the
absence of his son and heir Prince Edward in the Holy
Land. Owing to several impediments he was unable
to reach England before 2nd August, 1274. His coronation at Westminster followed on 19th of the same
month and year. After subjugating Wales, and during
his stay at Caernarvon, his Queen Eleanor was brought
to bed, on 25th April, 1284, of her fourth child, Prince

HISTORY OF EXETER.

Edward. The natives claimed him for their country-man, and their joy was unbounded when he was sub-sequently created Prince of Wales—a title usually conferred ever since on the heir-apparent to the British crown.

Our valiant monarch was ambitious to annex the crown of Scotland to his empire. A sanguinary and ruinous warfare, with varied success, was continued against that hardy and belligerent race for thirteen years; and in all probability he would have reduced Scotland to a province of England, if death had not interposed and cut him off at Burgh on the Sands, near Carlisle, on 7th July, 1307.

Our learned commentator on the laws (vol. iv. p. 418) writes thus:—"Edward the First may be justly styled the English Justinian; for in his time the law did receive so sudden a perfection, that Sir Matthew Hale does not scruple to affirm, that more was done in the first thirteen years of his reign to settle and establish the distributive justice of the kingdom, than in all the ages since that time put together." He might have added a reference to his enactment that "all judgments given against the Great Charter shall be void and holden for nought; that it should be read before the people in every cathedral-church twice in the year; and excommunication should be pronounced by the archbishops and bishops against all those that by word, deed, or counsel, do contrary thereunto."

But, to confine our attention to Exeter, our new Lord-Paramount, Edmund Earl of Cornwall, occasionally honoured this city with his presence. Such was his high character for fidelity and discretion, that the king his cousin, during two absences abroad, confided to him the government of the realm. But, for some unknown cause, our mayor and citizens had incurred in the spring of 1286 the earl's displeasure; for, in his

DEATH OF THE LORD-PARAMOUNT.

letter [or writ] dated Berkhampstede on the Monday before Midsummer-day of that year, he assured them of his pardon, and at the request of his cousins, the daughters of Edward the illustrious King of England, consented to give back 50 marks of the sum of 250 due by their bond; reserving, however, his right to reclaim it if they deviated from their duty towards him. He was a kind and religious prince—a considerate benefactor to the Franciscan establishment in this city, and the munificent founder of the Augustinian House of Ashridge, Bucks. Dying 1st October, 1300, he was buried in the choir of its conventual church; and, leaving no issue, his honours reverted to the Crown, and his splendid inheritance to the king, his first cousin, next akin and heir-at-law.

In the ninth year of his reign Edward issued a writ of quo warranto to try by what authority this city held its fee-farm and other privileges. The return of the burgesses before Solomon Roff and his companions, the king's justices, showed satisfactorily that they held the fee-farm since the reign of Henry I., by the yearly payment to the crown of 39l. 1s. 6d., and that they had enjoyed their privilege since the Conquest of a fair on 1st August, and a market on three days of the week, viz. Monday, Wednesday, and Friday. The king thereupon confirmed the whole under the great seal.

We may now direct the reader's attention to the homicide of the Precentor of Exeter, in November 1283. Hoker, and Izaacke (his copyist) contend, that King Edward I. and his queen (Eleanor of Castile), at Bishop Quivil's request, came hither and kept the Christmas[1] of 1285 within this city of Exeter, "chiefly

---

[1] They took up their residence in the Bishop's palace; but Mr. Jenkins states apparently upon his own authority (p. 49, History of Exeter) that they and their suite lodged in the convent of the Black Friars (lately Bedford House).

64 HISTORY OF EXETER.

occasioned through the death of one Walter Lichlade, the first chaunter of this church, who was murthered as he came from matins; that upon an inquisition Alphred Duport, late mayor, and the porter of Southgate, were both indicted, arraigned, found guilty, and executed accordingly, for that the Southgate was that night left open, by which means the murderer escaped." And they add, that the Close round the cathedral was formed in consequence of this murder.

Without noticing the incorrectness of the assertion that Walter Lechlade was the *first* precentor—for that office was in fact coeval with Leofric's translation of the See from Crediton to Exeter, in the year 1050; and both those writers had previously stated, that John the Chaunter, or precentor, had been advanced from that office to be the seventh bishop of this church, a century before this murder [2]—we had come to a conclusion that no such event transpired, and for the following reasons :—

First.—From the silence of the Register of Bishop Peter Quivil, who had collated the said Walter, a canon of his church, to the office of its precentor, on the 1st of August, 1282, void by the resignation of Henry de Somerset (Reg. 118). Walter held it until his death; which the obituary of the cathedral fixes on the 9th of November, 1283. The same register records the collation on the 19th of November, 1283, of Andrew de Kilkenny to the precentorship of the church of Exeter, void by the death of the same Master Walter (fol. 122), and on the very same day the bishop collated the Queen's nephew (James de Hispaniâ) to the prebend in this church, void also by the death of the said Walter de Lechlade. Now how could we account, in those days of clerical influence, that no

---

[2] Andrew Brice in his ' Mobiad,' written here in 1738, will have it that this John the Chaunter was murdered as he was going early to matins.

WALLING-IN OF THE CLOSE.

allusion throughout the register is made to such. an astounding act of violence?

Secondly.—In King Edward the First's charter, dated "*Exeter*, 1st day of January, fourteenth year of our reign," 1285-6, licensing the formation of the Close,[3] and also in the composition between our Dean and Chapter of the one part, and the Mayor and citizens of the other part, dated on the Monday after Lady-day, 1286, a perfect silence is maintained as to the sacrilegious murder of this dignitary.

Thirdly.—Several such licences for similar inclosures around cathedrals were obtained of the Crown by the deans and chapters of Lincoln, York, London, and Wells, at this very period, as a general measure of security. (See Prynne's Records, vol. iii., pp. 345, 346.)

Fourthly.—In a deed preserved in our chapter archives of Brother John,[4] Prior of St. John the Baptist's Hospital, Wells, bearing date the 30th of September,

---

[3] CARTA DOMINI REGIS de venellis claudendis portis ac posternis construendis.

Edwardus Dei gratiâ rex Anglie Dominus Hibernie et dux Aquitanie omnibus ad quos presentes littere pervenerint, Salutem. Sciatis quod cum per nocturnos incursus latronum et aliorum malefactorum per vicos et venellas in procinctu cimiterii cathedralis Ecclesie Sancti Petri Exonie et in cimiterio illo multociens de nocte vagancium homicidia fornicationes et alia mala pluries hactenus fuerint perpetrata, et formidetur quod adhuc consimilia vel majora pericula per hujus modi incursus in vicis et venellis et cimiterio ac procinctu predictis poterunt evenire nisi contra pericula illa remedium apponatur; nos ad honorem Dei et dicte Ecclesie ac sanctorum quorum corpora requiescunt in eadem nec non ad securitatem et quietem canonicorum et ministrorum predicte Ecclesie et suorum ibidem residentium, concessimus pro nobis et heredibus nostris quantum in nobis est dilectis nobis in Christo Petro Episcopo loci illius et decano et capitulo Ecclesie predicte, quod cimiterium illud et procinctum muro lapideo circumquaque includere et sic inclusa sibi et successoribus suis tenere possint sine occasione et impedimento nostri et heredum nostrorum imperpetuum. Ita tamen quod portas et posternas faciant in locis necessariis et competentibus ibidem et quod porte ille et posterne singulis diebus aperte sint ab aurora diei usque ad noctem. Ita quod omnes et singuli ibidem transire volentes pro voluntate sua et sine impedimento predictorum episcopi decani et capituli et successorum suorum seu ministrorum ejusdem Ecclesie quorumcunque liberum ingressum habeant per portas et posternas supradictas, et ita quod porte ille et posterne de nocte claudantur, et in aurora diei aperiantur sicut predictum est. In cujus rei testimonium has literas nostros fieri fecimus patentes. Teste me ipso apud Exon primo die Januarii, anno regni nostri quarto decimo. [1286.]

The great seal of England is appendant in green wax.

[4] This prior was unknown to the editors of the 'Monasticon Anglicanum,' vol. vi., p. 664.

HISTORY OF EXETER.

1292, is a minute statement of his expending the moneys which had been placed in his hands by the executors of the *late* Master Walter Lechlade, of happy memory—that he had succeeded in obtaining, through the kindness of Bishop Bitton, the advowson of West Down (in the North of Devon), for the maintenance of the perpetual obit of the said Walter in Exeter Cathedral—that the body of the deceased lay opposite St. Edmund's altar there—that a chantry priest would ever celebrate there " pro animâ supradicti defuncti "—that on his anniversary a distribution of money would be given to the clergy who should assist at the service; but no reference whatever is made to his murder.

Fifthly.—We could not reconcile it with the character of our English Justinian, King Edward I., to order the execution of Alfred Duport, who stood so high in the estimation of his fellow-citizens, as to elect him their chief magistrate eight several times. Moreover we have seen a deed witnessed by this Alfred,[5] the Sunday

---

[5] Indorsed "Carta W. de Doderigge" (late in Sept. 1285).

Die Dominica proxima post festum beati Mathei Apostoli, anno regni regis Edwardi tertio decimo, ita convenit inter Petrum Dei gratiâ Exon Episcopum, decanum et capitulum Ecclesie beati Petri ejusdem loci, ex parte una et Walterum de Dodderigg et Benedictam uxorem ejus ex altera, videlicet quod idem Walterus assensu et consensu dicte Benedicte uxoris sue, obstruere concesserit pro se, heredibus et assignatis suis, omnia hostia cujusdam tenementi sui, quod quando fuit Philippi Le Lorim de Exonia, que quidem hostia annexa fuerunt cimiterio beati Petri ejusdem loci; ita tamen quod prefati Walterus et Benedicta, heredes seu assignati sui, aliquem ingressum seu egressum imposterum habere non possint. Pro hac autem concessione gratis habenda, sepedicti Petrus episcopus, decanus, et capitulum, relaxaverant et imperpetuum quietum clamaverunt dictis Waltero et Benedicte, heredibus et assignatis suis quatuordecim solidos annui redditus, qui de pretextato tenemento dictorum Walteri et Benedicte prenominate Ecclesie annuatim debebantur: ita tamen quod idem Petrus episcopus, decanus et capitulum, aliquid juris seu clamii cujuscunque in redditu antedicto imperpetuum exigere seu vendicare non poterunt, nec aliquem alium redditum de memorato tenemento, quatuor solidis duntaxat exceptis. Ceterum licitum est sepedictis Waltero et Benedicte, heredibus et assignatis suis, domos suas ex parte cemeterii antedicti tegere ac meremia sua in eodem ponere et dirigere ad domos suas sustinendas quando necesse fuerit sine aliqua contradictione. In cujus rei testimonium tam sigilla predictorum Petri episcopi decani et capituli quam sigilla prefatorum Walteri et Benedicte, huic conventionali scripto bipartito sunt apposita. Hiis, testibus, magistro Hamundo tunc ballivo civitatis Exon, Johanne de Fenton, Aluredo de Porta, Richardo Aleyn, Thomâ de Gatepath, Johanne Rok, David Cissore, et aliis.

Dodderigge's seal is attached, a squirrel feeding on a nut.

MURDER OF WALTER LECHLADE.

after the Feast of St. Matthew (late in September 1285, nearly two years after the alleged murder), by which Walter de Dodderigge, and Benedicta, his wife, surrendered their right to the dean and chapter of egress and ingress, through the doors of their house in the High Street, into the cathedral cemetery.

Lastly, the silence of all our ancient chronicles disposes us to question, and even to discredit, the narrative of Messieurs Hoker and Izaacke.

There is, however, no reasoning against recorded facts ; and we cannot refuse our credit to the following letters to King Edward I., recently discovered in the Tower of London, by that indefatigable investigator of historical truth, Thomas Duffus Hardy. With his permission, we submit the following translations of them to the reader.

(No. 1855.)—First Letter of PETER QUIVIL, Bishop of Exeter.

To the most Serene Prince his Lord, Edward, by the grace of God, the illustrious King of England, Lord of Ireland, and Duke of Acquitaine, Peter, by the mercy of the same, Bishop of Exeter, health in Him by whom kings reign and princes exercise dominion. Whereas, John, called Pycot of Exeter, priest, arraigned for the murder of Mr. Walter de Lechelade, of happy memory, once precentor of our church of Exeter, and by your Justices then committed to our prison, has canonically purged himself before us of the murder aforesaid, by trustworthy and discreet men, according to the liberty of the Church and custom of the realm ; we humbly request and beseech your Excellency to order the restitution of his goods and possessions according to the demand of justice, if it be pleasing to you ; that as in person, so in goods and possessions, as the liberty of the Church requires, he may be restored to his former state and honour in all things. May the Most High preserve your Majesty to His holy Church and the realm for a lengthened period.

Given at Exeter, the 8th Kal. of August (25th of July), in the year of our Lord 1286.

(No. 1856.)—Second Letter of the said Bishop ; date the same.

To the most Serene Prince his Lord, Edward, by the grace of God the illustrious King of England, Lord of Ireland, and

F 2

68   HISTORY OF EXETER.

Duke of Acquitaine, Peter, by the mercy of the same, health in Him by whom kings reign and princes exercise dominion. Whereas, John de Christenestowe, priest, vicar of Hevetre, of our diocese, arraigned for the murder of Master Walter de Lechelade of happy memory, once precentor of our church of Exeter, and by your Justices then committed to our prison, has canonically purged himself before us of the murder aforesaid, by trustworthy and discreet men, according to the liberty of the Church and the custom of the realm; we humbly request and beseech your Excellency to order the restitution of his goods and possessions, if it be pleasing to you, according to the demand of justice; that as in his person, so in goods and possessions, as the liberty of the Church requires it, he may be restored to his former state and honour in all things. May the Most High preserve your Majesty to His holy Church and realm for a lengthened period.

Given at Exeter, the 8th Kal. of August, 1286.

(No. 1857.)—Letter of JOHN PECKHAM,[6] Archbishop of Canterbury.

To the most excellent Prince and the Lord Edward, by the grace of God illustrious King of England, Lord of Ireland, and Duke of Acquitaine, Brother John, by the Divine permission the humble minister of the church of Canterbury; Primate of all England, health and peace in Him by whom kings reign and princes exercise dominion. Whereas, our beloved son, Master Lucas, of St. Leonard, clerk, of our diocese, had been defamed as consenting to the death of Master Walter de Lechelade, once precentor of the church of Exeter, there sometime since barbarously slain, and before your Justices in the county of Devon convicted of this upon suspicion ("ymaginarie") and by the judgment of the Justices delivered up to us, as his ordinary, to be detained in safe custody; at length having summoned the parties concerned and proclamations made publicly and solemnly in fit place and time that all that wished to offer opposition or believed themselves interested, might appear before our official of Canterbury, our special Commissary in this matter, to propose or show legitimate or canonical evidence, if they had any, why the purgation of the said Luke, clerk, concerning the premises objected to him, should not be admitted in form of law. And whereas, against the admission of such purgation,

---

[6] Leland, in 'Scriptoribus Britannicis,' p. 328, describes this Franciscan as "magnus philosophus juxta ac theologus." Unquestionably he was one of the most intellectual men of his age, and few more zealous and self-denying prelates have adorned our English Church. After governing his see for fourteen years, he died on the 8th of December, 1292.

MURDER OF WALTER LECHLADE. 69

nothing was proposed or shown by any one, that could in the least degree impede such purgation or any wise retard it, the aforesaid Master Lucas appearing in person before our said Commissary according to the laws and custom of the realm of England hitherto used and obtained, purged himself legitimately and canonically of every thing imputed to him concerning the death of the aforesaid Walter. Wherefore, we humbly and devoutly supplicate your Royal Excellency, that you would vouchsafe to command that all the lands, possessions, the goods moveable and immoveable of the clerk aforesaid, taken and seised in your hands by reason of the counts of the indictment aforesaid, may be restored according to the custom of the realm without diminution, to the same clerk or his attorney, and that he may be set at liberty. May the Lord protect your Excellence for a lengthened period.

Given at Tenham, the 6th Ides of March (10th), in the year of our Lord 1285–6.

(No. 1858.)—Letter of Bishop QUIVIL.

To the most Serene Prince, his Lord, Edward, by the grace of God, illustrious King of England, Lord of Ireland, and Duke of Acquitaine, Peter, by the mercy of the same, Bishop of Exeter, health in Him by whom kings reign and princes exercise dominion. Whereas, John de Wolrington, priest, vicar of Ottery St. Mary,[7] of our diocese, arraigned for the murder of Master Walter de Lechelade, of good memory, formerly precentor of our church of Exeter, and by your Justices some time committed to our prison, has purged himself of the murder aforesaid, canonically before us by trustworthy and discreet men according to the liberty of the Church and the custom of the realm; we humbly request and beseech your Excellency that you would order his goods and possessions to be restored to him, if it pleaseth you, according to the demand of law, so that in effects and possessions, as the liberty of the Church requires it, he may be restored to his former state and honour in all things. May the Most High preserve your Majesty to His holy Church and the realm for a lengthened period.

Given at Exeter, the 8th Kal. of August (25th July), 1286.

With this superabundant evidence before us, no doubt can remain of the fact of the revolting murder; but,

---

[7] It is not generally known that the Dean and Chapter of Rouen leased to this precentor for his life their manor of Ottery St. Mary; and that Bishop Quivil, on the 6th of July, 1283, approved of his taking it. See his 'Register,' folio 121.

70   HISTORY OF EXETER.

perhaps, the name of the assassin may remain a secret until the final day of manifestation of all human guilt. We regret our inability to throw further light on the history of the mayor, Alfred de Portâ; yet we cannot bring ourselves to believe that the king, even from respect for his own character and the feelings of the citizens of Exeter, could be guilty of consigning their innocent and estimable chief magistrate to an ignominious execution.[8]

During his Majesty's stay in Exeter, at Christmas 1285,. he held a parliament, when a statute was enacted to remedy the abuses of coroners. At the period before us, inquests were taken not only in cases of murder, but also of felony and depredation. In consequence of the late turbulent times, these officers had become remiss in the discharge of their duties. By this " statute of Exeter " the strictest investigation of all inquests was demanded since his Majesty's accession to the Crown. The returns were to be forwarded to him, and he is authorised to punish the offending coroners according to the discretion of his justices.

The city assumed a new seal on 22nd August, 1292, representing the king crowned, with a lion passant and regardant on his breast, and a castle on either side, in allusion to his incomparable wife Eleanor, daughter to Ferdinand II., King of Leon and Castile. She died universally lamented, on 27th November, 1290. The legend on the obverse is—

S . EDW . REG . ANG . AD . RECOGN . DEBITOR . APVD . EXON.

(*i. e.* The seal of Edward King of England for the recognizance of debts at Exeter.)

The reverse of this beautiful seal bears a lion couchant, surrounded by CIVITATIS . EXONIE. This is

---

[8] [The complicity of these "purged" offenders is by no means negatived by the several writs above cited. The award of the civil courts was probably adverse to them.]

ACCESSION OF EDWARD II.

not to be confounded with the seal of the mayor of the staple of Exeter, which may not have been made until the statute was enacted anno 27 Edwardi III. (1353).[9]

In concluding this chapter, we must notice the great diocesan council held in this city by its bishop after the Easter of 1287. The Acts may be seen in Spelman and Wilkins; and we have not failed to dwell upon them in the biography of that energetic prelate in our Lives of the Bishops of Exeter, to which we refer the reader.

CHAPTER XII.

Accession of Edward II. — Recall of Piers Gaveston — Edward the Black Prince Lord-Paramount — Captivity of John, King of France — The Black Pestilence ; its disastrous effects on Exeter — Bishop Grandisson. His recognition of the distinction between the ecclesiastical and civil powers.

SCARCELY had the king breathed his last, when his son and successor, Edward II., in violation of his solemn promise to his late parent, recalled from banishment that worthless minion and evil counsellor, Piers de Gaveston ; and, as if to insult the nation, created him Baron of Wallingford, gave him his niece Margaret de Clare in marriage, appointed him regent of the realm during his temporary absence in France, and at his coronation, celebrated with unprecedented splendour, on St. Matthias' day, 24th February, 1308, assigned to him the honour of carrying the crown, and of walking in the procession immediately before the sovereign. The predilection manifested for this obnoxious favourite, combined with his elevation to the carldom of Cornwall, provoked the universal wrath of the country, and pre-

---

[9] [The above seal is in the usual form of such seals elsewhere, and was used by authority of a statute, and not by grant of the crown.] The common seal —the workmanship of one Lucas, and the gift of William Prudum, the founder of St. Alexius's Hospital, behind St. Nicholas's Priory, A.D. 1170; the Mayor's official seal; and the seal of the Provosts, will be described in the Appendix.

HISTORY OF EXETER.

pared the way for Gaveston's untimely fall and execution. From such a Lord-Paramount Exeter could not have derived honour or advantage. Our imbecile and vacillating sovereign continued to be surrounded with false friends and interested counsellors, with the honourable exception of that incorruptible loyalist and able minister Walter de Stapeldon, bishop of this city and diocese. But indeed the king was to be pitied; and the historian is almost disposed to overlook his errors and infatuations, when contrasted with the unnatural conduct of his profligate queen, and the lawless and perfidious excesses and unprincipled combinations of avowed traitors.

To our wise and irreproachable bishop we have endeavoured to do justice in our Lives of the Bishops of Exeter. In these perilous times this diocese clung with desperate fidelity to the cause of their ill-fated sovereign,[1] proud to emulate the noble example of its illustrious prelate.

We may now confine our attention to the immediate concerns of this city. In Bishop Brantyngham's Register (vol. i. p. 236) is inserted a composition between Bishop Stapeldon and his chapter on the one part, and the mayor and commonalty of Exeter on the other, concluded on the Monday after the Feast of St. Hilary (January, 1322), by which the former concede to the latter the right of surveying and repair-

---

[1] From a MS. account, taken from the Berkeley Records, we collect that this dethroned monarch was placed during the day-time in a room called the Dungeon Chamber, of Berkeley Castle; that this chamber is immediately over the vault or dungeon itself; in its floor is a trap-door opening into the dungeon below, which is twenty-eight feet deep, down to the very foundations of the castle. This dungeon was filled with putrid carcases of animals, &c., the rising fumes from which the keepers expected would produce fever, and accelerate the king's death. The unhappy prisoner bitterly complained of this to some carpenters at work upon the castle, from the window of that little bedroom to which he was taken every night, and in which he is stated to have been horribly murdered.

Sir Thomas de Berkeley, the owner of the castle, was tried by a jury of twelve knights for being instrumental in this murder, but was acquitted (Hatsell's Precedents, vol. iv. p. 81).

THE BLACK PRINCE LORD-PARAMOUNT. 73

ing the walls of the close abutting on the episcopal palace, and the residences of the chancellor of the cathedral, and of the archdeacons of Exeter and of Cornwall. As the document has been hitherto unpublished, we have inserted it in the Appendix to our work above alluded to. The turbulent reign of the ill-used father was redeemed by the triumphant career of his son King Edward III. The decisive victory of Halidon Hill over the Scotch on 19th July, 1333, and of Creci on 26th August, 1346, followed by that of Poictiers on 19th September, 1356, established the fame of our superior skill and valour, and must for ever immortalize our country in the pages of history. In the two last-mentioned engagements, our Lord-Paramount,[2] Edward the Black Prince, eclipsed the achievements of his gallant comrades. Yet there is no truth in the assertion of some of our modern writers, misled by the authority of Henry Knyghton and Polydore Vergil, "that the prince landed at *Plymouth* on 5th May, 1357, with John the captive king of France," and "from thence came to this city, where they were honourably received, and so conveyed to London." The fact is, they landed at *Sandwich*, and proceeded by easy journeys to the metropolis. This is incontestably proved by Froissart in his 'Chronicle.'[3] The fleet, with the royal prisoners on board taken at Poictiers, sailed for England from Bordeaux, and, after being detained at sea for eleven days and nights, reached Sandwich on the twelfth day of the voyage, viz., the

---

[2] John of Eltham, the second son of King Edward II. and Queen Isabella, was created by his royal brother, in 1328, the Earl of Cornwall. Soon after his death the earldom was formed into a duchy, of which Exeter was made a parcel, viz. 18th March, 1337, in favour of Edward the Black Prince, who now became the receiver of its farm-rent, 20*l.* per annum.

[3] John Froissart was born at Valenciennes, in 1337, and died about 1402. The best, as well as the rarest edition of his 'Chronicle,' was printed at Lyons, in four vols. folio. For a time he was chaplain to King Edward III., and attended the court at Bordeaux, where Richard his son was born 6th January, 1366.

74   HISTORY OF EXETER.

5th of May. After remaining there two days to refresh themselves, they proceeded to Canterbury, visited the cathedral, and made their offerings. Early the next morning they started for Rochester, where they passed on that day. The following day witnessed their arrival at Deptford, where every preparation had been made by the public authorities to give them an honourable reception. The entry into London on the ensuing day resembled a triumph. The royal prisoner was mounted on a white courser covered with the richest trappings, whilst his modest conqueror rode by his side on a black hackney. The cavalcade at last stopped at the Savoy Palace, which had been fitted up for John's residence, where King Edward and his queen frequently came to visit and console him; and shortly afterwards Windsor Castle was assigned to the French monarch and his suite, as may be seen in Froissart's Narrative, vol. i. chapter 173.

With the greater part of Christendom, our city had to experience the frightful ravages of the disease called the Black Pestilence. Its progress from India was marked with desolation to man and beast. From France it travelled to Southampton at Michaelmas, 1348; it soon reached Winchester, the coast of Dorset, Bristol, and thence was imported into this diocese. The episcopal registers here show its wide-wasting fatality among the population, and especially in religious communities.[4]

Of the numbers swept away by this disastrous visitation within this city we have no means of discovery; but we well know that it arrested the building of the cathedral nave, that it paralysed our woollen trade

---

[4] How frightful its ravages were in the diocese of Winchester, may be gathered from Bishop Edyngdon's Register, where, in 1349, not a single inmate of Sandown Hospital escaped death, and two abbesses, eleven priors, and very many canons fell victims. When in 1361 the plague broke out again, it carried off two abbesses at Wherewell, two abbesses at St. Mary's, Winchester, the abbot of Chertsey, and eight or nine priors of various houses.

THE BLACK PESTILENCE. 75

and all commercial enterprise, and suspended agricultural pursuits, and that its effects weighed heavily on our population for upwards of three years. It burst out again in 1361, but in a mitigated form. During this calamity, Exeter was fortunate indeed in possessing such a pastor and bishop as John de Grandisson. He had a commanding influence and large pecuniary resources; and he was never so happy as when he could console and relieve his afflicted and indigent fellow-creatures.

We close this chapter with observing, that this sterling English prelate, to whom Exeter and the diocese must ever be indebted, fully recognized and asserted the distinction between the spiritual and the temporal power of the Holy See. On reaching England in February, 1328, he hastened to meet his sovereign at York; and, though he had been provided to this see by Pope John XXII., he openly and expressly renounced, before his liege lord the king, every expression in the papal bulls that could entrench on the rights of the Crown of England. This act of renunciation had been required by our monarchs for a considerable period back, before they put bishops in possession of the temporalities of their respective sees; and it was a reasonable and expedient measure, distinctly marking the boundaries between the ecclesiastical and civil powers.

CHAPTER XIII.

Reign of Richard II. — Exhausted exchequer — Insurrection against the capitation tax — Energy of the King — His subsequent misgovernment and deposition — Accession of Henry V. — John Wickliffe — The Lollards.

EDWARD the Black Prince, the hope and darling of his country, died 8th June, 1376; his only surviving

76   HISTORY OF EXETER.

son Richard, now ten years of age, was acknowledged
by Parliament to be heir-apparent to the throne, and
to which he succeeded on the death of his royal grandfather a twelvemonth later. The protracted wars with
France had completely exhausted the treasury, but the
commons and the clergy were liberal with their subsidies, and, moreover, voted a capitation-tax, graduated
according to the rank and estate of each individual, to
meet the public exigences. The collection of this
capitation-tax gave occasion to the formidable insurrection in 1381, which threatened the life of the sovereign and the subversion of all constitutional government. In this critical conjuncture the youthful king
displayed a chivalrous coolness and courage far above
his years. But as he grew older he disappointed
the expectations of the country. He had been taught
by his mother and her friends to estrange himself
from his uncles, especially John of Gaunt, Duke of
Lancaster ; he grew mistrustful of the ancient nobility,
and seemed in his choice of favourites to have forgotten the memorable fate experienced by his great
grandfather King Edward II. His was a period of
national fermentation and turbulence, and of undefined
prerogative ; and in taking the reins of government
into his own hands, he was betrayed into errors and
lamentable excesses. His wars with France and Scotland, and the extravagant expenditure of his household,
gradually compelled him to be a humble suitor to Parliament to extricate him from pecuniary emergency.
His necessities threw him at their mercy ; and, by
occasional attempts to set himself above the law, he
weakened and at length forfeited the affection of the
people, without which a king is but a cipher in a constitutional monarchy. By degrees he sunk so low in
his own estimation as to consent to the act of his own
deposition, which was, in his case, almost tautamount to

DEPOSITION OF RICHARD II. 77

the signing of his own death-warrant. If sovereigns could anticipate what misfortunes they might avert from themselves, their dynasty, and their country, by pursuing a direct, conciliatory, and legal course, they would never calculate on that deceitful power produced by their passions, but solely on the moral strength founded on reason, justice, and integrity of character. They would act on the conviction that the maintenance of the rights of every member of the body politic would give stability to the whole ; and that encroachment on the liberties of the people must shake their thrones, if not subvert them. Could subjects, on the other side, foresee the wrongs, the bloodshed and ruin, entailed and perpetuated by revolutions, they would contract their ambitious views, and be satisfied that success may be purchased at too dear a rate. Well might King Richard II. exclaim on 13th August, 1399, " Alas, what trust in this false world ! "

During this disastrous reign, if Exeter was not distinguished by any important events,[1] it was exempted at least from many calamities that afflicted other parts of the kingdom. Its citizens remained tranquil and submissive to the legally constituted authorities; and amidst the defection of faithless statesmen and counsellors, they were content to be guided by the example of their irreproachable bishops, Thomas Brantyngham and Edmund Stafford. When ingratitude and violence had seated Henry of Bolingbroke on the throne, they quietly yielded to legalised usurpation, and acquiesced in the new order of things.

Unfortunately the country was heaving with the earthquake of religious and political feelings occasioned by the doctrines of John Wickliffe, who died rector

---

[1] On Michaelmas-day, 1397, the king created his uterine brother, John Holland, the first Duke of Exeter; but he held his honours but for a short time, being executed on the 9th of January, 1400.

78   HISTORY OF EXETER.

of Loughborough, 31st December, 1384, and of his
followers the Lollardists—doctrines partially borrowed
from the Poor Men of Lyons, from the Albigenses,
and the Bohemian Brethren.   Had their views been
confined to theory, had they not threatened disturbance, and even ruin, to public and private property,
the government might have left them unheeded.
Even Archbishop Parker (Antiq. Brit. p. 275)
contends, " that it was not without good reason that
the law of the second year of Henry V. was made to
suppress them, on account of their numbers and the
tumults they occasioned to the disturbance and even
to the terror of the civil government."   And most
certainly such licentiousness of teaching and practising levelling principles would not be tolerated, even
in these days, by the constituted authorities of our
country.   The Commons, in their address to King
Henry V., affirm, that these insurgents "sought
to destroy the Christian Faith, and the king, the
spiritual and temporal estates, and all manner of
policy and law."   The king himself announces, in his
proclamation, that "they had plotted to destroy him
and his brothers during the Christmas festivities at
Eltham, in 1413, with several of the spiritual and
temporal lords, and to confiscate the property of the
Church, and to divide the realm into districts, and to
appoint Sir John Oldcastle President of the Commonwealth."   Dr. Fiddes also, in his Life of Cardinal
Wolsey (pp. 35-39), maintains that in all these proceedings the Church acted in subserviency to the
authority of the State, and by virtue of standing and
express laws; and that "it was not for their speculative opinions, considered purely as such, but because
in certain respects these innovators maintained principles derogatory to the rights of the prince, injurious
to society, and contrary to the laws then in force."

HENRY VI. 79

For our own part, we must ever deem the sanguinary punishment of mental errors as a departure from the genius and spirit of the Founder of Christianity ; that it can only serve to provoke and embitter fanaticism, and is therefore irreconcileable with sound policy and even humanity.

CHAPTER XIV.

Henry VI. — His reception at Exeter — Civil war — Edward IV. assumes the crown — Visit to this city — Death of the King — Usurpation of Richard III. — Murder of the Princes in the Tower — The King killed at Bosworth Field — Perkin Warbeck repulsed at Exeter — His surrender at Taunton, and imprisonment in this city — Henry VII. at Exeter — Royal charters — Visit of Princess Catherine — Marriage with Prince Arthur, and subsequently with Henry VIII. — Progress of literature — Degeneracy of morals.

WE have had occasion already to lament the misfortune of the succession of minors to the throne in troublesome times. By the premature death of King Henry V., on 31st August, 1422, in the zenith of his military glory, the crown devolved to his son Henry, a babe but nine months old. It was indeed a critical period, for the council was divided, and his two uncles, John Duke of Bedford, and Humphrey Duke of Gloucester, stood in opposition to each other—the former one great in the field, the latter in council ; but the infant sovereign was permitted to be crowned at Westminster on 6th November, 1429, and even at Paris, on 17th November, 1431, where the French nobility swore allegiance to him. By the death of his uncles he lost the main pillars to his throne. Innocent, gentle, religious, and devoted to the cultivation and patronage of the liberal arts and sciences, he was little qualified to wrestle with such boisterous times ; he found himself the sport of the vicissitudes of fortune ; he beheld his father's conquests melting away before

80   HISTORY OF EXETER.

him, and eventually deprived of his crown and his life
by those who had sworn fealty to him.

Amidst the turmoils and carnage, amidst the alter-
nate reverses and successes of the Houses of Lancaster
and York, which for so many years spread disunion
and desolation in families, which revolutionized the
tenure of property, unhinged public credit, and plunged
the country into mourning, Exeter could not fail of
experiencing her full share of the general affliction.
Under the House of Lancaster she had prospered.
The sixth Henry had honoured her with his
presence, and she had abundant opportunities of
witnessing and admiring his benevolent and peaceful
virtues. The reception that he met with here must be
interesting to the reader. He had long cherished a
special regard for our bishop, Edmund Lacy; and in
his progress westward, in the early part of the summer
of 1452, he would testify his esteem of this aged and
venerable prelate and trustworthy friend by taking up
his abode in the episcopal palace within this city. On
entering Devon, he rested a night at Ford Abbey;
the next day he proceeded to St. Mary's collegiate
establishment at Ottery, where he stayed two days.
On Monday, 17th July, he left for this city, accompanied by a prodigious concourse of knights,
gentlemen, and yeomanry. The mayor and commonalty of our loyal city, in full state, were waiting
at Honiton Clist to welcome their sovereign. The
communities of the Franciscan and Dominican convents
and the rural clergy were assembled at St. Clara's
Chapel, Livery Dole, to join in the procession. On
reaching the great Cross without the Southgate, the
Benedictine Prior of St. Nicholas and the Augustinian
Prior of St. John's Hospital met him with the parochial clergy and chaplains, bearing two crosses before
them, and offered incense to the King, who saluted

HENRY VI. AND EDWARD IV. AT EXETER. 81

the cross. Then the Mayor delivered to him the keys of Southgate, and rode in advance, carrying the 'mace, before him. The streets were richly hung with silks and tapestry. At Broadgate he alighted, where the bishop, canons, and choristers were in full attendance, and in solemn procession advanced to the west door of the cathedral, and thence to the high altar. After spending some time in devotion and making his offering, he adjourned to the bishop's palace adjoining. The next day the judges in commission sat in the bishop's hall, where two men were indicted, arraigned, and sentenced to death for treason; but, at the intercession of the bishop and his chapter, the king graciously extended his mercy and forgiveness to the convicts. Hoker supposes that the king left the city for Honiton on the following Wednesday. Izaacke prolongs his visit for eight days; but Mr. Hardy collects, from records in the Tower, that he was actually in this city on 29th July. Perhaps he quitted on that day for Honiton; for he reached Gloucester, on his way to London, on the fourth day of August.

Eighteen years had not elapsed when King Edward IV. visited Exeter, viz., on Saturday 14th April, 1470. He had come in pursuit of the Duke of Clarence, the Earl of Warwick, and other leaders of the Lancastrian cause, but they had effected their escape, and embarked at Dartmouth. His heart was not disposed in favour of Exeter, which had afforded harbour and hospitality to his enemies, and successfully sustained a siege of twelve days very shortly before against his adherent Sir William Courtenay of Powderham, Knight; but he may have deemed it expedient to dissemble his displeasure, and try to conciliate the good feelings of those who had manifested fidelity to their old sovereign. The Mayor, with four hundred of the citizens in red gowns,

HISTORY OF EXETER.

received him respectfully. Thomas Douriche, the Recorder, complimented him in a set oration; a purse, containing one hundred nobles, was benignantly accepted; and the keys and maces were presented, but graciously re-delivered to the Mayor. The next day was Palm Sunday, when this stately monarch, the handsomest man of his age, walked in the customary procession bearing the blessed palm in his hand. From Bishop Stapeldon's Register (fol. 168) we learn that the yearly processions on Palm Sunday and Corpus Christi day extended beyond the eastern gate of the city from the cathedral, so that all had the opportunity of viewing and admiring their sovereign. After dinner on the Tuesday the King departed on horseback, "giving great thanks to the Mayor for his entertainment, as also showing himself very loving and bountiful to the people" (Hoker's MS.). His sword, which he is said to have presented to the city on this occasion, is still carefully preserved.

But such is the uncertainty of human affairs, that within six months afterwards Edward was a fugitive to the coast of Holland; and Henry VI. was conducted with great pomp from the Tower, and replaced upon his throne, and Parliament hastened to proclaim Edward an usurper, to attaint his adherents, and to repeal all the acts done under his authority. The ensuing Easter witnessed the fugitive and exiled monarch the conqueror at the battle of Barnet,[1] and again, within three weeks later, at the decisive battle at Tewkesbury, and the unfortunate sovereign Henry immured in the Tower,

---

[1] To show how slowly news travelled in those days, the issue of the battle of Barnet, fought on the 14th of April, 1471, was not known in Cornwall on the 23rd of that month and year. I have seen a deed dated Llandulph, on the banks of the Tamar, near Plymouth, on the 23rd of April, 1471, " Redemptionis regiæ potestatis anno primo." Henry had recovered possession on the previous 6th of October. But what is more surprising, the news of Queen Elizabeth's death, on the 24th of March, 1603, did not transpire in Ireland until the 9th day of April.

MURDER OF THE PRINCES.

83

whence his dead body was brought forth, shortly after, to be exhibited to the public previous to its interment.

King Edward IV. granted to our Mayor, Bailiffs, and Commonalty the goods of felons and outlaws, and the confiscated property of citizens and inhabitants of Exeter, and all fines; also a fair, to commence on 21st July, the eve of the Feast of St. Mary Magdalen, and to continue during the two following days. He also confirmed the incorporation of the Cordwainers' Company, which had been created nearly a century before, and incorporated the city guilds of the glovers, tailors, and bakers. Had he been less suspicious, less voluptuous and cruel, this king might have proved a blessing to the nation. Death marked him for his victim in the forty-first year of his age, 9th April, 1483. His unnatural and remorseless brother Richard is charged with the murder of the two youthful sons of the king, to clear his way to the Crown. He had first appointed the 4th of May for the coronation of his nephew Edward V.; then the 22nd day of June was ultimately fixed for the grand festivity; but this insidious Protector's object was to gain time for maturing his plans, for removing the most confidential ministers of his late sovereign in the interim, for assembling in the capital his friends as well as several of those whom he suspected to be his enemies, to be present at the coming coronation. Then he threw off the mask, and a parliament was found base enough to admit and support his pretensions. On 6th July, 1483, with extraordinary pomp, Richard was crowned with his queen Anne, daughter of Richard late Earl of Warwick. The list of dukes, earls, lords, and knights is given in S. Bentley's Excerpta Historica (p. 384). Our bishop, Peter Courtenay, with several others, especially Margaret, the mother of Henry of Richmond, the queen's trainbearer, must indeed have been

G 2

HISTORY OF EXETER.

sorely mortified to be obliged to assist at the ceremony, but they had no means of escaping the office. To ingratiate himself with his subjects, he spent several weeks in making a royal progress with the queen and court, dispensing honours and favours; and the whole ceremony of the coronation was repeated at York on Sunday the 8th of September of the same year.

But whilst the felon-king was indulging in expensive pageantry and dissipation in the northern part of his dominions, a widely extended confederacy was formed and matured against him in the southern and western parts, by the united friends of the Houses of York and Lancaster. The 18th day of October was marked for a general rising in favour of Henry, the young Earl of Richmond, who had pledged himself to marry the Princess Elizabeth of York. On the appointed day, Thomas Grey, Marquis of Dorset, proclaimed Henry in this city. The usurper lost no time in hastening to Exeter (having first caused the Duke of Buckingham's head to be struck off in Salisbury market-place on Sunday, November 2nd—Hist. Croyland) with a considerable force to surprise the daring insurgents. Early in November, John Atwill, the mayor, at the head of the municipality went forth to meet him beyond Eastgate; the recorder, Thomas Hexte, presented a congratulatory address, and a purse containing 200 nobles was then handed to his Majesty, and graciously accepted. The bishop's palace, which had been abundantly stored with provisions, was at once occupied by the royal retinue; for Peter Courtenay, the diocesan already mentioned, his brother Sir Walter, the dean, John Arundell, and a large concourse of political guests had succeeded in effecting their escape, and had reached the opposite coast. Comparatively few were executed here; for his brother-in-law, Sir John St. Leger, and Thomas Rame were

DEATH OF RICHARD III.

the only persons who suffered death for conspiring against him. And though, on his return to town, he met a parliament ready to confirm his title to the crown, and to enact a bill of attainder of his opponents, as "undoubted traitors, rebels, and enemies," yet he was haunted with alarms at the preparations which Henry Earl of Richmond was making in France. His mind was racked with suspicions of the fidelity of his professed adherents. On August 1st, 1485, Henry sailed from Harfleur, landed at Milford-Haven, and directed his steps towards Shrewsbury. A week elapsed before Richard heard of his landing. Staking his crown and his life on the issue of the battle at Bosworth on August 22nd, he lost both. He that went forth to the field, wearing his crown, was found a corpse hideous with ghastly wounds, and, with every circumstance of indignity, was thrown across a horse "with a halter hanging from his neck," as the continuator of the Hist. of Croyland informs us, and conveyed to Leicester for interment (p. 575); thus leaving an awful example of a name that will live only in his country's curses, and showing that guilty ambition provokes the wrath of Heaven (Ps. v. 6) ;—that there is no peace for the wicked—and that no measure can be either beneficial or honourable, which is not based upon justice and integrity.

With the unhonoured Richard were buried the glories of the House of Plantagenet; and by the fortunate union of the victorious Henry with Elizabeth, the eldest daughter of Edward IV., the feuds of the white and red Roses were closed for ever; unless we except the abortive attempt of the king's enemies in the person of their tool, Perkin Warbeck. That impostor's life and adventures may be read in Sir Frederick Madden's lucid dissertation, printed in vol. xxvii. of the Proceedings of the Archæological Society. Suffice it

HISTORY OF EXETER.

to say, that Warbeck landed from Cork at Whitsand bay, Cornwall, on September 7th, 1497, with a small force—that he appeared ten days later before this city, calculating only on a feeble opposition; but was wofully disappointed. "Such," says Hoker, "was the courage and valiant stomach of the citizens, that they decided on suffering every extremity, rather than submitting to a surrender. The enemy burnt Northgate, and actually forced an entrance into Eastgate,[2] as far even as Castle Lane; but were gallantly foiled and driven back with great slaughter. Hearing that Sir Edward Courtenay, Earl of Devon, was approaching with a considerable force, that the king was expected to join him with a formidable army, and that a proclamation had offered a reward of a thousand marks to the first person who should bring him alive to the King, he fled to Taunton, and thence, on September 21st, to Beaulieu Abbey for sanctuary; but was soon forced to surrender, and brought to the king at Taunton, October 5th. The king made his public entry into this city on October 7th. In a letter dated Exeter, Oct. 23rd, 1497, which he addressed to Don Rodriguez Gonzales, the Spanish envoy, the king informs him that he had sent to the queen the Lady Catherine Huntley (whom the impostor had married), "but we hold Perkins here, '*penes nos*,' in safe custody, and we shall bring him with us on our return to London, which we hope will be soon; when you will be able to see him." The king remained in Exeter until November 3rd, when he proceeded to Ottery St. Mary. During his stay at Exeter we learn from a deposition, made in 1554, that one Richard Beale, then 80 years

---

[2] Eastgate had been so much shaken by this assault, that in 1511 the Chamber resolved to rebuild it. Robert Poke, of Thorverton, mason, contracted to complete the job for 28*l.* The statue of Henry VII. was placed in a niche over the inner entrance.

ROYAL CHARTER FOR CIVIC GOVERNMENT. 87

old, remembered when eight of the sixteen trees that stood in St. Peter's Close between the north door of the cathedral and the treasury were taken down, that the king, standing in the new window of the treasurer's house, might see the rebels, who came bareheaded with halters round their necks before him, and that they cried out for mercy and pardon. The king then addressed them in a short speech, and granted them his clemency; upon which they made a great shout, hurled away their halters, and cried "God save the king!" (Hoker's MS.)

The King, who in the beginning of his reign had confirmed all the charters granted to Exeter by his royal predecessors, now presented his sword and his cap of maintenance, commanding both to be carried in state before the mayor for the time being for ever. On reaching London he granted a new charter for regulating the election of the mayor and for the better government of the city.[3]

Within four years Exeter was honoured with another royal visit, viz. of the Princess Catherine, daughter of Ferdinand King of Spain. She landed at Plymouth on October 9th, 1501, after a tedious and stormy passage. In her suite were the Archbishop of Compostella and many noble persons. Proceeding by Tavistock, Okehampton and Crediton, she arrived in this city on October 21st and made the deanery her headquarters,

---

[3] Here we lament the loss of the 'Black Roll,' made in 1489, which contained the ancient orders, privileges and customs of the city, and which was usually delivered to the mayor on being sworn into office. It was lent to Sir William Cecyll, secretary to King Edward VI., and could never be recovered. Many documents had also disappeared before the mayoralty of Mr. John Nosworthy, in 1521. Until his time the records lay abroad and in great disorder, "by which means all the records from the Conquest until the end of King Henry III.'s reign were entirely lost," says Hoker. The same historian informs us that he himself had found one of the Court Rolls of Henry III.'s reign (1216-1272) in a tailor's shop beyond the Eastgate, and that the above mentioned John Nosworthy caused a large press to be made, where the records might be kept in order and in safety.

for the See was then vacant, by the recent translation of Bishop Redmayne to Ely.

The noise of the weathercock surmounting the spire of the adjoining church of St. Mary Major so disturbed the princess during the first of the two nights she passed here, that it was taken down. By easy journeys she reached Lambeth on November 9th, and was married to Arthur, Prince of Wales, on the 14th. For their residence, Ludlow Castle was appointed; but, to the disappointment of the nation, the prince died there on April 2nd, within five months, in the sixteenth year of his age, without having consummated the marriage, as several matrons attested, and as she herself repeatedly declared. Under these circumstances, her father-in-law encouraged his surviving son Henry, who became passionately attached to her, to marry her. The king's increasing illness and his subsequent death on April 9th, 1509, delayed the nuptial ceremony; but, with the unanimous consent of the council, this union was eventually accomplished on June 3rd that year. Subsequent events make it not impertinent to notice that her bridal dress was that of a maiden. Afterwards, in public court, in the confidence of innocence and truth she made this significant appeal to her husband :—" God knows, when I came to your bed I was a virgin, and I put it to your own conscience to say whether it was not so."

In closing this chapter, the attentive observer of events in taking a retrospect of the fifteenth century,—notwithstanding the din of arms, bloody revolutions, multiplicity of attainders, and transfers of power and property from one family to another, notwithstanding the successes of the Turks, those barbarous foes of civilization,—cannot fail to discern that this western hemisphere was at this time irradiated by genius, learning, and the general cultivation of polite lite-

LITERATURE AND MORALS. 89

rature amongst the peoples. Italy, that "mercatura bonarum artium," of course took the lead. Thither the Greek fugitives, especially from Constantinople, found an asylum for classic literature, for architecture, painting and sculpture; and the happy discovery of printing served to unfold hidden treasures and to propagate science with electric rapidity. England was soon illustrated with numerous schools and colleges; insomuch that Erasmus, writing to Paul Bembi, declares that "amongst the English good letters triumph; and the royal court abounds with such eminent scholars, that it is rather a museum than a palace, and might vie with any school of philosophy in Athens itself."

On the other hand, the observer of the ambitious competitors and political characters of this period must often be shocked at their want of good faith, at their systematic dissimulation, and their disregard of their pledged word and solemn oaths whenever their interests were concerned, forgetful of the awful truth that unprincipled success ever engenders the cancer of self-destruction.

Lastly, the observer must lament the growing laxity and degeneracy of national morals. May not this in some measure be accounted for by the non-residence of the bishops in their respective dioceses—by those perpetual translations from one see to another—their cringing obsequiousness to the party in power, and the consequent neglect of vigilance over their charge, and thus suffering the tares to multiply? (Matthew vi. 24, xiii. 25; Osee iv. 9.) Translations of bishops, made without cogent reasons of necessity, had been condemned by the fifteenth canon of the General Council of Nice in the year 325, as introductory of ambition, sloth, and avarice into the sanctuary.

CHAPTER XV.

Prosperous state of the nation at the accession of Henry VIII. — The woollen trade of Exeter — Extravagance of the king — Embarrassed state of the exchequer — Appeal to parliament for pecuniary aid — Resistance to the proposal of a property-tax — Bridgeman the member for the city — Thomas Cromwell's influence with the king — Degradation of parliament — Oppressive taxation.

It may fairly be questioned if any of our preceding sovereigns mounted the throne with brighter prospects than Henry VIII. Foreign and domestic opposition to his title had equally died away; the leading powers of Europe courted his alliance; his deceased parent, who had confined all his expenses within his income, had left him a sum almost incredible in those times in ready money—one million seven hundred thousand pounds sterling (Walker's ' Hist. Discourses,' p. 299). A scholar himself, his court embraced a galaxy of literary characters; his cabinet was graced by sage and experienced statesmen; in truth, England had almost reached the zenith of her fame; and no nation enjoyed to a greater degree plenty, security of personal property and freedom, and commercial credit and prosperity, than the realm of England in the early part of his reign.

The staple trade of Exeter was wool. In the reign of Edward III. we find that the wools of Devon and Cornwall were reputed to be of inferior quality, and comparatively of little value : " Lanæ de Com. Cornub. et Devon. grossæ, et modici valoris existunt " (Grandisson's Reg., vol. i. fol. 23). From Westcote's View of Devon (p. 59) we learn that only frieze and coarse plain cloths were made of it until the time of King

WOOLLEN TRADE OF EXETER. 91

Edward IV., when an Italian, Anthony Bonvisi,[1] " taught us the knowledge of making kersies, and our women to spin with the distaff;" yet within a century an astonishing progress and improvement succeeded through the active energy and enterprise of our merchants. Hoker, in his MS. History, so often referred to, relates " this city to have been chiefly inhabited by clothiers and workers of broadcloths, which were of such good and substantial making that the names of *Exeter cloths* be yet had in remembrance in the south and Spanish countries." Antwerp was our principal market, and subsequently Calais. The Statute-book unfortunately shows how the trade was cramped and crippled by our sovereigns ; that the exportation of wool was made felony ; that the wearing of any cloth but of English manufacture was prohibited to all ranks, though the king, the queen, and royal children, who might be considered as giving the *ton* to fashion, were exempted from such prohibition. These coercive restrictions on free-trade, the frequent interference with the price of labour, and the confinement of exportation to a single town, argued a short-sighted policy, and cast a damp on commercial enterprise. But of this subject we may have to speak more at large when we treat of our haven or canal, for which an Act of Parliament was passed in 1539—said to be the earliest instance of artificial inland navigation in this country. Hitherto imported goods were generally unloaded at Topsham, and thence conveyed by carts into Exeter by Holloway, then called Carten Street.

The king gradually became so devoted to tournaments and pageantry, and so passionately fond of

---

[1] I suspect that he had a brother or son called Lawrence. In the privy purse expenses of King Henry VII., we read, " 1 June, 1494, delivered to Lawrence Bonvisi, for to bye wulles for the king's use, 1340l. 11s. 1d." In the previous month 2068l. 4s. 11d. had been ordered to be delivered to the same to be employed for the king.

HISTORY OF EXETER.

expensive warfare, that at length his thoughtless extravagance discovered to him an empty exchequer. In his embarrassments he applied to Parliament to supply the ways and means to continue his wayward career, but the nation still retained a portion of its early spirit, demurred, and declined to grant the exorbitant sums demanded by the minister. In the Convocation Richard Fox, the venerable Bishop of Winchester, exerted his powerful influence to ward off the extortion intended to be practised on the clergy; and when Cardinal Wolsey, in April, 1523, dictated to the Commons the imposition of a property-tax of 20 per cent. (Sir Thomas More then being Speaker of the House), the proposal " was received with a marvellous silence." His Eminence attended the House to overawe it by his presence; but, perceiving the reluctance of the Commons to proceed to business, retired much discontented. From Hoker (MS., p. 339) we find that at the debate on the motion " no man spake more earnestly and effectually against it than John Bridgeman, the representative of this city in Parliament—a wise man, and of great experience,—which thing being made known to the cardinal, he sent for him, and very sharply rebuked him for it; but he maintained his sayings. And at his next coming to the Lower House, when the said Bill was again read, Mr. Bridgeman spake against it. But he had little thanks for his labour; and, being again most sharply rebuked, he never enjoyed himself, but returned to his lodgings, fell sick and died, and was buried in the Savoy in the Strand, London." Yet Parliament, soon after the death of Bishop Fox and the Primate Wareham, lost its patriotic character, and sunk into the most abject subserviency to the royal dictation. Intoxicated with success and adulation, and, after the fall of Wolsey, guided by Thomas Cromwell, an upstart statesman of the Machiavellian school, the king adopted his suggestions on his divorce and on the spiritual supremacy. This unprincipled minister, transporting, as it were, his sovereign to the pinnacle of the Temple, displayed before him the fair possessions of the Church, of the religious houses, so numerous and wealthy, and the goodly manors of the bishops and the patrimony of the clergy—all of which but awaited and courted his gracious use; for the king had but to nod his pleasure, and parliament was ready to obey and enforce his every wish. To the lover of liberty and of country it is indeed revolting to witness the servility of an English parliament, degraded to become the mere automaton of royal caprice. The Statute-book proclaims that it was the instrument to say and unsay, to affirm and to contradict—that it consented that the king's proclamations should have the force of law—that it released him in 1529 (21st Hen. VIII. cap. 3) from the payment of a number of loans advanced to him by his subjects during the previous six years, though his securities had, by sale, by gift, or by bequest, passed into other hands — that the succession of the crown was several times altered—that the fundamental laws of the land were set at nought—that treasons were dangerously multiplied—that sport was made of the property, the rights, the freedom, and the lives of the people of England. In truth, this realm had never groaned before under such despotism; and no domestic, no foreign enemy, could have so humbled and enslaved it as its own Parliament. Yet, notwithstanding the incredible spoils voted to the sovereign, more taxes were imposed on the nation than by all preceding sovereigns together since the Conquest. " Like snow this vast sacrilegious accumulation had melted away," says Sir Edward Walker ('Historical Discourses,' p. 299). And Heylyn (p. 11, ' Hist.') remarks, " The king was neither the

94 · HISTORY OF EXETER.

richer in children by so many wives, nor much improved in revenues by such horrible rapines." And in page 17 he adds, that " the money of the realm was so imposed (counterfeit) and mixed, that it could not pass for current amongst foreign nations, to the great dishonour of the kingdom and the loss of the merchant; and that, soon after the universal spoil and dissolution of religious houses, he was feign to have recourse to parliament for moneys; that the clergy had to give a subsidy of six shillings in the pound, payable out of all their spiritual promotions; that he next pressed his subjects for a Benevolence, and shortly after he obtained a grant of all chantries, hospitals, colleges, and free chapels within the realm, though he lived not to enjoy the benefit of it."

This city was a mournful witness and victim of the innovations around her, of the invasions of Magna Charta, and of the removal of the ancient landmarks of her forefathers, by the proscription and dispersion of the Benedictine, Augustinian, Dominican, and Franciscan priories, and of St. Catherine's nunnery at Polslo. If it be a proof of innocence, as Dr. Burnet admits, when the members of religious communities were awarded pensions by the royal visitors and commissioners, we may fairly conclude that the monastic brethren and sisters in this city and diocese must have lived in good repute, for they were generally favoured and gratified with annuities. But the *poor* of Exeter, and the artizans and tradesmen, were the unhappy sufferers by the change of masters and owners. But, to their honour, *they* patiently submitted to their hard fate after the example of the primitive Christians, under the pressure of privation and persecution, without having recourse to violence. For details of this momentous revolution in property and religion we refer our readers to the Monasticon of this diocese; and we

NEW PRIVILEGES CONFERRED ON THE CITY.

submit to the justice of the assertion of a popular writer (see the Times of 17th February, 1823), "If Henry VIII. had not plundered the Church, the word *Poor's-rate* would never have been known in England."[2]

In dismissing this reign of blood and terror, we must not forget that Henry VIII., on 16th February, 1535, constituted our mayor, recorder, and aldermen justices of the peace for the city : hitherto the mayor and bailiffs only had possessed that privilege. He further confirmed the chartered rights of the citizens ; and, on the 23rd August, 1537, the twenty-ninth year of his reign, erected Exeter into a county of itself, separate and distinct from the county of Devon, with the exception, however, of the castle of Exeter and the adjoining county jail.

---

[2] "There was a principal parliamentary motive, which did facilitate the rest ; for it was propounded in parliament, that the accession of abbey lands would so enrich the Crown, as the people should never be put to pay subsidies again. This was plausible both to Court and country. Besides, with the overplus there should be maintained a standing army of 40,000 men, for a perpetual defence of the kingdom. This was safety at home, terrour and honour abroad. The parliament would make all sure. God's part, religion, hath been reasonably well preserved, but it hath been saved as by fire, for the rest is consumed and vanished. The people have paid subsidies ever since, and we are now in no very good case to pay an army."—Extract from Sir Benjamin Rudyard's speech, delivered in the House of Commons, on 21st June, 1641.

We may add, that if any one will read No. lxxix. Collection of Records, at the end of Collier's Ecclesiastical History, vol. i. p. 21, he will be satisfied, that in the division of the property of the Church, cunning stewards, pettifogging lawyers, and greedy courtiers obtained the lion's share ; and, as another expresses it, "the king's cheese was lost in the parings."

CHAPTER XVI.

Accession of Edward VI. — Changes in the tenure of land — State of the poor —Prayer-book of King Edward VI.— Resistance to its introduction — Siege of Exeter — Loyalty and fidelity of its inhabitants — Death of the King — The Lady Jane Grey — Queen Mary — Her marriage with Philip of Spain — Royal letter to the citizens of Exeter — Age of religious persecution — Its inconsistency with the spirit of Christianity.

THE death of Henry VIII., on 28th January, 1547, introduced a wonderful alteration in public affairs. His son Edward, a minor of weakly constitution, was in the hands of profligate ministers solely intent on their own aggrandizement. Within the realm discontent generally prevailed : the new practice of letting lands at rack-rents had driven from their homes numerous small farmers, with their families, whose fathers and grandfathers had leases of their estates on easy terms from the Church and monasteries. Numbers of poor, decrepit, blind, lame, and sickly objects craving relief swarmed in the streets of our populous towns, insomuch that laws to prevent the starving poor from soliciting charity were enacted at which humanity shudders. Then the inclosure of commons and wastes by the new landlords and non-resident court-harpies, and the violent means adopted to eradicate the faith of their forefathers, disgusted the feelings of the nation, propagated disaffection, excited insurrection in many counties, and threatened the subversion of all order and tranquillity. The Act of Edward VI.'s short reign, commanding that the new Book of Common Prayer should alone be used in every place of worship throughout England, in *Wales*, in *Calais*, and the Marches of the same, from Whitsunday, 9th of June, 1549, under severe

THE CITY BESIEGED. 97

penalties,[1] became the signal and tocsin for tumult and open resistance and rebellion. The first insurrection in this county commenced at Sampford Courtenay, about six miles from Okehampton, and it spread like wildfire. Reinforced by a large body of Cornishmen, and with a daily accession of numbers so as to amount to ten thousand, the rebels advanced to this city by the 30th of June, and, having duly invested it, summoned the mayor and his council to surrender and capitulate. Our historian, John Hoker, has left a graphic narrative of the event; he was an eye-witness to the proceedings, and was himself assessed, " by order of the magistrates, at 20s. the day, towards the common charges of the defence." This host of undisciplined insurgents were anxious to secure the city before the Government could assemble an adequate force to succour the besieged ; but, though the inhabitants were reduced to many privations and a great dearth of provisions, and though, as the historian confesses, " the mayor himself, John Blackaller, as well as Mr. William Hurst (of charitable memory), Mr. John Buller, Mr. John Britnell, Mr. William Periam, and others of the best and antientest families of the city were well affected to the Romish religion, and were at sundry times and in diverse ways and manners solicited to join with the rebels, yet it pleased Almighty God so to rule their hearts, that they again and again openly declared, that, as they had been brought up in the city, and all along therein dwelt, and got their living ; had sworn fidelity to their prince, and had faithfully hitherto served him, so they would continue to do so to the utmost of their power ; and so they did, and returned for answer to their overtures and to their threats, that they renounced and defied them as enemies

---

[1] [The Author's significant use of italics here seems to indicate a belief that the old *Latin* services were more intelligible to the Welsh, &c., than the new English ones.]

H

98   HISTORY OF EXETER.

and rebels against God, their king, and their country."
The siege, after a continuance of thirty-five days, was
abandoned. The royal army, under Lords Russell and
Grey, entered the city as deliverers on 6th August,
1549; the insurgent forces were scattered, very many
lives were forfeited and sacrificed, much private property rifled or confiscated, and the object of the rioters
entirely defeated and blighted.

The king was graciously pleased to acknowledge and
reward this exemplary loyalty and heroic gallantry of
Exeter. He renewed her charters, enlarged her liberties, and increased her revenues by the grant of Exe
Island, then valued at 29*l.* 18*s.* 10*d.* per annum, and
allowed them for ever sufficient timber towards the
maintenance of Calabeer Weir[2] and Hooper's Weir,
across the river Exe, from his woods called Cottey and
Pirage woods.

Heylin, in the Preface to his History, dates the
Reformation from the reign of King Edward VI.; but
he adds that, " his death I cannot reckon an infelicity
to the Church of England; for, being ill principled in
himself, and easily inclined to embrace such counsels as
were offered to him, it is not to be thought but that the
rest of the bishoprics (before sufficiently impoverished)
must have followed Durham,[3] and the poor Church be
left as destitute of lands and ornaments as when she
came into the world. Nor was it like to happen other-

---

[2] This, now called Headwear, was
originally called Calabeer. It had been
washed down by the floods about 1534-5,
whilst George Huett was rector of St.
Edmund's on Exeter bridge, who suffered a loss of nearly one-third of his
income; for the tithe of mills and fish
was valued at 3*l.* 6*s.* 8*d.* In 1568 the
wear was substantially rebuilt, but was
placed higher up the stream in 1609 to
form the new mill leat, mentioned in
Act 7th of James I. cap. 19.

Our readers are aware that Exe
Island, for several ages the property of
the Courtenays (at least from 1311), had
been forfeited to the Crown by the attainder of Henry Courtenay, Marquess
of Exeter, 31st December, 1538. Floy-
ersland had also been held of the
Courtenays by the service of half a fee,
or 50*s.*

[3] Amongst the private acts 7th Edward VI., is one for the dissolution of
this bishopric of Durham, and also for
the new erecting of the same bishopric, and one other of Newcastle. This
act was repealed in the first year of 2
Mary, Sess. 3, cap. 3.

ACCESSION OF QUEEN MARY.

wise in the reign of Queen Jane, if it had lasted longer than *a nine days' wonder.* For Dudley of Northumberland, who then ruled the roast and had before dissolved, and in hope devoured, the wealthy bishopric of Durham, might easily have possessed himself of the greatest part of the revenues of York and Carlisle, by means whereof he would have made himself more absolute on the north side of the *Trent* than the poor titular Queen Jane could have been suffered to continue on the south side of it. To carry on whose interest and title, the poor remainder of the Church's property was, in all probability, to have been shared amongst those of that party, to make them sure. But, the wisdom of this great *Achitophel* being turned to foolishness, he fell into the hands of the public hangman, and thereby saved himself the labour of becoming his own executioner."

Information of Edward's death at Greenwich, on Thursday, 6th July, 1553, was conveyed to the Princess Mary, at Hoddesdon in Hertfordshire, on the very evening of the king's decease, by Henry Fitz-Alan, the Earl of Arundel. "He had held intelligence with her since the first extremities of her brother's sickness," says Heylin, p. 163. At once she wrote to the Council, who, after much deliberation, returned the following reply :—

"MADAM,—We have received your letters, the 9th of this instant, declaring your supposed title, which you judge yourself to have to the imperial crown of this realm, and all the dominions thereunto belonging. For answer whereof, this is to advertise you, that, forasmuch as our sovereign lady, Queen Jane, is, after the death of our sovereign lord, Edward VI. (a prince of most noble memory), invested and possessed with the just and right title in the imperial crown of this realm, *not only by good order of old ancient laws of this realm, but also by our late sovereign lord's letters patent, signed with his own hand, and sealed with the great seal of England, in presence of the most part of the nobles, counsellors, judges, with divers others grave and sage personages, assenting and subscribing the same ; we must, therefore, as of*

H 2

100   HISTORY OF EXETER.

most bound duty and allegiance, assent unto her said grace, and to none other except we should (which faithful subjects cannot) fall into grievous and unspeakable enormities. Wherefore, we can no less do, but for the quiet both of the realm, and you also, to advertise you, that, forasmuch as the divorce made between the king, of famous memory, King Henry VIII., and the lady Catharine, your mother, was necessary to be had, both by the everlasting laws of God, and also by the ecclesiastical laws, and by the most part of the noble and learned universities of Christendom, and confirmed also by the sundry Acts of Parliaments remaining yet in their force, *and thereby you justly made illegitimate, and unheritable to the crown imperial of this realm, and the rule, and dominions, and possessions of the same*, you will, upon just consideration hereof, and *of divers other causes, lawful to be alleged for the same, and for the just inheritance of the right line*, and godly order taken by the late king, our sovereign lord, King Edward VI., and agreed upon by the nobles and great personages aforesaid, *surcease, by any pretence, to vex and molest any of our sovereign lady, Queen Jane, her subjects from their true faith and allegiance due unto her grace;* assuring you, that, if you will, for respect, show yourself quiet and obedient (as you ought), you shall find us all, and several, ready to do you any service, that we with duty may, and glad, with your quietness, to preserve the common state of this realm wherein you may be otherwise grievous to us, to yourself, and to them. And thus we bid you most heartily well to fare. From the Tower of London, in this 9th of July, 1553.

"Your ladyship's friends, showing yourself an obedient subject,

Thomas Canterbury.	Huntingdon.
Marquess of Winchester.	Darcy.
John Bedford.	Thos. Cheeny.
Will. Northampton.	R. Cotton.
Tho. Ely, Chancellor.	John Gates.
Northumberland.	William Petre.
Henry Suffolk.	William Cecil.
Henry Arundel.	John Cheek.
Shrewsbury.	John Mason.
Pembroke.	Edward North.
R. Rich.	Robert Bowes."

Against this traitorous answer, concocted in open violation of the settlement made by her royal father, and in virtue of which Edward VI. had succeeded to the crown, the princess boldly appealed to the nation;

EXECUTION OF NORTHUMBERLAND.

and her appeal was cheerfully responded to by many noblemen, knights, gentlemen, and yeomen. In a few days she found herself at the head of thirty thousand volunteers; nay, such was her confidence in her rights, and in the loyal enthusiasm of the country in her favour, that she offered, on the word of a queen, that whoever should arrest Northumberland and bring him into her presence, should be entitled, if a peer, to 1000*l.* in land, to him and his heirs. But if a knight should render her that service, she promised 500*l.* in lands, to him and his heirs, with a patent of nobility; if a private gentleman, 500*l.* in land, to him and his heirs, with the honour of knighthood; and if a yeoman, 100*l.* in land, to him and his heirs, with the rank of esquire. On the 20th the Lords united in sending an order to Northumberland to disband his forces, and to acknowledge Mary for his sovereign. This he did in the market-place of Cambridge two days later. During the night he was prevented from attempting to escape by his own men, and, on the following morning, was arrested by the Earl of Arundel at King's College, Cambridge, and conducted to the Tower. It required a strong guard to protect him on the way from the vengeance of the populace. On 22nd August he suffered the penalty of his treason.

And when, within six months after, a formidable insurrection was organized against her by Sir Thomas Wyatt and Sir Peter Carew, Knight, on the pretence of her intended marriage with Philip of Spain, she displayed the same presence of mind—the index of an invincible heart—before the mayor and citizens of London. In her harangue she reminded them that they had sworn allegiance to her as their lawful sovereign; that at her coronation she was wedded to the realm of England; that the ring she then wore, and ever would wear, was the solemn pledge of their

HISTORY OF EXETER.

mutual covenant; that her title to the inheritance of the crown was indisputable; that her people might confidently rely on her motherly affection; that the proposed marriage had been judged by her council to be expedient and honourable to the country, and that, if she could be satisfied it would be otherwise, she would withhold her consent; and, as a proof of her sincerity, she gave them the word of a queen that if her Commons and Peers were of a different opinion she would break it off altogether. She concluded by informing the Lord Mayor and Common Council that every assistance would be afforded them for the defence of her loyal city of London. The result speedily showed how the traitors had miscalculated on success—how loyalty and courage were an overmatch for rebellion. The marriage with Philip of Spain took place in the cathedral of Winchester on 25th July, 1554, and, strengthened by it, her Government, with the full sanction of both Houses of Parliament, succeeded in the restoration of the old religion.

But to confine ourselves to Exeter. In the first year of her reign she addressed the following letter to her trusty and well-beloved the Mayor and his brethren of her city of Exeter :—

"T(este) Marye the Queene.

"Trustie and welbeloved we grete you well. And understandinge bothe by the reporte of our cousen the Marques de las Navas and otherwise, the courteouse entretaynement and other good offices shewed unto him at our request, We have thought goode not onely to give you our hertie thancks for the same: but also t'assure you that we will not fayle to reteyne the same in our goode remembraunce, to be considered towards you and our citye, as any occasion may serve. Yeven under our signet at oure towne of Guildeford the xxii of June the first yere of our Reigne."

She confirmed our charters, incorporated our merchants, and did all she could to restore to the churches

PREVALENCE OF PERSECUTION. 103

their former rights and properties. "To her the cathedrals are indebted for a considerable part of their present revenues," says Brown Willis in his 'Scenery.' In the early part of her reign she had exercised a remarkable degree of clemency towards her opponents, especially when contrasted with the barbarous and promiscuous vengeance manifested towards the seditious of the two last reigns; but at length, worn out in mind and body by antecedent privations, sorrows, and persecutions—agonized by the indifference and absence of her husband—irritated by the plots forming against her—and wounded to the heart by the loss of Calais[4]— fearful of the political changes that were like to ensue after her death—instead of repelling with horror the re-enactment of the sanguinary statutes of her royal progenitors, kings Richard II., Henry IV., and Henry V., against heresy, she fatally consented to the detestable advice of her Cabinet in favour of persecution. But let us be just in our indignation, and not suffer her to be the scapegoat of the universal system of intolerance prevalent in her time; for all denominations of religion, when they gained the ascendency, forgot, though professing in tongue the Gospel of peace and goodwill, to do unto others as they could wish to be done by— *all*, by forming a false conscience, were persuaded that they were rendering a service to their common Redeemer by breathing out threatenings and slaughter against the

---

[4] Calais, the key of France, was lost by faction. "Bishop Gardiner being sent into France, had particular commission to see the state of Calais. On his return, he related that he had found the place so full of malcontents, as if Lord Wentworth, governor there, and some other chief officers were not removed, Calais would not be English one year together. The queen gave commission to Sir Edward Waldegrave and Sir Francis Englefield to go to Calais to change the governor and other officers; yet the other side (to which also was joined Sir William Corbett, Master of the Rolls, that could do most with the queen in her latter days) turned the matter again, and Calais was lost at Christmas after; and thus the Commonwealth and religion were infinitely hindered by the opposite faction."— From P. Robert Parsons's MS. 'Storie of Domestical Difficulties.'

Bishop Gardiner died 12th Nov. 1555.

104 HISTORY OF EXETER.

unbelievers of their individual creeds. In truth, this religious persecution of each other's conscience, this making hypocrites of men, was the crime of our forefathers. To each and to every party we may apply the words in Genesis, "They were instruments of cruelty in their habitations. Cursed be their anger, for it was fierce, and their wrath, for it was cruel." Mary too ought to have borne in mind that her Church was the first and the only Church that had disavowed and disclaimed for itself the right of enforcing her doctrines by sanguinary punishment. This was publicly done by the twenty-seventh Canon of the Third Council of Lateran, A.D. 1179,[5] and the Church proclaimed this truth at a time when the civil authorities enacted penal statutes against the Cathari, the Patarini, and others, who, not content with maintaining opinions endangering the public peace, proceeded to overt acts of violence and sedition, destroyed churches and monasteries, committed frightful massacres, and marked their progress by wanton devastation,—" more Paganorum omnia perdunt et vastant."

As Exonians and fellow Christians, we have to congratulate ourselves that but one person in this extensive diocese, Agnes Prest, is even alleged to have been the victim of this barbarous law. She is said to have suffered in August, 1557, on Southernhay; but I look in vain for any mention of such an occurrence in the Register of Bishop Turbeville, or the Act Books of our Common Council.

Nothing worse can be said of any religion than this, that, to secure it a legal establishment, the body of the people (if they adhere to their old opinions) must be deprived of their liberties and free customs, and be reduced to a state of civil servitude. Blessed be God for

---

[5] See Concilia, vol. xxvii., Paris edition, 1644.

ACCESSION OF QUEEN ELIZABETH.

having reserved us for these latter and enlightened days, and that the age of such cruelty and folly has passed away! What a light has irradiated the world since the Congress of the United States set the example of disclaiming all pretence to legislate for Heaven, or to lay an embargo on conscience! All classes of Britons no longer petition for toleration as a favour, but challenge it as an indefeasible right, of which no Government is justified in robbing the subject. Lamenting that our forefathers should have usurped the vengeance of the common Father of us all in persecuting the conscience of His children, let it be our business to follow peace with all men, to walk in love, to respect each other's sincerity of belief, and to cultivate benevolence and concord as becomes children of one family—disciples of the same Saviour and Redeemer.

CHAPTER XVII.

Elizabeth's persecution of the Catholics — Charters of the city confirmed — Loyalty of Exeter — Title of "Semper fidelis" conferred — Elizabeth's encouragement of commerce — First Act for the relief of the poor — Accession of James I. — His predilection for the Scotch — Parliamentary control over the Royal prerogative — Charles I. — Coronation repeated at Edinburgh — Plague of 1625 — Spread of disaffection — Intolerance towards the Catholics — Their adoption of the King's cause — Parliamentary party at Exeter — Capitulation to Prince Maurice — The Queen, a refugee at Exeter, gives birth to the Princess Henrietta — She embarks at Falmouth — Visit of the King to Exeter — The city surrenders to Fairfax — Puritan desecration of the churches — State prisoners and executions at Exeter — Barbary pirates on the west coast.

THE Act Book of our Mayor and Chamber, page 173, records "that Queen Mary died about five o'clock of Thursday morning, 17th November, 1558, and the same day about nine of the clock A.M. the Lady Elizabeth was proclaimed Queen of England, &c., first in Westminster Hall and then in other places; and that on the Tuesday following, being the 22nd of November, her Grace was

106   HISTORY OF EXETER.

proclaimed Queen at Exon between nine and ten A.M.,
Mr. Mayor and all the aldermen being in scarlet gowns,
and the rest of the twenty-four in decent and best array;
thence they proceeded to St. Peter's Church, where the
procession and *Te Deum* done, in solemn order they
returned." All this was accomplished legally and be-
comingly, and without a symptom of disloyalty.

She was crowned according to the form of the Roman
pontifical by Dr. Owen Oglethorp, Bishop of Carlisle,
at Westminster, on 15th January, but soon set at defiance
her coronation oath, which bound her to the maintenance of the liberties of the Church as then established
by law; she deprived the bishops of their sees; she prohibited all preaching without a special licence; she proceeded with the sanction of an obsequious parliament
to discard and put down the religion which she had
herself professed and found established by law; nay, a
new code was enacted against the professors of the
ancient faith, and thus her Catholic subjects were
subjected to legalized persecution, like Daniel, for
making their prayers and supplications to God as they
had done "aforetime." But Catholics alone were not
the victims of her intolerance. We may glance at
her writ for the burning at Smithfield of John Peters
and Henry Turwert, Flemings and anabaptists, dated
15th July, 1575, in Rymer's Fœdera (tom. xv. p. 741).
From these revolting scenes of inhuman and anti-chris-
tian severity, let us contemplate the useful and brighter
policy of her lengthened government.

On 2nd June, 1564, the Queen confirmed the charter
of King Edward for enclosing the cemetery of the
Cathedral referred to in our eleventh chapter, as also
the privileges granted by subsequent sovereigns to the
bishop, the dean and chapter, and the vicars choral of
the Cathedral. On 30th May, 1567, she ratified King
Henry VI.'s charter for the liberty of the Close and

CONFIRMATION OF CHARTERS. 107

St. Stephen's fee; and though she dismembered from the See of Exeter Bishop's Clist and the extensive Manor of Crediton, so recently recovered by Bishop Turbeville in her sister Queen Mary's reign, yet it must be admitted to her honour, that on 5th July, 1585, she restored to the dean and chapter the Chantry lands, tenements, and rents which had been appropriated to their maintenance of obituary services, of which the Crown had dispossessed them in 1547, reserving to herself, her heirs, and successors to the throne, in lieu thereof, a yearly pension of 145*l*.; and on the same day she re-granted similar property to the vicars choral of the cathedral, contenting herself with their yearly payment of fourpence to the royal exchequer for ever.

To this city, so renowned for its loyalty, she assigned the honourable title of "Semper fidelis"; she confirmed its rights and liberties, granted a charter for orphans, and appointed the mayor for the time being her escheator. To trade and commercial enterprise she gave an impulse and lent considerable encouragement. Some documents in the possession of Sir Thomas Trayton Fuller Elliot Drake, of Nutwell Court, abundantly prove that she adventured large sums in trading speculations, on one occasion as much as 20,000*l*.; and that she was keen enough in looking after the returning profits. Her example was imitated by her courtiers, and taken up by merchant adventurers and companies; and a spirit of commercial enterprise and emulation was fostered in the community. Our readers are aware that the haven, the new work, or canal, was now undertaken in earnest, and vessels of fifteen or sixteen tons burthen brought up goods and merchandise from Topsham to the City quay.

The general tranquillity enabled her government to apply its attention to establish a legal provision for

HISTORY OF EXETER.

the poorer classes of the increasing population. Since the dissolution of monasteries and the spoliation of church property, the aged, the impotent, the sickly and destitute were left for support to the charity of individuals and to voluntary collections. This proved a very inadequate resource in the altered circumstances of the times, and especially in seasons of dearth and epidemical visitation. It was therefore most just, and a measure of political expedience and even of imperative necessity, to provide a settled relief, chargeable on lands and tenements, for such as were really deserving objects in every parish; and this desideratum was accomplished by the Act of the 43rd year of Elizabeth (1601), chapter 11, entitled " An Act for the Relief of the Poor." The abuses, however, in working the machinery of the poor-law have been sometimes felt by the landed interests as threatening eventually to pauperize the country itself.

Within a few hours after the Queen's death James the Sixth, King of Scotland and son of the unfortunate Queen Mary, was proclaimed in London as the lawful and rightful successor to the English crown; and on the very next day, 25th March, 1603, the Privy Council despatched an order, signed by twenty-four of its members, to the mayor and aldermen of this city to make open proclamation of their new sovereign. This was obeyed speedily and cheerfully, and his Majesty graciously acknowledged their unequivocal loyalty and dutiful service. As a testimony of their gratitude for his royal courtesy, the Mayor and Chamber voted as a free gift the sum of 133*l.* 6*s.* 8*d.* some time afterwards, which was kindly accepted. But he soon disappointed the expectations of his subjects by his obnoxious grant of monopolies and patents; by his manifest predilection and invidious intrusion of hungry Scotchmen [1] into office:

---

[1] Their oppressive and avaricious conduct occasioned Cleaveland to write this satirical distich—

" Had Cain been Scot, God would have changed his doom,
Not made him wander, but confined at home."

ACCESSION OF CHARLES I.

and by his weak and vacillating policy. He was little aware of the reviving love of freedom and independence, and the impatience of control and the jealousy of the Royal prerogative that were growing up in the bosom of the nation. Parliament had become conscious of its strength, and was determined to exercise its powers and privileges. James would have played the despot if he could, but the time was gone by, and his pecuniary embarrassments at last compelled him to descend to a more moderate course both with his parliament and the corporate boroughs.

We now come to the eventful reign of Charles I., who ascended the throne on the day of his father's death, 27th of March, 1625. Exeter lost no time in tendering to the new Sovereign, as a free gift, the sum of 300*l.*; but the public joy was damped by a dreadful plague, which committed such ravages in families as to cause universal consternation. Lady Bevill Grenville, who had come up from Stow, in Cornwall, to visit her mother, Lady Grace Smythe, of Great Madford, in Heavitree parish, writes thence to her absent husband on 20th August, 1625 : — " The sickness increases here, and is much dispersed abroad in the city; and when it comes, it goes through the house and ends all. I am determined to leave to-morrow on account of the children. Mrs. Bampfylde is gone and her children, and Mrs. Isaac is gone from Polslow, &c., with sons and daughters, &c., and all the citizens that can possibly get horses do remove." In his fright and panic the mayor, Thomas Walker, abandoned his post; but his deputy, Alderman Ignatius Jourdain, nobly remained to do his duty. A pesthouse was established near Lion's Holt, in St. Sidwell's, and, as usual, public and private benevolence was exerted to administer relief to the sufferers. It is pleasing to witness the generous sacrifices which our fellow-citizens made to benefit the sick in other places,

HISTORY OF EXETER.

as the infection was propagated. Plymouth acknowledged to have received from Exeter in the winter of 1626 the sum of 92*l*. 11*s*. 5*d*.; Salisbury in the following year 40*l*.; Cambridge in 1630 45*l*. 10*s*.; Barnstaple 65*l*. 8*s*. 0½*d*.; Taunton 40*l*. in August 1640, and later the large sum of 185*l*. 17*s*. 4*d*. in money, besides corn, &c., to the value of 6*l*.

In the meanwhile the political horizon wore a threatening appearance. The king was thought to be insincere as well as arrogant and exacting, and it was generally circulated that he contemplated to abridge the liberties of the nation and to rule supreme without the intervention of Parliament. Discontent and disaffection gradually spread through the country, when the king, though he had been crowned at Westminster 2nd February, 1626, in order to ingratiate himself with his Scotch subjects announced a repetition of his coronation at Holyrood, Edinburgh, on 18th June, 1633, and summoned a meeting of the Scotch Parliament for the day after the ceremony. During its session "several Acts were passed," says a MS. letter (written by Rev. John Lesley, a shrewd observer, dated 30th September, 1633), "so manifestly obnoxious to the country that it was proclaimed by the popular voice, that whereas the king's coming to Scotland resembled Christ's triumphant entrance into Jerusalem amidst hosannahs of joy, so, after a few days, the multitude was as clamorous for his crucifixion." "This expression of altered feeling was related to Charles by the Bishop of the Isles on his departure, whilst actually dining on the borders of the two kingdoms; when the King became pensive, and ceased from eating." His return to England was not calculated to mend matters; he affected indeed a disregard of public opinion, but the friends of order and the monarchy trembled for the approaching crisis.

INTOLERANCE TOWARDS THE CATHOLICS. 111

At the period before us politics hinged on religion, and the bigots of all parties forgot that freedom of conscience was the natural and inalienable right of the subject—that no mortal being should dare to intrude between a fellow-creature and their common Creator—and that every claimant for such sacred liberty ought in fairness to concede it to his neighbour. Yet Charles refused toleration, the basis of public tranquillity, to his unoffending Catholic subjects. When his queen, Henrietta Maria, made suit to his Majesty (as we read in Rous's Diary, p. 49) "for several Catholics to be released from prison, who had been caught attending mass at her own privileged chapel and at the houses of the Catholic ambassadors ;" he replied, " Madam, I permit you your religion with your chaplains, I permit ambassadors and their retinue, but the rest of my subjects I will have them live in the religion I profess and my father before me." During his reign many of the Catholic clergy fell victims to the sanguinary laws against their adherence to the dictates of conscience and to the creed of *their* fathers. Even in the adverse posture of his affairs, he issued a proclamation against the employment of a Catholic subject in his army; but at last his eyes were opened to his error by the gallant Sir Arthur Aston. The fact is thus stated by Lord Castlemaine (Catholique Apologie, p. 15, ed. 1674). " Sir Arthur Aston, a Catholic of quality and experience, tendered his own and the services of many other Catholics ; the good prince sincerely thanked him, but, on account of their religion, durst not accept them, for fear that the rebels would use this as a pretence to discredit him with the nation. On this refusal the knight posted to London, and made a similar offer to the Earl of Essex, the General-in-Chief of the Parliamentary forces, who readily embraced the offer, and granted to Sir Arthur a formal commission. Posting back to the

HISTORY OF EXETER.

Court, he showed the commission to the King, who instantly decided on giving him a considerable command, and from that time declared all Catholics welcome, who presently hastened from all parts to his standard." It is an undeniable fact, that of the five hundred officers who fell in the Royal cause, no less than one hundred and ninety-eight were Catholics; and Dr. Stanhope, a Protestant divine, frankly avows " that a great many noble, brave, and loyal spirits of the Roman persuasion did with the greatest integrity, and without any other design than satisfying conscience, adventure their lives in the king's service; and that several, if not all of them, were of such souls that the greatest temptations in the world could not have prevented them or made them desert the king in his greatest distress."

It was now manifest that the nation was splitting into two great parties, the adherents to the Royal·cause, and its envenomed opponents—both suspicious and jealous of each other's intentions and movements. The diocese of Exeter, which includes Devon and Cornwall, was naturally disposed in favour of the Court; the tenantry entertained an hereditary attachment to their landlords, who, for the most part, represented ancient families and had not degenerated from the sterling merits of their progenitors; almost all the gentry were connected by intermarriages, especially in Cornwall, and the friendly interchange of hospitality was habitually practised. To dissolve such family compact, the covenanters against the Crown multiplied their emissaries, and even introduced armed reinforcements; they had tampered in towns with the municipal bodies, and their boldness gradually scared away the more timid members. After the 22nd of August, 1642, when the king raised his standard at Nottingham, loyal subjects could no longer demur which cause to maintain, however they might deprecate and lament the necessity of being in-

THE CIVIL WAR.   113

volved in that most dreadful of all human calamities, a
civil war.   From this epoch Exeter makes a distinguished figure in our English annals.

Under pretence of the public safety, Parliament had
ordered the trained bands and militia of the country, of
its own authority, to hold themselves in readiness, and
had dared to assign the command of the fleet to their
creature the Earl of Warwick, whilst the Earl of Essex
was appointed the Lord-General of the army. It is
lamentable to witness several members of both Houses
of Parliament, in whom the king had placed confidence
and treated with special favour, now turning against
their benefactor.[2] And it is curious to watch in the
Act Books of our corporation how insidiously the partisans of Parliament were weeding out the loyalists, how
they managed to introduce into the body persons of
their own views and principles, and even into subordinate offices, as the *porters* of the city gates; and
how adroitly they provided stores of corn and ammunition, and how they had prepared to defend the
city when once they had gained its possession. On the
11th January, 1642, these emissaries of mischief, after
misleading the inhabitants by the circulation of extravagant reports, succeeded in obtaining signatures

---

[2] Amongst these we may particularize
Philip Herbert, Earl of Pembroke and
Montgomery, Lord High Steward of
Exeter, to whom his Majesty had very
recently granted "Tobago and other
islands lying between the line and ten
degrees of northern latitude" (see the
Earl's letter to our Mayor and Chamber, dated Woodstock, 22nd August,
1638, inviting them to assist in establishing a plantation therein). Again,
Francis, Earl of Bedford, and William
his son and heir, owed everything to
the crown. Well might Sir Edward
Walker, in his 'Historical Discourses,'
p. 298, after pointing out the grants of
the lands and revenues of the suppressed monasteries to many of the nobility, and to others of mean families,
who thereby got to be ennobled,
thus express himself:—"This accumulation of wealth and influence put
their posterity in condition and
power to act against the sovereign
authority which first advanced them.
The original possessors were never in
the capacity to rebel. For example,
the Prior of Lees, in Essex, could never
have been in a posture to have usurped
the Admiralty, or been a rebel, as Robert, the Earl of Warwick, has been.
Nor could the Abbess of Wilton have
proved so ungrateful as the late Earl of
Pembroke; and the like may be said of
others possessing these lands."

1

114   HISTORY OF EXETER.

to a petition to Parliament, expressive "of several
dangers apprehended by them of the decay of their
trades, occasioned by the disturbances in London,
and by the bishops of the land, and by popish lords in
Parliament" (Act Book No. VII., p. 199). On 2nd
September following, they carried by vote the dis-
missal of Nicholas Hooper, the city chaplain, and the
substitution of Mark Downe, a noted Puritan preacher,
and to their great joy secured the services of Mr.
Edmund Prideaux as one of the learned counsel for the
city, on 3rd November, 1642, who was sworn into office
on 18th of April next ensuing. In the meanwhile, by
a majority of votes, they managed on the 14th of
February to get rid of the honest and loyal recorder,
Mr. Peter Balle, and selected for his successor the
same Mr. Prideaux. Accordingly we read in p. 146
of the Act Book:—"2nd May, 1643, Mr. Prideaux,
who was elected recorder 22nd April, was sworn
recorder this day, and admitted and sworn a freeman of this city, gratis." Everything seemed to
favour the wishes of the opponents of loyalty. On
10th January following the sum of 100l. was voted to
Henry Grey, Earl of Stamford, whom the Parliament
had appointed Lord-General for these western counties,
"as a small gratuity unto him;" and 4th July, 1643,
200l. more was presented to this governor of Exeter
"as a testimony of their due regard unto him." But
his government was doomed to be of short duration, for
Prince Maurice, the king's nephew, succeeded in in-
vesting the city; and as the Parliament was unable to
afford him any efficient succour, he capitulated on Wednesday, 5th September, 1643, and on the Friday marched
out *without* the honours of war. A new governor of
Exeter was provided in the person of that gallant
officer Sir John Berkley, knight. On the 21st September he was presented with the freedom of the city, with

THE QUEEN A REFUGEE AT EXETER. 115

500*l.* to be divided between himself and Prince Maurice; new blood was infused into the members of the body corporate, and they had courage to revise the case of the recorder, Peter Balle, who had been so informally and ungratefully dismissed after eleven years' service, to reinstate him, and to declare on 4th November "that the election of Edmund Prideaux was void and that he be henceforth clearly dismissed of and from the said office."

Exeter, now free to act, manifested such devotion to the Royal interests, that the King decided on confiding his Queen (whom the Parliament had voted on the preceding 30th April a *traitor* for her exemplary attachment to her husband) to the fidelity and protection of its inhabitants. She was advanced in pregnancy, and leaving Oxford 17th April, 1644, escorted by the King, the Princes Charles and James, and a cortège of the nobility, as far as Abingdon, the royal couple parted, never to meet again in this world! By easy journeys she was enabled to reach this city in safety by 1st of May. On the 2nd, the Mayor, Hugh Crocker, Esq., and the Chamber, voted 200*l.* to her Majesty in testimony of their respect. She kept her Court at Bedford House, and there was delivered of a princess, on Sunday morning, 16th June, who was solemnly baptised in our cathedral by the chancellor, Dr. Lawrence Burnell. Its register thus records the event :—"Henrietta, daughter of our Sovereign Lord King Charles and our gracious Queen Mary, was baptised the 21st of July, 1644." To escape the inhuman efforts of Parliament to get possession of her person, she was, within a fortnight after her confinement, forced to take her departure in secret. Her careful physician, Sir John Winton, waited upon her Majesty in her weak condition, and on the 1st of July they were enabled to reach Okehampton. In his interesting

I 2

116 HISTORY OF EXETER.

memorial he states, " that he had to make the greatest part of the journey from Exeter to Falmouth on foot by the side of her litter." The Earl of Warwick had issued orders from Torbay to the Vice-Admiral Batty to intercept the Queen. She managed, however, to embark at Falmouth in a Dutch vessel on 14th July, and to land at Conquest on the opposite coast on the 15th, notwithstanding "fifty great shot made at her by the Vice-Admiral," says the Micro-Chronicon. Her doctor was then ordered to return and take charge of the princess at Exeter, " she having convulsion fits; and afterwards she went away well recovered with the Lady Dalkeith and the Lord Berkeley." He stayed in Exeter until the town was surrendered upon the Lord Fairfax's Articles.

On Friday, 26th July, the King, in pursuit of the Earl of Essex, reached Exeter from Honiton. Apprised of his intention, the Corporation had met that morning and come to the following resolution:—"Whereas the King's Majesty is this day to make his access to this city, where, for many gracious favours to it, he ought to be with all duty and respect attended on by the citizens, which is heartily desired may be orderly done, it is further agreed and ordered that there shall be 500l. presented to his Majesty, and 100l. more to Prince Charles his Highness (who comes with him), as a testimony of the city's service and joy of his Majesty's presence here." Twenty pounds were also voted to their servants, viz.: 20 marks to the King's and 20 nobles to the Prince's. A short time before they granted 12l. to the Queen's servants at Bedford House.

After seeing his infant daughter and knighting our loyal mayor, the King proceeded to hold a great military council, and left the next day for Bradninch. On his victorious return from Cornwall, he made a short visit to Bedford House again on 17th September. In

THE CITY SURRENDERED TO FAIRFAX. 117

the exuberance of loyal generosity our Corporation granted 200*l.* towards *shoes* for the King's forces at Bristol, and a rate was ordered to be levied on the inhabitants for the maintenance of the soldiers of the garrison and for the efficient reparation of the city walls, and for seeing everything done for a proper state of defence. And such was the consciousness of growing strength from the successes of the royal troops in the west, that the Corporation excluded from their body some obnoxious members, who, from timidity or disaffection, had been remiss in attending their sittings.

But mark the instability of human affairs! The year 1645 set in big with disasters to the royal cause; fortress after fortress fell at the feet of the Parliamentary generals, especially the Lieutenant-General Cromwell; when the Generalissimo Sir Thomas Fairfax, only son to Ferdinand, Lord Fairfax, after sweeping all opposition as he advanced, and securing all the approaches towards Exeter, appeared before it 31st March, 1646, and sent a summons to Sir John Berkley, the governor, to surrender. The gallant knight convoked the City Council, and all being satisfied that resistance was unavailing, and anxious to save the effusion of human blood in a hopeless contest, an answer was returned on the following day, Wednesday, that he was disposed to negotiate on fair and honourable terms. The place of meeting for the Commissioners on both sides was fixed at Poltimore, the seat of Sir John Bampfield.[3] Negotiations commenced on Friday, 3rd April; on the Thursday following all the articles were amicably concluded and ratified by the respective parties, and on Monday, 13th, full possession was taken, when the governor and his forces marched out with the honours

---

[3] He was created a baronet by the king, 14th July, 1641, but turned violently against him. His grave-stone in Poltimore church shows that he died in April, 1650, æt. 40.

118 HISTORY OF EXETER.

of war. Colonel Hammond was now appointed the new governor. During the investment of the city a memorable event occurred, related by the Rev. Thomas Fuller [4] in his Worthies, p. 273. "When Exeter was besieged by the Parliament forces, so that only the south side was open to it, incredible numbers of larks were found in that open quarter, like quails in the desert. Hereof I was an eye and mouth witness. They were as fat as plentiful, and were sold for twopence a dozen and under."

The inhabitants soon ascertained the difference between a regularly constituted government and an arbitrary power, as to the security of person and property. The fifth article of capitulation had provided " that the cathedral church, nor any other church within the city, shall be defaced, nor anything belonging thereunto spoiled, or taken away by any soldier or person on either side whatsoever." But very soon great complaints were made to Sir Thomas Fairfax of the violation of this, and indeed of most of the twenty-four articles. In 1656 an Act or rather an ordinance of Parliament was passed " for the promotinge and more frequent preachinge of the Gospell and mainteynance of ministers in the cittie of Exeter, and unitinge of parrishes and parrish churches within the said cittie of Exeter." The cathedral was divided into two places of worship, East Peter's and West Peter's, at the instigation of Lewis Stukeley, the Independent minister and chaplain to Cromwell, and the service of the Directory was to be performed in but four other parish-churches, viz. : St. Mary Major's, St. Petrock's, St.

---

[4] This B.D., chaplain to the Princess Henrietta, had been appointed Bodleian Lecturer on 21st March, 1645-6, but was dismissed by the new authorities on the 17th of June following. He survived the restoration of monarchy, dying at his rectory of Cranford, 15th Aug. 1661, æt. 58. Was not the Rev. Wm. Fuller, elected to be the Bodleian Lecturer here, 19th Nov. 1648, brother to this Thomas Fuller?

DESECRATION OF THE CHURCHES. 119

Mary Arches, and St. Edmund's on the Bridge; the remaining thirteen being condemned as useless, and announced for sale [5] by the public crier : yet in the true levelling spirit of the fanatical Independents, the towers of the churches were to be taken down " clean to the roof by the purchasers and to be converted either into schools or burying places." The following extracts from the Acts of the Chamber may prove interesting to the reader :—

" The 11th day of August, 1657.

" It is ordered, and the respective churchwardens of the respective churches of *Trinity, Mary Steps, George's, Allhallows on the Walls, John's Bow, Olave's, Kerrian's, Pancras, Paul's, Allhallows in Goldsmith-street, Lawrence, Stephens*, and *Martin's*, and every of them are commanded that, within four days after notice of this order to them to be given, they bring in to the Right Worshipful the Mayor of this city, a true particular in writing of all the bells, goods, utensils, and implements whatsoever to the said respective churches belonging and appertaining. And also to give up unto the said Mayor the possession of the said respective churches by the delivery of the several keys of the doors of the same, to the end order may be further had and taken in the premises according to and in performance of an Act of this present Parliament, intituled 'An Act for the promoting and more frequent preaching of the Gospel and maintenance of ministers in the city of Exeter, and uniting of parishes and parish churches within the said city of Exeter;' hereof the said respective churchwardens may not fail at their peril. Which order Mr. Townclerk is appointed to sign with his own name, in the name and by the order of the Common Council, which was

---

[5] Namely :—

					£.	s.	d.
St. Stephen's Church, with the cellar under the same, sold, 11th May, 1658, to Toby Allyn, for					230	0	0
St. Kerrian's, sold to the parishioners, 11th May, 1658, for					66	13	4
St. Martin's,	do.	do.			100	0	0
St. George's,	do.	do.			100	0	0
St. Laurence's,	do.	7th June, 1658			100	0	0
All Hallows, in Goldsmith-street, sold to Dr. Vilvain, 19th June, 1658					50	0	0
St. Pancras, sold to the parishioners,		do.			50	0	0
All Hallows on the Wall, which was unroofed,		do.			33	6	8
Trinity, sold to the parishioners,		do.			100	0	0
St. Mary Steps, on the 14th Sept. 1658					100	0	0
St. John's, Bow					100	0	0
St. Paul's, purchased by the parishioners, 9th Nov. 1658					105	0	0
St. Olave							

120   HISTORY OF EXETER.

done accordingly. And the parties therein concerned to be served therewith.

"It is also agreed that the partition of the cathedral church of St. Peter's be made with a brick wall on the east part of the cross aisle, where the organs stood, closing up the body or middle aisle upon a foundation which is already there, and filling up the place where the doors stand in the aisle sides leading into the choir. And that the south tower be divided by a wall of * * foot high, and a passage made from the East Church through a chapel there into the belfry. And whereas Mr. Walter Deeble hath undertaken to make this partition wall [6] for 150*l.* well and sufficiently with brick, and plastering and whiting the same on both sides, it is also agreed and ordered that the said 150*l.* shall be paid unto the said Mr. Deeble out of the first monies that can be risen.

"And it is further agreed that John Parr, that keeps the seats in the church, and now dwells in the Treasury rooms, shall be removed thence, and that Ralph Cooze be likewise removed out of his house adjoining to the workhouse (treasury), and Peter Seelye to live therein, for that the said Seelye's room is to be pulled down for an avenue to be made to pass into the great church.

"And it is also agreed that the sum of ten pounds shall be given and paid unto the said Ralph Cooze as a gift or pension from the Chamber during his life, and his pay to begin from Michaelmas next, and then to leave his house and get another.

"And it is agreed that an avenue be made through the garden wall and outrooms of the late treasurer's house unto that part of the great church which some time was the Treasury, and the window thereof to be taken down and a door there made to pass into the eastern part of the said church, and that another avenue to come unto the same door be made close to the north part of the north tower into the said garden, through certain rooms now in the possession of the said Peter Seelye.

"Also it was proposed that 800*l.* should be raised and advanced by the members of this house, or any of the citizens that shall willingly subscribe thereunto, as a present supply for the repairing, enlarging, fitting, and commoding of those churches, whereto ministers are presented, and to which other parishes are united.

"The same **day** these several presentations were sealed with the common seal :—

"A presentation to Mr. Ferdinando Nicholls for Mary Arches Church.

---

[6] Rev. John Reynolds, in his sermon, 27th July, 1684, on the occasion of erecting the seats in the nave, calls it " the monstrous Babylonish wall."

ORDINANCES AGAINST CHURCH ORNAMENTS. 121

" The like to Mr. Thomas Downe for Edmund's Church.
" The like to Mr. Robert Atkins for Peter's the East.
" The like to Mr. Mark Downe for Petroch's Church.
" The like to Mr. John Bartlett for Mary the Moor.

" Also it is agreed that a seventh minister be added; and the endeavours of the ministers are desired to procure an able and godly man[7] to assist the several ministers at sacrament in the forenoon on the respective days of administration thereof, and every other Lord's day to assist Mr. Thomas Downe at Edmund's in the morning in case of absence or sickness, and in the afternoon to bestow his labour where he shall be appointed by the Chamber.

" Also it was agreed that Mr. Thomas Ford, minister, do carry on the Wednesday's lecture in *West Peter's* as hitherto he hath done. And that he do assist the other ministers as he finds strength and opportunity, which is left to his own free will. And that he shall have and enjoy the maintenance which formerly he had."

A few years before the surrender of Exeter, the Lords and Commons assembled in parliament had published two ordinances " for the speedy demolishing of all organs, images, and all manner of superstitious monuments in all cathedrals, parish churches and chapels throughout England and Wales." The ' Mercurius Rusticus, or the Countries Complaint,' by Dr. Bruno Ryves, printed at Oxford 1646, contains a detailed report of the wanton outrages, profanations, and abominations exercised by these fanatics in our cathedral; but in submitting it to the reader, a love of historical fairness and truth compels us to say that, nearly a century before, irreparable injury and mutilation had been inflicted here by Queen Elizabeth's Visitors, as early as September, 1559, viz. by William, Earl of Pembroke, Dr. Jewel, Henry Parry, and William Lovelace. " These visitors" (we give the words of Hoker, chamberlain of the city at the time) " lodged in the Dean's house, and

---

[7] The seventh minister, John Tickell, was brought from London. Ten pounds were allowed for his journey down. His salary was 100*l.* per annum, besides the rent of a house.

122 HISTORY OF EXETER.

during their stay defaced and pulled down and burnt all images and monuments of idolatry, which all were brought into the churchyard of St. Peter's; and they who in Queen Mary's days were accounted to be most forward in erecting and maintaining them were now made the instruments to make the fire and burn them. Amongst other good things which these visitors did, they did deface all the altars"! Yet notwithstanding such Vandal outrages, Rev. Thomas Barret commenced the visitation of his archdeaconry of Exeter on 6th April, 1583, by inquiring "whether all images and other superstitious things were clean defaced and·rood-lofts taken down; if not, through whose default it is so?" Queen Elizabeth even affected a decided aversion to cuts and pictures in the Common Prayer-book, as we learn from her conversation with Dean Nowell in the vestry of St. Paul's Cathedral. (Strype's Annals, from p. 238 to 244.)

With this preamble, we may submit to the reader Dr. Bruno Ryves' account, though highly coloured and magnified, of the horrors practised by the levellers and Independents in this cathedral. "Having demanded the keys of the cathedral and taken them into their own custody, they presently interdict divine service to be celebrated; so that for the space of three quarters of a year the holy liturgy lay totally silenced. The pulpit was open only to factious schismatical preachers, whose doctrine was rebellion and their exhortations treason; so that the people might hear nothing but what might foment their disloyalty, and confirm them in their unnatural revolt from their duty and obedience. Having the church in their possession, in a most Puritanical beastly manner they make it a common jakes for the exonerations of nature, sparing no place, neither the altar nor the pulpit. Over the communion table, in fair letters of gold, was written the blessed

PROFANATION OF THE CATHEDRAL.

name of Jesus : this they expunge as superstitious and execrable. On each side of the Commandments, the pictures of Moses and Aaron were drawn in full proportion : these they deface. They tear the books of common prayers to pieces, and burn them at the altar with exceeding great exultation and expressions of joy. They made the church their storehouse, where they kept their ammunition and powder, and planted a court of guard to attend it, who used the Church with the same reverence as they would an alehouse, and defiled it with tippling. They break and deface all the glass windows of the church, which cannot be replaced for many hundred pounds, and left all those ancient monuments, being painted glass and containing matter of story only, a miserable spectacle of commiseration to all well-affected hearts that beheld them. They struck off the heads of all the statues on all the monuments in the church, especially they deface the bishops' tombs, leaving one without a head, and another without an arm. They pluck down and deface the statue of an ancient queen, the wife of Edward the Confessor, mistaking it for the statue of the blessed Virgin Mary, the Mother of God ; so she was styled by the Holy Catholique Church many years before it was in danger to be voted blasphemy in that committee, where learned Miles Corbett sat in the chair. They brake down the organ,[s] and, taking two or three hundred pipes with them, in a most scornful and contemptuous manner went up and down the streets piping with them ; and meeting with some of the choristers of the church, whose surplices they had stolen before, and imployed them to base servile offices, scoffingly told them— ' Boyes, we have spoyled your trade ; you must goe and

---

[s] In the Lansdown MS. this organ is described by the Norwich tourist of the summer of 1635 as rich, delicate, and soft, and having more additions than any other, and large pipes of an extraordinary length.

HISTORY OF EXETER.

sing hot pudding pyes.' By the absoluteness of their power, they send forth their warrants to take away the lead off a conduit and a great cistern that stood in the midst of the Close, giving plentiful supplies of water to many hundreds of the inhabitants; and by virtue of the same warrant, they gave their agents power to take a great quantity of timber which was laid up and designed for the repairing of the church; as also a great stock of lead reserved for the same purpose, which warrants were accordingly put in execution to the full. They did enter into a consultation about taking down the bells, and all the lead that covered the church, to convert them into warlike ammunitions. They took down the gates of the Close, which gates they employed to help forward and strengthen their fortifications. They lay intolerable taxes on most of the members of the Church; and whosoever refused to submit to these most unjust and illegable impositions, were threatened to have their houses plundered and their persons sent on shipboard, where they must expect usage as bad as at Algiers or the galleys. Dr. Burnell, a grave learned man and canon of the church, refusing to submit to their taxations, they gave command (though he were at that time sick and confined to his bed) to take him in the night and bring him away to prison though they brought him in his bed; but upon much importunity, some of the best rank of citizens being tendered his security to render himself a true prisoner, for that time they left him. For the like refusal they took Dr. Hutchinson, another canon of the church, a man of weak infirm body, and violently carried him towards the ship there to imprison him. By the way, as they carried him along, he was (not only by the permission but by the encouragement of those that led him captive) blasted and abused and hooted by the boys, and exposed

BARBARITY TOWARDS THE CANONS.

to the affronts and revilings of the base insolent multitude. At twelve by the clock at night, they seized on Mr. Hilliar in his bed, another canon of that church, being almost ninety years old, because he would not dispense such sums as they demanded: they carry him first to the prison and then to the ship. In the way to the prison they threw dirt in his face, and beat the good old man so cruelly that his roaring and outcries were heard and pitied by all his neighbours; and at last, not able to endure, by reason of his extreme old age, the barbarous usage of the rebels, he was forced to redeem his liberty at 800*l*. And now, having dispossessed the owners, the rebels find new employment for the canons' houses. Some of them they convert into prisons, and, in an apish imitation, call them by the names of *New Gate, King's Bench, Marshalsey*; others they employ as Hospitals for sick or maimed soldiers; and for the Bishop's Palace they might have called it *Smithfield*, for in and about it they kept their fat oxen and sheep and all their plundered provisions. Other houses they set on fire and burn down to the ground. They burnt down the Gildhall, in St. Sidwell's, belonging to the Dean and Chapter, and as many houses more of their ancient inheritance and revenues as were worth 100*l.* per annum; making likewise great havoc and spoil of their woods and timber, malicious intending to disable them from re-edifying what they had most barbarously burnt down."[9]

---

[9] Those who wish to have further insight into the history of the wrongs and excesses of these brutal barbarians may consult Dugdale's ' Short Views of the late Troubles in England;' Walker's 'Sufferings of the Clergy;' even John Vicars' 'Parliamentary Chronicle:' the 'Journal of William Dowsing, of Stratford,' the parliamentary visitor of Suffolk. "At Clare, 6th Jan. 1643-4," he says, "we brake down one thousand picture superstitions. I brake down two hundred." Rev. Prebendary John Reynolds, in his sermon delivered in Exeter Cathedral, 27th July, 1684, on the occasion of pews erected in its nave, observes, "Many of us have been sorrowful witnesses to great disorders and profanations in this very House of God where we are now assembled. You cannot forget the monstrous Babylonish wall, which was raised here to divide the Cathedral into two parts. Many of us have seen not only the monuments

HISTORY OF EXETER.

But it is time to turn aside from this recital of wrongs and oppressions. The Corporation had become so moulded to the views of Parliament, that the 13th of April, the anniversary day of the surrender of Exeter, must be solemnized with a public thanksgiving. At the return of the day, 1647, Mr. John Bond, "Minister of God's Word," had so acquitted himself to their hearts' content, that they voted him a piece of plate to the value of 10*l.*, "as a testimony of their friendly acceptance and thankfulness too;" and they further resolved, "that the 13th of April shall be yearly here-after commemorated, in like manner as now, for the delivery up of this city from the *enemie* to the power of the Parliament."[10] This was quite in character with the authorities above, who, after purging the House of Parliament of above fifty of the members, brought their sovereign to the block, and to perpetuate their malice, caused his statue in the Royal Exchange to be thrown down, and in its stead to be engraved,

Exit Tyrannus Regum ultimus, Anno
Libertatis Angliæ restitutæ Primo,
Anno Domini 1648, Jan. 30.

Shortly before the commencement of the civil wars, Parliament had passed an Act to adventure plantations in Ireland; and the Mayor and Town Council of Exeter, as well as of other towns, under the impression that in such agitated times land would prove the best security for their funds, as well as for the moneys placed in their hands for charitable uses, determined on pur-chasing estates in the sister kingdom. After much

---

of the dead, but even the very ashes and bones of some of them, disturbed and violated."

[10] We wish we could credit a tradition in the respected Gould family, "that an ancestor, the wealthy merchant, James Gould, who filled the office of the mayor in the fatal period of 1648-9, and continued a justice of the peace until his death in 1659 (see Act Book ix. p. 126), ransomed the Cathedral from being plundered of its leaden roof, bells, and ornaments, at the ex-pense of many hundred pounds." Can it be traced back earlier than 1704 ?

RECREANT AND DESPOTIC GOVERNMENT. 127

negotiation our Corporation concluded, through their agent, Samuel Jones, merchant, in June 1654, a covenant with the Commissioners of Sale of Forfeited Estates, whereby, for the consideration of 9890l. 10s. 0d., they received a conveyance of 2583 acres 2 roods 32 poles of Irish measure, or of 4185 acres and 29 poles of English measure, lying and being in the barony of Middlethird, in the county of Tipperary and province of Munster. The purchase deed was enrolled in Chancery on the 20th of March next ensuing. But it proved a disastrous speculation, and they were contented to sell their purchase, within a twelvemonth, at a serious loss,[11] to Sir Ames Ameredith, Bart., Colonel Jerome Sankey, and Valentine Greatorix of Cornworthy, Esq. Relying also on the public faith, our Chamber, by order of Parliament, advanced considerable loans, amounting in the whole to 14,000l. and upwards; but the manner in which their petition on 3rd December, 1653, for payment was received and was treated in the sequel, abundantly showed that the Government of the day, like a desperate gamester, set at defiance every principle of honour and justice.

During this reign of military and religious despotism our city became crowded with prisoners taken at the injudicious and abortive rising in 1654-5. The list is given in the third volume of Thurloe's State Papers, pp. 306-8. They were headed by Colonel John Penruddock, of Compton, Wilts, and his neighbour Hugh Groves, Esq., of Chisenbury, in the parish of Enford. At first they proclaimed Charles II. at Salisbury, 11th March, and, not meeting with the encouragement they expected, they proceeded to Southmolton for the same purpose; but the *posse comitatus* being raised, they surrendered at discretion. On 18th April, 1655, the

---

[11] One account in the Act Book makes the expenditure of the Chamber in this purchase 15,728l. 10s.; and that they received for it but 3,360l.—See p. 336.

128 HISTORY OF EXETER.

prisoners were brought to trial; and on the 23rd judgment was pronounced upon twenty-six for high treason; yet the Attorney-General, Edmund Prideaux, recommended to Secretary Thurloe "the enlargement of the rest for fear of confusion" (vol. iii. 442, Thurloe's State Papers). The copy of the warrant for execution may interest the reader. It will be seen what a narrow escape John Duke, of Lake, Wilts, had. He had been sheriff of that county, was a noted loyalist, and though at seventy-eight years of age, had joined the party, had been convicted and intended for execution, with his friends Penruddock and Groves; but by some unaccountable oversight his name was omitted in the body of the warrant, then interlined, with the misnomer of Robert in two places; and on the discovery of the flaw, the Protector seems to have struck out the name altogether.

OLIVER, P.

Whereas John Penruddock, Hugh Groves, [Robert Duke] Richard Reeves, Edward Davy, Thomas Poulton, Edward Willis, Thomas Hillard, John Haynes, James Horsington als Herish, and John Giles als Hobbs, were indicted, convicted, and attainted of high treason, at a commission of oyer and terminer and gaole deliverie lately held at Exeter, in our countie of Devon, and have received sentence to be executed as traytors; We have thought fit, and our will and pleasure is, the said John Penruddock and Hugh Grove [and Robert Duke], instead of being hanged by the neck be put to death by sevaring their heads from their bodyes; and that the said Richard Reeves, Edward Davy, Thomas Poulton, Edward Willis, Thomas Hillard, John Haynes, James Horsington, and John Giles, be only hanged by the neck till they are dead, and that you forbeare all other and further corporall payne and execution of y° bodies of y° persons aforesaid, and for soe doeing this shall be your warrant. Given at Whitehall the third of May, 1655.

To JOHN COPPLESTON,[18] esq°. high sheriffe of our countie of Devon, or his deputie.

---

[18] Who he was, I have yet to learn. Certainly not of Copleston in Cole- | broke parish, for its register affirms that "Mr. John Copleston (the last of his

RAVAGES OF BARBARY PIRATES.

In the Appendix we shall give the parting letters between Colonel Penruddock and his wife. His execution took place at the castle on Wednesday, 16th May, 1655, and he was privately interred in St. Lawrence's Church. His fellow sufferer Mr. Groves was "privileged to be decently interred in St. Sidwell's Church, was thither attended," says Izaacke (p. 10), "by some thousand persons of a depressed party, of which number I then thought myself happy to be one." The brass plate to his memory there was erected after the restoration of monarchy.

In concluding this chapter, we may allude to the ravages inflicted on our western coasts, the injuries sustained by the merchants of this city, and the insults offered to the English flag by the pirates of Sallee, Algiers, Tunis, and Tripoli, during a series of several years.[13] These, however, were amply revenged on the

---

family here") was buried 3rd Sept. 1593. That he was an ardent supporter of the Protector, is manifest from his letter dated Exeter, 10th Mar. 1654-5, in vol. iii. of Thurloe's State Papers, p. 219. It is pleasing, however, to record his humanity and even courtesy to these unfortunate prisoners. A Sir John Copleston was returned to serve in parliament in 1656 for Barnstaple, says Hatsell, Precedents, vol. ii. p. 401.

[13] In Roberts's History of the Southern Coast (London, 1856), we read, p. 96, "23rd July, 1636, from Plymouth it is advertised that fifteen sail of Turks were upon this coast, and had done much mischief. That the Swan, of Topsham, was set upon by two great Turkish men-of-war near Scilly, and the crews were obliged to run ashore in order to save themselves. The Lark, of Topsham, of 80 tons, having fifteen men and a boy, was lately taken, and the master slain. The Patience, of Topsham, was taken two days after her setting out on her voyage to Newfoundland. The Rose Garden, a barque of Topsham, coming from Morlaix, and having aboard her 100 fardels of white ware, belonging to the

merchants of Exeter and other places, and the barque, goods and seamen carried away by them." P. 97, "A ship was taken by the Turkish pirates within three leagues of Dartmouth. 5,000l. loss was sustained by Exeter, besides the loss of the ship and the seamen. The merchants of the port-towns are utterly disheartened, nor can they get seamen, who say they had rather starve at home, than be brought under the tyrannous and Moorish subjection of those Mohammedans." These Mr. Roberts selected from the Sherren Papers. My kind friend, T. E. Drake, Esq., has furnished me with the following minutes from the archives of the justices of Devon :—

"1607. 5° Jac. The county justices complained to the lords of the council that the harbour of Salcomb was infested with pirates, who often landed and came into the town in great numbers armed, and that the inhabitants were in great danger.

"1623. The constables were ordered to make returns of all who are in Turkish captivitie, and what their friends will give to bring them home. "1625.

K

130 HISTORY OF EXETER.

aggressors by the gallant Admiral Robert Blake, in the year 1654. In memory of such services to his country, his ashes ought to have been left undisturbed at the restoration of monarchy.

CHAPTER XVIII.

Protectorate of Cromwell — His son Richard proclaimed his successor — Death of Richard near Winchester — Connection of General Monk, the restorer of monarchy, with Exeter — Charles II. recalled by the new Parliament — Rejoicings at his proclamation in Exeter — Visit of the Grand Duke of Tuscany to the city — Stay of the king at Exeter on his route to London — Character of his reign — His demand for the surrender of civic charters.

THE Lord General Cromwell, who had attained the summit of his ambition by being inaugurated Protector, on 16th December, 1653, was not permitted by death to retain his supreme authority long; for, on 3rd September, 1658, æt. 60, he was summoned to appear before that highest tribunal, before which there is no respect of persons, and where judgment without mercy awaits all who have not exercised mercy.

When the news of his death reached Exeter, our municipal body gave orders that "the manner of the proclaiming of his Highness Richard (eldest son of the Lord Protector) be at the Guildhall, and at the little conduit, and at Peter's churchyard; and that the seven companies be attending and present thereat." Numerous congratulations were voted to him by

"1625. Julian Vynton, of Topsham, having had her ship taken at sea by the pirates, and her son and sons-in-law and the rest of the crew carried captives into Barbary, applied to the justices for relief. Her loss she stated to be 700l. and more. The justices order her 10l. "1632. The bishop grants a licence for a collection in the diocese for the redemption of the Turkish captives."

THE PROTECTORATE. 131

the military of the three kingdoms, by all the Independent congregations, by the French, Dutch, and Italian Reformed Churches, and by most of the counties, cities, and principal towns in England, in such language as the following: "if his father had been Moses, to lead them out of the house of bondage, he was the Joshua to conduct and settle them in the land of promise; if his father, like Elijah, had been taken into heaven, he, like Elisha, survived the inheritor of his mantle and spirit,"[1] &c. &c. Fortunately his character was the very reverse of that of his dissembling, ambitious, and despotic father. His good sense and foresight made him shrink from intrigues, agitation, and contest. He was satisfied that the heart of the nation was not with him, and after a few months he cheerfully abdicated titles and honours to lead the life of a country gentleman on his estate near Winchester, where he peacefully ended his days on 12th July, 1712, at the venerable age of 80. We may be allowed to add, that we should have thought much better of Charles II., if, instead of warring with the dead and impotently revenging himself on the ashes of Richard's father, and above all of Admiral Robert Blake, he had imitated Louis XI. of France, who forbade the grave of his gallant foe, John Duke of Bedford at Rouen, to be treated with disrespect and indignity.

Under Divine Providence, Lieutenant-General George Monk, intimately connected with this city, was the principal instrument in restoring monarchy. He was the second son of Sir Thomas Monk, of Potheridge, knight, by his wife Elizabeth, daughter of Sir George Smyth of Exeter,[2] who filled its office of mayor in 1607,

---

[1] One of these proclaims him his Josiah, whose pious life is his never perishing pyramid; "Every man's heart being his tomb, and every good man's tongue an epitaph."

[2] He was a merchant here; filled the

K 2

132 HISTORY OF EXETER.

and gave the freedom of the city to his son-in-law Thomas Monk, who had been recently knighted. At an early period George adopted the military service, and for a considerable time supported the declining cause of his Sovereign, but at length was over prevailed to sacrifice his hereditary principles of loyalty to the pursuits of ambition. Cromwell rejoiced to see a man of his standing and military experience deserting his party, and, to attach him still more, he gave him the command of the forces in Scotland. He could not fathom, however, his phlegmatic coolness and profound taciturnity and reserve, and at last grew suspicious; but contented himself with putting him on his guard by this postscript to a letter—" 'Tis said, there is a cunning fellow in Scotland, called George Monk, who lies in wait there to serve Charles Stuart: pray use your diligence to take him, and send him up to me." To throw dust into the Protector's eyes, the inscrutable Monk actually sent him a letter, which Charles II. had addressed to him from Cologne, August 12, 1655. It is quite true that *verbal* negotiations occasionally passed, yet with extreme caution; and that the main channel of such communications was the General's brother, Rev. Nicholas Monk, Rector of Kilkhampton, Cornwall, and their kinsman, Sir John Grenville. We read in the memorial of Sir John Hinton, the royal physician—" General Monk, the day before he went to Scotland, dined with me, for I had contracted a great friendship with him when he was of our party; and after dinner he called me

---

mayoralty chair in 1586, 1597, and 1607; for several years represented Exeter in parliament; was knighted by King James I. 2nd June, 1604; and was appointed sheriff for Devon in 1614. He chiefly resided at Great Matford, where his arms, "Sable, a fess cotised between three Martlets Or," may still be seen.

In the archives of Exeter is a letter of Sir Thos. Monk, of Potheridge, of 5th Aug. 1622, claiming his share of the property of his deceased father-in-law.

RESTORATION OF CHARLES II. 133

into the next room, and after some general discourse, taking a lusty glass of wine, he drank an health to his Black Boy (as he called Prince Charles), and whispered to me, if ever he had power, he would serve his Majesty to the utmost of his life." We believe this was his object; but to succeed with safety, and without violence and bloodshed, what dissimulation! what circumspection! what tampering! what fencing! what anxious delays were resorted to! "Unus qui nobis cunctando restituit rem." And now the Rump Parliament having dissolved itself on 17th March, 1660, the new Parliament or Convention, summoned for 25th April, decided on the recall of the King. And yet, having the game in his own hands, the lovers of civil and religious liberty must ever lament and complain that Monk neglected that golden opportunity of insisting on the security of good government, and on a constitutional compact between the Sovereign and the nation—at once determining the fair rights of the Crown and the liberties of the subject—and thus preventing discord and future revolution!

To return to our city. On the news reaching the town, that the new Parliament had voted the restoration of monarchy, and that Charles II. had been proclaimed in the metropolis, the Mayor and Council ordered, that "on 11th May, 1660, about 2 P.M., on King Charles II. being proclaimed in several places within this city, that Mr. Marshall doe cause three hogsheads of good claret wine to be put into the cisterns of the three conduits, to be drunk out, to his Majesty's health." On 21st May the following address was voted by the municipal body to his Majesty :—

"May it please your Majesty—

"The sense of our late sufferings, whilst we were made to serve under the rage and tyranny of an usurping martial sword held over us, could not but much afflict us; the more for that

134   HISTORY OF EXETER.

we were made to behold the unparalleled treasonable violence offered to the sacred person of your Majesty's royal father, of glorious memory, which so deeply affected our hearts, as through the extremity of grief and just indignation, divers of us did quit our places of public trust, and betake ourselves to a solitary retired life, not knowing how to find our way in such a dismal confusion of affairs.

"Yet since it hath pleased God, who worketh all things after the counsel of His own will, so to dispose and order, as your Majesty's royal person, the only rightful heir to these kingdoms, hath been miraculously preserved in the midst of desperate perils and difficulties, and is now restored to the exercise of that regal power and trust which did by inherent birthright and undoubted succession lawfully descend upon your Majesty, we cannot look upon ourselves (when we compare our past and present condition) otherwise than as brought out of darkness to light, as raised from death to life.

"And upon the account of these glorious appearances of God in so blessed a change, we hold ourselves in all duty bound to congratulate your Majesty's happy restoration, with our most humble and hearty thanksgivings to the King of Kings, that hath been pleased to hear the prayers and answer the desires of your Majesty's loyal subjects.

"Now may it please your Majesty graciously to accept of us in this our most humble address, whereby we do engage in all sincerity, through the assistance of Almighty God, to continue and abide in our bounden duty, loyalty, and allegiance to your Majesty, humbly begging we may enjoy the happiness of your Majesty's gracious protection and favour, as we have formerly had of your royal and famous progenitors.

"We, as in duty bound, shall ever pray, that your Majesty may long reign in peace and prosperity over these nations, by ruling in the fear of God for the punishment of evil-doers and the praise of such as do well, to the glory of Him who is Lord of all; so as your name may be famous to all posterity, and the generations to come may call you blessed.

"CHⁱ. CLARKE, Mayor."

As a further proof of loyal devotion, a vote was passed on 25th June that a piece of plate of nearly 600*l.* value be presented to the new Sovereign.

To ingratiate himself with the nation, Charles granted a free and general pardon, indemnity, and oblivion, with the exception of the most notorious rebels and re-

VISIT OF THE GRAND DUKE OF TUSCANY. 135

gicides. Yet, notwithstanding the exemplary loyalty and unexceptionable conduct of the whole Catholic body, he suffered the sanguinary Act of the 27th of Elizabeth to remain in full force against the clergy of that communion. His own experience, as well as a retrospect of history, should have taught a very different policy: that the duty of every Sovereign is to consult and provide for the interests and freedom of *all* classes of his subjects; that to look only to the benefit of a *portion* of the community, and to neglect and abandon the rest, was to engender discord and perpetuate disaffection, undermine the stability of the throne, and foment convulsion and revolution.

In the spring of 1669, Cosmo III., Grand Duke of Tuscany, visited this city on his way from Plymouth to London. In vol. ix. p. 86, of the Act Books of our Chamber, occurs the following notice: "27th March, 1669, O.S. The Prince of Tuskey being expected to come to this citie this present day, Mr. Mayor (George Tothill) is desired to give him an invitation at the costs of the citie, and it is agreed that Mr. Mayor and the Aldermen and the rest of this Societie do present the respects of this citie to his Highness at his coming hither, and that he be lodged at the New Inne,[3] and also a present of 20*l.* or thereabouts be provided to be presented to him by the Receiver, as from this citie. For the more orderly doing thereof Mr. Mawdett, Mr. Brodridge, and Mr. Sparke be desired to assist the Receiver therein." From the quarto volume of the prince's Travels through England, published in London, 1821 (p. 128), we collect that the prince reached Exeter from Okehampton and Crediton on the evening of

---

[3] Sometimes called Merchants' Hall in Queen Mary's reign, and built in High-street, on land belonging to the Chamber and Chapter. Thomas Johnson was ejected from its tenure 25th July, 1582, and it was taken by Valentine Tucker.

136   HISTORY OF EXETER.

6th April, N.S.; that at Cowley Bridge several of the
principal gentlemen of the city awaited his arrival to
pay their respects; that he descended from his carriage
to answer them with his usual courtesy; that he
alighted at the New Inn; that, soon after, the mayor,
aldermen, and bailiffs arrived in full dress; that he
received them graciously in the saloon above stairs,
and desired the mayor to be covered. Having replied
to the congratulatory address, his Highness declined
the mayor's polite invitation to the entertainment on
the ground of his travelling incognito, and his impatience to reach London to pay his respects to their
Sovereign. The next day he visited the cathedral
and castle, and returned the call of Sir John Rolle
and of his two sons, John and Dennis Rolle, in their
house within the Close. The prince calculated that
the population of the city averaged from 20,000 to
25,000. On the morning of the 8th, after sending his
compliments to the mayor, his Highness departed for
Axminster.

The King himself in the course of the year 1671
honoured our faithful city with his presence. The
mayor, Benjamin Oliver, Esq., on 18th July, announced
to the council that he had received intimation that his
Majesty had arrived at Plymouth by a sea voyage from
London, and intended to return the same way. In
consequence, it was agreed that a deputation from the
municipal body should proceed to Plymouth, and present their humble duty and service to his sacred
Majesty ; and, as it was improbable that he would visit
Exeter on this occasion, to request his acceptance of
500*l.* in new gold " as a testimony of the city's gratitude
and loyalty." Before the deputation had arrived at
Plymouth the King had sailed. On 22nd July the
Council met again, and were informed, that, by contrary
winds, his Majesty had put into Dartmouth, and had

CHARLES II. AT EXETER. 137

decided to proceed onwards to London by land, and take Exeter in his way : " therefore it is this day agreed, that the gift of 500*l.* shall be presented *here* unto him, and that all possible care be taken by all the members of this house for his entertainment and accommodation, at the charges of the city." The next day, Sunday 23rd July, about 7 o'clock P.M., his Majesty reached the Deanery house, and was there waited upon by the mayor and his brethren ; the 500*l.* were graciously accepted, and the mayor was there knighted in honour of the city. The sword being delivered then to the King, with the keys of the city gates, were returned to the mayor ; and the aldermen and some others of the chief persons of the town attended on his Majesty at supper, bringing in the dishes. The next morning, about 3 o'clock, his Majesty departed, " being waited on by the Duke of Monmouth and divers other lords and the high sheriff of Devon in four coaches, with his servants on horseback."

During this Sovereign's reign the commercial interests of Exeter were much encouraged and extended, and great attention was directed to the improvement of the river, the quay, and canal; but this will be set forth in a distinct chapter. We may premise, however, that an Act of Parliament had been obtained for the purpose ; that a Mr. William Bailey of Winchester had been engaged to superintend the work, but decamped in a disgraceful manner ; that Mr. Daniel Dennett and Mr. Gilbert Greenslade were subsequently employed to direct the undertaking, which was occasionally interrupted for want of pecuniary resources ; indeed in the progress of the work the Chamber had to submit to many painful sacrifices. But at length the port was opened in 1725 ; and amongst the numerous persons specially invited to attend the ceremony were Dr. Blackburn, Archbishop of York, formerly bishop

138   HISTORY OF EXETER.

of this See, Lord Walpole, and Lord Chief Justice King.

Whilst all must admit that during this reign the arts improved, commerce increased, as well as the wealth and comforts of the people, and that literature was encouraged, yet we cannot sufficiently regret that liberty of conscience was so much obstructed and violated. A petition in the State-Paper Office, of the year 1683, records that thirty-eight men and four women were confined at one time in Exeter Gaol for *nonconformity!* It states that they had been much engaged in manufacturing serges; that they gave employment to five hundred persons in the trade, who, by their imprisonment, were thrown out of work. Had the King been a man of energy and business-like habits—had he been of inflexible integrity and of unimpeachable morality—he would have added grace and dignity to the crown, proved a blessing to the nation, and averted manifold calamities to his dynasty and his country; but he showed himself fitter to be a jovial companion than to wield the sceptre of a mighty empire.

In the course of 1684 Charles required of many corporate cities and boroughs the surrender of their ancient charters, and amongst others that of Exeter. His object was to increase the influence of the Crown; but, though an ungracious measure, it did not affect the public rights so much as the privileges of individuals. Our charter was returned on 22nd October of the same year, but from the informality of not being enrolled it proved unavailable.

CHAPTER XIX.

James II. — His character — Rebellion of the Duke of Argyle — Landing of Monmouth at Lyme Regis — His defeat at Selgmoor and subsequent execution — Judge Jeffreys and the "Bloody Assize" — National discontent with James's rule — Birth of a prince royal — Landing of William Prince of Orange at Torbay — His reception at Exeter and progress to London — Abdication of the king.

On the death of Charles II. on 6th February, 1685, his brother the Duke of York was proclaimed by the Lords as the new and rightful Sovereign by the title of King James II. On the 25th February this corporation voted an address of congratulation to him, and three members of the body were deputed to present it. The coronation was conducted with the usual splendour on the feast of St. George, 23rd of April next ensuing. James possessed several qualities to recommend him to the nation. He was personally brave and fearless, very skilful in naval tactics, and remarkable for industry and economy ; but unfortunately he was stern and headstrong, and his temper had been soured by the unrelenting persecution of a party who had intrigued, during the preceding reign, to separate him from the society and court of his royal brother, and exclude him from the House of Lords. Their envenomed hostility reminds us of the text, "His citizens hated him and sent a message after him, saying, We will not have this man to rule over us" (Luke xix. 4). They denied to him the right, which they all individually claimed for themselves, of openly professing and practising a religious creed. Even some of his own Privy Council and confidential Ministers proved false and treasonable, and boasted, like Sunderland, how successfully they had cajoled him, and at last driven him to extremities.

140   HISTORY OF EXETER.

The standard of rebellion was first unfurled in Scotland by Argyle. It was an ill-concerted attempt; he was made prisoner, and paid the forfeit of his treason on 30th June, 1685.

The expedition of James Duke of Monmouth[1] to dethrone his presumed royal uncle threatened more formidable results to the King's government. Landing at Lyme Regis, within thirty miles of this city, on 11th June, 1685, a blue flag was planted in the market-place; and to the multitude was read a proclamation of the most virulent and seditious character, describing the King as the usurper who had snatched the crown from the head of his brother, as a murderer, traitor, and tyrant, the patron of idolatry, against whom the Duke protested and declared war until he should have brought him and all his adherents to condign punishment. Proceeding to Taunton he assumed the title of King, "and set a price on the head of the usurper of the crown, James Duke of York." In the meanwhile Parliament pronounced Monmouth "a traitor for levelling war against the Sovereign, contrary to the duty of his allegiance" (Statute 1° Jacobi Secundi, cap. 11). The defeat at Sedgmoor baffled all his projects; his subsequent flight and capture, his cowardly fear of death and meanness of spirit, excited pity and contempt; and on 15th July he fell a victim to the justice of his country.

From the Act Books of our corporation we learn that in this city " the thanksgiving-day for the happy victory obtained over the Duke of Monmouth was celebrated with great joy and exultation." Soon followed

---

[1] His name was James Crofts, and he was supposed to be an illegitimate child of Lucy Barlow, but fathered on Charles II., " though all the knowing world, as well as myself, had many convincing reasons to think the contrary, and that he was Robert Sidney's child."—See the Life of James II., vol. i. p. 494, compiled from the Stuart Papers in 1816. It is true that he was a most ungrateful subject, a false friend, and an infamous husband.

JEFFREYS' "BLOODY ASSIZE."

what is often called the Bloody Assize, against those who were implicated in that rebellion. On the 14th September the harsh and inexorable Chief Justice Jeffreys opened his commission in this city. John Fouracres and Robert Drower were the first arraigned: they pleaded not guilty, but were convicted; and Jeffreys ordered Fouracres for immediate execution. The rest, twenty-six in number, pleaded guilty. Thirteen were executed as traitors, and, to inspire terror, in different parts of the county: at Exeter three, viz., John Fouracres, Thomas Broughton, and John Gosling; at Honiton six, viz., John Oliver, Henry Knight, Samuel Potts, John Knowles, — Port, and Rev. J. Evans; at Colyton two, viz., John Sprake and William Clegg; at Axminster one—John Ross; at Crediton one—Thomas Hobbs.

The names of three hundred and forty-two persons who were then at large were proclaimed in order to their apprehension, but they seem to have escaped discovery. Such disgusting and tragical exhibitions of heads and quarters remind us of the brutal massacre of the insurgents near this city by John Lord Russell in 1549, and of the sanguinary campaign of the Earl of Sussex within a quarter of a century later, in the reign of Elizabeth, after the Northern Rebellion, when, in the county of Durham alone, more than three hundred suffered death; and between Newcastle and Wetherby there was not a town or village in which some of the inhabitants did not expire on the gibbet, as a warning to their fellows. (See Sir Cuthbert Sharp's Memorials of that rebellion.)

James had now apparently reached the zenith of power and prosperity, but a smouldering volcano of national discontent lay under his feet; and instead of proceeding with caution, instead of temporising and adapting himself to circumstances, instead of seeking to

142   HISTORY OF EXETER.

conciliate the affections of his subjects, his high notions
of the royal prerogative made him forget his speech to
the Privy Council on the day of his accession,—" I know
that the laws of England are sufficient to make the
King as great a monarch as I can wish to be;" and he
suffered himself to rush blindfold into the most obnoxious and unconstitutional measures. We know not
still how to blame him for his proclamation to all his
loving subjects for liberty of conscience, dated from
Whitehall, 4th of April, 1687 (Wilkins, Concilia,
vol. iv. 614-15), but we are bound to protest against
his attempt to set aside the Habeas Corpus Act, that
great bulwark of the constitution for the security of
personal liberty. And what could be more obnoxious
and illegal than his intrusion of Roman Catholics into
the offices of the Universities, and his encroaching on
the rights of the Church established by law? The
time had gone by for the exercise of the royal prerogative in these cases; the attempt betrayed infatuation,
and even madness.

William Prince of Orange, Stadtholder of Holland,
the King's nephew,[2] and also his son-in-law (he had
married Mary, the eldest daughter of James, on 14th
November, 1677), now coveted the splendid prize of
the English crown. The ill success of Argyle and
Monmouth had served to favour his prospects; and no
wonder that he could afford to tender his congratulations to his uncle on the victory of Sedgmoor. With
his political duplicity he went on with preparations
to dethrone him, and with that view fomented intrigues;
and all was now nearly ripe for the execution of his
design, when the queen of our misguided monarch was
announced to have been safely delivered of a son and

---

[2] He was the posthumous child of William of Nassau, by Mary his wife,
eldest daughter of King Charles I.

LANDING OF THE PRINCE OF ORANGE. 143

heir-apparent to the crown on Sunday 10th June, 1688. This unexpected event proved to William and his partisans a cruel disappointment; but he mastered his vexation, and actually despatched an envoy to his father-in-law to congratulate him on this auspicious occurrence.

The loyalists, however, could not dissemble their joy; and Exeter, with its characteristic fidelity, on June 19th voted an address of their warmest congratulations to his Majesty " on the birth of the young prince." The Mayor, Thomas Jefford, Esq., was deputed to present the address, which was graciously received, and he returned to the city with the honour of knighthood.

During the interval before his descent on England, the Prince of Orange grew pensive and disheartened at the prospect of the difficulties of his enterprise. Writing to Bentinck on August 29th, 1688, he says, " My sufferings, my disquiet, are dreadful; I hardly see my way. Never in my life did I so much feel the need of God's guidance." But reassured by his partisans in England—who claimed for themselves the prerogative of dispensing with their oaths of allegiance to their lawful sovereign, and with all obligations of honour and gratitude,[3] and even the ties

---

[3] We must make an honourable exception in a gallant youth, George Granville, who, writing to his father, the Honourable Bernard Granville, from Wear, near Doncaster, county York, 16th Oct., 1688 (in which county the prince originally had intended to land), thus expresses himself :—" Sir, your having no prospect of obtaining a commission for me can no way alter or cool my desire, at this important juncture, to venture my life in some manner or other for my king and my country. I cannot bear living under the reproach of living obscure and idle in a country retirement, when every man who has the least sense of honour should be preparing for the field. You may remember, Sir, with what reluctance I submitted to your commands upon Monmouth's rebellion, when no importunity could prevail upon you to permit me to leave the academy. I was too young to be intrusted. But give me leave to say, it is glorious at any age to die for one's country, and the sooner, the nobler sacrifice. I am now older by three years. My uncle Bath was not so old when he was left among the slain at the battle of Newbury; nor you yourself, Sir, when you made your escape from your tutor's to join your brother at the defence of Scilly. The same cause is now come round again. The king has been misled; let those who have misled him be answerable for it. Nobody

144 HISTORY OF EXETER.

of nature itself—that he would meet with powerful support, he took leave of the States of Holland on October 16th, and with a large armament sailed from Helvoetsluys. For several days his fleet encountered a violent tempest, and he was necessitated to return to port, and repair damages. This disaster occasioned some delay, but on November 1st, taking advantage of a favourable wind, he set sail. It was generally supposed that his destination was the coast of Yorkshire; but he suddenly tacked and bore down Channel, and on Sunday, November 4th, the anniversary day of his birth and marriage, anchored in Torbay. In the course of the two next days, the landing of the troops and stores was accomplished at Brixham. In the meanwhile great excitement and agitation prevailed in this city; the bishop and dean took their departure; the clergy and magistrates were generally faithful to their sovereign; and when the vanguard of the invaders under the command of Lord Mordaunt reached the west gate, they found that orders had been issued by the civil authorities for the closing of all the gates. The next day, Friday 9th, the prince made his public entry.

---

can deny but he is sacred in his own person, and it is every honest man's duty to defend it. You are pleased to say it is yet doubtful if the Hollanders are rash enough to make such an attempt; but be that as it will, I beg leave to insist upon it that I may be presented to his Majesty, as one whose ambition it is to devote his life to his service and my country's, after the example of my ancestors. The gentry assembled at York to agree upon the choice of representatives for the county, have prepared an address to assure his Majesty they are ready to sacrifice their lives and fortunes for him upon this and all other occasions; but at the same time they humbly beseech him to give them such magistrates as may be agreeable to the laws of the land, for at present there is no authority to which they can legally

submit. They have been beating for volunteers at York and the towns adjacent, to supply the regiments at Hull, but nobody will list. By what I can hear, everybody wishes well to the king, but they would be glad his ministers were hanged. The winds continue so contrary, that no landing can be so soon as was apprehended; therefore I may hope, with your leave and assistance, to be in readiness before any action can begin. I beseech you, Sir, most humbly and most earnestly to add this one act of indulgence more to so many other testimonies which I have constantly received of your goodness, and be pleased to believe me always, with the utmost duty and submission, your most dutiful son and most obedient servant, "GEORGE GRANVILLE."

THE PRINCE OF ORANGE AT EXETER. 145

"The magistrates had been pressed to receive him in state at the entrance of the city, but steadily refused," says Macaulay. But it must have been a most imposing spectacle. The deanery had been hastily prepared for the prince's reception; after some refreshment, the prince repaired in military state to the cathedral. Dr. Burnet, the prince's chaplain, had previously informed the Chapter that a solemn service must be performed in honour of the safe arrival of the prince, and that the prayer for the Prince of Wales must be omitted. The prince occupied the bishop's throne; but the canons did not choose to take their stalls; and "when Dr. Burnet began to read the prince's declaration," continues Macaulay, "prebendaries and singers crowded in all haste out of the choir." Such a stupor had come over men's minds, that he felt disappointed and mortified at the coolness that attended him, and "he was indeed so indignant that he talked of falling back to Torbay, re-embarking his troops, and leaving those who had betrayed him to the fate which they deserved" (vol. ii. p. 493, Macaulay, 5th ed.). After a few days the prospect brightened; many persons of rank and consideration joined his standard. On the 20th he left Exeter[4] for Honiton: his progress towards the capital resembled an ovation, and he sent an order on December 18th, for James to quit his palace. The king, humbled, unnerved, and deserted—mindful of his father's words, "The distance is short between a king's prison and his grave," and believing there was no faith in man—forsook the kingdom, and on Christmas-day reached Ambleteuse on the coast of France.

---

[4] Many of his soldiers on the sick list were left behind, and the Chamber had to expend the sum of 345l. 4s. 2½d. Repayment was frequently applied for at the Treasury, as appears by the Act Books, but unsuccessfully.

L

CHAPTER XX.

The Revolution — Character of the reign of William III. — Former neglect of sanatory measures in Exeter — Provisions for lighting the city — Preservation of the peace — Supply of water — The Workhouse — Pictures contained in its Board-room.

THE Revolution having been accomplished by the legislature, and by the national voice, it became the duty of every good citizen to submit to the new order of things, and to yield obedience to King William III.[1]

---

[1] It is fashionable to uphold King William III. as the champion of civil and religious freedom, and Macaulay asserts (vol. ii. Hist. of England, p. 593, 5th ed.), " No body of men had so much reason to feel grateful to William as the Roman Catholics. It would not have been safe to rescind formally the severe resolutions which the peers had passed against the professors of a religion generally abhorred by the nation; but by the prudence and humanity of that prince, those resolutions were practically annulled." To this assertion we may answer in the words of Cicero (l. 3, Tuscul. Quæst. 20), " Quid verba audiam, cum facta videam?" Why should I listen to words, when I have facts staring me in the face? It is very true that amongst the troops he brought over with him were some Catholic regiments, and that he caused it to be proclaimed at Brussels that he had no intention of molesting the Catholics, nor would he ever do so, " nihil se in Anglia contra Romano-Catholicos moliri, neque moliturum," and that his only object was to bind Great Britain to the continental confederacy against Louis XIV. How he redeemed this pledge, we have but to consult the statutes enacted in his reign against his Catholic subjects. And what can be said in excuse of the violation of the treaty of Limerick? or of the warrant for the massacre of the Catholic M'Donalds of Glenco? " A warrant,' says Dalrymple (Memoirs, vol. i. p. 488), " signed both above and below with his own hand." And what defence can be offered for his depriving Charles, the third Lord Baltimore, that champion of civil and religious freedom in Maryland, of his noble patrimony, granted absolutely to his family by King Charles I. in Jan. 1632 ? Why did he not imitate the example of Charles II., who by his charter, dated 8th July, 1663, guaranteed inviolably to the people and inhabitants of Rhode Island and the colony of Providence plantation, in New England, " that they should never be called upon to conform to the exercise of religion according to the forms and ceremonies of the Church of England, or take and subscribe to the oaths and articles made and established in that behalf; but should freely have and enjoy their judgments and conscience in matters of religious concernment"? Nor was religious freedom better understood and encouraged by his successor, Queen Anne, as the statute book demonstrates. The truth is, it was not till the reign of King George III. of happy memory, that liberty of conscience dawned upon all classes. Witness the previous imprisonments and persecutions of the inoffensive Society of Friends. Witness the brutal indignities to which the Methodists were exposed, not by the mob only, but by justices of the peace in this very city, during May, 1745.—See the account published by John Canning, London, 1745.

and his protecting government. And it is much to the honour of this city and to the county of Devon, that they were never disgraced by those intestine divisions and overt insurrections against the public order and tranquillity, which subsequently convulsed the more northern parts of the kingdom and overwhelmed so many families with mourning and irretrievable ruin. Yet we should have thought better of King William III. if he had abstained from passing that act "for the attainder of the *pretended* Prince of Wales" in 1701, a youth of twelve years of age, "that he suffer the pains of death, and incur all forfeitures as a traitor convicted of high treason." What a contrast to the generosity of King George IV., who erected a monument to this royal prince's memory in St. Peter's Church at Rome, with this inscription to departed greatness!—

JACOBO TERTIO, JACOBI SECUNDI
MAGN. BRIT. REGIS, FILIO:
CAROLO EDUARDO,
ET HENRICO, PATRUM CARDINALIUM DECANO,
REGIÆ STIRPIS STUARDIÆ POSTREMIS.

Let us now confine our attention to Exeter. Though this city was the capital of the west of England, and the hive of commercial industry, yet its approaches were narrow, steep, and incommodious; and the vast majority of the population was so engrossed in the wool trade, as to pay little attention to the fine arts, or even to the ventilation of their houses and prisons, to the draining, cleansing, and lighting the streets, and, above all, the providing of a supply of that essential article, river-water. In turning over the Act Books of the Chamber, we find, indeed, an order in 1599, that " the deep way between the Wynard's House and the Maudlyn Hospital be filled up and paved," and another of October 20th, 1619, that " the Hollow-way be

148   HISTORY OF EXETER.

filled up with the rubbish of the city." In consequence
of the gross neglect of all sanatory precautions, Dr.
Edward Kellett,[2] a canon of Exeter, in his Tricœnium,
published in 1641, enters into a detail of the filthy inde-
cencies and abominations which he had witnessed in the
churches, in the cloisters, and the cathedral-cemetery,
and then recounts " as a *wicked wonder*, with grief and
indignation of heart, that whereas the city of Exeter is
by its natural situation one of the sweetest cities of
England, yet, by the ill use of many, is one of the
nastiest and noysommest cities of the land; but for my
love to that city, I do forbeare to say more." Who can
cease to be surprised, then, that it should have so often
been the victim of malignant fever and pestilence ?[3] As
to lighting the streets, the corporation was satisfied
with ordering on November 24th, 1635, " that every
inhabitant of this city shall, in every dark night,
between All Hallow tyde (November 1st) till Candlemas (February 2nd), set forth a light at their door, so
to continue until nine of the clock in the night, upon
pain of everyone making default to pay 6d., to be
levied by distress." And for security of person and
property and the preservation of the peace, " Ordered
December 14th, 1641, that proclamation be made by
the bell, that all the inhabitants of this city shall have
a club, or some other fitting weapon in readiness for
the preservation of the peace, according to the ancient
order of this city; which is a thing of late much

---

[2] This learned divine was admitted a
prebendary of this cathedral 4th Aug.
1630, at the nomination of King
Charles I., on the promotion of Dr.
William Murray to the see of Llandaff.
He must have died in the spring of
1641, for Bishop Hall collated Francis
Bampfylde, clerk, to the prebend and
canonry, on 15th May, 1641, which
had become void "per mortem natura-
lem venerabilis viri Edwardi Kellett,

S.T.P."

[3] Horace, in his first book of Epistles,
observes on the importance of attention
to cleanliness at Rome :

           " Grave virus
    Munditiæ pepulere."

And every friend to Exeter should join
in his aspiration—

" Pauperies immunda domûs procul absit ! "

THE WATERWORKS. 149

neglected." Again, March 6th, 1654—"Two pits of water without Southgate, near the drawbridge, be forthwith filled up with earth to prevent future danger to people coming that way."

We may now allude to three memorable events connected with Exeter in the reign of William III.

1. According to Izaacke, attempts were made as early as 1635 to introduce river-water into the city, but all ended in disappointment. Within 60 years later, the long-contemplated scheme was determined upon to convey the Exe water by wooden pipes to the houses of such of the inhabitants as should agree to take in the same at a reasonable rate. On February 12th, 1695, the Mayor and Chamber contracted with Jonathan Pyrke of Stourbridge, county Worcester, gentleman, Richard Lowbridge and Ambrose Crowley of the same place, ironmongers, and Daniel Dennett of Gloucester, carpenter, for this purpose. These undertakers agreed at their own charge to erect and maintain a water-engine in the New Mill Leat; and, in consideration of their expenses, and of the benefit and safety to accrue to the city from their useful enterprise, they were to pay down a fine of 5s. to have a term on their water-works of 200 years, and to make an acknowledgment of a pepper-corn, if demanded, at every Michaelmas. We can well remember how inadequate was this supply, —what leakage there was in the wooden pipes—the stoppages during floods and summer droughts. Consequently the proprietor, Mr. Rous, derived but little profit from public encouragement. The late Mr. James Golsworthy [4] became the lessee of the water-

---

[4] This friendly neighbour and very useful citizen died on the 27th Jan. 1850, æt. 74. The head source of the water which supplied the city conduits and the Close was derived from wells in the vicinity of Lion's Holt in St. Sid-well's parish. We well remember when the supply perceptibly diminished, and finally ceased in 1835. At the request of the Chapter and Chamber he remedied this defect by sinking the wells deeper, by clearing the springs, by lay-

150 HISTORY OF EXETER.

works in 1808, and his ingenious and energetic mind immediately set about increasing the power of the engine and introducing that great original improvement of substituting iron pipes instead of wooden ones, for the conveyance of water ; but the history of his exertions for nearly twenty-five years, when he at length parted with his interest to the new water company, is admirably given in Dr. Shapter's valuable work on the Cholera in Exeter A.D. 1832 (chapter iv.), to which we must refer our readers. Suffice it to say, that no city can boast of a more regular or copious supply of this necessary luxury, and at a cheaper rate, than Exeter.

2. It is not generally known, that on April 10th, 1604, a suggestion was held out tö our Mayor and Chamber, that "a Mint could be obtained for Exeter by suit to the King's Majesty ;" but as they could not determine whether it would prove beneficial to the city, and were left in ignorance of the amount of the expenses, they declined all interference on the subject (Act Book v. p. 62 b). The currency after the Revolution had become for all practical purposes notoriously depreciated by clipping, and in 1695, now that the times had subsided into comparative tranquillity, a grand recoinage of silver in the following year was determined on, and wisely confided to the charge and superintendence of our immortal Sir Isaac Newton. By his energy no less than nineteen mills were set going in the Tower ; and, as men could be trained to the work, bands of them were sent off to other parts of the kingdom. Mints were established at York, Chester, Norwich, Bristol, and at Exeter, to expedite this national work. The mint here was in Hele's Hospital, Mary

---

ing the conducting pipes at the bottom instead of the surface of the wells, and at the end of nine months brought to the city a superabundant supply. From the surplus of the great conduit in Milk Lane he brought pipes to a font erected at his own expense in St. Mary Arches Lane, in 1839, for the benefit of the neighbourhood. All this public service was rendered without fee or reward.

THE WORKHOUSE. 151

Arches Lane, and its coinage is distinguished by the letter E in the exergue.

3. About this time the new Corporation of the Poor obtained the fee-simple and inheritance of the land possessed by the old workhouse and hospital at the bottom of Paris Street, subject to the yearly rent-charge of 30*l.*; and, shortly after, that corporation succeeded in acquiring the residue of a term of 1940 years, commencing from Christmas-day, 1707, of a parcel of land in St. Sidwell's parish belonging to the feoffees of the said parish, under the clear yearly rent of 20*s.*, payable quarterly. In a commanding and airy situation on the old London Road was erected an extensive workhouse, after a design of Ralph Mitchell. No situation could be more eligible; and we believe no similar establishment can be better conducted so far as regards the comfort and welfare of the objects of charity.

In the board-room of this imposing and convenient structure are several pictures or portraits which are worthy of notice.

1st. On the right of the President's chair is the portrait of Mr. Paul Micheau in crayons. He was a native of Barnstaple, whose real name was Mitchell. In early life he settled himself in this city, and was celebrated as a scientific mechanic and organ-builder. For several years before his death he was afflicted with blindness. His wife Eleanor was interred in St. Paul's burying-ground, Exeter, on July 29th, 1791. Their only child, Anne, followed her to the grave on August 27th, 1795. His own remains were laid over them November 18th, 1824. He died at the advanced age of 89.

2nd. Rev. John Bury, D.D., canon of Exeter Cathedral and rector of St. Mary Major's, the principal

152 HISTORY OF EXETER.

founder of the old workhouse on the left hand at the bottom of Paris Street. He died on the 5th and was buried on the 9th of July, 1667, æt. 87, in our cathedral. His will was proved in the principal registry here, August 1st, 1667. This portrait was the gift of his son, the Rev. Dr. Arthur Bury, who requested that it might be set up in some convenient place in the house. On November 6th, 1705, it was ordered by the committee that the said picture be set up in the hall at the workhouse, according to the Doctor's desire, and that there be a handsome frame made for it with a suitable inscription in letters of gold.[5] By his wife Agnes, who was buried in our cathedral, November 16th, 1644, he had two sons :—John, a colonel, who took an active part on the side of the Parliament during the civil wars ; and Arthur, a learned divine and canon of Exeter, and rector of Exeter College, Oxford.

3rd. Behind the chair is the portrait of King William the Third, in whose reign this new workhouse was commenced in virtue of the Act of Parliament in 1699. His Majesty's reign extended from February 13th, 1689, to March 8th, 1702.

4th. Arthur Bury, D.D., the canon of Exeter beforementioned.

5th. Colonel John Bury, before-mentioned.

6th. Sir Thomas Bury, knight.

7th. Over the door is Ralph Mitchell, architect, whose plan of the house was approved of by the committee, February 7th, 1699. He may perhaps have been related to Paul Micheau, No. 1.

In the Chapel are two portraits :—
1st, of Sir Edward Seaward, knight, alderman of

---

[5] The statue of the Doctor was erected in 1681, over the foregate of the old workhouse. It was intended to remove it to the new workhouse, but we cannot ascertain whether this was done.

PICTURES IN THE WORKHOUSE. 153

Exeter, and mayor in 1691; a great promoter of this hospital and workhouse, its first governor, and the principal donor of Berry Meadow, near St. David's Church. He died March 1st, 1703-4, æt. 70, and was buried in St. Paul's Church, in this city, where his monument may still be seen.[6] At the foot of the picture appears the following inscription :— "1702. This picture was made and given by Mr. Wm. Gandy." On April 20th, 1703, a vote of thanks was passed by the committee " to Mr. Wm. Gandy, for his gift of Sir Edward Seaward's picture to the new hospital." This eminent painter was buried a St. Paul's, Exeter, on July 14th, 1729.   He will be again noticed hereafter in our account of the Guild Hall.

The 2nd is supposed to represent Sir John Elwill, knight, elected the second governor on May 27th, 1701.   He was created a baronet in 1709, and served the office of sheriff of Devon in 1694.

CHAPTER XXI.

OBSERVATIONS ON SOME OF THE CHURCHES IN EXETER.

WHILST we gratefully admit the disinterested zeal and piety of our forefathers in providing places of divine worship in this city, yet their very multiplication must have detracted from their ornamental character, and have prevented them from affording a decent maintenance to the incumbents.   At the conclusion of our

---

[6] In St. Mary Major's parish book of christenings, I read "1682, May 19th. Hannah, the daughter of Mr. Edward Seaward, marchante, living in Bradnage [Bradninch], within the city walls, and of Mrs. Hannah, his wife."

154   HISTORY OF EXETER.

fifth chapter we have referred to the payment of the
silver penny within fifteen days after Easter, and
again on the octave of St. Martin, which sum King
William had granted from the collection of the city
taxes for ever, through the hands of the Wic-reeve
or Provost of Exeter. We know that St. Mary's
prebendal Chapel existed in Exeter Castle at an early
period, and that in a deed of Bishop Henry Marshall,
who was consecrated early in 1194, we find mention
of St. Michael's, SS. Simon and Jude, St. Clement's,
and S. David's.[1] The following document in the reign
of King John will interest our readers.

"Let all present and future persons know, that I, Peter de
Palerna, with the consent of Ysabel, my wife, and of my heirs,
have granted and given a rent of 28*d.* from a messuage which
Stephen of Wales holds, which lies between the land that was
Baldwin Bulmer's and the land of Ralph Helffren's, unto the
twenty-eight Chapels underwritten:

St. Sativola (Sidwell)	St. George
St. Bartholomew	St. John
St. Stephen	St. Edward
St. Martin	St. Edmund
St. Peter the Great	St. Thomas
St. Mary the Great (Major)	Allhallows
St. Mary the Little (St. Mary Steps?)	St. Olave
	St. Mary (Arches?)
St. Peter the Little	St. Cuthbert
St. Petrock	St. Kieran
St. James	St. Pancras
Holy Trinity	St. Paul
St. Mary Magdalene (the Leper's Hospital)	Holy Trinity
	Allhallows
St. Leonard	St. Laurence

To be received and had by the same chapels for ever; so that
the foresaid Stephen and his heirs shall yearly pay the said rent
at the two terms, to wit on Lammas Day (1st of August) and
Candlemas Day (2nd of February) to the Chaplain of St.
Laurence for the time being, as the Procurator, whom I appoint

---

[1] Preserved in Bishop Bronescombe's Register, fol. 45.

PARISH CHURCHES.

to distribute the same rent to the Chapels aforesaid. And the Chaplain of St. Laurence for the time being, for the burthen of his procuration and labour, shall receive the relief from the land aforesaid when it shall fall in. And this same Chaplain of St. Laurence shall faithfully pay the rent aforesaid to the said Chapels for the keeping of my anniversary and that of my wife, Ysabel, and the memory of my predecessors and successors, every year on the morrow of St. Blase (4th of February). And that this my gift may continue stable, I have confirmed it by the present writing and the addition of my seal. Witnesses, Eudo de Bello Campo, then Sheriff; William Dirling, then Mayor; Roger Fitz-Henry and Nicholas Gervase, then Provosts; William Hastement, Roger Baubi, Laurence Taylor, Robert Painter, Emesius Bruteville, and many others."

The seal represents a man kneeling on one knee, with his left hand placed on his breast, in the act of presenting a cup with his right hand to a person seated. The legend is " S. Petri de Palerna." The seal of Peter de Palerna.

The original document was formerly in the possession of my late friend, Pitman Jones, Esq.

The taxation of Pope Nicholas IV., completed before the end of the same thirteenth century, shows how many of these parochial chapels had disappeared, and how stinted and insufficient were the means to support their ministering clergy. We cannot doubt, however, that the conventual church of St. Nicholas, the subsequent one of St. Francis (originally opposite the Snail Tower and its successor, beyond the south gate), and the Dominican Church of St. Peter (in Bedford Circus) did honour to the city. Indeed the destruction of our monastic churches led to a vast change and degradation of our national architecture. We may now be permitted to make a few observations referable to some of those parish churches. And first on St. Olave's.

This is specially mentioned in the Domesday Survey, and was granted by William the Conqueror to his foundation of Battle Abbey in Sussex, and may

156   HISTORY OF EXETER.

perhaps have been erected in the reign of Canute.
Olave was King of Norway when he received the
light of faith from English missionaries, but, according
to Bishop Grandisson's legend, was baptized at Rouen.
He exerted himself with commendable zeal to induce
his subjects to share in his happiness; but a powerful
faction rose up in arms against him, and he was finally
slain on July 29th, 1028, or more probably two years
later, and was buried at Drontheim.   His son Magnus
recovered his throne, and is ranked amongst the most *
illustrious of Norway's sovereigns.   The present structure has little to recommend it.

How the parochial church of St. Olave was disposed
of after the dissolution of St. Nicholas Priory we are
unable to say ; we suppose it was sold by the Parliamentary commissioners, during the Commonwealth, to
the parishioners on the usual condition of being "used
and employed for a burying-place, or free school."
After the revocation of the Edict of Nantes several
French Protestants sought refuge in this city, and they
were kindly allowed the use of this church for about
the space of seventy years under four pastors, Messrs.
Tonsal, Obing, André Majendie, and Jean Courtail who
was buried October 24th, 1759.

2. St. Stephen is also referred to in Domesday as
an appurtenance to the bishopric with several houses
and high rents, which obtained the name of St.
Stephen's Fee.   The old church, at the auction of
such sacred edifices in 1658 by our Mayor and Chamber,
was knocked down "with the cellars under the same"
(except the bells, the lead, and the taking down of the
tower as far as the roof), on May 11th, to Mr. Toby
Allyn for the extraordinary sum of 230*l.*   After the
restoration of the monarchy, the present fabric was
substituted in 1664.   We well remember that, early
in May, 1826, an interesting discovery was made in

PARISH CHURCHES.

digging the foundation for a new pillar at the east, the workmen coming upon some solid masonry ; and on clearing away the rubbish, two Saxon stone columns of the ancient crypt made their appearance. They were about five and a half feet high and nearly four feet distant from each other, and in perfect preservation. One was enriched with scroll-work; the other, nearly four inches higher, had a cornice ornamented with dentils. Nothing now appears of the ancient structure but the exterior arch or bow, above which stood formerly the altar of St. John.

3. Nearly opposite to St. Stephen's, in the High Street, is St. Laurence. The first time that we meet with it is in a deed of about the year 1202, when it belonged to the abbot and convent of St. Mary de Valle, in the diocese of Bayeux, Normandy. That community, with the consent of King Henry III., alienated their property in England about the year 1275 to the Augustinian priory and convent of Merton in Surrey. These new possessors, at the request of Bishop Peter Quivil, agreed to surrender their right of patronage of St. Laurence's Church in favour of St. John's Hospital, under a reserved pension of 26s. 8d., which was regularly paid until the dissolution of religious houses. During the Commonwealth the parishioners were deprived of their church, but on September 21st, 1658, succeeded in purchasing it with its three bells for the sum of 100l., and they are entitled to much credit for their zeal and attention to its respectable appearance. A small conduit, bearing the city arms with the date 1590, stood near the church. It was removed in 1674, and with the materials the church porch was erected; but has recently been restored in better taste, and the statue of Queen Elizabeth placed in a niche.[2]

---

[2] Rev. Thos. Long.

158   HISTORY OF EXETER.

4. St. Martin's in the Close. Its ancient Missal abundantly proves that a church in honour of the saint existed here just before the Conquest. "In the year of our Lord's Incarnation MLXV, July 6th, this temple was dedicated to the honour of our Lord Jesus Christ, and of His holy Cross, and of St. Mary the mother of Christ, and of St. Martin the Bishop, and of all the Saints of God." This saintly Bishop of Tours died November 8th, 397; the translation of his relics took place in July, 604 years after his death; and his memory was held in special veneration by our British and Saxon forefathers. In a former chapter we have alluded to the Chapel of St. Martin near Canterbury, which Venerable Bede describes at the end of the sixth century as "antiquitùs facta." Owing to the concurrence of festivals in the beginning of July, Bishop Stafford transferred the Wake to the Sunday next following the 7th of that month by his ordinance of July 13th, 1409. Of the present edifice nothing challenges attention but the graceful perpendicular window at the west end, introduced by Bishop Edmund Lacy, the successor of Stafford.

.5. St. Mary Arches, or de Arcubus. Its nave is of great antiquity. The day of its dedication was the Eve of Trinity Sunday, and Bishop William Brewer in 1232 granted an indulgence of twenty-four days to all true penitents who, from a motive of piety, should assist at its anniversary. At the head of its north aisle was the chantry of the Holy Trinity, and in the south aisle was another founded by Thomas Andrew, who filled our mayoralty chair in 1505 and 1510, and died, as his monument records, on March 9th, 1518. From the Chantry Rolls we learn that the yearly value of its lands and possessions amounted to 19*l.* 4*s.* 8*d.*, out of which the annual stipend to its priest was 5*l.* 6*s.* 8*d.*; and that twelve poor men yearly were to be provided

PARISH CHURCHES. 159

with "12 gownes of fryze, 12 pair of hosen, 12 pair of shoes, and 12 pair of woolen socks." Rev. Thomas Poter was its last stipendiary, and was pensioned off at 5*l.* per annum for life.

Ferdinando Nicholls, who was the rector of this church on November 12th, 1634, took the Covenant in 1648, grew into high favour with the Parliamentary faction, and secured the Bodleian Lectureship; but was turned adrift by the Bartholomew Act. At his funeral in the church in April, 1663, a great riot ensued; we find that "a dozen men were bound over April 13th, 1663, for disturbance of the public peace and committing a rout in the parish church of St. Marie Arches at the interment of the corpse of Mr. Ferdinando Nicholls, late minister of that parish, without a minister to do the same in the night time; and when the minister came to do his office, carrying away the lights and making such a noise by *hemming,* &c., as hath not been heard; and divers of the persons then present laying violent hands on the grave-maker and others." The deceased had been collated to the rectory by Bishop Hall on November 12th, 1634. On his deprivation, Gideon Edmonds was admitted his successor on March 22nd, 1662-3.[3]

6. The central church of St. Petrock was always regarded as amongst the wealthiest and most respectable in the city. Before encroachments were suffered to disfigure and obscure it, it was lighted on both sides; "ex utrâque parte." The churchwardens' accounts from 1425 are the best preserved of any in the city. In the inventory of 1485, we discover that its gold plate amounted to $18\frac{1}{2}$ ounces and its silver to 281 ounces; and its treasures went on increasing until the Reformation. Owing to several alterations in the edifice, we learn from Bishop Oldam's Register (fol. 48) that

---

[3] See Bishop Gaulden's Register, fol. 55.

160   HISTORY OF EXETER.

it was reconsecrated on July 22nd, 1513. Near it was the dwelling-house of Thomas Elyot, Esq., Comptroller of the Royal Customs in the ports of Exeter and Dartmouth, which he gave to this parish August 5th, 1505. Its handsome front looked into the Close, of which we gave an engraving in vol. i., p. 80, of our Ecclesiastical Antiquities. This has been removed, and now forms a graceful and ornamental feature in the front of the Episcopal Palace.

7. Allhallows in Goldsmith Street was redeemed from demolition by a parishioner, Robert Vilvaine, Esq., M.D., on May 11th, 1658, for 50*l.* This ancient church had been much neglected; its bells were even taken down in 1767 and sold to St. Sidwell's. This occasioned the lowering of the tower, and we may remember that the performance of divine service was discontinued from 1807 to 1822. The late rector, Rev. Matthew Vicars, but especially his successor the Rev. Charles Worthy, aided by his zealous churchwarden, Mr. Joslin, have exhibited much judgment and spirit in the work of its restoration and improvement.

8. Allhallows on the Walls required to be rebuilt in 1448. Two centuries later it suffered much during the sieges of the city, and a resolution was passed by the Corporation 27th October, 1657 : " Whereas the roof of the parish church of Allhallows on the Walls and a decayed wall adjoining thereto is become very dangerous and likely to fall, to the great danger and hurt of people passing near, it is hereupon agreed and ordered that the roof be taken down and such part of the said wall, as shall be conceived necessary." It was sold, however, to the parishioners on the 11th May following, for 33*l.* 6*s.* 8*d.* The three bells in its tower were subsequently sold for 30*l.*, and the unserviceable church continued an eyesore and nuisance until the decision to erect the Exeter new bridge, when it was utterly de-

PARISH CHURCHES. 161

molished in May, 1770. The foundation stone of a new parochial church was laid by Henry, the present lord bishop, on 4th April, 1843, in St. Bartholomew's cemetery, and was consecrated for public worship on 22nd September, 1845. It is from a design of Mr. I. Hayward, architect, and, whilst it reflects credit on all concerned in the work, is really an embellishment to the city. We have lately witnessed a becoming zeal for improvement in the rebuilding of several parish churches, among others St. Sidwell's, St. Edmund's, and Heavitree; and though in others the style adopted varies from that of the older structures, they are preferable to their predecessors, in respect of space, convenience, and ventilation; and the same credit is due to the chapels of the other denominations of our Christian brethren.

CHAPTER XXII.

Devon and Exeter Hospital — Labours of Dr. Alured Clarke to secure its establishment — Opened January 1st, 1743 — Portraits in the Board-room — The County and City Prisons — Cemeteries — Avenues and approaches of the city — Bridge over the Exe — Markets — General advantages of the city — Extensive nature of the physical and moral improvements effected.

In the 20th chapter we have remarked on the gross disregard of all sanitary provisions in Exeter and its suburbs in times gone by, and on the inattention of our citizens to domestic comfort. Their only thought was trade; their motto—

" O cives, cives, quærenda pecunia primum ! "

The idea of a commission of improvement would have been scouted as folly. But if Dr. Kellett could come to life again, how his heart would rejoice at witnessing such a blessed revolution in the minds of our

162   HISTORY OF EXETER.

Exonians, and what wonders their Herculean labour,
combined with judgment and good taste, have accomplished! He would in rapture proclaim Exeter one of
the most refined, salubrious, and cheerful cities of the
land. In the first place, let us look at the progress of
humanity; at the treatment and attention of our unfortunate fellow-creatures of the same flesh and blood as
ourselves, who are victims of acute internal complaints,
or are sufferers by accidents. It is true there had existed a small hospital at the bottom of Paris Street, then
an unhealthy situation, for the reception of patients of
the city. But when Dr. Alured Clarke, Prebendary of
Winchester and Westminster, who had already founded
a noble public hospital at Winchester for the benefit of
that city and the county of Southampton, and had made
judicious regulations for its government and witnessed
their blessed effects in the restoration of many to
health and to their families—no sooner was **this** good
Samaritan elected to the deanery of Exeter on Jan.
7th, 1740-1, than he determined not to give sleep to
his eyes nor slumber to his eyelids until he had secured
the same blessings for the county of Devon and its
metropolis. Though of a weak and delicate constitution, yet by indefatigable energy and winning manners
he succeeded so far in securing the generous support of
the charitably disposed, as to lay the foundation of this
philanthropic establishment on the 27th August in the
same year, on a convenient site on Southernhay, given
by his friend John Tuckfield, Esq. Nine months later
this truly good and great man "of happy and most
amiable memory," as Brice describes him, sank under
his exertions; but the work prospered, and was opened
for the reception of patients on the first day of the year
1743. The benedictions of Heaven have rested on the
labours of this benefactor of his species. Of several of
the medical practitioners of this institution we shall have

DEVON AND EXETER HOSPITAL.

163

to treat in the sequel of this volume. In fact, when we look to this Hospital, to the Eye Infirmary, the Asylum for the Deaf and Dumb, and the Dispensary, we have cause to rejoice at the provident provision for the relief of the infirm and the sick in all cases, and that Exeter abounds with skilful and humane professors of the healing art.

Of the Portraits in the Board-room of the Devon and Exeter Hospital we offer to the reader the following account :—

1. Behind the chairman's seat is *John Tuckfield*, Esq., of Little Fulford, holding in his hand the deed of gift of the site of the Hospital, indorsed to Dean Clarke and others, 22nd Sept. 1741. This gentleman represented Exeter in Parliament from 1745 till his death in 1766. This, as well as his other portrait in the Guildhall, was painted by our townsman, Thomas Hudson, who died at Twickenham in 1779, aged 78.

2. *Dr. Alured Clarke*, Dean of Exeter and Prebendary of Winchester, whose name is identified with this charitable institution. He originated it, and laid its foundation stone on the 27th Aug. 1741. His death occurred on the 31st May following, æt. 46, and he was buried at Westminster. The portrait was taken by James Wills, then a professional artist; but who subsequently became a clergyman, and died rector of Little Stanmore, Middlesex, in 1777.

3. *Michael Lee Dicker*, M.D., painted by Thomas Hudson. This student under the immortal Boerhaave, of Leyden, was elected one of the five first physicians on the 24th Sept. 1741. His death occurred in 1752, since which time the number has been limited to four only. He left a legacy of 50*l.* for wainscoting the Board-room, and directed this picture to be placed there, to which sum his widow added 20*l.* more, to complete the deficiency and to set up the two marble

M 2

164 HISTORY OF EXETER.

chimney-pieces. The doctor was a Quaker, and the smart house in Magdalen Street which he built was his residence.

4. *Ralph Allen*, Esq.,—painted by Thomas Hudson. Mr. Allen was the son of an innkeeper on the roadside, called *St. Blazey's Highway*, in Cornwall. From a clerk in the post-office by his judgment and persevering industry he became a farmer of the cross-posts at a certain yearly payment to the State, and eventually realised a splendid fortune. He built the mansion of Prior Park, near Bath, where he exercised munificent hospitality, and was truly a father of the poor. Dying on 29th June, 1764, aged 71, he was buried at Claverton.

5. *John Patch*, jun., Esq., over the entrance door— painted by James Opie. Mr. Patch, a native of St. Paul's parish, Exeter, baptized 8th Aug. 1723, was chosen on the 24th Sept. 1741, to be one of the four first surgeons of this Hospital, and his skill and zealous attention proved a blessing to its inmates. Dying on the 2nd Jan. 1787, he was buried in the family vault within the church of St. Paul in this city. This portrait was engraved by our townsman, Mr. Ezekiel.

6. *John Sheldon*, F.R.S., a first-rate anatomist, elected 25th July, 1797, one of the surgeons of this Hospital. He died 8th Oct. 1808, aged 56. This portrait, taken by Keenan, has been engraved by Barnard.

7. *John Patch*, sen., Esq. He completed his studies at Paris, then considered the first school of surgery in Europe, and was afterwards settled in Exeter; and we find him elected surgeon of the new workhouse, on 2nd. Sept. 1718, with a salary of 20*l.* On the 24th Sept. 1741, he was chosen senior surgeon of the Devon and Exeter Hospital, with his son John, already mentioned, Mr. Bartholomew Parr, and Mr. John Pillet. Mr. Patch was the first of the profession in the West

THE PRISONS. 165

of England who practised lithotomy. This picture was a tribute of gratitude to him from our townsman, the celebrated painter, William Gandy, who had derived essential benefit from his skilful treatment, as Dr. Musgrave's inscription on the back of the picture asserts. Mr. Patch was carried off by apoplexy, on the 11th May, 1746, aged 55, and was buried near his wife Hannah, grandniece of Bishop Burnet, in St. Paul's Church, Exeter.

8. *Thomas Glass*, Esq., a learned and scientific physician, died the 5th Feb., 1786, aged 76, and was buried in St. David's churchyard. This portrait was painted by Opie, at the expense of the medical gentlemen of Exeter, and was engraved by Ezekiel.

The County and City Prisons were a disgrace to humanity—mere nuisances and dens of pestilence. In our account of the Castle, in which lay the county prison, we shall relate the frightful ravages occasioned by the gaol fever at the assizes, 1585, which long bore the name of the *Black Assizes*, and spread consternation through all classes. Lord Bacon tells us (says Brice in his Universal Gazetteer, p. 540), that " next to the plague, the most pernicious infection is the smell of the gaol, when prisoners have been long, and close, and nastily kept, whereof we have had in our time experience twice or thrice, when both the judges that sat upon the gaol business, and numbers that attended, sickened thereupon and died." In truth such visitations were not unfrequent. In Pennant's London, p. 232, we read that the havoc produced in the Sessions House of the Old Bailey, even in May, 1750, " by the effluvia of that dreadful disorder, the gaol fever, was a melancholy admonition. My respected kinsman, Sir Samuel Pennant, Lord Mayor, Baron Clarke (own brother to that friend of mankind, Dean Alured Clarke, of Exeter), Sir Thomas

166 HISTORY OF EXETER.

Abney, Judge of the Common Pleas, the Under Sheriff, some of the counsel, and several of the jury and other persons, died of this putrid distemper. Several of these fatal accidents have happened in this kingdom, which makes the surprise the greater, that the neglect of salutary precautions was continued till the time of this awakening call." The legislature in 1787 sanctioned the erection of a new county gaol. It was subsequently deemed expedient to unite the House of Correction and the ward for debtors all under the inspection of one governor. We believe a more airy, healthy, cheerful, and convenient situation could nowhere be found, and the range of buildings well becomes the site. Every attention is paid to the reasonable comforts of the persons detained, and we are satisfied that no better administration can be conducted.

As to the City Prison, in South-gate, it was, in the opinion of the benevolent John Howard—who, in his active zeal, devoted the best years of his life to visiting and closely inspecting the prisons of England and Wales, and very many such establishments on the Continent—one of the most unwholesome and most dismal places of confinement he had ever seen. We heartily rejoiced at witnessing the keystone over the archway let in and drop in its place towards the bottom of Northernhay in 1818. Thank God! we live in times when the human heart and the feelings of the public are open to the afflictions of others, and eager to assuage sorrow and to ease each other's burthens. Instead of slighting and despising the oppressed, all of us should remember that it is the gratuitous favour of God that has protected us from falling into their temptations and calamities; and we should show them that we cherish the spirit of Christian charity, as we hope to find mercy from Him at the last day, knowing, as we do, that the same measure is to be meted

THE CEMETERIES. 167

to us as we shall have meted to our poor fellow-creatures.

Our readers are aware that the general custom of the civilized Jews, Greeks, and Romans was to bury their dead without the town walls. " In urbe ne sepelito neve urito," was dictated by a wise consideration for the health of the living population. In Exeter the common poliandrum or place of interment was, long before the Conquest, in the Close ; nay, amongst the archives of our chapter we find an ordinance of Pope Innocent III., between January 1198 and 1216, " ut nulli liceat construere cemeteria infra terminos parochiæ Exoniensis ecclesiæ sine assensu Capituli et Episcopi." This privilege had been conceded, however, to the religious houses, and Bishop Grandisson, on 31st March, 1354, extended this licence to St. John's Hospital. (See his Register, vol. i., fol. 184.) But the Close, which Bishop Grandisson styles " commune civitatis poliandrum," became at last an intolerable nuisance, and especially during the pestilence of 1636. The accumulation of corpses and the mounds of earth, to use the energetic language of Bishop Joseph Hall, threatened to bury indecorously the very cathedral. From the confinement of space he had strenuously exerted himself with the Corporation, in mercy to the living and decent respect for the dead, whose members before decomposition had often been thrown up to make room for others. This led to the opening of the new cemetery in the old Prisonhay, on 24th August, St. Bartholomew's Day, 1637.[1] We have seen the composition be-

---

[1] The first person buried there was a respectable citizen of Exeter, Christopher Tothill, on this day of the opening. We remember the gravestone of Alexander Pratt, who died 2nd Sept. 1637; of Emmanuel Jennings, who died 1st Oct. 1637 ; and of Thomas Waring, schoolmaster, 22nd July, 1638. But to show the animus of the puritanical Corporation a few years later, it was ordered, 23rd Nov. 1648, " that the inscription on the new churchyard, purporting the consecration thereof, be defaced."—Act Book, No. viii. p. 25.

HISTORY OF EXETER.

tween the Mayor and Chamber on the one part and the Dean and Chapter who had contributed 150*l*. toward the new enclosure on the other, and are surprised that the former should have insisted that the citizens and inhabitants, at the expiration of sixteen years from the levelling of St. Peter's cemetery, " should receive free and absolute power to bury in the said ancient churchyard, as they had heretofore done without any contradiction." The increase of population had rendered it imperative to open another burying-place on 27th October, 1654; so that the same parties, still insisting on their former right of interment in as ample a mode and form in St. Peter's yard, agreed to defer it until the year 1684. They seem, however, not to have exercised it, and on 30th May, 1689, gave liberty to the inhabitants to bury their dead in St. Bartholomew's churchyard, " in regard the churchyard near Southernhay was overfilled."

Another and much more spacious cemetery in the field near the Snail Tower adjoining Bartholomew yard, was opened on 24th August, 1837, precisely two hundred years after Bishop Hall had consecrated its predecessor ; but such has been, and is likely to be, the increase of population, that our constituted authorities are admonished to provide another receptacle or dormitory for the dead of Exeter.

The Avenues and Approaches to this Metropolis of the West were notoriously incommodious and disgraceful, and every one grew satisfied that the city walls and its gates could afford no protection to the inhabitants in case of attack, in those days of advanced military science. Gradually passages were opened through the city walls into Southernhay and Northernhay. The North-gate was the first doomed to demolition, in June 1769 ; but the steep declivity in this

THE APPROACHES TO THE CITY. 169

quarter was not relieved by the iron bridge (through the exertions mainly of the late Mr. James Golsworthy), until many years later, in 1831. The East-gate shared its fate in October 1784; the West-gate and Quay-gate were levelled in 1815; and the South-gate, the fairest and most imposing, was swept away with its horrible prison in 1819. But the grand desideratum was a new bridge over the Exe—a very tedious, difficult, and expensive undertaking. The current of the river, especially during floods and rapid thaws, was perpetually interrupted by the numerous and contracted arches of the old bridge; the thoroughfare over it from Fore Street through West-gate by St. Edmund's Church, and from St. Thomas's suburb, was then circuitous, confined, precipitous, and dangerous.

Mr. Joseph Dixon, of the parish of St. James's, Westminster, was called in to suggest plans and prepare specifications. His design for erecting a bridge of three arches only over the Exe, in a direct line from Cowyck Street to Fore Street, to remove the church of All Hallows on the Walls, and to raise up the intermediate space on walls and on five arches, to afford a fresh passage for the water of the mill-leats, was approved of; and a large dry arch under the new road towards the centre, with a flight of steps on the north side, would afford easy communication with Frog Street, Exe Island, and Tedder Bridge.[2] The foundation stone of the intended bridge was laid by John Floud, Esq.,[3] the mayor of Exeter, on Thursday, 4th October, 1770, with due solemnity and with the following inscription:—

---

[2] Under this arch may be seen the date, 1774.

This small bridge derives its name from William Tedder, a brewer. For exchange of two lives in a tenement on Exe Island he had to pay, 21st May, 1689, to the Chamber a fine of 15l.

[3] He was uncle to Thomas Floud, Esq., who was elected chief magistrate of this city in 1801 and 1818, and whose lamented death occurred 24th April, 1842.

170 HISTORY OF EXETER.

"The first stone of this Bridge
was laid by JOHN FLOUD, Esq., Mayor of Exeter,
on Thursday, October 4th,
in the Tenth year of the reign of King George III.,
in the presence of several of the Nobility and Gentry
of the County of Devon, and Citizens of Exeter,
MDCCLXX."

For some months the work proceeded rapidly, when
the Bridge Committee began to entertain suspicions
that Mr. Dixon was deviating from the terms of his
contract, and they desired Mr. Robert Stribbling, an
experienced builder, of North Street, to report on the
progress of the work at the meeting to be holden on
13th August, 1771. After mature deliberation, he
gave in his report, in writing, " that in the presence
of some of the trustees he had examined the work—
that there had been a considerable departure from the
contract—that the pier is in no way regular in courses,
or wrought fair—that the course of Portland stone
which should have been solid on the upper course, now
tails back on the rough masonry, and is, in many
places, raised by small stones to keep them in course,
which in my judgment will within a short time be
fretted out by the water ; and the consequence will be
the water will gully under, and be the means of endangering the whole pier. The upper course of Portland stone, which should have been two feet six inches,
is only two feet and one inch ; and from the appearance
of the abutment at the Bonhay, there seems to have
been a total neglect in the workmanship, as far as can
now be viewed. " Robᵗ· Stribbling."

On this report Mr. Dixon called for his arbitrator, a
Mr. Lowther, who having given it as his opinion that
all had been executed in a very workmanlike manner,
and much to the honour of the contractor, a majority
of the Bridge Committee unfortunately directed Mr.

THE BRIDGE. 171

Dixon to proceed with his work; but to be sure to cramp the stones with iron run with lead, according to the eighth condition of the contract.

The sequel proves that Mr. Dixon was unfit for his work, that he had superficially provided for the stability of the foundation, and was unacquainted with the velocity and vehemence of the occasional floods in this mountainous district. A tremendous inundation came down on 9th March, 1774, followed by another in the middle of January, 1775, when the work had made considerable progress. The result of the latter may be seen in No. 573 of Trewman's paper. "On Monday, 18th January, 1775, it entirely destroyed the foundation and carried away all the arches of the new bridge, and greatly terrified the neighbouring inhabitants lest it should damage the old bridge. The loss on this occasion must have been very considerable. An arch over the mill-leat had fallen on Saturday, 16th January." Fortunately, every precaution was taken to save the old bridge, and it stood the shock and straining. Mr. Waddilove, Mr. Dixon's foreman, and Mr. Walker, the clerk of the works, returned to London by his direction on 16th February, 1776. Mr. John Goodwin, who had been employed in the erection, and had seen his master's error, now undertook to remedy all defects. By raising a strong dam, he turned the current into a channel below the old bridge, and by the aid of powerful machinery cleared the old bed, and prepared a foundation for the piers on the solid rock, and the first stone was laid on 15th July, 1776, by the Rev. Chancellor Nutcombe. In No. 650 of the above-mentioned journal, after stating the relaying of the foundation of the new bridge on Monday, 15th July, 1776, it adds, that "from the number of hands employed and the steps taken to obviate the many difficulties which have hitherto attended this work, we

172　　　　HISTORY OF EXETER.

have the pleasing prospect of its being expeditiously completed with strength and elegance." In accomplishing this Mr. Goodwin derived material assistance from that judicious builder, the late Mr. Joseph Row, and from the practical advice of James Templer, Esq., of Stover ; and so rapid was the advancement of the works, that on 5th May, 1777, it became necessary to begin breaking up the pavement at the bottom of Fore Street, and to prepare the approach and avenue to the bridge from the city walls. At the following Epiphany Sessions, 1778, a committee of the justices of Devon was appointed to meet our Mayor and Chamber to determine their respective boundaries. This was soon decided by the agreement of a perpendicular line sunk in the central pilaster of the bridge, with the word EXON on one side of the said line of demarcation, and DEVON on the other.

We regret to say that we have sought in vain for the precise date of the opening of the new bridge. We have been told that the first carriage that passed over from Fore Street was at the funeral of Sir John Elwill, Bart., who had died on 1st March, 1778: so that it must have been early in that month. A proposal was made to exact a toll for foot-passengers over the bridge ; but the measure was so generally obnoxious, and was so steadily opposed by Sir Charles Warwick Bamfield and the new member, John Baring, Esq., that it was abandoned, and this great accommodation and improvement to the city was effected at the expense altogether of 30,000l.

We have lived to see the happiest changes in the Markets. The cattle and pig markets, originally in the High Street, a notorious grievance, were removed to what was called Little Bretayne Street and Bartholomew Street, on 10th November, 1691. Here, to

THE MARKETS. 173

the great discomfort of the neighbouring houses and
the risk of passengers, this sad nuisance continued,
with a pound, for more than a century and a quarter,
when an excellent situation was provided in the island.
The necessity had long been felt of transferring the
market for goods and provisions from the long thoroughfare of High Street and Fore Street; and at last it was
determined that two spacious market-houses, of an ornamental character worthy of the city, should be erected
and opened. This afforded an opportunity of clearing
away the incumbrances of several blind alleys and
crowded courts, and of introducing perfect ventilation
and cleanliness, whilst the health and comfort of the
buyers and sellers were attended to, and the vendible
articles were protected from the changes of the
weather. It is a singular coincidence that, in excavating the ground for the lower market for meat and
corn, a medal of Nero, the Roman emperor, was
discovered on the spot, with a reverse of an edifice
not very dissimilar from the front of the present
structure.

In erecting these buildings the following inscriptions
on parchment were placed in glass bottles, in which
were deposited coins of King William IV., and were let
into the corner stones; viz. in the Lower Market :—[a]

This stone was laid on the fourth day of April, in the fifth
year of the reign of His Majesty King William the Fourth, and
in the year of our Lord one thousand eight hundred and thirty-
five, by Philip Chilwell de la Garde, Esquire, Mayor of this
city, in the presence of several members of the Corporation of
Exeter, and numerous other persons. Architect, Charles Fowler,
Esquire, Bristol. Builders, Messrs. W. H. and W. Hooper,
Exeter.

This was opened 9th December, 1836. During the

---

[a] A medal of the front of this Lower Market, bearing on the reverse the arms of the city, was struck by B. Wyon, and is worthy of the skilful taste of that admirable artist.

174 HISTORY OF EXETER.

building of it the conduit was removed from South Street to its neighbourhood.

Inscription in Higher Market :—

This stone was laid on the eighth day of May, in the fifth year of the reign of His Majesty King William the Fourth, and in the year of our Lord one thousand eight hundred and thirty-five, by Philip Chilwell de la Garde, Esquire, Mayor of this city, in the presence of several members of the Corporation of Exeter, and numerous other persons. Architect, Mr. George Dymond, Bristol. Builders, Messrs. W. H. and W. Hooper, Exeter.

It was opened 24th July, 1838.

How can we praise too much the anxiety of our magistrates to administer justice with promptitude and impartiality ?—the care of the trustees of all the public charities to consult the comfort and benefit of the poor ? Where can be discovered more active zeal for the diffusion of education ? Where do the constituted authorities display more considerate liberality in providing places of recreation, and beautiful and airy walks, like Northernhay, Bury Meadow, Bonhay, &c.? What town can boast of more convenient locomotive communication with our charming watering-places, and of conveyance to every part of the kingdom ? Where shall we find a city freer from popular commotion ; whose inhabitants are more orderly, patriotic, and obedient to the laws ? Where find a climate more mild, more equable and salubrious, and where superior medical relief is more accessible ? We may perhaps close our catalogue of advantages by claiming for Exeter almost entire [5] exemption from all physical convulsions of nature.

---

[5] We say "almost," for the register of St. Pancras mentions the shock of an earthquake felt in all the houses of Exeter, between four and five o'clock in the morning on the 19th July, 1727, but without any material damage. "It was felt," adds the register, "all over England, and in some places beyond sea." In the granite district of Dartmoor a sensible shock was experienced about seven P.M., on 28th Sept. 1858. In the neighbouring county of Cornwall repeated shocks have been lately felt.

ADVANTAGES OF THE CITY. 175

During more than half a century the writer has witnessed with inconceivable delight the progressive alterations effected by the Boards of Commissioners of Improvements, Trustees of the Turnpikes, and Directors of the Water Company, to whom Exeter owes a heavy debt of obligation. Rejoicing in the welfare and advancing prosperity of the city, the writer can say with admiration and gratitude, that vast as its physical improvement has been, its moral revolution in the expansion of liberal and Christian feeling has been still greater; and that no reasonable being need seek elsewhere a residence more salubrious, comfortable, polite, and friendly.

HISTORY OF EXETER.

PART II.

PART II.

—o—

CHAPTER I.

THE CASTLE OF EXETER.

OUR Chronicles agree, as Bishop Grandisson observes in the letter he addressed to King Edward III. (Register, vol. i., fol. 286), that King Athelstan was the first of our monarchs who surrounded the city of Exeter with walls and erected a castle. " Si ·len regarde bien les cronicles, len trovera que le Roy Adelstan fist enclore la vylle D'Excestre, et fist le chastel." This enclosure must therefore have been between A.D. 925–941. About seventy years later, the whole of these fortifications, with the city itself, were utterly demolished and levelled by Sweyn ; but, under the auspices of the Kings Canute and Edward the Confessor, Exeter arose like a phœnix from its ashes, and, at the period of the Conquest, was regarded as a city (*civitas*) of considerable importance for its population, its strength, and the riches of its inhabitants. William the Conqueror,—provoked at the honourable reception which Githa, the mother of King Harold, and several noble ladies of her court had experienced from the authorities here, and, in consequence, at their successful escape to Flanders from his grasp ; furious also at the ill-treatment which the citizens had inflicted on a fleet of his mercenaries driven by a tempest into the river Exe, and at their daring to refuse the admission of a garrison, or perform any other services to him than they had hitherto rendered

180   HISTORY OF EXETER.

to their Anglo-Saxon monarchs—determined at once
to crush this rising spirit of resistance, and to visit
them with exemplary vengeance. In the spring of
1068 he advanced towards Exeter with a numerous
army, a great part of which was composed of Englishmen. At some distance he was met by the magistrates,
who implored his clemency, proffered the surrender of
the place at discretion, and gave hostages for their
fidelity. With five hundred horse he approached
one of the gates, and, to his astonishment, found it
barred against him, and a crowd of combatants bade
defiance from their walls. It was in vain that, to
intimidate them, he ordered one of the hostages to be
deprived of his eyes. The siege lasted eighteen days;
the Royalists suffered severe loss in different assaults;
but, as we learn from the Domesday Survey,[1] forty-
eight houses (about a sixth part of the whole city) were
destroyed. At last the citizens submitted, but on conditions which could hardly have been anticipated.
They took, indeed, an oath of fealty and admitted a
garrison; but their lives, their property, and municipal
privileges were secured; and, in order to prevent the
opportunity of plunder, the besieging army was removed from the vicinity.[2]

In the following year Exeter was besieged by the
malcontents of Cornwall; but, in return for the
sovereign's clemency and confidence, the citizens offered
a gallant resistance, and at length were relieved by the
fleet of Brian and the forces of William Fitz-Osbern,
Earl of Hereford, the king's relative and most favoured
general, whose brother shortly after was appointed the
second bishop of our diocese.

---

[1] This record shows that Lidford did
not submit to the Conqueror until forty
houses of the burgesses were demolished, nor Barnstaple until twenty-
three houses were laid waste; a proof
of the deadly hostility of the townsmen
against the Norman invaders.

[2] For the correctness of this narra-
tive, Dr. Lingard, in his History of
William I., refers to Ordericus and the
Chronicon Lombardi.

THE CASTLE. 181

A site had been selected by the king for his citadel within the walls, admirably adapted to overawe and protect the town. It was on the north-east summit of its highest ground, called *Rougemont*, from the redness of its soil. In deeds of the thirteenth century, in the possession of the Dean and Chapter of Exeter, we find it described as "rubeus mons extra portam aquilonarem civitatis Exoniæ;" and William of Worcester, in his Itinerary of 1478, designates the castle itself by the name of Rougemont. "Castrum de Excestre vocatur Castellum Rougemont." De la Beche,[3] in his Report on the Geology of Cornwall, Devon, and Somerset, 1839, p. 203, says, "Continuing a course from Broadclist to Exeter, along the boundary of the Series, red sandstones and conglomerates are observed to rest upon the edges of the older rocks to that city, where another patch of similar igneous rock occurs, forming the hill on which Rougemont Castle is situated."

This castle is not indeed mentioned in the Domesday Survey, as are the castle of Okehampton in this county, and the castles of Trematon and Dunhevet or Launceston in Cornwall. Perhaps it was not completed until the following reign, as Henry de Knyghton insinuates; but no one views its elevated massive gateway with its triangular-headed openings without pronouncing it to be an early specimen of the Norman architecture in this country.

To Baldwin de Molis, or De Brioniis, or De Sap, who had married Albreda, the Conqueror's niece, was assigned the charge of superintending the work; and the custody of the castle, with the office of Sheriff of Devon, was granted him as an hereditary appendage to his Barony of Okehampton. The historian, however, of

---

[3] Sir Henry Thomas de la Beche, the distinguished geologist.

182   HISTORY OF EXETER.

Ford Abbey contends that this grant was made to Richard, the son of the same Baldwin. From the Patent Rolls, the Charter Rolls, and the Close Rolls of King John, it is evident that this sovereign at least exercised the power of appointing the governor of the castle at pleasure; [4] and that the expenses of repairing the fortifications, of sinking the well, of making the fosse, and the costs of maintaining the garrison, were defrayed by the Crown.

Scarcely had the Conqueror breathed his last, on 9th September, 1087, æt. 64, when England was threatened with the calamity of a disputed succession. Robert was the eldest son, though not the faourite one like William, of the deceased monarch. According to Ralph de Diceto, the majority of the barons was disposed to maintain the claims of the elder brother, and he enumerates amongst them Robert de Avranches, a grandson of Baldwin de Sap, above mentioned, who had the command of Exeter. Fortunately for the public welfare, an amicable arrangement took place between the brothers. William was to retain the crown for his life, and Robert was contented with the Dukedom of Normandy and an annual pension besides.

The death of King Henry I., at St. Denys le Froment, in Normandy, on 1st December, 1135, was the signal for another civil commotion. The barons were divided between the king's only legitimate

---

[4] Mandamus, 1st March, 1201, to William Briwere, to deliver to Ralph Morin, sheriff of Devon, the castle of Exeter. Mandamus of the King, 17th June, 1203, to the said Ralph Morin, to deliver without delay to the said William Briwere our castle of Exeter. Order on the Treasury, 5th Oct. 1204, to pay the account of the sheriff of Devon in "operatione Castri nostri Exon per preceptum nostrum." Order on the same, 19th June, 1205, to pay William Briwere the expenses "in puteo Castri nostri Exon faciendo per preceptum nostrum." Order to the Sheriff, dated 17th March, 1208, to provide stone and lime "et quod facias fieri fossatum ejusdem Castri." An order of 9th Sept. 1215, for the payment of thirty pounds and nine pence "Balistariis et servientibus qui sunt in Castro Exon." In 1216 he directed Robert de Courtenay, the governor, in case he could not defend the city, together with William Briwere, against the attacks of the barons, "tunc ipsum Willielmum et omnes suos infra Castrum Exon. receptet."

THE CASTLE. 183

daughter, Matilda,[5] on whom the succession to the crown had been settled nine years before, and Stephen, Earl of Mortaigne[6] and Boloigne, the king's nephew. The latter aspirant to the throne had lost no time in securing the royal treasures; the citizens of London proclaimed him king, and by his bountiful generosity and liberal promises of freedom to the clergy and people he succeeded in procuring his coronation by the Primate William, on the feast of his patron, St. Stephen, the Proto-Martyr, on the 26th of December that year. But very soon the new sovereign had to encounter a most formidable opposition; and Baldwin de Redvers, Earl of Devon, grateful for the favours received from the late king, and mindful of his oaths, was the first to raise the standard in the cause of Matilda. " Primus quidem omnium Baldewinus de Redvers caput suum levavit in Regem, firmato contra eum Castello Exoniensi." (Chronica Gervasii.) Retiring into the castle of Exeter, he spared no exertions to render it impregnable, and fully determined to suffer every extremity rather than consent to surrender. In the course of 1136 Stephen invested the city, and for nearly three months pressed the siege with unabated vigour. The garrison offered a desperate defence; but at length were compelled to capitulate for want of water.[7] Their protracted resistance, which had cost the king the immense sum of more than 15,000 marks, might have been expected to meet with exemplary vengeance; but he exercised the greatest clemency to

---

[5] She married the Emperor Henry IV. of Germany; was his wife eleven years, but had no issue by him, except a daughter, Christina. In 1129 she married Geoffrey Plantagenet, and by him had three sons – 1, Henry, surnamed Fitz-Empress, afterwards Henry II. King of England; 2, Geoffrey; 3, William. Matilda died at Rouen, 10th Sept. 1167, and was buried at Bec.

[6] [*Mortain*, Moritonium, is probably meant; not *Mortagne*.]

[7] The present well in the castle is 104 feet deep, and affords an abundant supply. We have already referred to the Close Rolls, where King John, on 19th June, 1205, orders the treasurer to settle the account of William Briwere for making this well " per preceptum nostrum."

184   HISTORY OF EXETER.

the citizens and the garrison; he indemnified the cathedral clergy -for the damages inflicted on their property, and contented himself with the banishment of Baldwin, who retired to his Castle of Nehou, in Normandy (see Recherches sur les anciens Châteaux de la Manche, par M. de Gerville, p. 101), but was shortly after restored to his English honours and possessions; for we find him, as Earl of Devon, on his return, founding the Priory of St. James, near this city.

To his brother Henry, the Bishop of Winchester, the king now committed the custody of Exeter Castle; but the government was soon replaced in the hands of the family of Redvers, and, with partial interruptions, so continued until 1232, when King Henry III. detached it from the Barony of Okehampton.

From the Charter Rolls we collect that lands were held of the Crown by the service of guarding the castle. Thus, on 7th July, 1216, King John granted to Richard Malherbe, and his heirs by his then wife, the estates of Wyke, Ailrichestan, and Slaucombe, by the service of providing in the time of war, at his own charges, "unum servientem ad haubergellum," [8] for forty days in our castle of Exeter.

King Henry III., having granted to his only brother Richard the earldoms of Poitou and Cornwall, also granted to him and his heirs on 10th August, 1231, the whole county of Cornwall with the stannaries and all franchises appurtenant, as well as the city and castle of Exeter, as an appendage to his earldom of Cornwall. Nevertheless, the said king, in 1266, committed the custody of the castle to Ralph de Gorges; and his successor to the crown, Edward I., in 1287, appointed

---

[8] For the Feudum hauberticum, see Spelman's Glossary, pp. 260, 333. The hauberk or coat-of-mail service was sometimes extended to a complete suit of armour, with horse, breastplate, shield, spear, sword, and helmet; and the period of serving was also enlarged.

THE CASTLE. 185

Matthew Fitz-John to be the castellan for his life—an appointment attested by his cousin *Edmund, Earl of Cornwall and Lord-Paramount of Exeter. When the earldom of Cornwall was raised into a duchy by King Edward III., on 17th March, 1337, the city fee-farm of twenty pounds, and the manor of Bradninch with the castle of Exeter, which was then reputed to be *the manor-house, or mansion of the said manor*, were constituted parcels of the said duchy. The enclosure with its ditches, called in the Duchy leases the Castle Close, still retains the title of "the Precinct of Bradninch."[9]

Early in 1470, during twelve days, the city was invested with a strong force by Sir William Courtenay, Knight, the first of that name settled at Powderham, for receiving within its walls the Duke of Clarence and his father-in-law the Earl of Warwick, and some leaders of the Lancastrian party; but these noblemen contrived to reach Dartmouth and to sail for the French coast before King Edward IV. could arrive at Exeter on 14th April that year.

Twenty-seven years later (viz. 17th September, 1497) Perkin Warbeck attempted to take the city by a *coup-de-main*. He actually set fire to Northgate; but the citizens fed the flames with fresh fuel, whilst digging a deep ditch behind it. Directing his force against the east gate, he effected an entrance, and advanced as far as Castle Lane, when he was repulsed with considerable loss. Discouraged by this failure, and at the reports of a rising of the gentry in aid of the citizens, as also of the advance of the royal army, he solicited a cessation

---

[9] Survey made 25th Nov. 1650, of the honour, manor, and borough of Bradninch, in the possession of George Pearse, of Bradninch, Esq.

The Act for the enlarging the liberties of Exeter, 2nd and 3rd of King Edward VI., provides that "the castle of Exeter, and the *soil within the walls of the said castle*, and also the common gaol of the county of Devon adjoining, shall be accepted, reputed, and deemed to be within and parcel of the said *county* of Devon only."

HISTORY OF EXETER.

of hostilities, and then decamped towards Taunton. On the 7th of October King Henry VII. entered the city in triumph.

After the gallant defence of the inhabitants against the rebels in the reign of King Edward VI., from 2nd July to 6th August, 1549, the castle of Exeter was suffered to fall into decay. Westcote, who wrote about 1630, several years before the Civil Wars, describes it in his View of Devon, p. 139, as "an old ruinous castle, whose gaping chinks and aged countenance presageth a downfall ere long. The amplitude and beauty thereof cannot be discerned by the ruins; but for former days was of good strength; but now, as the poet said, 'magnum nil nisi nomen habet.'" To the same purpose, his contemporary Risdon, in his Survey, p. 116—"The castle sheweth the fragments of the ancient buildings ruinated, whereon time hath tyrannized." When Cosmo III., Duke of Tuscany, visited the site on the 7th of April, 1669, he found it to be a square enclosure, dismantled of guns and devoid of troops. At a subsequent date something was done to fortify the castle, and a drawbridge was made in Castle Lane.

Though this was one of the royal castles, yet we cannot discover that any of our sovereigns occupied it as a residence in their occasional visits to this city; but it must have proved a safe, convenient, and cheerful mansion for the castellan, or keeper. Like other ancient fortresses, as described by Dr. Lingard on the authorities of Du Cange, King, and Grose (Life of King Stephen, 8vo. edit., vol. ii., p. 171), it had its keep, or house for the governor, encompassed by an embattled wall, and flanked with towers. Beyond this wall, towards the city, was excavated a deep and broad fosse,—here of necessity a dry one,—over which a drawbridge was thrown, protected by the barbican tower on the other

THE CASTLE. 187

side towards Castle Lane. The keep was usually a strong square building of five stories. The lowermost consisted of dungeons for the confinement of captives and state-prisoners; the second contained the stores; the third served for the accommodation of the garrison; in the fourth were the best apartments, for the governor and his family; and the uppermost was portioned off for chambers. The only portal, or entrance, was fixed in the second or third story, and generally led through a small side tower (as in Rochester Castle) into the body of the keep. The ascent was by a flight of stone steps, carefully fortified, and protected by a portcullis, to prevent the entrance of an enemy. About the middle stood a strong gate. On the landing was a drawbridge, and then appeared the door itself, protected by a portcullis, which ran in a groove, and was studded with spikes. Hoker, in his MS., p. 294 (who wrote in Queen Elizabeth's time), states "that John Holland, Duke of Exeter" (who was uterine brother to King Richard II., beheaded in 1400), "had within the castle of Exeter a very fair and a princely house, but now destroyed, and scarcely any monument left thereof," and says that he had another mansion at Dartington, near Totnes.[1]

Within the precincts of the castle, we suppose, was the Mint. For the history of the Exeter coinage we refer the reader to Mr. Richard Sainthill's work (pub. London, 1844, p. 180). Here also were kept the stamps for marking the blocks of tin assayed by the officers of the earldom or duchy. These were heavy hammers, with the die of its arms on the hammer end. Thus we find, in the Charter Rolls, p. 101 b., 1st March, 1201, King John's mandamus to William Briwere, to deliver to Ralph Morin, sheriff of Devon,

---

[1] [The above must be taken as descriptive of such castles in general, and not of Exeter Castle in particular, of which no detailed account has yet been found.]

188   HISTORY OF EXETER.

the castle of Exeter, and the coinage-stamps of the
Stannary—" cuneos de Stannariâ."

The area of the castle witnessed, in November, 1483,
the execution, by order of King Richard III., of Sir
Thomas Leger, who had married his sister, the Princess
Anne, Duchess of Exeter,[2] and of his squire, Thomas
Rame ; though Hoker asserts they were executed at the
Carfoix (or Quatre Voies), near the Great Conduit in
High Street. And here again, on Wednesday, the
16th of May, 1655, John Penruddock and Hugh
Grove, Esqrs., suffered decapitation, by order of the
Lord Protector, for proclaiming their lawful sovereign,
Charles II., at Southmolton.

After the restoration of monarchy a magazine was
erected within the castle. The arms and ammunition,
which for some time had been kept in the chapel of
St. John's Hospital, were ordered, on the 4th of September, 1663, to be removed thither. The order was
signed by John Drake, sheriff of the county of Devon,
and by John Northcote, John Rolle, John Bampfylde,
and Henry Ford.

Dr. Stukeley, who visited the castle on the 19th of
August, 1723, relates in his Itinerary, vi., p. 157, that
a narrow cavity runs quite round its outer wall, perhaps
for the conveyance of sound from turret to turret.

Andrew Brice, in his Geographical Dictionary, published in 1759, describing the castle, says, " It had a
sallyport, with a drawbridge, and the former yet stands
not quite ruinous, and by the rude vulgar has been
called the Devil's Cradle." This was towards Northernhay, the ditches of which are claimed as belonging to
the Mayor and Chamber, and not to the Duchy of
Cornwall. In page 266 of the Act-Book, 28th of

---

[2] Sir Thomas St. Leger (says Weever, p. 284) was entombed with his wife in the collegiate church of Windsor. | Query, Were their two children, Anthony and Anne, born in the castle of Exeter ?

THE CASTLE. 189

January, 1600-1, the Mayor and Chamber admit that "Exeter is parcell of the Duchie of Cornwall." But for this they paid a consideration to the Crown.

On the 18th July, in the first year of King Edward VI., the corporation leased Northernhay to John Tuckfield, his wife and daughter, Katharine Rykard, during their several lives, for a fine of 40s., and a yearly rent of 20s., and a heriot of 5s. In October, 1560, a lease was again granted, but with a proviso " that every man shall have free liberty, as in times past, for walking and recreation on Northernhay." [3]

In 1612 Northernhay was levelled at the expense of the Chamber, and a pleasant walk made thereon, and upon the mount over against *Gallant's Bower* seats or benches of timber were erected (Izacke's Memorials). And again, " The elm-trees in Northernhay of above one hundred years' growth were felled in 1642." And again, in 1664, " A pleasant walk made on Northernhay, and above two hundred young elms on each side thereof planted in 1662." And in the Act-Books of the Chamber is an order, dated 21st July, 1696, " to pay thirty shillings to George White, the painter, for drawing a map of the Castle ditches;" and another of " 8th March, 1698, for filling up the ditch at the lower end of Northernhay with rubbish." The whole of the castle fosse, from the city wall in Dr. Pennell's premises, along the inner sweep, to the city wall just below the eighth and last house in Bradninch precinct, belongs to the duchy of Cornwall. We learn also from Brice that John Fortescue, Esq., a leaseholder of a part, had converted the castle gateway into " a pleasure-house." His portion afterwards passed into the

---

[3] The ancient fosse, called Crolditch, probably commenced below the city wall towards Eastgate, and ran in nearly a parallel line towards Southgate. Much of an old wall is said still to remain, though the ditch was gradually filled up to make way for the handsome row of houses on Southernhay. The Lammas fair was partially removed from Southernhay in 1793, in consequence of this prospective improvement.

190   HISTORY OF EXETER.

hands of Mr. John Patch, a surgeon, who tastefully profited by the inequalities of the ground in forming walks and plantations, and erected a fair dwelling-house. On his death, in 1787, it was purchased by the late Edmund Granger, Esq., who improved and enlarged the premises. This beautiful and unique free-hold residence, which had been sold by the duchy officers for the redemption of the land-tax, as also a leasehold property of a house and garden on North-ernhay held under the Town Council, were purchased on the 18th March, 1847, for 6300*l*., by Richard Sommers Gard, Esq., M.P. On the other side of the gate-way, now the premises of Dr. Pennell, we recollect a choice vineyard, planted and cultivated by the late Mr. Frankpit.

By permission of the Dukes of Cornwall, the Courts of Assize and General Quarter Sessions of the Peace for the county of Devon were holden within the castle of Exeter from an early period. "The county jail lay just below it, a living tomb—a sink of filth, pestilence, and profligacy,"[4] and where several perished from sheer starvation. In 1608 a complaint was made to the justices of Devon, "that, by reason of the then dearth of all things, the number of prisoners had greatly increased, and their allowance found was so small that

---

[4] In F. Henry More's History of the Provincia Anglicana, S. J., p. 391, is the following description of the old county jail in 1604 :—"Erant 80 viri fœminæque unum in locum varia ob flagitia inclusi. Viros a fœminis disjungebat clathrum ligneum tam latis spatiis laxum, ut non manibus solum et capiti, sed integro penè corpori pateret exitus. Singulos tamen unco ferreo impliciti compedes ita astringebant, ut sedendi quidem jacendive esset copia, non vero se de loco movendi. Duobus ex eo numero fiebat potestas obeundi locum cum situlis ad requisita naturæ. Libertas in atrio perangusto et fœtenti obambulandi emi debebat duobus assibus in dies singulos, pendendis custodi."

Sir William Pole, in his Description of Devon, p. 163, Risdon, p. 50, and Westcote, p. 239, contemporary writers, Brice and the Rev. Richard Polwhele, misled by King Henry I.'s grant of Bicton manor to John, called "Janitor" from his office, to be keeper of the county jail, imagined that the jail itself was at Bicton. The Close Rolls and the Crown Pleas abundantly prove that the service of Geoffrey Balistarius, as Lord of Bicton, consisted in keeping the county jail at Exeter, "custodiendi gaolam comitatus Exoniæ." Innumerable documents prove the fact, and in a deed dated 20th March, 1459, we find this prison designated as the old jail, "vetus gaola."

THE CASTLE. 191

divers of them of late had perished through wante :" upon which the justices ordered the constables " to be diligent in collecting the money for the gaole, that the poor prisoners do not perish thro' their default." Our annals record the melancholy fate of the judge, Mr. Serjeant Flowerby, eleven of the jury, and five of the magistrates—viz., Sir John Chichester, Sir Arthur Basset, Sir Bernard Drake, Robert Cary, and Thomas Risdon, Esquires,—victims of the gaol-fever at the trial of the prisoners at the Lent Assizes for Devon of 1585. In consequence of this frightful visitation, the Assizes were held for a time in other places. For the transaction of special business the justices were allowed to assemble in the Chapter House ; and we find Bishop Woolton, and his successors Bishops Babington and Cotton, occasionally presiding at their meetings.

In 1607, at a meeting of the magistrates in the Chapter House, it was resolved that every knight in the county, being a justice, and every esquire that had been sheriff, should pay towards the building of a convenient Session House within the castle of Exeter the sum of 40$s.$; and every esquire, being a justice, 20$s.$, with every gentleman within the county, being lawyers, whose names hereafter follow, viz. — John Hele, Elles [Elizeus ?] Hele, William Martyn, Hugh Wyat, Robert Davye, Thomas Lee, Humphry Weare, Alexander Maynard, Thomas Risdon, Philip Risdon, James Welche, Nicholas Duck, Richard Martyn, John Molford, Philip Molton, John Hatche, George Stafford, Esquires—and all other gentlemen not herein named, being lawyers within the county, should pay towards the same 13$s.$ 4$d.$; and a committee was appointed to take order about building the Session House. It appears that several of the persons ordered to pay demurred to contribute their quota, insomuch that in 1609 the Judges of Assize, Fleming and Tanfield, addressed letters to the defaulters to make good their payments before the 26th of August

HISTORY OF EXETER.

that year; and in 1610 the same two judges ordered warrants of distress to be executed on those who remained in default. In 1614 the justices held their Sessions at Bedford House; but ten years later they were enabled to sit in "the Grand Jury Howse," which Westcote (p. 141) describes as "the spacious hall and rooms newly re-edified."

After this it was in contemplation to build a House of Correction "upon the lands of the Prince's Highness in the Castell of Exon," and negotiations for the purpose were opened with the Lords of the Council; but the premises "redye builte" of the late Sir John Whyddon, Knight, on the left side of Cowick Street, in St. Thomas's, being offered for sale by that judge's grandson, William Whyddon, Esq., they were purchased of him, in 1637, for 600*l.*, and fitted up for a county Bridewell by the liberality of Elizeus Hele, Esq. As such it continued to be used for a hundred and seventy years. In process of time many alterations and additions were required for the transaction of the increasing business at the castle; but all proving inadequate, plans were advertised for rebuilding the public courts. In 1772 a county meeting was called to consider them. The Crown, which in 1710 granted a lease of the castle for a term of ninety-nine years, was petitioned to grant the fee; and an Act of Parliament was obtained (13th Geo. III., 1773), which vested the fee of the castle in certain justices, as commissioners in trust for the county of Devon, subject to the yearly rent of 10*l.*, payable at Michaelmas to the duchy of Cornwall. Upon this the commissioners entered into a contract with Messrs. Stowey and Jones, builders, to take down the old courts, and erect the present; the first stone of which was laid by the Viscount Courtenay, on the 25th of March, 1774. A direct approach to the castle had been previously made from High Street, in lieu of the old road, which is described in

ANCIENT CHURCH WITHIN THE CASTLE. 193

the Act as " so very narrow, steep, and dangerous, that it is impossible for two carriages to pass by each other, and is very hazardous for foot-passengers."

In 1787 the Legislature sanctioned the erection of a new county jail;[5] and the site of the old horrible pit, with the materials of the jailer's house, were purchased on the 1st of March, 1796, by the late Mr. Shirley Woolmer for 420*l*., to make room for the present Independent chapel. Its first minister was the Rev. John Giles.

The interesting plans, of which, by the kindness of Mr. Holmes, facsimiles were printed in the Author's memoir on the Castle, in Vol. 7 of the Archæological Journal, A.D. 1850, are preserved in the British Museum. The more detailed of these was taken by Norden, in 1617 (Add. MS. 6027).

CHAPTER II.

ANCIENT PREBENDAL CHURCH WITHIN THE CASTLE OF EXETER.

WE now subjoin the history of the ancient church of St. Mary, founded for four prebendaries, at a very remote period, within the castle of Exeter. In letters patent addressed by William Avenel to Robert Chichester, Bishop of Exeter, it is styled " Ecclesia de castello Exonie cum quatuor Prebendis."—Mon. Dioc. Exon., p. 136. Robert Chichester was bishop of the see from 1138 to 1150. We have not been able to meet with the original grant, but tradition attributes

---

[5] [In the author's History of Exeter, ed. 1821, p. 111, he laboured under the error noticed by him, and corrected ante, p. 190, n. [2]; and strongly censured the release of Bicton manor from the burden of the keepership in 1787. It is needless to say that the transaction there denounced was quite misunderstood by the worthy author, and in every respect desirable and beneficial to the public.]

194   HISTORY OF EXETER.

the foundation of the church to the family of **De
Briwere** : it is not improbable, however, that its existence was coeval with that of the castle. It was
dedicated to the Virgin Mary, and not to the Holy
Trinity, as stated in the Chantry Rolls. Annexed
to the church were the four prebends, Hayes, Cutton,
Carswell, and Ashclist, the patronage of all belonging
to the Barony of Okehampton.

In a deed dated 14th of February, 1259, is mentioned
a spot of ground " in prebendâ de Heghe," charged
with the yearly payment of threepence at Easter,
"luminari B. Marie in Capella B. Thome Martyris."
This chapel stood " in capite pontis Exonie." Amongst
the obligatory yearly payments of the Prior and
Brethren of St. John's Hospital, Exeter (Cartulary, p.
37), is half a pound of wax to be offered at St. Mary's
Chapel within the castle of Exeter on the feast of her
Assumption (15th of August).

1. HAYES or HEGHE, as it stood first in rank, appears
also to have been the richest of the prebends. John
Stephyns, prebendary thereof, in consideration of a fine
of 40*l.*, leased it on 10th of October, 1543, to Anthony
Harvey, of Culm-John, Esq., for a term of twenty-one
years, at the yearly rent of 37*l.* 7*s.* 11*d.*, which was
its yearly value in King Henry VIII.'s taxation eight
years before. The same prebendary, on the 22nd of
September, 1548, alienated the fee, described as the
prebend of Hayes and Manor of Hayes in Cowick, and
of Clistmoys (Cliston Hayes in Broadclist parish), to
Robert Kelweye, Esq., his heirs and assigns; and this
alienation was ratified, approved, and confirmed on the
30th of November next ensuing, under the hands and
seals of Edward, Duke of Somerset, " the verye and
indubitate patrone thereof," and of John Veysey,
" Byshope of Exeter." On 1st of April, 1550, Robert

ANCIENT CHURCH WITHIN THE CASTLE. 195

Kelweye conveyed this estate to King Edward VI., who granted it at Greenwich on the 8th of the same month to Nicholas Wadham, Esq., to hold it of the Crown in capite, by the service of the fortieth part of a knight's fee. From Nicholas Wadham it passed to his only sister, Jane, who married John Foster, Esq., of Baddesley, in Hampshire. The above-mentioned Anthony Harvey, on the 12th of January, 1557, disposed of the residue of his term to the said John Foster for 166*l*. 13*s*. 4*d*., who, with his son and heir-apparent, Andrew Foster, on the 1st of October, 1563, covenanted to sell the whole prebend and manor of Hayes to John Petre, Esq., of Exeter, younger brother of Sir William Petre, Knight. In the conveyance, dated 5th of November, 1563, the purchase-money is stated to be 800*l*. The Fosters had previously sold to the same purchaser Clistmoys, in Broadclist, which had produced the yearly rent of 13*l*. 16*s*. In Hilary Term, 6 Elizabeth, 1564, a fine was levied at the castle of Hereford, between John Petre, Esq., plaintiff, and John Foster, Esq., and Jane his wife, and Andrew Foster, son of said John and Jane, deforciants, of the "manor and late prebend of Hayes with the appurtenances, and of 4 messuages, 4 gardens, 100 acres of land, 60 acres of meadow, 100 acres of pasture, and 8*l*. rent, with the appurtenances in Hayes within the castle of Exeter (infra Castrum Exon.), Stoken-Tynhed, Okehampton, Ken, Cutton, Aysshe-Clyste, and in the parish of St. Thomas the Apostle, without the west gate of the city of Exon."

The whole estate descended to the purchaser's nephew, William Petre, Esq., of Tor-Newton in Tor-Brian, whose son, Sir George Petre, Knight, sold Hayes to William Gould, Esq., of Exeter, and by the marriage of Elizabeth Gould, in August, 1739, with James Buller, Esq., of Shillingham, it passed into that

o 2

196   HISTORY OF EXETER.

family, and is now in the possession of James Wentworth Buller, Esq., of Downes.

2. CUTTON. This prebend, in Henry VIII.'s taxation, was rated at 8*l.* After passing through the hands of Brushford and Turberville in the reign of Queen Elizabeth, it shortly after came into the possession of the Aclands, the present holders. The lands of the prebendal manor lie in the parish of Poltimore, and consist of 290A. 1R. 6P. Hoopern pays 3*l.* 3*s.* 4*d.* ; the rectory of Whimple 13*s.* 4*d.* ; and the rectory of Hemington in Somersetshire, 13*s.* 4*d.*

3. CARSWELL or CRESSWELL. This prebend consisted of about 141 acres in the parish of Kenn, but the revenues have passed into lay hands. To the prebendary is doled out the trifling yearly sum of 2*l.* 13*s.* 4*d.*

4. ASHCLIST. This prebend was alienated to Tor Abbey by Robert Courtenay in 1238, and formed part of its possessions until the suppression of the monastery, when it was valued at 12*l.* 10*s.* 10½*d.* per annum, after deducting its yearly payment of 6*s.* 8*d.* to the prebendary of Hayes. The Crown bestowed the Ashclist estate, which lay in the parish of Broadclist, on Thomas Godwyn, who, on 29th of August, 1543, was licensed by Henry VIII., in consideration of a fine of 3*l.* 17*s.* 3*d.*, to alienate it to John Petre the younger, Gentleman, of Tor-Brian. On 1st of September, 1626, Sir George Petre, Knight, was empowered by King Charles I., in consideration of a fine of 5*l.* 6*s.* 8*d.*, to alienate it to Sir Simon Leach, Knight, and John Vigures, Gentleman. The royal letters patent were duly enrolled in the Exchequer. The property afterwards came into the family of Evans; and in 1768 was purchased by Sir Thomas Dyke Acland, the grandfather of the present baronet of the same name.

When Westcote wrote, soon after 1630, St. Mary's

ANCIENT CHURCH WITHIN THE CASTLE. 197

Chapel was "ruinous." A few years later, in 1639, Bishop Hall was requested to assign it "for the buryall of such prisoners as shall dye in the gaole." And the justices resolved that "Mrs. Biglestone, the lessee of the Castle, be paid out of the county stock, for her content-ment, such sums as the Lord Bishop should think fit."

Towards the end of the reign of King Charles II. Bishop Lamplugh, at his own cost, undertook to repair and beautify the chapel; and the justices voluntarily tendered some pecuniary aid, "but soe that the same be accepted as a free gift, and noe obligacion for the future for the like benevolence."[1] The building appears to have been used for prayers during the periods of quarter sessions, until the rebuilding of the Shire Hall, by the "Act of Parliament passed in 1773 for taking down the Shire Hall of the County of Devon, and for rebuilding a new Shire Hall in a more com-modious manner,"[2] and in which a new chapel was provided. Another Act of Parliament for making and declaring the gaol for the county of Devon, called the High Gaol, a public and common gaol; and for discharging Denys Rolle and John Rolle, Esqrs., and their respective heirs and assigns, from the office of keeper of the said gaol, and for improving and en-larging the same, or building a new one, and also for taking down the chapel in the castle of Exeter, and for other purposes, was passed 27 Geo. III., 1787. In 1792 the ancient building, consisting of a chancel and nave, was removed. There is an engraving of it from a sketch by the late R. S. Vidal, Esq., which indicates no architectural beauty; indeed, all its later reparations appear to have been most unsightly.

A quantity of ancient armour which had been de-

---

[1] A resolution of the magistrates to give for the beautifying of this chapel 10l., and 6l. yearly to any one whom the bishop shall appoint to read divine service and to preach a sermon therein on the first day of the sessions, to begin at 8 A.M., was published in folio, Exeter, 1683.

[2] The new work was begun on Lady-day, 1774.

198   HISTORY OF EXETER.

posited in the chapel was given by Lieutenant-General
Simcoe, the commander of the district, to John Houlton,
Esq., of Farleigh Castle, Colonel of the Wiltshire
Militia; an act of questionable legality, and much to
be regretted by those who take an interest in the
preservation of local vestiges and memorials of by-
gone times.

Though a well-endowed chapel within a royal
castle, it would be an error to suppose that it was
exempt from the visitation of the Ordinary, as the old
prebendal chapels of our sovereigns were at Wolver-
hampton, Gnoushale in Leicestershire, St. Mary's at
Stafford, Penkridge, Tetenhall, Bridgenorth, St. Mary's
at Shrewsbury, All Saints Derby, Bosham in Sussex,
St. Martin's London, and Wimburne Minster (Stapeldon's Reg. fol. 28), and, subsequently, St. George's at
Windsor. That our bishops did exercise their right
of visitation and jurisdiction here is manifest from
their registers; it is sufficient to specify the one so
publicly made by Bishop Stapeldon in relation to its
neglected condition :—" Memorandum quod xix die
Januarii 1321 Dominus existens personaliter in Castro
Civitatis Exon' ingressus est in capellam ejusdem
Castri, que prebendalis est, assistentibus sibi Henrico
de Walmesford, tunc tenente locum Vice-Comitis Devon,
Domino Roberto de Stokhay, milite, Henrico de Bo-
kerel, et aliis in multitudine copiosa, et vidit eandem
capellam, in quâ singulis diebus celebrari consueverant
divina, ruinosam et in nonnullis partibus ejusdem
discoopertam, hostiâ fractâ, et quasi penitus sine cele-
bratione divinorum desolatam. Dicebat quod remedium
super hoc, quamcitius commodè posset, apponeret
oportunum." Register, fol. 164. We may mention
also Bishop Lacy's commission on 26th of August,
1438, " ad inquirendum de et super defectibus in
prebendâ de Cutton," the return to which is not to be
found in his Register.

ANCIENT CHURCH WITHIN THE CASTLE. 199

LIST OF PREBENDARIES OF HAYES.

Thomas de Wimundesham, translated from the Prebend of Asheclyst, 7 February, 1261, "ad prebendam de Heghes ultra Exham;" on the presentation of John, Lord de Courtenay.

Robert de Littlebury, admitted 4 June, 1278. Patron, Hugh de Courtenay. This prebendary is mentioned in Pope Nicholas' taxation, 1288-1291.

William de Strete succeeded on 20 June, 1309. Patron, Lady Alianora de Courtenay. He died on 14 February, 1313.

John de Skodemer appears to have been instituted 5 March, 1313, on the presentation of the same Countess (Stapeldon's Register, folio 70), yet we find in the next folio that

Walter de Wereminster was instituted 6 April, 1313, on the presentation of the last Patroness.

Robert de Sambourne . . . on whose death,

Patrick Wode followed, 21 June, 1382. Patron, Edward Courtenay, Earl of Devon.

Richard Buttelkys, 16 March, 1395-6. Patron, King Richard II.

Nicholas Bubbewith, 16 June, 1396; he was afterwards Bishop of London, and then of Sarum. Patron, King Richard II. On Bubbewith's resignation,

Richard Courtenay, LL.B., eldest son of Sir Philip Courtenay, Knt., of Powderham, by Margaret Wake, succeeded, on 3 July, 1403. Patron, Edward Courtenay, Earl of Devon. On his resignation for the See of Norwich,

Thomas Henderman succeeded, 3 September, 1413. Patron as before. He became Chancellor of Exeter, and exchanged his prebend for the Rectory of Crukern, with

Walter Collys, 18 December, 1427. Patron, *hâc vice* King Henry VI. He died Precentor of Exeter, and on his death,

Thomas Mannyng was instituted 22 May, 1457. Patron, Thomas Courtenay, Earl of Devon.

John Symons . . . died 30 May, 1497; buried at Stokeinteignhead.

John Rhese, or *Rise*, Treasurer of Exeter; he died 9 May, 1531. Hoker, his grandson, says he was about 90 years of age.

John Stephyns, instituted 22 May, 1531, on the presentation of "The Noble Henry Courtenay, Knight of the Garter, Lord of Okehampton and Plymton, Earl of Devon and Marquis of Exeter." We are not to confound this John Stephyns with the Canon of Exeter Cathedral of the same name, Rector of Doddiscombesleigh, who died 21 March, 1560, and was buried in the chancel there. This prebendary of Hayes must have lived to a great age, for in Bishop

200 HISTORY OF EXETER.

Woolton's Register, folio 49, we find that on 17 December, 1591, Queen Elizabeth presented

Walter Herte, A.B., " ad prebendam de Hayes juxta pontem Exon' in Castro Exon' ab antiquo fundatam," void by the death of John Stevens, the last incumbent—nomen sine re.

LIST OF PREBENDARIES OF CUTTON.

Henry de Esse, admitted 20 December, 1260, " ad prebendam Capelle Castri Exon, de Cuteton vacantem, ad presentationem Johannis de Curtenay veri patroni." He was inducted 5 April, 1261. Bronescombe's Register, folios 16th and 17th, occurs in Pope Nicholas' taxation.

John Moriz . . . on whose death,

Walter de Clopton, Rector of Kenn, instituted 29 July, 1322, " ad presentationem Domini Hugonis de Courtenay." Bishop Grandisson, on 21 August, 1328, licensed the celebration of divine service " in capella manerii sui de Cutton infra parochiam de Poltymore," in favour of this prebendary. Reg. vol. 2, folio 59. We believe the chapel was dedicated to St. John the Baptist.

Thomas de Courtenay, second son of Hugh, Earl of Devon, by Margaret de Bohun, admitted 30 November, 1346, on the presenta-tion of his father, Hugh de Courtenay, Earl of Devon and Lord of Okehampton. Grandiss. Reg. vol. 3, folio 59. He was buried in the Augustinian church, London.

Robert de Paston succeeded " ad prebendam de Cutton vacantem," 11 December, 1348. Patron, the same.

Otho de Northwode, Archdeacon of Exeter, followed, 9 May, 1350. The same Patron.

Philip de Courtenay, a relative of the above-mentioned Thomas, was admitted on 15 November, 1360, " ad prebendam vacantem." The same Patron.

Robert Vaggescombe succeeded, 2 October, 1366. The same Patron. On his resignation,

William Bermyncham was admitted ; on whose death,

Robert Vaggescombe was reappointed on 30 April, 1382 ; but dying shortly after his second induction,

Henry Cole was admitted 29 June, 1382, on the presentation of Edward Courtenay, Earl of Devon. Brantyngham's Register, vol. 2, folio 72.

Thomas Kerdyngton . . . on whose resignation,

John Radeclyff was admitted on 15 May, 1400. Patron, Edward Courtenay, Earl of Devon. This prebendary exchanged for Clare, the second portion in the church of Tiverton, with

PREBENDARIES OF CUTTON.

Walter Robert, who was admitted on 2 August, 1406. Patron of both preferments, the aforesaid Earl.

Thomas de Kerdyngton was reappointed on 11 February, 1407-8. The same Patron.

Richard Donscombe, or *Dunscombe*, admitted 1 August, 1419, on Kerdyngton's death. The same Patron. Dunscombe died 7 June, 1421.

Richard Aldryngton, a Canon of Exeter Cathedral, was admitted on 14 June, 1421. On the preceding day it had been found by inquisition that Hugh Courtenay, Earl of Devon, was the true patron, jure hereditario—that this prebend paid 6s. 8d. yearly at Michaelmas to the prebendary of Hayes—that Cutton was taxed at 5l. 13s. 4d. per annum—and that Richard Aldryngton was 70 years of age and more. Inquisition in Lacy's Register, vol. 2, folio 34 b.

Robert Felton . . . on whose death,

Richard Beauchamp, afterwards Bishop of Salisbury, was admitted on 25 August, 1438. Patron, Thomas Courtenay, Earl of Devon.

Thomas Bekyngton, LL.D., afterwards Bishop of Bath and Wells, admitted 13 December, 1441. The same Patron. On Bekyngton's resignation,

John de la Bere succeeded, 31 October, 1443. The same Patron.

Geoffry Motte, a Canon of Exeter, followed on 24 April, 1448. The same Patron.

Thomas Copeland was admitted 25 April, 1450, on Motte's resignation. The same Patron.

Thomas Copleston, a Canon of Exeter, admitted 1 July, 1460, on the death of Thomas Copeland. Patron, Thomas Courtenay, the second of that name, Earl of Devon.

John Fulford, afterwards successively Archdeacon of Totnes, Cornwall, and Exeter; on whose resignation,

Thomas Gilbert, D.C.L., was admitted 8 February, 1494-5. Patron, Edward Courtenay, the second of that name, Earl of Devon. Arundel's Register, folio 9.

Thomas Harryes succeeded, 10 September, 1503, on the death of Gilbert. The same Patron. Harryes was Archdeacon of Cornwall and Treasurer of Wells, and died Precentor of Exeter late in 1511.

John Skelton . . . on whose death,

John Touker, admitted 27 December, 1529. Patron, Henry Courtenay, Marquis of Exeter, K.G. This prebendary was living when the taxation was made in 1535. His prebend was then valued at 8l. a-year.

John Blackston, a Canon of Exeter Cathedral, collated by Bishop Turberville, per lapsum, on 24 May, 1556. On his deprivation,

Richard Tremayne, D.D. (a younger son of Thomas Tremayne, of

HISTORY OF EXETER.

Collacombe, by Philippa, daughter of Roger Grenvile, of Stow in Cornwall), Treasurer of Exeter Cathedral, was admitted 21 February, 1560-1, on the presentation of Reginald Mohun, John Trelawney, Peter Courtenay, John Vyvian, and John Killigrew, as Trustees of Alexander Arundel. Tremayne's will was proved 15 December, 1584.

John Bradford succeeded Tremayne on 27 January, 1584-5. Patron, Nicholas Turberville, Gent., of Crediton.

John Bradford, jun., instituted 8 October, 1619, by simony of the preceding prebendary. Patron, King James I.

Thomas Atwill . . . on whose death,

Humphry Saunders, M.A., was admitted 19 January, 1634-5. Patron, John Acland, Esq.

John Procter was admitted 10 February, 1662-3, on the deprivation of Saunders. Patron, Margaret Acland, widow, of Killerton.

Bernard Galard was admitted on 6 May, 1671, on the death of Procter. Patron, Lady Margaret Acland, widow, of Killerton. This prebendary died at his Rectory at Poltimore, and was buried in the parish church, 23 November, 1693.

Thomas Bate succeeded on 21 August, 1694. Patron, Sir Hugh Acland, Bart., of Killerton. On his resignation,

Thomas Acland, M.A., admitted 25 September, 1703. Patron as before.

Edward Reeks followed on 2 October, 1735, on Mr. Acland's death. Patrons, Sir Thomas Acland, Bart., of Killerton, Rev. Thomas Troyte, and Dame Cicely Acland, *alias* Troyte, his wife.

George Drake was admitted on 15 June, 1748, on Reeks' death. Patrons as in the preceding presentation, only the first is called Sir Thomas Dyke Acland, Bart., of Culm-John.

John Pitman, admitted 20 July, 1752, on the death of Drake. Patron, Sir Thomas Dyke Acland, Bart. Mr. Pitman died 2 February, 1768, aged 50.

John Acland succeeded 10 June, 1768. Same Patron. Mr. Acland was buried at Broadclist, 16 August, 1795.

John Pitman, jun., admitted 26 November, 1795. Patrons, Sir Thomas Dyke Acland, Bart., an infant, with the consent of Hugh Acland, Esq., the Hon. Sir Francis Buller, Bart., and John Rolle, his trustees.

Francis Huyshe, M.A., instituted 4 July, 1831, on the death of Mr. Pitman, which happened on 29 December, 1830, aged 81. Patron, Sir Thomas Dyke Acland, Bart.

William Barker, M.A., was admitted 27 February, 1840, on the death of Mr. Huyshe, on 28 August, 1839, aged 71. Patron the same.

PREBENDARIES OF CARSWELL.

The Hon. *Charles Leslie Courtenay*, M.A., fourth son of William Courtenay, second Earl of Devon, was admitted 17 June, 1842, on Mr. Barker's death, which happened on 31 March, 1841. Patron the same.

Peter Leopold Dyke Acland, M.A., instituted 30 December, 1845, on Mr. Courtenay's resignation, 22 August, 1845. The same Patron, his father.

LIST OF PREBENDARIES OF CARSWELL.

Philip de Dutton occurs in Pope Nicholas' taxation.

William Strete held the preferment about a month, together with Hayes, but at the end of the month ceded the preferment. Patron, Lady Alianora de Courtenay.

Henry de Soler, afterwards Rector of Kenn, was then admitted on 18 July, 1309. Patron, the same lady.

Robert de Brandone succeeded 26 April, 1312. Patron, the same lady.

John Aleyn . . . on whose resignation,

John Southdon, 1 November, 1376. Patron, Hugh Courtenay, Earl of Devon.

Richard Danyell . . . on whose resignation,

Robert Good was instituted 16 July, 1414. Patron, Edward Courtenay, Earl of Devon.

John Cole . . . on whose death,

John Seger succeeded 15 April, 1457. Patron, Thomas Courtenay, Earl of Devon.

John Caperton admitted 10 October, 1477, on the death of Seger, at the presentation of George Duke of Clarence, Earl of Sarum, Lord of Richmond, and Great Chamberlain of England.

Peter Courtenay, afterwards Bishop of Exeter and Winchester, on whose death,

John Courtenay, described as "Senior." We apprehend that he was the fourth son of Sir William Courtenay, Knt., the second possessor of that name of Powderham, but perhaps of the Molland branch. He succeeded on 2 March, 1492-3, on the presentation of Edward Courtenay, the second Earl of that name, Earl of Devon.

John Pampyng was admitted on 3 August, 1495, to the vacant prebend. Patron ut supra.

John Walrond, on Pampyng's death, succeeded on 13 December, 1512, on the presentation of the most noble Lady Catherine, Countess of Devon. He was probably the second son of Humphry Walrond, of Bradfield, by Eleanor, daughter of Henry Ogan, Esq.

David Hensley, Rector of Kenn, was admitted on 24 September,

HISTORY OF EXETER.

1566, on the death of the last Incumbent. Patron, Geoffry Tothill, Gent. Queen Elizabeth, on 10 June, 1564, had granted to William and John Killigrew, brothers, the advowson and patronage of Carswell, which they sold the next day to William Floyer and Geoffry Tothill. Mr. Hensley died on 3 September, and was buried at Kenn on 7 September, 1573.

Geoffry Collyns, "a layman," was admitted on 19 January, 1573. Patron as the last. On his death,

Thomas Barrett, Archdeacon of Exeter, was collated by his father-in-law, Bishop Woolton, on 28 May, 1584. Register, folio 17. On his resignation,

John Bridgeman was admitted 20 February, 1603. Patron, Jasper Bridgeman.

George Bridgeman succeeded on John's resignation, 27 July, 1613. Patron as the last.

Thomas Baker, collated by Bishop Valentine Carey, per lapsum, on 6 October, 1624. On his death,

John Snell, afterwards Canon of Exeter Cathedral, 10 January, 1660-1, on the presentation of Hugh Potter, Esq., and George Potter, merchant. On Snell's death, which happened 15 April, 1679,

George Snell, afterwards Archdeacon of Totnes, was instituted 10 August, 1679, on the presentation of his brother, John Snell, of Exeter, merchant.

Thomas Snell . . . on whose death,

Thomas Snell, jun., on 25 March, 1718. Patron, John Snell, Clerk.

Chichester Tomkins, 22 April, 1758. Patrons, Sir John Colleton, Bart.; Wenman Nutt, of London, and Mary his wife; and Gertrude Snell, of Exeter.

John Vye, admitted 5 May, 1781. Patrons, Wenman Nutt, Esq., and Mary his wife; Gertrude Snell, spinster; and Louisa Colleton, spinster.

Jonas Dennis, B.C.L., admitted 29 July, 1799. Patrons, Wenman Nutt, Esq., and Mary his wife. He held this single preferment until his death, on 6 December, 1846.

William Ludlow, instituted 3 April, 1847, on Dennis's death. Patrons, Edward Erskine Tustin, and Frederick Pratt Barlow, Esqrs., on the death of General Richard Dickinson, on 5 December, 1846.

LIST OF PREBENDARIES OF ASHCLIST.

In the Episcopal Register of the See of Exeter, two institutions only to this Prebend are noticed after its appropriation to the Abbey of Tor, viz. :—

THE GUILDHALL. 205

Thomas ˜de Wimundeham, who was promoted 7 February, 1261, to *Hayes*. On his resignation,

William Stanfer was admitted by Bishop Bronescombe, 7 February, 1261, on the presentation of John Lord Courtenay. Bronescombe's Register, folio 16 *b*.

CHAPTER III.

DESCRIPTION OF THE GUILDHALL.

FROM all the evidences that my late friend Mr. Pitman Jones and myself examined, we were fully satisfied that the Guildhall of the City invariably occupied its present situation within the parish of St. Pancras.

In a deed of the 13th century we found an annual rent of seven shillings granted to St. Nicholas' Priory from certain lands and shops in the High-street, near the Guildhall, "*de terris et seldis in magno vico juxta Gialdam*." In the Patent Rolls of 1389 it is mentioned again as situate in High-street. In the rental of St. Mary's Priory, at Marsh Barton near this city, made on 2nd November, 1421, occurred a similar payment issuing from two shops lying and being on the east side of the Guildhall, in the High-street of Exeter, "*in orientali parte Gyhaldæ in magno vico Exoniæ*." And, not to multiply authorities, a document of the middle of the 15th century described the *Eagle House* (where the Cloth-hall was kept) as being in the High-street of the city, and opposite to the Guildhall, "*in summo vico civitatis Exoniæ ex opposito Gialdæ ibidem*."

The present structure, according to Hoker, was rebuilt in 1466; who adds, that Thomas Calwodelegh, a gentleman born and learned, governed the city to his great commendation and the benefit of the commonwealth, but severe against notorious and evil offenders, and such as escaped corporal punishment paid in moneys,

206   HISTORY OF EXETER.

which were employed in building of the front and chapel of the Guildhall. This chapel in front was dedicated to St. George and St. John the Baptist; for so it is stated in a deed of the Mayor and Chamber, dated 22nd of March, 1512, "*capella Sanctorum Georgii Martyris et Johannis Baptistæ, situata in anteriore parte Gildæ Aulæ Civitatis Exoniæ.*" Over the chapel was the priest's apartment, who was obliged to officiate, in person or by deputy, every day.

Towards the chaplain's better maintenance, John Kelly, by will, dated 16th November, 1486, and proved on the 16th of the following January, left a tenement to the Mayor, Bailiffs, and Commonalty of Exeter, "*ad subsidium salarii sacerdotis sive capellani divina celebrantis in capellâ noviter edificatâ in fronte Gildæ Aulæ.*" On 4th November, 1521, the Chamber agreed "that Sir William Asshe, the city Chaplain, should have yearly 4*l.*, and to sing in St. George's chapel as he used to do, and no place elsewhere, except obits and trentals; and also, every day that the Mayor goeth in procession to St. Peter's church, the said chaplain to say mass before him and his brethren at St. Catherine's altar, or else another priest for him."

The chapel contained two altars, St. John's and St. Bartholomew's; and it appears from Archbishop Wareham's letter to the Mayor and Chamber, bearing date Lambeth, 5th July, 1531, to have been respectably fitted up, "*condecenter ornata.*" At the suppression of chantries, soon after the accession of Edward VI., the plate of this chapel was sold (3rd December, 1547) to William Smythe for 22*l.* 5*s.* 8*d.* In the Chamber Act Book, No. 1, p. 1, is the inventory of the plate, vestments, and ornaments belonging to this chapel, taken 10th October, 1541, and delivered by Mr. Lake, the chaplain, to William Bucknam, mayor. Probably the fabric stood until the present tasteless substitute, which masks and disfigures the Guildhall, was piled up in its

THE GUILDHALL. 207

stead in the year 1593.—The Act Book, p. 114, November 2, 1592, shows " it was agreed that the forepart of the Guildhall, now in a ruinous and decayed state, shall be re-edified at the city's expense, and a committee be appointed to confer with trusty and proper persons as to the plan and expense, and to report to the body the result." John Sampford was appointed overseer of the building 18th April, 1594.[3]

On the 8th October, 1594, Mr. Receiver was directed with all convenient speed " to planche, plaister, glase, and finishe the forepart of the Guildhall."

In the Act Book, No. 1, p. 150, we find that on 12th July, 1556, "a house was ordered to be built in the back court behind the Guildhall for the safe keeping and imprisoning of such as shall at any time be commended to the ward of the mayor for the time being, or otherwise by any other who hath lawful authority therein."

" A strait prison in the pit of the Guildhall" is mentioned in the Act Book, No. 2, p. 77, to which Richard Sweete was consigned on 19th December, 1561, for 40 days in solitary confinement, there to be fed on Wednesday and Friday on bread and water, for incontinence. There he continued till 12th January, when the mayor, on his repentance, ordered his release. It is 17 feet long by 15 wide and 6 high, but the window of the court is now closed.

The chapel bell is still preserved with the following legend :

"Celi Regina me protege queso ruinâ."

The Guildhall is a bold and handsome structure, and measures in the interior length 62½ feet, by 25 in breadth. The roof rises to 37 feet 4 inches in height,

---

[3] [The like metamorphosis of a pointed into a quasi-Italian building was effected about twenty years before on the Town Hall of Cologne, with results equally unsatisfactory.]

HISTORY OF EXETER.

and is gracefully formed. At the head and sides of the hall are emblazoned the armorial bearings of several of the mayors, recorders, benefactors, and trades of the city. Many of the escutcheons, originally depicted under the direction of the celebrated John Hoker, were described in Hollingshed's Collections, lib. v., and copied thecne into Westcote's View of Devonshire.

At a subsequent period (perhaps after the order of the Chamber on 10th March, 1663, "that the Guild-hall be repaired and the fair brass candlestick, lately provided by Mr. Isaac Maudit the elder, be hung up in the Guildhall, and be paid for by the Receiver") several of the original shields were effaced to make room for others. Some have been strangely altered by painters, who were ignorant or regardless of heraldic distinctions. We shall attempt to throw what light we can on the series; and for this purpose begin from the Mayor's seat to the right, and then proceed from the left.

1. Over the Mayor's seat,[4] England and France quartered; under which is the crown and double rose.

2. On the right of the Mayor's seat were the arms of the City of Exeter :[5]—Party per pale gules and sable, a castle triple-towered with a portcullis or ; but *now* occupied by the arms of the Company of the BREWERS.

3. DENNIS.—Ermine, three Danish battle-axes erect gules.

---

[4] By an Act of Chamber, 4th Nov. 1521, it was agreed that Master Mayor shall have for his pension 40 marks, and every Mayor to have as much hereafter. Originally the pension was £5, which was increased to £6 13s. 4d. in 1421, "in consideration that the Mayor should not ask any further allowance for his dyet." In 1450 it was raised to £8, "in consideration that he should keep 2 dinners for the 24 members of Council, and all his officers—the first on the Monday of his election; the second on the election of his successor." In 1460 it was raised to £10. See pp. 301, 309, 313, Hoker's MS. History.

[5] By grant of the Heralds' College, 6th of August, 6 Eliz. 1564, the city of Exeter bears upon a wreath, gold and sable, a demi-lion gules, armed and langued azure, crowned, supporting a ball thereon, a cross botoné gold, manteled azure, doubled argent, and for the supporters two pegasuses argent, their hoofs and manes gold, their wings wavy of six, argent and azure. A countryman showing these supporters to a stranger, is reported to have observed, " These be the two race-hosses that rinned upon Haldon, wi' names of 'em put under, Scamper and Phillis," i.e. *Semper Fidelis.*

THE GUILDHALL. 209

4. MOORE.—Now a chevron azure, three cinquefoils, but formerly ermine on a bend sable.

5. COLSHULL.—Checky, or and sable, on a chief argent, five goutes.

6. HOKER.—First, VOWEL of Pembroke; or, a fess vair, between two lions passant gardant sable. Second, HOKER; gules, a fess engrailed argent, charged with two fleurs-de-lis azure, between three cinquefoils or. Third, BOLTER; ermine, now argent, a chief azure, charged with three bird-bolts argent. Fourth, DRUELL; sable, a chevron argent, between three bunches of daisies argent. Fifth, KELLY; argent, a chevron gules, between three billets of the second. Sixth (COMYNS?), gules, a chevron argent, between three gards or.

7. CALWODELEIGH.—Azure, on a pair of wings in lure argent, a bar gules.

8. DUKE.—Party per fess, argent and azure, three chaplets counterchanged.

9. BLUNDELL.—Paly undy of six, ermine and gules. (Qy. argent and gules?)

10. SHILLINGFORD.—Argent, a bend gules, a label of five points azure.

11. HULL.—Sable, a chevron between three talbots' heads erased argent, langued gules.

12. FITZHENRY.—Argent, a cross engrailed sable. This was formerly HELE.

13. SPICER.—Party per pale gules and sable, three castles or; on a bend wavy between two cotises ermine, a border engrailed of the same.

14. LEVERMORE.—Argent, a bar and two barulets sable, between three tufts of leaves vert; now pine-apples proper.

15. HELE.—Argent, a bend of five fusils gules.

16. DREW.—Ermine, a lion passant gules.

17. TOTHIL.—Azure, on a bend argent, cotised or, a lion sable.

P

210 HISTORY OF EXETER.

18. CHARLES.—Party per fess undy, gules and ermine, in chief an eagle displayed or. (Now destroyed.)

19. STURE.—Or, now argent, a star of eight points sable.

20. HARRIS.—Sable, three crescents argent within a bordure of the same.

21. WYNARD.—Argent, a bend azure, charged with three mullets of the first. Now argent, a chevron azure, between three mullets gules.

22. HOLLAND.—Azure, a lion saliant guardant, between five lilies argent. Now within a bordure argent.

23. DOWRISH.—Argent, a bend cotised within a bordure sable.

24. HEXT.—Or, a castle triple-towered between three battleaxes sable.

25. HUNT.—Azure, on a bend or, now argent, three leopards' faces gules between two water-bougets or.

26. HUDDESFELD. — Argent a bar sable, charged with a crescent for difference between three boars sable.

27. GANDY.—Gules, three saltiers argent, now or; formerly SOMASTER—Argent, a castle triple-towered between seven fleurs-de-lis sable.

28. CROSSING.—Argent, a chevron azure, charged with three bezants between three crosslets gules; formerly WEEKES—Ermine, three battle-axes sable.

29. WALKER.—Azure, a griffin segreant, armed and ungued or; now argent, a bordure engrailed ermine, now argent; formerly NEWCOMBE.

30. GRAY?—Or, on a bend azure, three martlets argent; now quarterly, first and fourth sable, a chevron argent, charged with five goutes between three martlets argent; second and third argent, a chevron between three cross-crosslets gules.

31. BURGOIN.—Azure, a talbot passant argent, langued and collared gules, chained or.

THE GUILDHALL. 211

32. TICKELL.—Ermine, on a chief indented gules, three crowns or.

33. KITSON.—Sable, three fishes hauriant argent, a chief or ; now gules, three fishes hauriant argent.

34. BATISHULL.—Azure, a cross-crosslet saltier-wise between four owls argent.

35. DUPORT.—Barry of six or and sable ; now azure, a saltier within a bordure, both engrailed, gules.

36. BRADESTONE ?—Argent, a chevron between three boars' heads couped sable.

37. NOBLE.—Or, two flanches, and on a bar sable, between two lions passant azure, incensed gules, three besants ; now argent, two flanches sable, and on a bar sable, three roundlets between two lions passant sable, incensed sable.

38. CHALONS ?—Or, two bars between an orle of martlets gules ; now BRIDPORT—Argent, a bend azure, between six double roses gules.

39. OXENHAM.—Ermine, a bar between three crescents gules ; now BAMPFYLDE—Argent, a bend azure, charged with three mullets argent.

40. HELION ?—Or, on a bend sable three martlets argent ; now argent, a fess between three crescents gules.

41. GOULD ?—Party per pale argent and sable, a lion salient gules, within a bordure counterchanged.

To the left of the Mayor's seat.—

1. SMITH.—Sable, a fess between two barulets, and three martlets or ; now argent.

2. PERIAM.—Gules, a chevron engrailed between three leopards' faces or.

3. HURST.—Argent, an étoile of eight points wavy gules.

4. POLLARD. — Argent, a chevron sable between three mullets—now escalops—gules.

5. TUCKER.—Barry-wavy of twelve azure and argent, on a chevron crenelle or, between three sea-horses

P 2

212 HISTORY OF EXETER.

sable—now or—finned, trailed, and maned, of the third, five goutes of the fourth—goutes now omitted.

6. PRESTWOOD.—Sable, a lion salient, now rampant, between two flanches or.

7. PRIDEAUX quartered with ROACH. — First and fourth argent, a chevron sable a label gules; second and third, three roaches—two, one—naiant—argent.

8. BULLER.—Argent, on a cross sable, pierced of the field, four eagles displayed sable.

9. Arms of the JOINERS' Company.

10. HILL of Hill's Court.—Gules, a saltier vairy, now argent, between four mullets pierced argent, now or.

11. BALL.—Argent, a chevron gules, between three fire-balls sable, fused gules.

12. NEWCOMBE.—Argent, a fess crenelle, in chief three escalops sable; now gules; a chevron or between three escalops or.

13. Arms of the TAILORS' Company.

14. HUTCHINSON.—Per pale azure and gules, in fess a lion rampant argent, semée with twelve crosslets or; now sable, a lion rampant argent, between fifteen cross-crosslets or.

15. WHITE.—Gules, on a canton ermine, a lion saliant, now rampant, sable, within a bordure sable, charged with stars argent; now or.

16. GERVIS.—Argent, six ostrich feathers in pile—three, two, one—sable.

17. BERRYMAN.—Argent, a chevron sable between three talbots sable.

18. BONVILE.—Sable, six mullets—three, two, and one—pierced gules, now argent.

19. GILBERT.—Argent, on a chevron sable three roses of the field.

20. CHAMPNEYS.—Argent, a lion salient, now rampant, within a bordure engrailed gules.

21. AMERIDETH.—Gules, a lion rampant regardant or

THE GUILDHALL. 213

22. ATWILL.—Argent and sable, a pile chevron voided.

23. MAINWARING ?—Barry of ten or and gules, with an annulet for difference gules.

24. PETRE.—Gules, on a bend or two cinquefoils azure between two escalops argent, charged with a Cornish chough between two cinquefoils azure, with a crescent for difference argent, a chief or, charged with a double rose gules, between two demi fleurs-de-lis or.

25. DUCKENFIELD.—Argent, a cross sarcelly sable, voided of the field.

26. HAYDON.—Argent, three bars gemelles sable, on a chief gules a bar dancette or.

27. PLEA.—Party per pale azure and gules, now azure and sable; a lion passant, now rampant, argent, crowned or, with a label of three points azure for difference.

28. ————. Barry of eight sable, a chief gules, charged with three leopards' heads or.

29. Arms of the WEAVERS and FULLERS' Company.

30. ———————— GLOVERS' Company.

31. ———————— BAKERS' Company.

32. ———————— HABERDASHERS' Company.

33. ———————— ARMOURERS' (?) Company.

34. ———————— COOPERS' Company.

35. ———————— BUTCHERS' Company.

36. ———————— TAILORS, the most ancient Company, incorporated by King Edward IV.

37. ———————— MERCHANT ADVENTURERS trading to France, incorporated by Queen Mary.[e]

When Scipio Squire visited Exeter, in James I.'s time, he saw the coat of LIMPENNY, in the Guildhall of Exon, viz :—Per pale gules and sable, a cat passant between three roses or.

---

[e] [The arms of the Merchant Adventurers and of the Armourers are not now to be found in the heraldry of the Hall.]

214   HISTORY OF EXETER.

Let us now examine the portraits.

1. Opposite the mayor's bench is a full-length picture of SIR CHARLES PRATT, son of Mr. John and Mrs. Elizabeth Pratt, baptized at Kensington, 21st March, 1714; painted by T. Hudson, 1764. None of the memoirs of this great lawyer, which have been hitherto published, mentions the place or (with accuracy) the time of his birth. His father, M.P. for Midhurst, also a lawyer of great eminence, was made a Judge of the King's Bench in October, 1714, and in 1718 was promoted to be the Lord Chief Justice of that Court. Charles Pratt, his third son, was bred up to his own profession. It is said that he had been nine years at the bar without distinguishing himself, when a favourable opportunity brought into prominence those talents which raised him to the highest honours of his profession. He was made Attorney-General in 1757, Lord Chief Justice of the Common Pleas in 1762, and in 1766 Lord High Chancellor of England. · In these high stations he conducted himself with singular ability and integrity. In 1765 he was created Baron Camden,. of Camden Place, Kent. In 1782 he was President of the Council, and in 1786 he was raised to the rank of an earl. Lord Camden died on the 18th of April, 1794, having completed his 80th year. It appears that his father, Lord Chief Justice Pratt, resided at Kensington several years (Lysons's Environs of London, vol. iii. p. 218). Lysons (Devon, pp. 128, 418) says that some of the Pratts resided at King's Mill, Cullompton, and at Green End, Plymptree.

The cities of London, Dublin, Bath, and Norwich also have portraits of him.

In the Act Books of Exeter we find the resolution following :—

"27th February, 1764. Resolved unanimously,—

"That the Right Hon. Sir Charles Pratt, Lord Chief Justice of His Majesty's Court of Common Pleas, be presented with the

THE GUILDHALL. 215

freedom of this city, and he he most respectfully requested to accept thereof as an expression of our profound veneration for his consummate abilities, and as a testimony of that gratitude which he hath merited at the hands of every Englishman, by the unshaken courage and inflexible integrity which he hath so singularly displayed in the public administration of justice, and in maintaining and vindicating the public liberty and property of the subject, which makes so essential a part of the legal and constitutional rights of this free people " (Act Book, No. 12, fol. 276).

" 17th March, 1764.

" Mr. Mayor having communicated to the chamber a letter he had received from John Walter, Esq., one of the representatives in parliament for this city, where, in expressing his grateful acknowledgements of the repeated honour done him by the city in twice electing him their representative in parliament, he begs the Chamber's acceptance of the portrait of a truly right honourable person, who, from the circumstance of his being our countryman, merits, with a peculiar propriety, every sort of regard from us ; and who, besides, lately from his standing up so gloriously in defence of the liberty of the subject, hath made himself the object of almost admiration to every true Englishman, and must endear his memory to the latest posterity. It is unanimously resolved that Mr. Mayor would be pleased to return the grateful thanks of this body to Mr. Walter for the very obliging present he proposes to make them, and to acquaint him that they shall receive it from him with the highest satisfaction, as the most acceptable one that could have been made them at the present juncture, and that the Town Clerk do lay before the Right Honourable the Lord Chief Justice Pratt the humblest respectful services of this body, with their request that he would favour them so far as to sit for his portrait to Mr. Hudson, in order that it may be set up in their Guildhall as a monument to posterity of their unfeigned veneration for his unbiassed integrity and superior abilities, and of the great honour done this city by his permitting himself to be enrolled among the number of our citizens " (Ibid. fol. 276.)

In page 100 of the Universal Magazine, 20th February, 1768, we read that " a beautiful whole-length picture of Lord Camden has been lately finished by Mr. Hudson, and is sent down to Exeter in order to be put up in the Town Hall at the expense of the corporation. It was the gift of John Walter, Esq., in

216   HISTORY OF EXETER.

memory of the great asserter of the English laws and liberties, 1764."[7]

2. On the left of the earl is a copy, by Robert Edge Pine, of the original portrait of BENJAMIN HEATH, LL.D., made in virtue of a resolution of the Mayor and Chamber 22nd September, 1766. This able lawyer was the Town Clerk of Exeter for fourteen years, and was uncle to the late Mr. Justice Heath. He died 13th September, 1766, æt. 63.

> "22nd Sept. 1766.
>
> "Resolved unanimously that a full-length portrait of Benjamin Heath, Esq., late Town Clerk of this city, from an original painting, be copied by Mr. Pyne and fixed in a conspicuous part of the Guildhall, to perpetuate his memory and testify the obligations of this body to the unwearied exertion of his great abilities in that office "[8] (Act Book, No. 12, fol. 291).

This portrait was engraved in mezzotinto by J. Dixon.

3. On the right of Earl Camden is General MONK, Duke of Albemarle,[9] K.G., by Sir Peter Lely,—not by Vandyke, as Lysons supposes in his Devonshire, p. 193. He was chosen High Steward of the city on 2nd December, 1662, with the usual pension of 10l. Born at Potheridge near Torrington, Devon, 6th December, 1608, he died 3rd January, 1670, at his own house near Whitehall. His duchess, Anne, survived him but three weeks. His son and heir, Christopher Duke of Albemarle, was elected High Steward on 1st February, 1676, and died s. p. in Jamaica in 1688. The picture was engraved for Lodge's Portraits.

4. On the left of the mayor's seat is JOHN ROLLE WALTER, Esq., who represented the city of Exeter from 1754 to 1776; ob. 1779, æt. 66. He was admitted

---

[7] [It was the recent judgment in *Wilkes's* case which caused this outburst of popularity.]

[8] This Mr. Pine is said to have died in 1790, æt. 48. Another account by Naylor states with more probability that this native of London died in 1795, æt. 65.

[9] The Duke of Albemarle's brother, Sir Thomas Monk of Potheridge, in the parish of Merton, knight, was made free of this city in the mayoralty of his father-in-law, Sir George Smith of Matford, knight, in 1607.

THE GUILDHALL. 217

to the freedom of this city 6th Sept. 1753. The portrait was painted by Leaky, and presented, in 1835, by the late Lord Rolle, his nephew. The original, by Sir Joshua Reynolds, is at Bicton.

5. KING GEORGE II., by T. Hudson. Andrew Brice, in his Geographical Dictionary, page 545, calls this portrait " the ingenious work and generous present of the celebrated Mr. Thomas Hudson, heretofore of Exeter." It was engraved by J. Faber in 1745.

6. REUBEN PHILLIPS, Esq., æt. 84, presented to the Mayor and Chamber of Exeter in 1831, as a testimonial of the esteem of his fellow citizens. It was painted by Sharland. In 1784 he married Jane Knight, spinster, of Ebbesbourne in Wilts.[1] Dying 29th November, 1833, in the 87th year of his age, at Exeter, he was buried at Honiton-Clist.

7. On the right of the mayor's seat, JOHN TUCKFIELD, Esq., of Little Fulford, founder of the hospital, and from 1745 to 1766 a representative of Exeter in Parliament; painted by Hudson.

8. The PRINCESS HENRIETTA, Duchess of Orleans. This illustrious daughter of King Charles I. was born at Bedford House in this city on Sunday morning, 16th June, 1644; baptized in the cathedral 21st July following; married 31st March, 1661, to Philippe of France, Duke of Orleans, brother of Louis XIV.; and died 29th June, 1670. The suddenness of her death excited a suspicion of poison, but it was utterly groundless. (See King James the Second's Life, vol. ii. p. 451.) It is the work of Sir Peter Lely,[2] and was presented by King Charles II. in 1672.

On 22nd November, 1660, the Chamber voted 200l. to buy a piece of plate for the Princess Henrietta, to

---

[1] She died at Honiton-Clist, 23rd Feb. 1854, aged 93.

[2] Mr. Jenkins, p. 319, History of Exeter, will have it that this portrait was painted by the celebrated Vandyke, who died in London 9th Dec. 1641, aged 42, two years and a half before the Princess Henrietta was born.

218   HISTORY OF EXETER.

be presented to her highness in the name of the city by Sir Peter Balle, knight, the Recorder of Exeter.

9. HENRY BLACKALL, Esq., thrice Mayor of Exeter; painted in 1833 by Leaky. He died 19th, and buried 25th February, 1845, at St. Mary Major's, Exeter, æt. 75.

In the Council Chamber are the following portraits.[3] On the right of the Mayor :—

1. WILLIAM HURST, A.D. 1568, æt. 96, with the inscription following :—

> "Non mihi lingua data quâ possim dicere nomen
> Qualis eram, paucis versa tabella notat."

2. JOAN TUCKFIELD, A.D. 1573, æt. 67.—Argent, three fusils in fess within a bordure sable, and quarterly ; the arms of ATWILL.

3. SIR THOMAS WHITE. This founder of St. John's College, Oxford, and benefactor to the public, died 11th February, 1566, æt. 83. He bore—Gules, an annulet in fess or, a bordure sable entoized with mullets on the second ; on a canton ermine a lion rampant of the third. "Auxilium meum a Domino." He was buried in St. John's College Chapel. On the picture are the following verses :—

> "Cernitur hic Thomas Whitus, sub imagine pictâ
> Cernitur hic Vitæ melius sub imagine verâ.
> Et Pater et Prætor Londini, miles in illo ;
> Providus Oxoniæ fautor, fundator in illâ ;
> Bristoliæ decus eximium, laus prima Redingi ;
> Gloria Tunbrigiæ ; tibi causa, Coventria, famæ ;
> Urbis honos, orbis prudentia, gemma senectæ."

Portraits of Sir T. White may be seen in the halls of Leicester, Salisbury, Reading, Merchant Taylors', London, and St. John's College, Oxford.[4]

---

[3] Besides these, in an Act of the Chamber 30th June, 1605, we find that *Laurence Seldon's* picture and that of his wife was ordered to be set up in the Council Chamber at the costs of the city. Laurence Seldon and Elizabeth Hackwill were married at St. Kerrian's 1st Oct. 1566: he was buried at St. Mary Major's 22nd May, 1598.

[4] [It is not apparent how Sir T. White's portrait found a place in the chamber? He was not a native of Exeter, nor did he found any scholarships there, as at Bristol, Reading, and elsewhere.]

THE GUILDHALL. 219

4. JOHN PERIAM, knight, who died about the year 1616.[5] On the 3rd July, 1705, Periam's portrait was allowed by the Chamber " to be lent to Mr. Gandy the painter to copy for the use of Exeter College, giving a note to return it in a reasonable time." He was a citizen of Exeter and a benefactor to that College.

5. JOHN HOKER, the Chamberlain, born in 1524, member for Exeter in 1571, died in Nov. 1601, " ætatis 76, A.D. 1601." Every lover of antiquity must wish to see an engraving of this valuable and original portrait.[6]

6. WALTER BOROUGH, 1626, æt. 72. He was buried in the cathedral 20th August, 1632.

7. LAWRENCE ATWILL, A.D. 1588, æt. 77. By an Act of Chamber, 12th December, 1599, it was agreed " that Mr. Atwill's picture, which·cost twenty shillings, shall be paid for."

On the left of the mayor we find,—

1. THOMAS JEFFORD, a wealthy dyer of this city, who was said to have built Great Duryard House, where he died in 1703, having been knighted by King James II. on presenting the congratulatory address on the birth of the Prince of Wales, afterwards called the Pretender. The painter of this was perhaps William Gandy, son of the James Gandy, whose finest portrait is that of Tobias Langdon, now in the hall of the priest-vicars of the cathedral. William Gandy the painter was buried 14th July, 1729[7] (see the Register of St. Paul's, Exeter).

---

[5] Quære if this uncouth portrait was not painted by John Browcke?

[6] He is described as John Hoker the *Younger* in St. Mary Major's Register, to distinguish him from his grandfather, John Hoker. He was buried 8th Nov. 1601.

[7] [The author assigns to William Gandy the portraits of Jefford and Oliver, Nos. 1 and 5, *infra*, upon what grounds does not appear. These and No. 2 (Mrs. Flay) resemble one another in style, treatment, and composition, and may perhaps be by the same painter; but that of Oliver was probably a copy, *if* by W. Gandy; for Oliver died before W. Gandy is said to have settled at Exeter. The great talents of the two Gandys are noticed in the late biographies of Reynolds, who is said to have owed more to W. Gandy than to his reputed master, Hudson. There is a short notice of Gandy in Northcote's Life of Reynolds.]

220 HISTORY OF EXETER.

2. ELIZABETH FLAY, who died 20th November, 1673, æt. 86, widow of Thomas Flay, apothecary, who founded the almshouses in Goldsmith's Street, now removed to St. Sidwell's. She improved this her husband's foundation. As the inscription on their gravestone in the nave of the cathedral has been inaccurately given by Prince and Polwhele, we now subjoin a correct copy :—

> "Here lieth the body of THOMAS FLAY, Alderman,
> sometime Mayor of this citie of Exon,
> who departed this life the second day of July, 1634.
> Here also lyeth the body of ELIZABETH FLAY,
> his wife, who departed this life
> the 20th day of November, 1673,
> in the 86th yeare of her age."

Below is his coat of arms—Ermine on a pale azure, three doves argent.

This charitable lady gave to the Chamber of Exeter a silver gilt bason and ewer, parcel gilt.

3. HUGH CROSSING, A.D. 1621, æt. 55, founder of St. John's Hospital.[8]

4. The portrait of a nobleman, taken in 1618, æt. 66. The person represented is open to question. It may represent William Compton, Lord Northampton, elected High Steward of Exeter, June 1615, and created Earl of Northampton, 2nd August, 1618. Or it may be Thomas Lord Howard, Earl of Suffolk, made Lord High Steward 1st June, 1615 (Cartulary of St. John's Hospital).[9]

5. SIR BENJAMIN OLIVER, knighted when mayor by King Charles II., 23rd July, 1671, on his passing through Exeter on his road from Dartmouth to London. His marriage licence, with Jane Richards of Dunkswell, spinster, is dated on 8th February following.

---

[8] Alderman Francis Crossing was buried in the Cathedral 7th Nov. 1638.

[9] Some have thought that it was Charles Howard, Earl of Nottingham, Lord High Admiral of England; but this is not likely. It may be Thomas Lord Howard de Walden, created Earl of Suffolk in 1603, 1st James I. Obiit 28th May, 1626. Qy. if painted by Nicholas Hillyard who died in 1619?

THE GUILDHALL. 221

Died 2nd November, 1672, æt. 71, and his will was proved by his son and executor, Benjamin Oliver, on 27th of the same month and year. He lived in the house on Fore-street Hill now occupied by Mr. Davey, oil and colourman ; his country-house was at Exwick. Quære, if painted by W. Gandy ?

NICHOLAS SPICER, A.D. 1610, æt. 78. Not now in the collection. This portrait is, or lately was, in the hall at Courtlands, and was presented to the family as one of the first acts of the Town Council after passing the Reform Bill. But the property has lately passed out of the family.

Before quitting the Guildhall we may observe,

1. That payments between the citizens in ancient times were often made, for greater publicity, between the four benches or forms here, " *inter quatuor bancos seu scamna Gihaldiæ.*" [1]

2. That to recover possession of a free tenement, or to receive arrears of rent, it was customary for the claimant to produce seven turfs in court, one at each successive law term, at the end of which, after public proclamation to show cause to the contrary, and none sufficient appearing, the mayor's bailiffs put the claimant in possession, or saw justice done him, by giving him tenure of the premises for one year and a day ; at the expiration of which, if the debtor does not appear and make full satisfaction, then the fee of the tenement was adjudged to the creditor.

---

[1] Fol. 19 :—John Grubbi in the early part of the 13th century received for the sale of some property to the Hospital quatuor marcas argenti in Gihaldia, Exon, inter quatuor scamna." Ibid. :—Tiphania, relict of Hamelin the goldsmith received 5 marks and a half in Gihaldia, Exon, inter quatuor scamna." Fol. 24 :—" Serlo, Archdeacon of Exeter (made our first Dean in 1225), paid to Richard Horwude duas marcas argenti inter quatuor scamna Gihalde Exon." Fol. 32 :—" Philip Fitzralph received 21 marks inter quatuor Banches Gyhall die Lune ante Festum S. Margarete Virginis (July), 1251."

Deeds of conveyance of property were sometimes sealed, delivered, and confirmed here ; v. g. Lucas de Culums about the year 1220.

222 HISTORY OF EXETER.

3. The wills of citizens were frequently proved in the Mayor's Court, certainly up to the reign of Henry VIII.; even the wills of clergymen holding houses in Exeter, viz., the wills of John Hardy, clerk, in April, 1349, and of William Combe, clerk, 25th November, 1354.[2]

When Cleaveland published his Genealogical History of the Courtenay Family, in 1735, the arms of Henry, Marquess of Exeter, were in a window of the Council Chamber (p. 254).

CITY SWORDS AND CAP OF MAINTENANCE.

When King Edward IV. visited Exeter, on 14th April, 1740, he presented his sword to the city. This sword, covered with black crape, was formerly borne before the mayor in the procession on the 30th of January. King Henry VII.,[3] at his visit here, 7th October, 1497, gave his sword also, with a cap of maintenance, for the vigorous resistance the citizens made to Perkin Warbeck's army. A new scabbard was provided for King Henry the Seventh's in 1634, according to Izacke, who seems to intimate that a new cap of maintenance was made at the same time; but the former is merely covered with new embroidered velvet. The Act Book on 13th May, 1624, records an order to provide a new hat for the swordbearer, either at London or elsewhere, of a comely fashion as it is now used in London or Bristow. On 6th July, 1843, Sir Samuel Meyrick saw these swords, in company with the late Mr. Pitman Jones, General Meyrick, Captain Cumming, and the writer; and afterwards expressed his opinion that they were the only swords of our early English

---

[2] [These and other customs of Exeter, detailed in Izacke's 'Exeter,' are similar to those of London, Winchester, and many other cities.]

[3] The king was at Taunton on the 4th, arrived at Tiverton on 6th Oct., and at Exeter the 7th, where he remained till the 3rd Nov., when he went to Ottery. See Privy Purse expenses of Henry VII., Bentley's Excerpta Historica, page 3.

THE GUILDHALL.

kings in existence. The present mounting of that of Edward IV. was made in the time of King Charles II., when the sword was put in mourning to be carried on the anniversary of his father's martyrdom. The other was altered in King James the First's time, as is evident from one of his gold coins appearing on the pommel. The mayor's cap, said to have been given by King Henry VII., was covered with crimson velvet when the sheath was made for the sword of Edward IV., in the latter part of the 17th century. The original cap, made of black felt, is still inside the velvet one. On the 6th November, 1634, an order was given for a new cap of maintenance, "as they use in London." It appears that William Birdall, being discharged from his office of swordbearer on 24th March, 1641-2, with a pension of 10*l.*, his successor, Robert Bletchinden, found neither cap nor sword; for on 26th July, 1642, it appears that Mr. Sheriff White brought into this House the *blade* of a new sword, and on information that the late sword-bearer had converted the old cap of maintenance to his own use, it was ordered that his pension be denied until he make satisfaction for the same. On 6th January, 1651-2, another hat was ordered for the swordbearer to be by him worn at such time chiefly as he waits on Mr. Mayor, and not otherwise. Another hat and a satin doublet were voted on 22nd December, 1668. On 9th March, 1685-6, the Receiver was ordered by the Council to procure a beaver hat for Mr. Swordbearer, and therein to lay out the sum of 4*l.*, or thereabout. So that we are now no longer in a condition to determine as to the originality of either cap or sword.

After much altercation between the Dean and Chapter, and the Mayor and Chamber, it was at length agreed, on 16th July, 1708, that if Divine Service should have commenced before the mayor's arrival at the cathedral, then the royal sword was to be dropped

224   HISTORY OF EXETER.

at the entrance of the choir, and the cap of maintenance to be taken off; but otherwise the sword was to
be carried erect, and the cap of maintenance be worn
before the mayor on entering into and coming out of the
choir, as had been used for some time past; and that
convenient places be appointed and made for placing
the sword and cap of maintenance before the mayor
and his successors, or near their right side, during
Divine Service.

The four sergeants at mace wear their ancient silver
collars, and bear their handsome silver-gilt maces of
George the Second's time before the mayor on court
days.   Order was given by the Chamber on 20th
October, 1730, to pay for " the new maces."

The following description of the city seals will perhaps interest the reader :—

1. *Common Seal.*—A circular seal, displaying an
edifice, possibly intended to represent a council-house
or guildhall, of an uncouth and fantastic style of architecture so greatly resembling the Chinese as to render
it difficult, if not impossible, to give an adequate description of it.   This edifice, standing in the back-
ground, is thrown open to view from between two
lofty circular embattled towers, each surmounted by a
pennon, connected by a very low parapet, and termi-
nating, on each side, an embattled wall, in each portion
of which is a recess containing a cross fleurée, and
over each portion is a key erect; the whole device
being surmounted by a representation of the sun between a planet, on the right, and a crescent, on the
left of it.   In the exergue is a fleur-de-lis between two
dragons passant respecting each other.   Inscription, in
a circle—" SIGILLVM . CIVITATIS . EXONIE ;" preceded
by a Calvary cross.   On the reverse—

" + WILL' . PRVDVM . ME . DEDIT . CIVITATI . EXONIE.
    CVJUS . ANIME . PROPITIETUR . DEVS . AMN."

THE GUILDHALL. 225

The handle of the matrix is like a fleur-de-lis, and is inscribed—" LUCAS . ME . FECIT." All the letters are Roman capitals. Quære, if this William Prudum or Prodom be the founder of St. Alexias' Hospital, behind St. Nicholas' Priory, A.D. 1170 ?

2. *The Mayor's Seal of Office.*—An oval one. In a Gothic niche and canopy of elegant design and elaborate workmanship, composed of stall-work and pinnacles, including a trefoil arch crowned by a pyramidal weather-moulding enriched with crockets and a bold finial, is the half figure, from the waist upwards, of an archbishop, habited in a chasuble, and wearing a mitre of great height issuing from a ducal coronet, uplifting in his right hand a church, and in his left holding an archiepiscopal cross. The figure stands behind a low parapet of masonry, in the centre of which is a doorway of very minute dimensions, having a pair of folding-doors thrown wide open. In each of the two interstices, between the pinnacles and the crown of the arch, is a star. In base, and under an arch, in each of the spandrils of which is a similar star, is the head of a lion or leopard crowned with a ducal coronet. On the right of the niche is a sword erect, and on the left are two keys erect, accosted. Inscription, in a circle— " S' . MAIORATVS . CIVITATIS . EXONIE."

3. *The Bailiff's* (or Provost's) *Seal.*—An octagonal one, representing an embattled tower of three stories, with a round-headed arch of entrance, and the gate closed, over which are two other similar arches, with a trefoil window between them. Above the tower is a lion passant between two banners displayed on the extremities of the battlement. Connected with the tower is a line of embattled wall, ranging and parallel with the first floor only, and unsupported by anything beneath it. On each side the tower, in chief, a star ; in base, a lion passant. Inscription, in a circle—

Q

226

HISTORY OF EXETER.

" s' . PREPOSITORVM . CIVITATIS . DE . EXONIA," preceded by a Calvary cross.

4. Another seal, (originally a seal of the staple) was
occasionally used by the mayor at a later period. I
find it appendant to a bond of 3rd January, 1528. The
device is,—On a diapered ground a castle triple-towered,
having a large gateway in the centre tower, with a
portcullis raised, and under it a lion couchant, with a
fleur-de-lis in base beneath the castle. The inscription,
in a circle, is—" s' . MAIORIS . STAPVLE . CIVITATIS .
EXON." See Weever, p. 341–342.

CHAPTER IV.

LISTS OF MAYORS, RECORDERS, SHERIFFS, TOWN CLERKS, CHAMBERLAINS, SWORDBEARERS, AND MEMBERS OF PARLIAMENT, OF EXETER.

MAYORS.

FROM the Conquest until the reign of King John,
the chief officer of Exeter was called Wic-reeve, Port-
reeve, Præpositus, Provost; but no records exist to
enable us to furnish a series. William Hoel held the
office of provost during several years of King Henry
the Second's reign.

We have met with—

1. Johannes, filius Theobaldi, præpositus.

2. Herbertus, filius Rogeri, præpositus.

3. Wilielmus, præpositus, 21st February, 1159–60.

4. William Hoel, præpositus civitatis Exon, with his
chaplain Baldwin.

5. Ralph Osbert, præpositus in 1170.

6. Gilbert Boschet, præpositus.

LIST OF MAYORS.

King John granted to the city a mayor, who was assisted by two officers called provosts. This arrangement continued until 1258, when another was added. Five years later the number was increased to four, one of whom was to be appointed receiver of the rents, issues, and profits of the body. The name of "provosts" was afterwards changed for stewards ("seneschali"); but their court, in which the mayor presided, has retained the name of the Provost's Court. Both mayor and stewards had their proper seals.

Formerly a residence was attached to the mayor for the time being. John Heath, Esq. agreed to sell his house in High Street at the corner of Gandy Street in May, 1759, and the purchase was concluded in July that year for 600*l*.

In the Memorials of Exeter (improperly described in the title-page as being originally collected by Richard Izacke, when nearly all that is valuable in them is borrowed from the MS. history of John Hoker) the series of mayors commences with the year 1200, assigning seven consecutive years of mayoralty to Henry Rifford, and the five following to John Fitz-Robert; upon what authority we cannot discover.

The custom of the city was to elect a mayor yearly on Monday next before Michaelmas. By charter of 10th July (13th Hen. VII.), 1498, the mayor is not to be re-elected for two successive years. Since the Reform Bill of 1836, elections of mayor, sheriffs, and other officers take place on 9th November every year.

The following list has been carefully drawn up from original records :—

The first mayor, a nameless one, we have met with in the Close Rolls (seventh year of King John, 1206); and again, between the year 1210 and 1216, in Eudo de Bello Campo's, or Beauchamp's, Shrievalty of Devon we meet with—

Q 2

228   HISTORY OF EXETER.

William Dirling, whose provosts were Roger Fitz-Henry and Nicholas Gervase. John Turburn[1] and Thomas de Gatepath[2] also were mayors unnoticed by Izacke.

*Those marked * are from Hoker.*

1216 Walter Turburt.*
  17 Roger Fitzhenry.*
  18 Walter Gervase.*
  19 Walter Turburt.*
1220 Walter Turburt.
  21 Roger Fitzhenry.*
  22 Roger Fitzhenry.*
  23 Philip Dyer.
  24 Walter Turburt.*
  25 Walter Turburt.*
  26 Roger Fitzhenry.*
  27 Hilary Blund.
  28 Walter Turburt.*
  29 Roger Fitzhenry.*
1230 Roger Fitzhenry.*
  31 Walter Gervase.*
  32 Walter Turburt.*
  33 Hilary Blund.*
  34 Martin Rof.*
  35 Roger Fitzhenry.*
  36 Walter Turburt.
  37 Martin Rof.*
  38 Martin Rof.*
  39 Walter Gervase.*
1240 Martin Rof and Philip Dyer.
  41 Martin Rof.*
  42 Martin Rof.*
  43 Martin Rof.*
  44 Adam Rifford.*
  45 Martin Rof.*
  46 Martin Rof.
  47 Adam de Rifford, Pentecost and Dec.
  48 Adam de Rifford.
  49 Walter Hastement.*
1250 Adam Rifford.*
  51 Adam Rifford.*
  52 Martin Rof, Oct.

1253 Martin Rof, Dec.
  54 Adam de Rifford, Easter.
  55 John de Okeston, Aug.
  56 Philip Dyer, June, and Walter de Okeston, Mich.
  57 Philip Dyer.
  58 Philip Dyer.
  59 Nicholas de Ilchester, Dec.
1260 Philip Dyer, Dec.
  61 Hilary White.
  62 Walter de Okeston, *Izacke.*
  63 Nicholas Ilchester, Dec.
  64 Philip Dyer.*
  65 Walter Okeston.*
  66 Walter de Oxton.*
  67 Nicholas Ilchester and Walter Chawe.*
  68 Walter de Okeston, Dec.
  69 Walter de Okeston, June.
1270 Martin Derling.*
  71 Walter de Okeston, Mich.
  72 Martin Dirling.
  73 Roger Beynim.
  74 Martin Dirling.
  75 Alfred de Porta, July.
  76 Alured de Porta.
  77 Alfred de Porta.
  78 Alfred de Porta, Martin Dirling, 25th July.
  79 Alfred de Porta, Aug.
1280 John Feneton.*
  81 Alfred de Porta.*
  82 Martin Dirling.*
  83 Alfred de Porta.*
  84 Alfred de Porta.*
  85 David Taylor.
  86 Richard de Aleyne.

---

[1] *John* Turburn occurs Mayor, circ. 1230.
  William Hastement was Mayor when Hilary White and Walter Probus were his Provosts.

[2] Thomas de Gatepath occurs Mayor with his Provosts Alfred de Porta, Richard Tantifer, in a dateless deed.

LIST OF MAYORS. 229

1287 David le Tailleur.
88 John South, 10th Aug.
89 Richard Aleyn,* we find Martin Dirling. *
1290 Richard Aleyn.
91 John Soth.
92 Richard Tantifer.*
93 William de Gatepath.
94 John South.
95 John South, Soth.
96 John South, April, William Tantifer, Oct.
97 Walter Tantifer, Feb.
98 Walter Tantifer, Dec.
99 William Gatepath.*
1300 John Horn.
1 William Tantifer.*
2 William Tantifer.
3 Roger Whetene.
4 Roger le Whetene.*
5 Roger Beynim.*
6 Roger Beynim, Benyn.
7 Roger Whetene.
8 Richard Seler.
9 Roger Whetene.
1310 Walter Tantifer.*
11 Walter Tantifer.
12 Walter Langdon.
13 William Gatepath.
14 Roger Beynin.
15 Roger Benym.
16 Philip Lovecock.
17 Philip Lovecock.
18 Roger Beynin at Easter; Robert Wotton, Whitsuntide.
19 Philip Lovecock.
1320 Roger Whetene.
21 Philip Lovecock.
22 Philip Lovecock.
23 Robert de Wotton.
24 Robert Wotton.
25 Robert Wotton and Philip Lovecock, Sept.
26 Philip Lovecock, Oct.
27 Richard le Seler.

1228 Richard le Seler, Oct.
29 Philip Lovecock.*
1330 Philip Lovecock.
31 Philip Lovecock.
32 Philip Lovecock, Sept., and Martin le Ken in July 33.
33 Thomas Gervays.
34 Martin le Ken and Thomas Litchfield.
35 Hen. Hughton.*
36 Hen. Hughton, 29th Sept.
37 Hen. de Hughton, 25th Feb.
38 Hen. Hughton.
39 Thomas Lichfied.*
1340 Hen. de Hughton.
41 Thomas Fourbour at Michaelmas, 1342.
42 Henry de Hugheton.
43 Thos. de Fourbour.*
44 Thos. Fourbour.
45 Henry de Hugheton.*
46 Henry de Hugheton, Dec.
47[a] Henry de Hugheton.*
48 Thomas Fourbour.
49 Robert Noble in May, and Robert Bridport.
1350 Henry de Hughton, July, Robt. Bridport.
51 Robert Bridport.
52 Robert Bridport.*
53 John Spicer, Jan., Robert Bridport.
54 John Gist.
55 John Gist.
56 John Gist, 24th Dec., Robert Noble.
57 Robert Bridport, Feb., Aug.
58 John Spicer.
59 Robert Noble.
1360 Roger le Wetheyn.
61 John Spicer.
62 Roger Plente.

[a] "1347. Mem.—It was ordered by a common consent of the Mayor and Commonalty that from henceforth none should be chosen nor admitted to be a Mayor except he be a wise, grave, sober, and honest man, and have been tried a steward of the city for one whole year."—Hoker's MS. p. 277.

230 HISTORY OF EXETER.

1363 John Gist.
64 John Gist.*
65 Nich. Taverner.
66 Nich. Brittestonwe.
67 John Gist.
68 Warin Bailif.
69 Roger Plente.
1370 ———
71 Martin Batyshull in Oct.
72 Roger Plenty.
73 John Gist.
74 Roger Plente.
75 Robert Wilford, Nov.
76 John Grey.
77 Robert Wilford.
78 John Atwill.
79 Robert Wilford, 2nd April, John Atwill, 3rd July.
1380 Robert Wilford.
81 John Grey, Feb., and John Nymet, Dec.
82 John Nymet in Dec.
83 Robt. Wilford, Dec.
84 Robt. Wilford.
85 Adam Scut.
86 Robt. Wilford.
87 Robt. Wilford, June.
88 Roger Beyn.
89 Richard Bozoun.
1390 Robt. Wilford, Feast of St. Mark, 25th April, 12th Rich. II.
91 Robt. Wilford.
92 Richard Bosin, 7th Sept.
93 Richard Boson.
94 Robert Wilford in the summer.
95 Rob. Wilford in 1396, Sept., 19th Richard II.
96 Simon Grendon, Aug.
97 John Talbot.
98 Adam Scot.
99 Adam Scot and John Grey.
1400 John Grey.
1 William Wilford.
2 William Oke.
3 ———
4 Henry Hull, 6th Jan.
5 William Wilford, Simon Grendon.
6 John Battyn, March.

1407 William Wilford.
8 Adam Scut, Easter.
9 Richard Bozon.
1410 Richard Boson.
11 William Wilford.
12 Adam Scut.
13 Peter Sturt in Oct., Henry Hull.
14 Peter Sturt.
15 Thos. Easton, Peter Sturt in Nov.
16 Thomas Easton.
17 John Batyn.
18 John Coke.
19 Thomas Easton.
1420 John Batyn.
21 Thomas Easton.
22 John Coke, August.
23 Thomas Eston, July.
24 John Batyn, John Coke, Nov.
25 John Coke, 25th March, Robt. Veysy, Oct. 19.
26 Robt. Veysy, Feb., Aug. 4th, Henry VI., and John Cook, Sept.
27 Thomas Easton.
28 John Hulle.
29 John Shillingford.
1430 John Shillingford.
31 William Cook, John Hull in March.
32 John Hull, Rich. Boson, 3rd April.
33 John Salter.
34 Thomas Coke.
35 William Frost.
36 William Coke, Thos. Coke, 20th Feb., 15th Henry VI.
37 John Coteler.
38 John Hull.
39 Benedict Drewe, 21st June.
1440 William Cook.
41 William Upton, Aug.
42 Thomas Cook.
43 Hugh Germin.*
44 Hugh Germin.
45 John Shillingford.
46 John Hull.

LIST OF MAYORS.

1447 John Shillingford.
  48 John Shillingford.
  49 John Coteler.
1450 Hugh Germyn.
  51 Hugh Germyn and Wm. Crymell.
  52 Hugo Germyn.
  53 Walter Pope. .
  54 John Germyn.
  55 Richard Oreynge.
  56 Hugo Germyn at Michael-mas.
  57 William Duke.
  58 John Kelly.
  59 Rob. or Rich. Druell.
1460 William Duke.
  61 John Kelly.
  62 Hugo Germin.*
  63 Richard Druell.
  64 Hugh Germin.
  65 Richard Druell.
  66 Hugh Germyn.
  67 Hugh Germyn.
  68 Thomas Calwodeley.
  69 John Hamlyn.
1470 Robert Smith.
  71 Hugo Germyn, 9th Jan., 49th Henry VI.
  72 Richard Geffray.
  73 Richard Clerk.
  74 Richard Ronewyll.
  75 Hugo Germyn.
  76 John Oreynge.
  77 John Atwill.
  78 John Kelly.
  79 William Obley.
1480 John Atwill.
  81 Thomas Calwodeley.
  82 Roger Worth.
  83 Richard Druell.
  84 Matthew Jubbe, John Atwill.
  85 John Atwill, 15th Jan., 1st Richard III.
  86 Robert Russell.
  87 Thomas Calwodeley.
  88 Robert Newton.
  89 Richard Clerk.
1490 Ste. Ruyggeway, June.
  91 John Hulle.*
  92 Robert Chubb.

1493 John Atwill.
  94 John Colshill.
  95 William Obeley.*
  96 John Calwodeley.
  97 John Atwill.
  98 William Frost.
  99 Richard Undey.
1500 Nicholas Hamlyn.
  1 Walter Yorke.
  2 John Calwodeley.
  3 Walter Champeneys.
  4 Rob. Newton, John Danaster, and Wm. Frost, 10th May.
  5 Thomas Andrew.
  6 William Crugge.
  7 Richard Huet.
  8 John Calwodeley, 1st Mar. 1508-9, John Lympany.
  9 J. Lympany and J. Buck-nam.
1510 Thomas Andrew.
  11 William Wilford and Wm. Crugge.
  12 Richard Symons.
  13 Richard Hewet.
  14 John More.
  15 William Crugge.
  16 John Bucknam.
  17 Thomas Hunt.
  18 William Crugge.
  19 Geoffrey Lewis.
1520 John Bradmore.
  21 John Noseworthy.
  22 Richard Duke.
  23 John Symons and Thomas Hunt.
  24 William Hurste.
  25 William Benet.
  26 Henry Hamlyn.
  27 John Britnall.
  28 Robert Buller.
  29 Robert Hooker.
1530 John Blackaller.
  31 Gilbert Kirk.
  32 William Peryam.
  33 Richard Martyn.
  34 John Britnall.
  35 William Hurste.
  36 John Blackaller.
  37 Thomas Hunt.

232 HISTORY OF EXETER.

1538 Henry Hamlyn.
39 Gilbert Kirk.
1540 Thomas Spurway.
41 William Buckenam.
42 John Buller.
43 Robert Toker.
44 Thomas Prestwode.
45 William Hurste.
46 John Britnall.
47 John Midwinter.
48 John Blackaller.
49 John Tuckfield.
1550 Thomas Prestwode.
51 William Hurste.
52 William Tothill.
53 William Smith.
54 John Midwinter.
55 Morice Levermore.
56 Walter Staplehill.
57 John Petre.
58 John Buller.
59 Robert Midwinter.
1560 John Blackall.
61 William Hurst.
62 John Peter.
63 John Peryam.
64 Maurice Levermore.
65 John Wolcott.
66 Thomas Richardson.
67 John Smith.
68 Robert Chaff.
69 William Chaple.
1570 Simon Knight.
71 Thomas Bruerton.
72 John Peryam, John Blackaller.
73 William Tryevet.
74 Nicholas Martin.
75 John Peter.
76 Thomas Prestwood, Robt. Chaffe.
77 George Perryman.
78 Richard Prouze.
79 William Chappell and Simon Knight.
1580 Thomas Bruerton.
81 Thomas Martyn.
82 Michael Germyn.

1583 Geoffry Thomas.
84 John Davy.
85 Nicholas Martin.
86 George Smithe.
87 John Periam.
88 Thomas Chappel.
89 Richard Prous.
1590 William Martin.
91 Michael Germyn.
92 Nicholas Spicer.
93 Thomas Spicer.
94 John Davey.
95 John Chappel.
96 John Levermore.
97 George Smith.
98 John Periam.
99 John Howell.
1600 William Martin.
1 Thomas Walker.
2 Richard Beavis, to 26th Aug., Wm. Martyn.
3 Nicholas Spicer.
4 John Davy.
5 Henry Hull.
6 Richard Dorchester.
7 Sir Geo. Smyth, Knight.
8 John Prous.
9 Hugh Crossing.
1610 Walter Borowe.
11 John Lant.
12 Wm. Newcombe.
13 Geoffry Waltham.[4]
14 Thomas Walker.
15 John Marshall.
16 John Shere.
17 Ignatius Jurden.
18 Thomas Martin.
19 John Prouse.
1620 Hugh Crossynge.
21 Walter Borowe.
22 John Modyford.
23 John Gupwill.
24 Thomas Crossing.
25 Thomas Walker.
26 John Tailler.
27 John Acland.
28 John Lynne.
29 Nicholas Spicer.

[4] Geoffry Waltham died 6th April, 1626, as I found on his gravestone in the nave of Exminster Church.

LIST OF MAYORS. 233

1630 Thomas Flay.
31 Nicholas Martin.
32 John Hakewell.
33 Gilbert Sweet.
34 Francis Crossing.
35 Adam Bennet.
36 Roger Mallock.
37 Thomas Crossing.
38 James Tucker.
39 Robert Walker.
1640 John Pennye.
41 Richard Saunders.
42 Christopher Clarke.
43 Sir Hugh Crocker, knighted by King Charles I.
44 Nich. Spicer.
45 John Cupper.
46 Walter White.
47 Adam Bennet.
48 James Gould.
49 Richard Crossing refused to act. Richard Saunders and Adam Bennet acted as Deputy Mayors.
1650 Richard Evans.
51 Richard Sweet.
52 Ralph Herman.
53 Simon Snow.
54 Richard Crossing.
55 Nicholas Brooking.
56 Thomas Ford.
57 James Pearse.
58 James Marshall.
59 Christopher Clarke.
1660 Christopher Lethbridge.
61 Henry Gandy.
62 John Martyn.
63 John Butter.
64 Alan Penny, Anthony Salter.
65 Nicholas Isacke.
66 John Acland.
67 Sir Thos. Walker, knighted on presenting an address.
68 George Tuthill.
69 Peter Hagedot.
1670 Sir Benjamin Oliver, knighted 23rd July, 1671.

1671 William Sandford.
72 Henry Gandy.
73 Isaac Mawditt.
74 Chris. Brodridge.
75 John Parr.
76 William Glyde.
77 George Tuthill.
78 William Sandford.
79 John Collyns.
1680 Henry Smith.
81 Isaac Mawditt.
82 Endymion Walker.
83 Christ. Brodridge.
84 James Walker.
85 Robert Dabynott.
86 George Saffin.
87 John Snell, 18th Oct. Sir Thos. Jefford, 14th Dec.; on 2nd Aug. 1688 he was a Knight.
88 Sir Thos. Jefford, Knight. Christopher Brodridge.
89 John Snell.
1690 Edward Cross.
91 Edward Seaward.
92 Christopher Coke.
93 John Gandy.
94 Robert Dabynott.
95 Gilbert Yarde.
96 Christopher Bale.
97 John Curson.
98 John Burell.
99 Joshua Hickman.
1700 John Snell.
1 John Cholwell.
2 John Gandy.
3 John Newcombe.
4 Gilbert Wood.
5 Thomas Baron.
6 Nicholas Wood.
7 Edward Daly.
8 Edward Spicer.
9 Edward Collins.
1710 Thomas Salter.
11 Josh. Hickman.
12 Jacob Rowe.
13 John Newcombe.
14 John Gandy.
15 William Sanford.
16 Nath. Dewdney.
17 Philip Pear.

234   HISTORY OF EXETER.

1718 John Burell.
  19 Thomas Coplestone.
1720 William Gandy.
  21 John Phillips.
  22 Thomas Salter.
  23 Philip Bussel.
  24 Humphrey Bawden.
  25 Anthony Tripe.
  26 Emanuel Hole.
  27 John Elston.
  28 Robert Lydston.
  29 William Stabback.
1730 Nathaniel Dewdney.
  31 Ethelred Davie.
  32 Richard Vivian.
  33 Samuel Symons.
  34 John Newcombe.
  35 Matthew Spry.
  36 Samuel Symons.
  37 Arthur Culme.
  38 Thomas Heath.
  39 Nicholas Blake.
1740 Nicholas Lee.
  41 William Newcombe.
  42 Nicholas Medland.
  43 Philip Elston.
  44 John Hawker.
  45 Francis Brayne.
  46 Matthew Spry.
  47 John Manley.
  48 Lewis Portbury.
  49 Thomas Heath.
1750 William Trosse.
  51 Nicholas Lee.
  52 Robert Dodge and Nicholas
     Lee.
  53 John Luckett.
  54 Nicholas Arthur.
  55 Lewis Portbury.
  56 William Trosse.
  57 Joseph Elliot.
  58 Richard Densham.
  59 Richard Jackson.
1760 Samuel Pierce.
  61 Samuel Dix, Francis
     Brayne.
  62 James Crossing.
  63 Edward Walker.
  64 Jacob Rowe.
  65 John Bussell.
  66 Humphry Hill.

1767 William Collins, James
     Crossing.
  68 Philip Dacie.
  69 Thomas Dodge.
1770 John Floud.
  71 Thomas Coffin.
  72 Gregory Jackson.
  73 Henry Kitson.
  74 John Dennis.
  75 John Eyles Pierce.
  76 Charles Edwards.
  77 Thomas Dodge.
  78 James Grant.
  79 Charles Furlong.
1780 Samuel Moore.
  81 Nicholas Brooke.
  82 John Bussel.
  83 William Ilbert.
  84 Benjamin Honeycombe
     Walker.
  85 George Westlake.
  86 Nathaniel Elias Cosserat.
  87 Richard Jenkins.
  88 Jonathan Burnet.
  89 William Bate.
1790 Edward Ragueneau.
  91 Reuben Phillips.
  92 John Pinhey.
  93 Richard Chamberlain.
  94 Richard Hart,
  95 John Balle.
  96 Charles Upham.
  97 John Brake.
  98 Joseph Gattey.
  99 Jonathan Worthy.
1800 Richard Jenkins.
   1 Thomas Floud.
   2 Charles Collyns.
   3 John Pinhey.
   4 Joseph Greenway.
   5 John Thomas Wright.
   6 Samuel White.
   7 Charles Collyns.
   8 Joseph Gattey.
   9 Edward Upham.
1810 John Hore.
  11 William Lee.
  12 Benjamin Wm. Johnson.
  13 Burnet Patch.
  14 John Hart.
  15 John William Williams.

LIST OF RECORDERS.

1816 Samuel White.
17 Charles Brake.
18 Thomas Floud again.
19 Henry Blackall.
1820 Robert Rogers Sanders.
21 George Galloway.
22 John Harris.
23 William Crockett.
24 Humphry Hill Pinhey.
25 William Payne.
26 John Hart.
27 Henry Blackall again.
28 John Haddy James.
29 Robt. Roger Sanders again.
1830 Paul Measor.[5]
31 William Kennaway.
32 Henry Blackall again.
33 Edward Woolmer.
34 Philip Chilwell Delagarde, who continued Mayor under the Reform Bill till
36 Samuel Kingdon was elected, 1st Jan. 1836.
37 William Kennaway again.
38 William John Playters Wilkinson.

1839 Edward Macgowan, M.D., ob. at Jerusalem, 5th Feb. 1860.
1840 William Drewe.
41 John Carew.
42 Charles Henry Turner.
43 William Page Kingdon.
44 Henry Hooper.
45 Edward Woolmer again.
46 Charles Brutton.
47 William Denis Moore.
48 Thomas Shapter.
49 Christopher Arden.
1850 Edward Andrew Sanders
51 William Wills Hooper.
52 William Wills Hooper again.
53 Robert Stribling Cornish.
54 John Daw.
55 John Daw again.
56 Thomas G. Norris.
57 William Buckingham.
58 Henry Hooper again.
59 Thomas Tanner.
1860 Thomas E. Drake.
61 Frederick Franklin.

RECORDERS.

In old time some one of the city officers was accustomed to advise the courts and the mayor according to the laws of the land and the customs of the city. The increase of business led to the appointment of a Recorder, to be attendant upon the courts, and to advise the Mayor and Corporation in all matters of law. John Weeks, was chosen the first Recorder, in 1354. The following is a list of Recorders :—

1354 John Weeks, Esq.
1379 John Hull, Esq., with a fee of 3l. per annum.
1404 William Wynard, Esq.[1]
1453 Nicholas Radford, Esq.

---

[5] Paul Measor died 9th Oct., and was buried in the cemetery 13th. He was postmaster here 50 years.
[1] On resigning office he spent the residue of his days in his own alms-house, Magdalen Street (Hoker's MS. fol. 303.)

236　　　　HISTORY OF EXETER.

1454　John Moor, Esq., of Collumpton.
1468　Thomas Dowrish, Esq.
1479　William Huttesfeld, Esq., afterwards the King's Solicitor.
1482　Thomas Hext, Esq.
1496　William Burgoyn, Esq.
1498　Roger Holland, Esq.
1514　Sir Thomas Dennys, Knight, 14th Nov.　Ob. 18th February, 1560-1.
1544　John Harris, Esq., Sergeant-at-Law.
1548　Lewis Pollard, Esq.,[2] grandson of the Judge.
1554　Edmund Sture, Esq.
1558　John Charles, Esq.
1563　Jeffery Tothill, Esq.
1576　Sir Robert Dennys, Knight.　Ob. Bicton, 4th Sept. and was buried at Holcumb Burnell, 15th Sept. 1592, near his father, Sir Thomas Dennys.
1592　Edward Drew, Esq., Sergeant-at-Law, six weeks; afterwards Recorder of London.　Buried at Broadclist in 1600.
1593　John Hele, Esq., Sergeant-at-Law, 29th June.
1605　William Martin, Esq.　Ob. 7th, buried 12th April, 1617, at St. Petrock's.
1617　Nicholas Duck, Esq., 25th April.　Ob. 28th August, and was buried in the Cathedral, 9th Sept. 1628.
1628　Richard Waltham, Esq., resigned in 1632; was buried at Kenn, 4th March, 1636.
1632　Peter Ball, Esq., 21st August; afterwards Solicitor and Attorney-General, and knighted.　In the Civil War he was sequestered for his loyalty, 14th Feb. 1643.
1648　Edmund Prideaux, Esq., 2nd May, 1643, ejected 13th Nov. Ob. 19th August, 1659, and was buried at Ford Abbey.
1654　Thomas Bamfield, Esq.
1660　Sir Peter Ball, Knight, restored 11th Oct.; resigned 27th April, 1676.　Buried at Mamhead 4th September, 1680, æt. 82.
1676　Sir Thomas Carew, Knight.　Elect. 9th May.
1681　Edward Seymour, Esq.[3]　Elect. 6th Aug.
1684　[3]Thomas Gibbon, Esq.　Appointed by the Crown on the surrender of the City Charter.
1688　Hugh Westlake, Esq.
1689　Edward Seymour, Esq., restored.　Ob. 1707.
1707　Sir Nicholas Hooper, Knight, Sergeant-at-Law to the Queen. Buried at Barnstaple in 1731.
1728　John Belfield, Esq., Sergeant-at-Law, 21st Sept.
1751　John Cholwich, Esq.

---

[2] Lewis Pollard preceded Sir Thomas Dennys according to the Act Book, and resigned for a Judgeship of the Common Pleas.　His pension had been raised to £4.

[3] Sir Edward Seymour resigned the office, and in consequence of his earnest recommendation, John Beare was elected his successor the last day of Feb. 1682-3, but on 3rd July following Sir Edward Seymour was resworn into the office on Beare's free resignation.

LIST OF SHERIFFS.

1764 John Glynn, Esq., Sergeant-at-Law. Ob.16th September, 1779.
1779 John Heath, Esq., Sergeant-at-Law, el. 25th Sept.; afterwards, viz., 8th July, 1780, a Judge of the Common Pleas. Ob. 16th January, 1816, æt. 83.
1780 Stephen Hawtrey, Esq. Elect. 7th August.
1794 Charles Fanshawe, Esq., 31st July.
1814 William Courtenay, Esq., M.P. Elect. 23rd June; resigned 20th Dec., 1820. Afterwards Earl of Devon.
1820 Thomas Moore Stevens, Esq. Elect. 30th Dec.; died 14th, and buried at Little Torrington, 19th Jan. 1832, æt. 49.
1832 John Taylor Coleridge, Esq., 26th Jan.; afterwards a Judge of the King's Bench, in March, 1835.
1835 Francis James Newman Rogers, Esq., Q.C., 27th May. By the 5th and 6th Wm. IV., c. 76, the power of appointing the Recorder was taken from the Corporation and vested in the Crown. Ob. 19th July, 1851, æt. 59.
1851 John Alexander Kinglake, Esq., Sergeant-at-Law, July ; on whose resignation
1856 John Shapland Stock, Esq. was appointed, 28th Nov., and sworn into office on 3rd Jan. 1857.

SHERIFFS.

The most eminent dignity from the Conquest to the 11th Edw. III. was the Earl or Count; and of ancient time earls were the rulers or governors of shires or counties under the king, having committed to them from the king the same charge and custody of the county which the Vice-comes, or Sheriff, now has.

A sheriff being the governor of a county, it is obvious Exeter could not have a separate sheriff until it was erected into a county, which was done by King Henry VIII., 23rd August, in the 29th year of his reign, A.D. 1537; before which time Exeter was under the control of the sheriff of Devon; but since its erection into a county it has been subject to its own sheriff, like other counties.

The following is a list of the sheriffs of Exeter, from the first appointment of that officer to the present time :—

1537 William Burgoyn.	1539 Robert Tooker.
38 William Buckenam.	1540 William Hurst.

HISTORY OF EXETER.

1541 John Midwinter.
42 Thomas Prestwood.
43 John Woolcott.
44 John Waye and John Helmer.
45 John Maynards.
46 Nicholas Lymett.
47 John Tuckfield.
48 John Drake.
49 William Tothill.
1550 William Smith.
51 John Hurst.
52 Moris Levermore.
53 John Peryam.
54 Walter Staplehill.
55 Griffith Amerideth.
56 John Peter.
57 Robert Midwinter.
58 John Blackall.
59 Richard Prestwood.
1560 Thomas Richardson.
61 John Dyer.
62 Hugh Pope
63 Edward Bridgman.
64 Thomas Richardson.
65 John Smith.
66 Robert Chaff.
67 Edward Lymett.
68 Richard Hellyar.
69 Simon Knight.
1570 Thomas Bruerton.
71 William Trivett.
72 Nicholas Martin.
73 Thomas Prestwood.
74 George Peryman.
75 John Pope.
76 Richard Prowse.
77 Thomas Martin.
78 Henry Ellicott.
79 Jeffery Thomas.
1580 Thomas Raymond.
81 John Davy.
82 John Peryam.
83 George Smith.
84 William Martin.
85 John Levermore.
86 Thomas Chappell.
87 Nicholas Spicer.
88 Philip Yard.
89 Thomas Spicer.
1590 John Chappell.

1591 Richard Beavys.
92 John Howell.
93 Thomas Walker.
94 Henry Hull.
95 Christopher Spicer.
96 Richard Dorchester.
97 Alexander Mayn.
98 William Spicer.
99 John Prowse.
1600 Thomas Edwards.
1 John Ellicott.
2 Walter Borough.
3 Hugh Crossing.
4 Alexander Germyn.
5 William Newcomb.
6 John Lant.
7 Jeffery Waltham.
8 Robert Parr.
9 John Marshall.
1610 John Sheer.
11 Ignatius Jurdain.
12 Thomas Martin.
13 John Modyford.
14 John Gupwill.
15 Thomas Crossing.
16 John Tayler.
17 Thomas Amy.
18 Peter Collaton.
19 John Acland.
1620 George Pyle.
21 John Lynn.
22 Thomas Wakeman.
23 John Jurdain.
24 Nicholas Spicer.
25 Thomas Flay.
26 Nicholas Martin.
27 John Hakewill.
28 Gilbert Sweet.
29 Francis Crossing.
1630 Adam Bennett.
31 Roger Mallock.
32 John Crocker.
33 James Tucker.
34 Robert Walker.
35 John Hayn.
36 John Penny.
37 Richard Saunders.
38 Thomas Tooker.
39 Christopher Clark
1640 Henry Battishill.
41 Walter White.

LIST OF SHERIFFS. 239

1642 Richard Yeo.
43 John Cupper.
44 Richard Yeo.
45 John Martin.
46 Ralph Herman.
47 Richard Crossing.
48 Nicholas Broking.
49 Francis Lippingcott.
1650 Richard Sweet.
51 James Pearse.
52 James Marshall.
53 Thomas Ford.
54 Christopher Clark.
55 Christopher Lethbridge.
56 Bernard Bartlett.
57 Henry Prigg.
58 Henry Gandy.
59 Walter Deeble.
1660 William Bruen.
61 Nicholas Isacke.
62 John Acland.
63 Isaac Mawditt and Stephen Olivean.
64 Thomas Walker.
65 George Tuthill.
66 Peter Hagedot.
67 James Slade.
68 Benjamin Oliver.
69 William Sanford.
1670 Isaac Mawditt.
71 Christopher Brodridg.
72 John Parr.
73 John Collins.
74 William Glyde, jun.
75 Andrew Quash.
76 Henry Smyth.
77 Christopher Bale.
78 Endymion Walker.
79 Robert Dabynot.
1680 George Saffin.
81 John Snell.
82 John Carwythen.
83 John Colwell.
84 Edward Cross.
85 Malachi Pyne.
86 Humphrey Leigh.
87 Christopher Coke, removed by order of King James, and Rich. Cunningham appointed in his room.

1688 Edward Seaward.
89 John Gandy.
1690 John Curson.
91 Gilbert Yard.
92 Richard Peryam.
93 John Burel.
94 William Bolithoe.
95 Daniel Ivie.
96 Isaac Gibbs.
97 Joshua Hickman.
98 George Yard.
99 Edward Dally.
1700 John Gandy.
1 John Newcomb.
2 Oliver Mustyn.
3 Thomas Baron.
4 Edward Spicer.
5 Nicholas Wood.
6 Edward Collings.
7 Thomas Salter.
8 Jacob Rowe.
9 John Pyle.
1710 Nathaniel Dowdney.
11 William Sanford.
12 Philip Peer.
13 William Gandy.
14 Nathaniel Bussell.
15 Thomas Copleston.
16 John Philips.
17 Philip Bussell.
18 John Elston.
19 Arthur Culme.
1720 Anthony Trype.
21 Humphrey Bawden.
22 Emanuel Hole.
23 Robert Lydstone.
24 William Stabback.
25 Etheldred Davy.
26 Richard Vyvyan.
27 Samuel Symonds.
28 John Newcombe.
29 John Haddy.
1730 Jonathan Waad.
31 Matthew Spry.
32 Thomas Heath.
33 Benjamin Pear.
34 Joseph Cheeke.
35 Nicholas Blake.
36 John Score.
37 Nicholas Lee.
38 Nicholas Medland.

240

HISTORY OF EXETER.

1739 William Newcombe.
1740 Philip Elston.
41 John Trevethick and John Thomas Heath.
42 John Hawker.
43 Francis Brayne.
44 Nicholas Medland.
45 John Manley.
46 Lewis Portbury.
47 Robert Dodge.
48 William Trosse.
49 John Luckett.
1750 Nicholas Arthur.
51 Charles Northcote
52 Robert Cornish.
53 George Lethbridge.
54 Joseph Elliott.
55 Richard Densham.
56 Richard Jackson.
57 Samuel Pierce.
58 Samuel Dix.
59 James Crossing.
1760 Edward Walker.
61 Jacob Rowe.
62 John Bussell
63 Humphrey Hill.
64 Edward Walker.
65 Philip Dacie.
66 Thomas Dodge.
67 John Floud.
68 Thomas Coffin.
69 Gregory Jackson.
1770 Henry Kitson.
71 Thomas Willcocks, who died 9th April, 1772, and Henry Kitson elected 11th April for the rest of the year.
72 John Dennis.
73 John Eyles Pierce.
74 Charles Edwards.
75 John Codrington.
76 James Grant.
77 Charles Furlong.
78 Samuel Moore.
79 Nicholas Brooke.
1780 John Bussell.
81 William Ilbert.
82 Benjamin Honeycombe Walker.
83 George Westlake.

1784 Nathaniel Elias Cosserat.
85 Richard Jenkins.
86 Jonathan Burnett.
87 William Bate.
88 Edward Ragueneau.
89 Reuben Phillips.
1790 John Pinhey.
91 Richard Chamberlain.
92 Richard Hart, jun.
93 John Balle.
94 Charles Upham.
95 John Brake.
96 Joseph Gattey.
97 Jonathan Worthy.
98 Benjamin Walkey.
99 Thomas Floud.
1800 Charles Collyns.
1 Samuel White.
2 Joseph Greenway.
3 Jonathan Worthy.
4 Samuel Trist.
5 William Bickford Jackson.
6 Joseph Gattey.
7 Edward Upham.
8 John Hore.
9 William Lee.
1810 Benjamin Wm. Johnson.
11 Burnet Patch.
12 John Hart.
13 John William Williams.
14 Robert Trewman.
15 Charles Brake.
16 Joshua Williams.
17 Henry Blackall.
18 Robert Rogers Sanders.
19 George Galloway.
1820 John Harris.
21 William Crockett.
22 Humphrey Hill Pinhey.
23 William Payne.
24 Charles Hamilton.
25 Henry Blackall.
26 John Haddy James.
27 John Harris.
28 Paul Measor.
29 William Kennaway.
1830 Henry Leslie Grove.
31 Edward Woolmer.
32 Philip Chilwell De La Garde.
33 Joseph Were.

LIST OF TOWN CLERKS.

1834-6 Charles Henry Turner.[1]
36 James Jones Tanner.[2]
36-7 John Hull Terrell.[3]
37-8 Joshua Hickman Stab-
back.
38-9 Daniel Bishop Davy
39-40 Richard Bastard.
1840-1 Henry Hooper.
41-2 William Kingdon.
42-3 William Hooper.
43-4 Benjamin Salter.
44-5 William Denis Moore.
45-6 Joseph Sheppard.
46-7 Henry Wilcocks Hooper
47-8 John Follett.

48-9 Thomas Floud.
1849-50 William Denis Moore.
1850-1 Frederick Franklin.
51-2 John Evomy Norman.
52-3 Thomas Edward Drake.
53-4 Joseph Sheppard.
54-5 Thomas George Norris.
55-6 Wm. Buckingham.
57-8 Christopher Arden.
58-9 Thomas Coulson Sanders.
Samuel Steele Perkins,
elected Sheriff 9th Nov.,
· 1858.
59-60 Augustus Drake, M.D.
60 Henry Sparks Bowden.

TOWN CLERKS.

The office of Town Clerk is of very great antiquity, and seems to have been coeval with the institution of Corporations, which required the assistance of a permanent officer to enter and keep the records of their proceedings, and to assist the mayor and other functionaries in the discharge of their corporate duties.

The list of Town Clerks, from 3rd Hen. VIII. (1511), is as follows :—

1511 John Clyff, elected 5th April.
1521 William Burgeyn, elected 14th August, on whose cession,
1538 Richard Hert, elected 23rd Dec.; on his resignation,
1574 Edward Hert, elected 11th Feb.; on whose cession,
1620 John Martyn, elected 22nd April.[4]
1624 Samuel Isacke, elected 4th May; deprived in 1647; reinstated
at the restoration of Monarchy; resigned shortly before his
death.   Buried at Ottery St. Mary, 14th Feb., 1681-2.
1647 John Farthing, elected 9th Dec.; deprived.
1648 Thomas Westlake, elected 21st Sept.
1681 Richard Isack, elected 15th Dec.   Died 13th March, 1697-8,
æt. 74.
1698 John Mannington, 21st June.[5]

---

[1] The last Sheriff elected under the City Charter, he continued in office until 1st Jan. 1836, when the first election of Sheriffs was made under the Act for the Regulation of Municipal Corporations in England and Wales, 5 & 6 Will. IV. c. 76.
[2] Elected 1st Jan. 1836, under the above-mentioned Act, and continued in office until 9th Nov. 1836.
[3] Elected 9th Nov. 1836.
[4] He was buried in St. Martin's Church, Exon, 20th April, 1624.
[5] He was buried in St. Martin's, 16th Dec. 1700.

R

242   HISTORY OF EXETER.

1700 John Carwithen,* elected 25th Feb. 1700-1.
1733 Henry Gandy, elected 31st July, 1733 ; died early in 1752.
1752 Benjamin Heath, elected 23rd March; died 13th Sept. 1766.
1766 Thomas Coffin, who held the office twenty days and then
       resigned it.
1766 John Heath, Esq., elected 11th October; afterwards Recorder
       of Exeter, and subsequently a Judge of the Common Pleas.
1775 Henry Ley, elected 1st June; resigned 6th Sept. 1814.
       Buried at Kenn, 29th Dec. 1824.
1814 Edward Gattey, elected 10th Sept. ; resigned.
1836 John Gidley, elected 1st January.

CHAMBERLAINS.

Hoker, who was the first Chamberlain, states that
the officer is of late erection, and was made and ordered
by Act of Parliament.

His office chiefly and especially concerned the
orphans, but he was also to see the records safely
kept, to enter the acts of the Corporation in the absence of the Town Clerk, to attend the city audits, to
survey the city property, and to help and instruct the
Receiver.

The following is the list of Chamberlains, from the
institution to the abolition of the office :—

John Hoker,	elected	21st Sept. 1555,[7] died 1601, aged 76.
William Tickell,	..	15th Sept. 1601.
John Martyn,	..	7th June, 1613.
William Prous,	..	26th June, 1624.
Richard Tickell,[8]	..	21st April, 1629.
John Crewkerne,	..	14th April, 1636.
John Dore,	..	1st Dec. 1646.
Richard Izacke,	..	25th Oct. 1653.
Edward Malet,	..	3rd April, 1683.
John Pratt,[9]	..	16th Feb. 1691.
Samuel Izacke,	..	26th Feb. 1693.

---

[6] Buried at St. Petrock's 25th July,
1733.
  [7] In his MS. Hist. of Exon, p. 351, I
read it 1555. "This yere at Michaelmas the Writer hereof entered ynto the
office of the Chamberlain of this citie,
having the fee of £4 by the yere, and
his liveries, which made up 32 more,—

£5 12s. in all."
  [8] The marriage licence of Richard
Tickell, of Exeter, Gent., to Mary Ma-
powder, of Exeter, is dated 18th June,
1627.
  [9] The father of Lord Camden mentioned *suprá*.

LIST OF SWORDBEARERS. 243

George Philips, elected 16th Dec. 1729.
Humphry Leigh, .. 5th July, 1748.
Adam Pierce, .. 3rd Nov. 1760.
Edward Gattey, .. 17th Nov. 1795.
Samuel Mortimer, .. 15th Sept. 1814; resigned 1825. Died 5th
    Nov. 1856, æt. 82.
Hugh Myddelton⎫ .. 25th May, 1825. On whose resignation
  Ellicombe,   ⎭   27th April, 1836, the office of Cham-
    berlain ceased, about 282 years after
    the first appointment of that officer.

SWORDBEARERS.

The following account of the origin of the office of Swordbearer is taken from Hoker's MS. p. 329 :—

" 1497. 13 & 14 Henry 7th, Memorandum that yn this yere there lacke twoo Rolles of the recorde of the courte yn wch ar sett downe and written the manner and order of the election of the Mayor Stewards and Sergeaunts made and established by the Kinge hymselff. For yn these dayes the tymes were no more troblesome than was the manner of the election of the Mayer and Officers of this Citie wch beinge advertysed unto the Kinge and he desyrouse to have the Goverment of this Citie quiet and peaceable had the Mayer and commen counsell of this Citye before hym. And when he had by theym lerned the manner of theire elections and the many trobles wch ensued thereof dyd of hymselff devyse and sett downe an order wch he dyd establyshe to contynewe and delyvered the same ingrossed yn parchement under his privie seale wch from hensforth hathe benne dewlye kepte and observed. And to begyne this order he named one Willm Froste to be now the first Mayer who had benne one of the bayliffes of the Citie yn the yere before past, but a servant unto the Kinge. And further to encorage the Mayer and Citisens to be myndefull of theire duties and to contynue dutyfull and obedient subgectes hensforth, as before they had donne, he toke his Sworde wch he then wore about his mydle, and gave it to the Mayer together with a hatt of mayntenaunce to be borne before hym and his Successors as it is used in the Citie of London." See ante, p. 87.

The list of Swordbearers is as follows :—

1498 Francis Gilbert, elected 25th July.
1509 William Downe, .. 10th Oct.
1510 William Somaster, .. 19th Aug.
1536 William Beamont, .. 22nd April.
1546 Richard Prous, .. 4th Oct.

R 2

HISTORY OF EXETER.

1553	John May,	elected	19th Oct.
1567	Richard Bartlett,	..	30th Sept.[1]
1586	Lobert Harrison.		
1592	John Woode.		
1593	Robert Northecot.		
1611	Thomas Toker.[2]		
1612	John Clerke,	elected	12th Sept.
1613	Leonard Cranebury,	..	23rd Nov.
1618	William Byrdall,	..	10th Oct.
1641	Robert Bletchinden,	..	24th March.
1646	John Cogan,	..	17th Dec.
1666	Thomas Willinge,	..	23rd Oct.
1685	Richard Rous,	..	27th Oct.

1687 Joseph Bradshaw, appointed by King James II., on removal of Richard Rous, 28th Nov.

1688 Richard Rous, restored 1st Nov.

1703	Israel Stafford,	elected	21st Sept.
1710	Philip Westcott,	..	27th Feb.
1724	Matthew Pear,	..	9th March.
1765	Simon Gandy,	..	24th Oct.
1772	William Marler,	..	5th May.
1786	James Grant,	..	22nd Aug.
1808	Richard Strong,	..	3rd May.
1830	Hugh Cumming,	..	19th Oct.

—In 1836 (25th May) Mr. Cumming ceased to perform the duties of the office, he being then appointed Superintendent of Police. No person was appointed Swordbearer in the room of Mr. Cumming; but the Sword has since been borne before the Mayor, and the cap of maintenance worn by the Senior Serjeant at Mace.

---

[1] He was allowed, 2nd Dec. 1586, as a retiring pension, 2s. per week, and was buried in St. Martin's Church 27th Jan. 1591.

[2] The history of this man is a melancholy one. He was dismissed from his office 12th Sept. 1612, "for his incontinens lyvinge with the late wief of Steven Toker deceased." In the same year he was arraigned and convicted before the Judges of Assize for the murder of his wife, and was executed at Heavitree. He must have married another wife (probably his paramour) immediately after the murder, as appears by her application to the Chamber, as his widow, for restoration of his goods, forfeited by his attainder.

CHAPTER V.

REPRESENTATIVES OF EXETER IN PARLIAMENT.

WE regret that for upwards of two centuries after the year 1264 (the first year of summons) we are incapable of supplying the returns;[1] but we know that the recorder was usually one of the representatives. Originally fit persons were selected from the most discreet and respected of the inhabitants to do the work of the public; yet, in process of time, several gentry of this neighbourhood were invited to become delegates. At length the Mayor and Chamber, on the 6th of October, 1554, took upon themselves to pass the following resolution :—" That from henceforth there shall be no burges for the Parliament chossen for thys cytte unless he be a cytteson inabytent, and also a ffreman of the same." These burgesses were paid for undertaking and discharging their office; first, at the rate of 2s. per day, which sum was gradually raised to 3s. 4d., 4s., and 5s., before the end of the 16th century. By the statute of the twenty-third of King Henry VI. (1444) the wages of the knights of the shire were ordered to be assessed by the sheriff in the next county court after the delivery of the writs by proclamation; and by the statute of sixth of Henry VIII. (1514) members departing without licence of the Speaker were to forfeit their wages. The allowance to the members was made only for their journies, and the days of attendance or session; and, as Hatsell observes, such payments were to be levied on the personalty of the constituents and not upon Corporation property. The Receiver of Exeter was the officer employed to settle our burgesses' fees. Thus, in the

---

[1] [The chasm might certainly have been supplied from the public records in the custody of the Master of the Rolls.]

246 HISTORY OF EXETER.

accounts of Mr. Thomas Flay, Receiver of Exeter from 1624 to 1625, we find—

	£.	s.	d.
"July 26—Paid Mr. Ignatius Jurdaine, one of the burgesses, for his fees and expenses at Parliament, as per his note . .	18	5	0
"Oct. 4—Paid him more for his fees and expenses at Parliament, kept at Oxford, as per his note	5	16	0
"Paid Mr. Recorder (Mr. Nicholas Duck[2]) one of the burgesses, for his fees at Parliaments, both at London and Oxford, as by his note appears	24	5	0
	£48	6	6

This custom of paying such wages continued until Sir Harbottle Grimstone, Master of the Rolls, on the 3rd of March, 1676, brought in a bill to repeal the statute of wages to knights and burgesses. Andrew Marvel, who died in 1678, is supposed to have been the last member who accepted wages. With this preamble, we venture to offer the best series we can of the Burgesses of this ancient and faithful city.

1466 Thomas Calwodelegh and Richard Clerk.
      John Hoker was burgess under three kings—Edward IV., Richard III., and Henry VII. He died in 1493. See his grandson's MS. history (of the same name), fol. 326.
1509-10 Thomas Andrew and John Orenge, elected 9th January.
1512 William Hewett, elected on the 11th of January, vice Orenge deceased.
1515 John Symons, elected on the 30th of December.
1522 John Nosworthy and John Brydgeman.
1524 John Nosworthy and John Bridgeman re-elected.
1539 John Hull and William Hurst occur members.
1543 Thomas Spurway and William Kirk.
1545 John Grynfeld occurs with William Hurst, 23rd November.
1549 Griffin Ameredyth and John Hull.
1555 Sir John Pollard, Knight.
1557 Walter Staplehill and John Gryncfeld.
1559 Sir John Pollard, Knight, and Richard Prestwood, elected 10th January.
1562 Jeffry Tothill and Thomas Williams; but the latter being elected in June, 1562, the Speaker of the House of Commons, was re-elected, and continued to represent the city until his death in September, 1566, when
      Sir Peter Carew, Knight, was chosen burgess in his place.
1571 Jeffry Tothill and John Hoker, the historian.

---

[1] The remittance of money in his time was a difficult service. In Mr. J. Prowse's letter dated London, 28th June, 1622, to the Corporation, he says, " I have now received of Sir John William Pole £70, his due upon the decree. I do intreat to be authorized by warrant to whom I shall paie it here ; for I dare not send it by the carryer, neyther dotho Mr. Recorder (Nicholas Duck) think itsafe."

REPRESENTATIVES IN PARLIAMENT. 247

1581 Simon Knight and Geoffry Ameredith.
1586 John Peryam and Edward Drewe, elected in October.
1592 John Peryam and Edward Drewe, elected 19th February.
1597 John Hele and William Martin.
1603 George Smith and John Prowse.
1614 and 1617 John Prowse and Thomas Martin occur.
1618 John Prowse and Nicholas Duck.
1624 Nicholas Duck and Ignatius Jurdain.
1628 Ignatius Jurdain and John Lynn.
1640 Simon Snow and Robert Walker. During this Long Parliament, Robert Walker, refusing to take the League and Covenant, was dismissed, and Samuel Clarke substituted.
1654 Thomas Gibbons occurs a Burgess in October.
1656 Thomas Bampfylde and Thomas Westlake.
(With the Restoration difficulty ceases.)
1660 John Maynard, Sergeant-at-Law, and Thomas Bampfylde.
1661 Sir James Smith, Knight, and Thomas Walker.
1670 Sir James Smith, Knight, and Robert Walker.
1678-9 William Glyde and Malachy Pyne. Re-elected in the following year.
1681 Sir Thomas Carew, Knight, and Thomas Walker.
1685 James Walker and Edward Seymour.
1688 Sir Edw. Seymour, Knight and Baronet, and Henry Pollexfen, on whose promotion to the Bench Christopher Bayle replaced him.
1690 Sir Edward Seymour and Christopher Bayle.
1695 Joseph Tilly and Edward Seward.[2]
1698 Sir Edward Seymour and Sir Bartholomew Shower, Knight.
1701 Sir Edward Seymour. On the death of Sir Edward in 1707, John Harris replaced him; and Sir Bartholomew Shower, who, dying shortly after his election, was replaced by John Snell.

---

[2] The reader will perceive that we omit all reference to the severe contests of candidates aspiring to the honour of representing this venerable city. "Detur digniori"; yet we cannot resist the temptation of giving Lord Macaulay's account of the election of 1695 :—" Exeter, the capital of the west, was violently agitated. It had been long supposed that the ability, the eloquence, the experience, the ample fortune, the noble descent of Seymour, would make it impossible to unseat him. But his moral character, which had never stood very high, had, during the last three or four years, been constantly sinking. He had been virulent in opposition, till he had got a place. While he had a place, he had defended the most unpopular acts of the government. As soon as he was out of place, he had again been virulent in opposition. His saltpetre contract had left a deep stain on his personal honour. Two candidates were therefore brought forward against him; and a contest, the longest and fiercest of that age, fixed the attention of the whole kingdom, and was watched with interest even by foreign governments. The poll was open five weeks. The expense on both sides was enormous. The freemen of Exeter, who, while the election lasted, fared sumptuously every day, were by no means impatient for the termination of their luxurious carnival. They ate and drank heartily; they turned out every evening with good cudgels to fight for Mother Church or for King William; but the votes came in very slowly. It was not till the eve of the meeting of Parliament that the return was made. Seymour was defeated, to his bitter mortification, and was forced to take refuge in the small borough of Totness."—(pp. 617, 618.)

248   HISTORY OF EXETER.

1708 John Harris and Nicholas Wood.
1710 Sir Copleston Warwick Bampfylde, Bart., and John Snell.
1713 John Rolle and Francis Drewe.
1714 John Bampfylde and Francis Drewe.
1722 John Rolle and Francis Drewe.
1727 Francis Drewe and Hon. F. Mollineux. On the death of the
         latter, John Belfield, Serjeant-at-Law, succeeded.
1734 Hon. John King; but in July he succeeded to the peerage,
         when Sir Henry Northcote, Bart., was elected, and Thomas
         Balle, Esq., of Mamhead.
1741 Sir Henry Northcote and Humphrey Sydenham. Sir Henry,
         dying 21st May, 1743, was succeeded by Sir Richard War-
         wick Bampfylde, Bart.
1747 John Tuckfield and Henry Sydenham.
1754 John Tuckfield and John Rolle Walter.
1760 John Tuckfield and John Rolle Walter. On Mr. Tuckfield's
         death, in 1766, William Spicer served till the end of the
         session.
1768 John Buller and John Rolle Walter.
1774 Sir Charles Warwick Bampfylde, Bart., and John Rolle Walter.
         The latter resigned to stand for the county of Devon, and
         John Baring was elected for the city, 9th Nov. 1776.
1780 Sir Charles Warwick Bampfylde and John Baring.
1784 Sir Charles Warwick Bampfylde and John Baring.
1790 James Buller and John Baring.
1796 Sir Charles Warwick Bampfylde and John Baring.
1802 Sir Charles Warwick Bampfylde and James Wentworth Buller.
1806 Sir Charles Warwick Bampfylde and James Wentworth Buller.
1807 Sir Charles Warwick Bampfylde and James Wentworth Buller.
1812 James Wentworth Buller and William Courtenay, afterwards
         Earl of Devon.
1818 William Courtenay and Robert William Newman.
1820 William Courtenay and Robert William Newman.
1826 Samuel Trehawke Kekewich, 9th February, in the room of
         William Courtenay, appointed Assistant Clerk to the House
         of Lords; and at the General Election in the same year (10th
         June), Samuel Trehawke Kekewich and Lewis Wm. Buck.
1830 Lewis William Buck and James Wentworth Buller.
1831 Lewis William Buck and James Wentworth Buller.
1832 James Wentworth Buller and Edward Divett.
1834 Edward Divett and Sir William Webb Follett, Solicitor-
         General.
1835 Sir W. W. Follett and Edward Divett.
1837 Sir W. W. Follett and Edward Divett.
1841 Sir W. W. Follett, re-elected September, and Edward Divett.
1844 Sir W. W. Follett, re-elected as Attorney-General.
1845 Sir John Thomas Buller Duckworth, Bart., vice Sir W. W.
         Follett, who died 28th June, 1845.
1846 Edward Divett and Sir John T. Buller Duckworth, Bart.
1852 Edward Divett and Sir John T. Buller Duckworth, Bart.
1857 Edward Divett and Richard Somers Gard.

CHAPTER VI.

HISTORY OF THE HAVEN OR CANAL OF EXETER.

[The following account is almost entirely derived from a 'Memoir of the Canal of Exeter, from 1563 to 1724,' written by Mr. Philip Chilwell De la Garde;[1] and continued by Mr. James Green, C.E.]

PREVIOUS to the reign of Henry III. the tide came up as far as Exeter, and barges and small craft ascended the river Exe to the Water-gate of that city.

About that time Isabella de Fortibus, Countess of Devon, built a weir, called after her, Countess Weir, in which an opening of 30 feet was left for the passage of vessels. In the twelfth year of Edward I. this passage was closed. Other weirs were added by the Courtenays, earls of Devon. Legal proceedings were taken by the citizens, and verdicts were gained, but the power of the earls was greater than the law.

In the thirty-first year of Henry VIII. (1540) an Act of Parliament was obtained for restoring the navigation. Many attempts were made, and much money was expended, without effect, in that and the two succeeding reigns.[2]

In 1563[3] the Chamber engaged John Trew, of Glamorganshire, in Wales, as their engineer. Trew, instead of clearing the river, rendered the city accessible by a canal. This work was a true pound-lock canal, similar, in all essential points, to canals of the present day.

The above statement may be supported by the existing evidence of contemporaneous public documents.

---

[1] The 'Armorial of Jersey' informs us that this respected writer is the only child of Rev. Philip De la Garde, Rector of St. Martin's, Jersey, in which island the family had long flourished, and of Sarah his wife, daughter and coheir of Jonathan Chilwell, Esq., of Westerham and Hadlow, in Kent. He married Susan, second daughter of the well known Rev. John Lemprière, D.D. Mr. De la Garde was sheriff of Exeter in 1832, and mayor in 1834, and laid the foundation of our excellent Lower and Higher Market-places. A more detailed account of the early history of this canal was contributed by him to the Society of Antiquaries, vol. 28 of the Archæologia. G. O.

[2] The Act Book, No. 11, of the Corporation, p. 117, shows that the plate of the parish churches of the city, to the amount of £228 12s. 4½d., was subscribed to the undertaking.

[3] Pp. 354–56 of John Hoker's MS:— "1563. This yere John Trewe came to this citie and toke the haven in hand to be brought to this citie."

250 HISTORY OF EXETER.

In the Act Book of the Chamber, No. 2, is a curious paper, entitled, 'The whole order and process of the covenants, bargains, communications, and other dealings had between the mayor, bailiffs, and commonalty of the city of Exon of the one party, and John Trew of the other party, for and concerning the river of Exe and conducting the same,' which affords a summary of proceedings to the second week of the fourth month after the commencement of the work.

The following passage shows a change in the plans of the engineer:—"Item, the 15th of December, 1563, Mr. John Peryam, mayor, the said John Trew, after sundry views of the ground about Exe, being before minded to have gone to the east side of the river, did now change his mind and thought it better to take the ground and way by the west side of Exe."

On reference to the map published in the above Memoir, it will be observed that a mill-leat extends from St. James's Weir to the Weir Mills. These mills are situated a little above the original and lowest obstruction, Countess Weir. Probably this weir had been already removed. By placing a lock near the lower end of this mill-leat, a canal would have been formed, conveying vessels above St. James's Weir, at that time the obstacle nearest to Exeter.

To those who are acquainted with the locality, and remember the high and, for the most part, precipitous bank, which extends from Wear to Exeter, it will be obvious that there was scarcely any other mode of going by the eastern side.

The following memorandum confirms this opinion:—" 28th of September, 1563. At which day order and agreement was had and made with John Cove and Nicholas Crowne, for and concerning certain wears placed and fixed in the watercourse from St. James's Wear to the Wear Mills; that is to say, the said John and Nicholas do covenant and grant consent and assent, that one John Trew, who hath taken in hand the conducting of the river or haven, shall have all stakes and other stuff as he or his men shall pull up, for the conducting of the said water, without any denial of them, or any of them, or their assignees, and of their own free gift. And further it is by the said John and Nicholas covenanted, and with their full assent and consent agreed, that not they, nor any of them, nor their assignees shall in anywise intermeddle with the wear called

THE HAVEN OR CANAL. 251

St. James's Wear, to pull up or take away any stake or stakes, or any stuff there."

The clearance of the mill-course, the conservation of the weir at its head, and the formation of the ground, appear conclusive. The plan might have been executed at a small cost in a short time, yet Trew's change of mind was creditable both to his boldness and sagacity. Until Trew's weir was erected, the current of the Exe must have been difficult to stem. Its rapidity is shown by the existence of the Tucking Mills, and its channel, near Exeter, was apparently shallow and rocky. Besides, whatever additional expense was incurred, the purchase of the weir mills, or at least compensation for damage, was avoided.

The conveyances of the land purchased, the map in Braun's 'Civitates,' the manuscript map called Havill's Map, and various other contemporaneous authorities, prove that the original canal took the same course as the present canal, as far as the deep pill or outlet of Matford brook.

The following extract from Act Book No. 3 furnishes the length, as well as some other very important particulars; and although, owing to the negligence of the clerk, it is imperfect, the deficiencies may be supplied from other sources.

"12th of March, Anno Eliz., &c., xv. . . . . Mr. Knight, Mr. Bruarton, Nicholas Martyn, William Trevet, Richard Prowse, Richard Hellier, Jeffry Thomas, William Martyn, John Webbe, and Michael Germin, shall measure the watercourse and work of the haven, all the length and breadth of the same, and of the pools, and to sup at Walter Jones, and the receiver to pay for their supper there." Then follows, at the bottom of the page, "which persons before named have measured the said watercourse, and do find the same to contain as followeth :—

"First, the length of the whole ground wrought is	. 9360 foot.
The length of the banks	. 6720 foot.
The breadth at the lower sluice and downwards	. 16 foot.
The depth there and below	. 3 foot.
The breadth of the lower pool . . .	. 23 foot.
The length of the lower pool . . .	. 189 foot.
The depth of the said pool ; . . .	. 5½ foot.
The breadth " . . ; . . .	

The length of the present canal to the Pill, or Matford brook, is just 9360 feet—a coincidence confirming the identity of its course with that of the original canal.

252 HISTORY OF EXETER.

From the several conveyances it appears that the land purchased for the canal was as follows:—

Owners.	Parishes.		Breadth.	Total.
Floyre,	St. Leonard, and St. Thomas,	from the Exe to Bole pool . . 68 ft. at and by Bole pool . . . 151		A. P. 3½ 20
Coffyn,	Alphington .	. . . . . no breadth given		120
Penrudocke and Loveys,	Alphington	through old Exe (apparently) . 68 from old Exe to higher of middle sluices . . . . . 68 from thence to 25 feet below Trew's house . . . 100 from thence to Alphington brook 76 from Alphington brook to Adelbury wood 68		8¾ 31¼
Mohun and others,	Exminster	from Alphington boundary to lower pair of sluices . . . 68 at and between the sluices and twenty feet below . . . 100 from thence to the pyll . . 68		6½ 6
Holland,	Exminster .	. . . . . no breadth given		1

That the breadth of 16 feet was continued throughout is shown by the fact that the breadth of the ground which it occupied varied but little, except where the locks were situated.

That the depth of 3 feet was continued throughout is proved by the following passage, " Also to talk and confer with them for the full depth of 3 foot from the Pyll to Adelbury wood, and to continue the same level to Old Exe." By "Old Exe" is probably meant the " Old river of Exe;" but if by "Old Exe" is meant an estate so called, through which the canal passed, it will still give that depth for five-sixths of its entire length.

That the breadth of the lower pool, or lock, was repeated at the middle lock, may be assumed on the same grounds; the land appropriated to each being 100 feet in breadth. There is no reason for supposing any difference in length or depth.

Considerable vestiges of these locks were discovered during the late improvements by Mr. James Green. They consisted of the western walls of the chambers of the locks, partially buried in the western bank of the canal of 1699. No remains of the upper lock were found ; but its position was fixed in the map at Bole Pool. The breadth of the ground was, however, 51 feet wider than at the two lower locks. Its pool, or chamber, was probably much wider, in order to serve as a floating dock for vessels, which, during floods, could not proceed at once to the

THE HAVEN OR CANAL.   253

quay. The reasons for regarding the pools as chambers of locks will be given subsequently. Their inordinate size, according to modern notions, was for the purpose of receiving several vessels at the same time, and allowing them to pass each other—for which the breadth of the canal was insufficient. The following item, from a specification for enlarging the canal in 1699, puts this beyond doubt:—" For digging a pool between the said two gates, which must be 300 foot in length at least, and about 80 foot in breadth at the top or surface of the water, and 50 foot broad at the bottom, and for walling the same on both sides, for the convenient and necessary passing of ships one by the other." The waste of water was great, but the engineer had the river Exe at his disposal.

That the pools, or, as they are elsewhere termed, "pairs of sluices," were real pound-locks, might be safely inferred from the last quotation; but as that applies to alterations undertaken more than a century later, it is desirable to prove the fact by contemporaneous evidence.

In the conveyance of the joint property of Robert Penrudocke and Leonard Loveys, Esquires, the following measurement occurs:—"From the said house upwards, to the head of the higher sluice, of the two middle sluices, there lately made one hundred foot, and from the said head upward," &c.

In the conveyance of the land of William Mohun, Esq., is the following description:—" Unto the lane or way there leading towards Countess Wear, where one pair of sluices now are lately made, called the lower pair of sluices, and so downward from the said lane or way to and until a place near or over against the Mansion House of William Holland, Esq., called the pyll or deep pool. And in breadth upwards from the said pyll or deep pool at and under twenty foot next adjoining and beneath the said lower pair of sluices, and by all the said way four perches, and in breadth, where the said pair of sluices be, and between the said pair of sluices, and the said twenty foot next beneath the said pair of sluices, one hundred foot, and in breadth upwards from the head of the higher sluice of the said pair of sluices to the higher part of the said ground and soil granted by these presents four perches."

Such dimensions can hardly apply to any structures excepting locks. But when it is observed that elsewhere, instead of being called " a pair of sluices," the last of the above-mentioned works

HISTORY OF EXETER.

is styled a "pool," which pool is described as being two feet and a half deeper than the canal, it must be evident, without referring to the specification of 1699, that the work mentioned could be none other than a lock, having between its sluices, or gates, a chamber 189 feet in length by 23 feet in breadth, with a lift of $2\frac{1}{2}$ feet; and that it belonged to a canal 16 feet wide and 3 feet deep.

It has been stated that there were three locks, although two only are mentioned in the conveyances, and one only in the Act Books. This might be assumed from the terms "lower and middle pairs of sluices," which may be received as implying an upper pair. The question is, however, set at rest by documents relating to the case of the Mayor and Chamber *versus* George Browning. From these the Rev. Dr. Oliver ascertained, some years before these researches were commenced, that the canal had seven sluices. The lower and middle locks account for four of these, and the King's Arms Sluice, which is shown in contemporary maps, for a fifth. The remaining two of course belonged to the upper lock.

The situation of the upper lock was determined by the breadth of the ground purchased at the confines of St. Thomas and Alphington, and that of the middle and lower locks by the masonry, which protected the western sides of their chambers.

Instead of removing any weirs, Trew added that which is known by his name. It is also called St. Leonard's Weir. It is thus mentioned in the conveyance of the property purchased of William Floyre, Esq.:—"Some part lyeth and adjoineth next and unto the new wear lately made by John Trew, crossing over the said river of Exe; and some part thereof is that whereupon the said wear is lately made, set, fixed, and erected, for the better continuance and maintenance of the said new watercourse, and for the rebounding of water into the said new watercourse."

This wear was originally a stake wear, as may be seen in Havill's, Braun's, and other maps; but it was subsequently re-constructed of stone.

Close adjoining to the Water-gate of the city (the place at which, previous to the time of Edward I., vessels had been accustomed to unload), a quay was erected. It is thus described in an address of the corporation to Lord Burleigh:—"The wharf

THE HAVEN OR CANAL. 255

or key now made . . . the same city to their like great charges containeth in length 150 foot, all of ashlerwork; and in breadth 80 foot of like work, little more over, with a convenient crane thereupon builded."[4]

As Trew's account of the progress of the work, and of his expenses, states, that " the first month ended the 6th of March, 1563" (O.S.), it is clear that it was commenced early in the February of that year.

The time occupied in completing the work, and the sum expended on it, are indicated in the following passage:—" The citizens of Exon have now made the said port, and made a fair and open key, which cost about three thousand pounds. And have laden and unladen their merchandises there these fourteen years."[5] The "fourteen years," which would allow about a year and a half, is not quite exact; for at that time the quay had not been commenced, as may be inferred by the following proceedings of the Chamber.[6] " An Act made the 25th of July, 1565, for making of the key." Then comes the order, and at the bottom of the page is added, " which Act was renewed the 10th of September, 1565," &c.; so that it seems not to have been begun at that time.

In about two years after the commencement of the work, it was evidently approaching completion, as may be collected from " An Act made the 25th of January, 1565 " (O.S.)[7] " By whom it is ordered, that all such duties shall be paid for every ton of wares, discharged at the water-gate and key of the city, as is usually paid and received at Topsham, &c. And further, it is concluded, that Thomas Rawlyns, tailor, shall be the porter and keeper of the said water-gate," &c.

It may be presumed, that these appointments were made in anticipation; for as the quay had not been begun in the preceding September, a very short time would have been thus allowed for constructing such an extent of ashlerwork.

The real date may be inferred from an Act made the 2nd of December, 1566. " And further it is agreed, that in consideration, that Mr. Oliver shall and truly collect and gather all such

---

[4] Lansdowne MS., No. 25, Article 2, superscribed "20 June, 1577. The answer of the mayor, bailiffs, and commonalty of Exeter, to the complaint of Richard Sandford, of Topsham." D.L.G.

[5] Lansdowne MS., No. 28, Article 12, superscribed "June 20, 1579, touching the Haven at Exon." D.L.G.

[6] Act Book, No. 3, fol. 160.

[7] Ibid., fol. 165.

256   HISTORY OF EXETER.

sums and sums of money, as shall be due for any kind of wares and merchandises discharged and unladen at the key of the water-gate, and to answer the same from the feast of St. Michael last past, until the same feast next coming, shall have for his pains the sum of 40*s.*"

The last order is on the 8th of January, 1566 (O. S.) "Who have fully condescended, that Mr. Smyth, receiver, shall build a crane or some other engine, for the charge or discharge of all wares and merchandises to be laden and unladen at the key."

It may therefore be concluded, that, in the autumn of 1566, the navigation was open, and that in the spring of 1567, the works were finished—having been commenced in February, 1564.

It may not be uninteresting to show on what terms the engineer, who was likewise the contractor, undertook the work :—

"Order, agreement, and a full conclusion is made, that in consideration that John Trew shall·and will conduct and make the haven of the city in such sort, as boats and vessels, laden with ten tons weight at the least, shall at all tide and tides pass and repass to and from the seas unto the city walls, and according to such articles of agreement between the said John Trew of the one party, and the mayor, bailiffs, and commonalty of the other party, agreed upon and sealed, he shall have the sum of two hundred pounds paid unto him, as also twenty-five pounds in money for the discharge of one hundred loads of timber, by him demanded, for saving of the Tucking Mills. And that, the works being finished, he shall take no more for transporting, lading, and unlading of any wares and merchandises, but after the rates as followeth :—

	s.	*d.*
"For every ton of tonnage from Colepool, Powderham, and Exmouth, to Exeter	2	8
For every ton of kyntaledge from any of the said places .	2	0
For every ton of tonnage from Topsham to Exeter . .	2	0
For every ton of kyntaledge from thence, to and from . .	1	8
For every boat loading with beer, shillingstones, lime, wood, coal, fish, corn, or grain, being not above six tons lading, shall have from Exmouth or elsewhere within Exmouth bar	0	4 " [a]

---

[a] From a MS. belonging to the corporation of Exeter entitled, "An Abstract of all the orders and ordinances extant, made, enacted, and ordained, by the mayors and common council of the city of Exeter for the time being for the good government of the said city and commonwealth of the same, by John Vowell, alias Hooker, and chamberlain of the same."

THE HAVEN OR CANAL. 257

John Trew is described in legal documents as a " Gentleman," and William Stroude, who preceded him, as an "Esquire," titles not lightly accorded in the days of Elizabeth, and which show the estimation in which the civil engineer was then held.[9]

Trew's work gave little satisfaction. It could not be entered "at all tide and tides"—which might have been foreseen. Besides, no barge canal can successfully compete with an ordinary road in a distance of only three miles or four miles. The double transfer, and the injury of goods, outweigh the advantage of the cheaper conveyance. There is reason for believing that the canal was deepened on the occasion of its being cleansed, or when new sluices were required.

About 1675 the Chamber commenced the extension of the canal to the Topsham Sluice, called in later documents after its keeper, Trenchard's Sluice.[10] On the 16th of July, 1698, they "Resolved that the old work for the bringing up of ships be forthwith widened and deepened from the key to Trenchard's Sluices."[11] Also "This day (12th September), certain articles made between the Chamber and Mr. Wm. Baly, for widening and digging the new canal or river, making a stone wear, and

---

[9] [John Trew, the artificer of this first of lock canals, seems to have realized no money by his work. Some unfortunate failure in the execution of his agreement involved him in litigation with the Chamber, which must have been expensive, and, for the time, ruinous. In MS. Lansd. cvii. art. 73, he addresses Lord Burleigh relating to his suit against the Chamber of Exeter. The first passage contains a melancholy picture of the state to which he was reduced. "The variableness of men, and the great injury done unto me, brought me in such case, that I wished my creditors satisfied and I away from earth, what become may of my poor wife and children, who lie in great misery, for that I have spent all." Perhaps his canal when finished was found not to be accessible by vessels of ten tons *at all tides*. But this partial failure might have been overlooked when vessels of fifteen and sixteen tons, by Hoker's admission, discharged their cargoes at the quay. It may however be satisfactory to state that in 1573 this harassing suit was brought to a con-

clusion. I have seen Trew's release to the Corporation, "in consideration of an annuity or yearly rent of thirty pounds, and the sum of two hundred and twenty-four pounds." There is a reciprocal release on the part of the Chamber of the same date, saving "harmless the said John Trew against the owners of the ground," &c. In MS. Lansd. xxxi. art. 74, are "Reasons against the proceedings of John Trew in the works of Dover haven, 1581." After this nothing seems to be known of him. *Note kindly communicated by Mr. De la Garde.*]

[10] See the estimate for finishing the work sent to Parliament, 1699, wherein the distance along the course of the canal proves that the Topsham and Trenchard sluice were identical. In Act Book, No. 11, we find, 13th of May, 1701—"Ordered that Mr. Way do take care of the works till further order, and that the sluices be not opened but when he is present, and he is to have inspection over Comb and Trenchard."

[11] Act Book, No. 11.

258   HISTORY OF EXETER.

digging the broad from the key thereunto, passed the common seal." [12]

Troubles now began to multiply. Bayly, having proceeded so far as to render the canal impassable, ran away with the money. The Chamber applied for an Act of Parliament under the circumstances detailed in the statement of their case.[13] Having recited the Act of the 31st of Henry VIII., the petitioners proceed, —" By virtue of which power the said mayor, bailiffs, and commonalty, did then, to their great cost and charge, cut and make a new channel, or haven, through which boats and lighters did with merchandize, on spring tides only, pass and repass to and from the said city, and in length of time, trade increasing, and that boats and lighters might have a free passage to and from the key of the said city upon all sides, the said mayor, bailiffs, and commonalty, did at several times within five-and-twenty years last past, by enlarging, lengthening the said channel, making of new sluices, erecting a new wear and building of a new key with conveniences thereunto belonging, lay out and expend the sum of ten thousand pounds, and within two years last past that ships of the burden of two hundred tons may come up to the said city, did agree to have the same done for nine thousand pounds: but the person with whom such agreement was made being fled, they were forced, by his so far proceeding thereon, to endeavour to complete the same, which they did, and therein have laid out the further sum of eleven thousand pounds, which said sums of money are still due and owing from the said mayor, bailiffs, and commonalty—the revenue that hath accrued thereby not having been sufficient to pay the interest of the same as it became due. Which works, being of late by the violence of fresh waters and other accidents, much impaired and damnified, the same cannot be completed under the further

---

[12] Act Book, No. 11.

[13] This and the " Estimate," which is given entire, belong to a set of extremely curious and interesting papers, which were found in 1834 by John Gidley, Esq., town clerk, in a drawer, where they had apparently lain undisturbed ever since they were written. They consist of original draughts of this statement of their case, with many corrections—of the petition to Parliament, with various alterations—of a second draught, with further correc-

tions — of rough draughts of correspondence with the Bishop, the Dean, the representatives of the city, the Council and solicitor, with numerous corrections, and the draught of the estimate, which is transcribed *verbatim et literatim*. A map is mentioned in the correspondence, but this probably was never returned. Perhaps this may be the map of the New Haven by Thomas Jennings, for which he was voted by the Chamber £3 on 26th Jan. 1669? See Act Book of the time, p. 85.—D. L. G.

THE HAVEN OR CANAL.

sum of ten thousand pounds, as by men of judgment therein has been computed. And if the said works be not completed, it will be the ruin of this city in all matters of trade, the extraordinary charge of land-carriage of goods between this city and Topsham, being already three thousand pounds per annum; besides, the great damages and losses sustained by the carriage of the said goods. And the said mayor, bailiffs, and commonalty, being so indebted as aforesaid, and likewise in a further sum of five thousand pounds, they are in no way able of themselves to proceed further on in the said work, so that now, and for six weeks past, the same has lain in a ruinous condition, no boat whatsoever being able to pass or repass, &c." [14]

In a letter to Sir Edward Seymour, they promise to send a map, plan, and estimate. This estimate, with all its erasures and interlineations, throwing much light on the work, is too curious to be omitted:—

" ESTIMATE

" *To what may be the charge of finishing the Kay with its appurtenances, & making of it compleat in every respect.*

" For finishing [walling] *walls of* [15] the Kay . . £264.00.00	
" Levelling and paving thereof 106.00.00	
" 2 new Cranes 100.00.00	
" Finishing the bridge between the wharfe and the Kay . . . . } — " Making of slipp to land timber & other bulky goods . . . . } —	} 85.00.00
" Making of a Dock for the security of the merchants' shipps and goods . . } 750.00.00	750.00.00
" Making of severall Bayes for the cleansing & finishing the Broad, & securing the bankes thereof } —	50.00.00
" Finishing the wall of the [same for] for the security thereof, and removing the gravell below the same . . } —	50.00.00
	£1405.00.00

[14] From a MS. endorsed "The case of an Act of Parliament relating to the Water-works."
[15] In the original the word between brackets is erased, and those *in italics* are inserted. This remark will apply to the various erasures and insertions throughout the document.

s 2

HISTORY OF EXETER.

" Other side	£1405.00.00
" Removing the Bay att the mouth of the Canall, & finishing the sluce there	100.00.00
" Repairing the breaches *in the said Canall* occasioned by a floud, removing the gravell, making good the bankes, *raising* & securing the same from the mouth of the Canall to the Lock, which is about a mile & half in length	705.00.00
" For another pair of gates at Kings Armes . .	700.00.00
" Finishing the upper gates of the intended Lock, the masonry, and other worke thereunto belonging, making of the lower gates of the same Lock, which must be 25 foot it height, & each leafe thereof twenty foot broad, with the iron *& brass* worke [thereunto belonging], ground ffloor & apron thereunto belonging	1382.[08.09]
" For digging of a foundation [of] *for* the said lower gates, making of [a] *the* floud & sufficient for such gates, with timber & other materialls to bee used in the same, [and for digging] . . . " For digging a poole between the said two gates, which must bee 300 foot in length att least, & about 80 foot in breadth [att] *on* the topp or surface of the water, & 50 foot broad att the bottom, & *for* walling the same on both sides, for the convenient and necessary passing of shipps one by the other	181.00.00
" For walling the poole as above	605.00.00
	£5078.00.00

" Other side	£5078
" For deepning the Canall, making and securing the bankes from the said Lock to Trenchard's Sluce, being *more than* a mile & ½ in length . .	407.[9].00
" For diverting and carrying off a Backwater, or Brooke, called Alphington Brooke, & two other Brookes, [which] thereby to prevent *frequent* damages which may *otherwise* happen to the *said* Canall	150.00.00
" For repairing the ground-worke & hanging of a gate att the said sluce, called Trenchard's Sluce, smyth's worke, masonry & carpentry, and materials .	55.00.00
" For removing severall ridges of gravell, sande, & mudd, between Trenchard's Sluce and the Kay of Topsam, which otherwise would obstruct the passage of shipps, fixing of poles and markes there for the secure passage of ships [Bordelling] .	100.00.00
" For new making & repairing & finishing of 4 [horse] *Turn* Bridges for horses & carriages, & 2 foot Bridges over & athwart the said Canall & the walls thereof	200.00.00
" For [though] throwing off the gravell att a considerable distance from the margent of the bankes to prevent falling & slipping in of the same into the said Canall	350.00.00
	£6340.00.00

THE HAVEN OR CANAL. 261

	" Other side	£6340.00.00
" For filling upp severall cutts[16] made in the landes adjoyning, for diverting the water during the tyme that the Broad & Canall were deepning		300.00.00
" For damages to the owners of the landes adjoyning to the Broad and Canall from the time of the beginning *of the said worke untill* [to] the same *shall* be compleated		
" For the purchase of several [through which] landes used in widening of the said Canall, and in banking the same		700.00.00

	" To Topsham	£7340.00.00
" For making of a new cutt from [Trenchard's slu] a place called Goffen's poole to a place called [Powderham poole], *Turfe poole*, being [near three] [ne] *two* miles in length, & making a sufficient Lock and poole at the mouth thereof & walling the same, that shipps of considerable burthen may come up *to the City*		
" For the purchase of all the landes through which such new cut shall bee made and the bankes of same		£6000.00.00
" For two [new] Turne Bridges for horses & carriages over the said new intended Canall, & walling the same on both sides "		

Through the opposition of petty interests in Exeter and Devon, the application for the Act failed. The popular triumph was complete, and not less costly than complete; for the Chamber with great difficulty, after a lapse of 25 years,[17] accomplished a work, the imperfect character of which will best be understood from Mr. James Green's Reports. It would be a very moderate calculation to set down the consequent loss to the town in delays, injuries, and repairs, at 250,000*l*.

Sympathy is due to the Chamber of that day, whose opinions were too far in advance not only of their city, but of the Legislature. It was no small matter for a corporate body, in a corner of the empire, to conceive and, as far as it was permitted them, to execute (more than 50 years before the Sankey Cut) a canal of 10 feet in depth—a canal in all other respects coinciding with the still greater work, which they were enabled to complete before their final extinction in 1835, and which remains a monument of the courage, integrity, and zeal, with which, for 700 years, they had directed the commercial affairs of their city.

---

[16] One of these cuts, which was never filled up, occupied part of the site of the present basin.

[17] In Act Book, No. 11, on the 27th of Dec., 1724, a committee is appointed, who " are desired to pen a letter to the Lord Walpole and such other persons as shall be thought proper for the opening of the port." On the 3rd of the ensuing January similar letters are directed to be sent to the Lord Chief Justice King and the Archbishop of York.

It must not, however, be supposed that the canal was wholly impassable during this long period; for there is abundant evidence to the contrary.

262 HISTORY OF EXETER.

The subsequent resumption and continuation of the works on the Exeter Canal, will be best described in the language of Mr. Green, the engineer to whom they were entrusted :—

"Previous to the year 1820, the canal had been for many years, only capable of passing vessels drawing 9 feet of water from the tideway of the river Exe, about a mile above the town of Topsham, to the quays in the river Exe, at Exeter; but the increase in the size of the canal, although accomplished by great perseverance on the part of the Chamber, and at a vast expense, had been effected in a very imperfect manner, and the several works had become greatly impaired and dilapidated.

"The canal from the King's Arms sluice at its entrance into the Exe, near the city, to what is called the "double lock," and which is nearly on the site of the highest, or third sluice,[18] or pool, described in Mr. De la Garde's Memoir, was a level pond. It had been originally so constructed that the water should be 10 feet deep, but the banks had been much washed down.

"The double lock had become greatly decayed, although it was still capable of passing several vessels simultaneously.

"The course of the canal, from the tail of this double lock to its entrance into the tideway, above Topsham, which was about 2 miles in length, was nearly the same as at present; at its junction with the tideway there was a sluice, with only one pair of gates, pointing inwards, so that vessels could only pass this sluice when the water in the pond above it was level with the tide outside the gates; and as the bed of this lower pond of the canal formed the only outlet for the several brooks which constituted the exclusive drainage of an extensive tract of meadow land, it was requisite that this accumulation of water should flow away every low tide.

"The cill of this sluice was laid 2 feet above the bed of the tidal channel; and the level of the lower gate cill of the double lock was 4 feet higher than the cill of the lower sluice; so that it was necessary to raise this lower pond of the canal for 2 miles in length with water at least 4 feet deep drawn from the upper pond of the canal, before a vessel, which was carried by the tide over the cill of the lower sluice, could pass that of the

---

[18] As no remains of the masonry of this third or upper lock were found by Mr. Green, he conceived the masonry near the double lock to indicate its site. There is no doubt, however, that this was the middle or second lock, and that the third was much nearer the King's Arms sluice at the head of the canal.— D. L. G.

THE HAVEN OR CANAL.   263

double lock. This lower pond of the canal might therefore be aptly compared to a lock 2 miles in length, with a rise of at least 4 feet. The disadvantages of such a mode of ship navigation to an important commercial city may be easily conceived.

"The first, and perhaps the most important, object was to repair the double lock, and in doing this, care was taken so to lower the cills of the gates as to facilitate any further improvements in the canal which might be considered desirable.

"In October, 1820, in a very full report on the state of the canal, and the improvements of which it was capable, it was shown that the increasing trade of the city required that vessels, drawing at least 10 feet of water, should approach the quays with facility. This report recommended that the lower reach of the canal, from the double lock to the tideway of the river, should be converted into a regular pond ; that side channels and culverts under the canal should be constructed, so that the brooks, which drained the marshes into the tideway, should be enabled to traverse beneath the canal by means of these side channels and culverts. The erection of an entire new lock, with complete gates, a little lower down the tideway than the then lower and very imperfect sluice, was also recommended.

"The subsequent improvements were chiefly confined to repairing the banks and bridges, and dredging the upper pond of the canal, until 1824, when the demands for a more perfect navigation became so general that the authorities were constrained to enter on an entire revision of the works ; and as it was evident for the interest of the trade of the city that facilities should be given for bringing up larger vessels, further surveys were made, and on the 1st of March, 1824, a report was presented, stating that it would be practicable to extend the canal to Turf, two miles lower down the estuary than had before been contemplated, and to which point vessels drawing 12 feet water could navigate on all tides. This report was approved and adopted, and the works were soon afterwards commenced.

"In executing these works, it was necessary to carry a considerable portion of the extended line over mud-lands, which were overflowed by the sea at every tide ; much difficulty was therefore experienced in maintaining the embankments to the required height, and some extraordinary high tides and floods which occurred, having made extensive breaches in the shore

HISTORY OF EXETER.

which separates the estuary from the sea near Exmouth, it was found that the tide rose several feet higher within the' estuary than it had been accustomed to do before these breaches in the sands of the shore had occurred. In consequence of this, it became necessary to raise the embankments over the mudlands 3 feet higher than had been originally intended.

"The raising of these banks on such a foundation was a work of considerable difficulty and expense, and it could only proceed slowly ; but, its completion being imperative, it was accomplished by the persevering energies of the Chamber. This induced the idea and the determination of increasing the depth of water in the canal to 15 feet, and of constructing the entrance lock at Turf of dimensions adapted to vessels drawing 14 feet of water ; hence arose also the necessity of adapting all other parts of the canal to vessels of that class. These works would have been in a great measure useless, unless the larger class of vessels could arrive at the river basin at Exeter. An entire new and walled basin, capable of accommodating such vessels, independently of the river, was therefore made at the upper end of the canal close to the city, and was opened for trade on the 29th of September, 1830. Experience has shown that this increase of the depth of water in the canal was not greater than was necessary. It was found, during the progress of the works, that as the depth of water in the canal increased from time to time, the demands for a still greater depth became more urgent, and the success of the exertions of what may almost be called a private corporate body 'in a corner of the kingdom,' is proved by the fact that the revenues of the canal have trebled since the commencement of the extension of the works. The only Act of Parliament obtained by the Chamber was passed in 1829, for legalizing the tolls. This Act provided for a lock between the canal and the river Exe at Topsham, which was accordingly executed ; so that the necessity for land-carriage between Topsham and Exeter was entirely superseded.

"In an engineering point of view there is nothing of a very novel character in the construction of these works; it may, however, be observed, that, with a large and constant trade upon the canal, the process of repairing, widening, and deepening it would be attended with hindrances, delay, and great expense; and some circumstances attended the execution of the works which deserve notice.

THE HAVEN OR CANAL. 265

"The excavation for the entrance lock at Turf proceeded very favourably, through a stiff alluvial clay, without water, to a depth of nearly 20 feet below the surface of the marshes, when, on the occasion of a pile being driven to ascertain the depth at which a harder foundation would be obtained, water forced its way up around the pile, and the following morning the sides of the excavation were found to have sunk perpendicularly at least 10 feet, and the bottom of the lock-pit had risen to a greater height than the sides, exhibiting on its surface peat-moss, roots of trees, and a great variety of marine plants, rushes, fern, &c., but with very little water. It was, however, now evident that there would be much water to contend with in sinking to the required depth for the foundation. In order to accomplish this, a complete close kirbing of whole timber piles was driven, enclosing a space for the invert and the side walls of the lock; these piles were well strutted by transverse whole timbers. The excavation was then made, and the lock was founded in short lengths between the tranverse struts. It was presumed that the pressure of water from the tide without the lock would have a tendency to force up and raise the invert and the gate platform; several flues, formed of elm-plank trunking, were therefore laid in the rubble masonry which formed the bed for the invert; these flues were carried under and throughout the lock, and terminated in a vertical well, beyond the upper gates of the lock; thus the sub-water was allowed to circulate, and to rise, without obstruction, to a corresponding height with the tide. This had the desired effect, for the platforms never exhibited any tendency to rise, and there was no settlement in the masonry.

"Mr. Telford, who saw this work in progress, declared he had never seen so troublesome a foundation, and he highly approved of the method adopted for preventing the upward pressure of the sub-water.

"Circumstances occurred of a very similar character in forming the canal from the lock upwards across the mud-lands in the tideway. This was accomplished by excavating the bed of the canal through the mud, which was tolerably stiff, and embanking the sides. When the tide was once excluded, there was very little trouble with the water in the cutting; the work stood well for some months, and did not subside to any remarkable extent; but suddenly the substratum in several places rose up

266   HISTORY OF EXETER.

in the bed of the canal, to the height of 9 feet, or 10 feet, exhibiting peat and vegetable deposit, similar to that found in the
lock-pit and the banks on the sides sunk perpendicularly to a
depth equivalent to the rising of the bottom. In these places
strong piles were closely driven in the lines of the bottom of
the canal. These piles were supported by transverse inverted
arches of rough stone, about 6 feet in width, and were laid about
20 feet apart; when these were finished, the excavations were
re-made, and the banks were re-formed; after which the work
stood well."

The principal circumstances attendant on the progressive
extension and enlargement of the canal, since the year 1820,
down to June 1826, are detailed in the several Reports of Mr.
Green and Mr. Telford, appended to the original Memoir from
which this notice has been abstracted.[19]

It is worthy of remark, that, so early as the year 1698, the
Chamber of Exeter contemplated the extension of their canal
to Turf, the point at which it now enters the estuary of the
Exe,[20] and that they were only foiled in their attempts to effect
this by a successful opposition to an Act of Parliament for the
purpose. It is also somewhat extraordinary that this fact
remained unnoticed until it was discovered by Mr. De la Garde,
in 1834, while preparing his Memoir.

The basin or floating dock was opened on 29th September,
1830.

[21] The Exeter canal is now upwards of five miles and a half in
length. It has two entrance locks, one at Turf and another
opposite Topsham. The Turf lock is built on piles driven
through the fluid bog into the subjacent rock, 20 feet beneath
the inverted arch. It is 131 feet in length and 30 feet 3 inches
in breadth. Its lower cill is 2 inches under Exmouth bar, with
16 feet of water on the upper cill. Vessels of great burden pass
through this lock in three minutes. Between these entrance

---

[19] Mr. Green was the projector and
engineer of the Bude haven and canal,
of the canal and aqueduct on the Tor-
ridge, besides bridges and other important works in this county. He also
invented a very ingenious and powerful
lift, to supersede the use of locks on
canals where there is a scarcity of

water. These lifts are used on the
Taunton canal, and are described in
the Transactions of the Institute of
Civil Engineers, vol. ii., p. 185.
[20] Vide ante, p. 257.
[21] For the concluding part of this
chapter the reader is indebted to Mr.
De la Garde.

locks and Exeter there is only one other lock, the old double lock altered and improved. Opposite Exeter is a basin 900 feet long, and gradually increasing from 90 to 120 feet in width. It is deeper than the canal; so that if the water were lowered in the latter several feet, the vessels in the wet dock would still continue to float. In this basin those vessels lie which are too large to proceed to the old quay through the King's Arms sluice, or which cannot approach it during floods. The canal is 34 feet wide at the bottom, and 94 at the surface of the water, with 15 feet of water throughout; so that in depth it is surpassed in Great Britain only by the Caledonian and Gloucester canals, whilst its sectional area is exceeded only by the former.

Unfortunately this great work was undertaken just before steam navigation at sea was adopted. The proportions of the Turf lock are therefore not such as would now be observed.

The large sum of 113,000l. was spent on these additions and improvements; partly owing to the great dimensions of the canal itself, but still more because (the original plan having been abandoned) the work as it advanced was progressively enlarged. Such a deviation always produces a disproportionate expenditure. Moreover, the unforeseen unsoundness of the ground through which the new portion of the canal, between Topsham and Turf, was cut, added, it is believed, not less than 25,000l. to its contemplated cost.

But the steadily increasing revenue of the canal, whilst under the direction of the Chamber, so far exceeded their expectation as fully to justify this outlay.

		£	s.	d.
The receipts were for	1829			
,, ,,	1830			
,, ,,	1831			
,, ,,	1832			
,, ,,	1833			
,, ,,	1834			
,, ,,	1835			

The Chamber, however, had always regarded their canal not as a mere water-communication for the use of Exeter, but as a great trunk whence branches were to be carried into the remoter inland districts, so as to connect them with the English Channel. They had for a very long period given countenance to every practicable scheme for effecting this object. Canals to Crediton, and even to Barnstaple, had their sanction; and, when these had failed and were forgotten, they rendered whatever assistance

268   HISTORY OF EXETER.

they could to a railway from Crediton to their canal, when railways elsewhere were dreaded or ridiculed. How they were defeated few remember, and the inquiry need not be revived.

But even within these few years, the Bristol and Exeter Railway Company desiring to carry their rails as far as the basin of the canal, the Chamber afforded every facility. They avowedly regretted that they could not—regard being had to the temper of the times—give such of their land as was required for this purpose; but they pledged themselves to take the lowest price they could justify in the public mind. Before the Railway Company could give effect to the liberal intention of the Chamber, the Corporation of Exeter was reformed. Their successors, the Town Council, viewed the affair as it was then generally viewed, and eventually succeeded in inducing the Company to forgo the rights comprised in their Act, and to stop at the Red Cow village half a mile from the basin. To connect the railway system with the canal is now a very difficult task, and it is not easy to foretell when these great engineering works, which were planned for beneficial co-operation, shall cease to be antagonistic.

APPENDIX

OF

DOCUMENTS AND ILLUSTRATIONS.

[Of the following articles, only Nos. I. and II. were left in a state for publication by the learned author of the History, and of these No. I. was supplied to him by Mr. Gidley, Town Clerk, and has been kindly corrected by him for the press. It will be seen hereafter, under article No. III., that the list of Acts might perhaps have been a little enlarged. The remaining articles have, with the assistance of the same intelligent and experienced officer of the city, and with the permission of the Mayor, been added, for the purpose of further illustration, by the Editor.]

No. I.

CHRONOLOGICAL TABLE OF ACTS OF PARLIAMENT

RELATING TO THE COUNTY AND CITY OF EXETER, AND THE DEVON COUNTY PRISONS SITUATED AT EXETER.

15 Henry VI.—The Act of Parliament for the bounding of Saint Sidwells. [Printed in the Appendix to the first edition of Oliver's ' History of Exeter.']

6 Edward IV.—An Act for paving the streets of Exeter.

31 Henry VIII., c. 4.—An Act for the mending of the River of Exeter.

32 Henry VIII., c. 18. —For re-edifying of Towns—Excester being one.

4 Edward VI.—The Acte of Parliament for the boundaries of the Countie of the Citie.

5 Elizabeth, c. 30. — An Acte for the Confirmation of certain Liberties granted to the Citie of Exetour.

23 Elizabeth, c. 17.—An Acte that Gavelkind Landes within the Cytye of Exceter maye be enheritable as Landes at the Common Lawe.

27 Elizabeth, c. 3.—An Act touching divers assurances made by the Bishop and Dean and Chapter of Exeter.—Private Act.

HISTORY OF EXETER.

4 James I., c. 9.—An Act to explain a former Act made in the last Session of this Parliament, intituled " An Act to enable all His Majesty's lovinge subjects of England and Wales to trade freelie into the Domynions of Spaine, Portugal, and France." Note.—This Act recites the letters patent of Queen Elizabeth, dated 17th June, in the second year of her reign, whereby she incorporated certain merchants, therein named, and their successors, being citizens and inhabitants of the City and County of Exeter, by the name of "the Governor, Consuls, and Society of the Merchants Adventurers of the Citye and Countye of Exceter traffiqueing the Realme of Fraunce and the Dominions of the French Kinge;" and also recites the Act of the said last Session; and then enacts that "the said General Law shall not dissolve, annihilate, or impeach the said Charter or the said Companie in any their privileges, liberties, or immunities granted unto them by the said Charter."

7 James I., c. 24.—An Act for the continuance and reparation of a new-built Weare upon the river Exe, near unto the City of Exeter.—Private Act.

18 and 19 Charles II., c. 9.—An Act for Reliefe of Poore Prisoners and setting of them on worke.

> [Exeter is not mentioned in this Act; but it gives power "to the Sheriffs of Counties, and to the Mayor, Bailiffe, and other head officer having the custodie of the Common Gaol within any Corporation," and therefore includes the County and Corporation of Exeter. Sec. 4 makes certain regulations respecting a messuage intended to be used as a Common Gaol and Workhouse in the parish of St. Thomas the Apostle, near the City of Exon.]

1 William and Mary, c. 32.—An Act for better preventing the exportation of woole and encouraging the woollen manufactures of this kingdome.

> Sec. 5 provides that "no wool shall be shipped from the kingdom of Ireland but from these ports following, viz.: Dublin, Waterford, Youhall, Kingsale, Cork, and Drogheda; and that noe wooll shall be imported from the kingdom of Ireland into any ports but these following, viz.: Liverpool, Chester, Bristoll, Minehead, Barnestaple, Bidiford, and Exeter."

> This Act was continued by 4 W. & M., c. 24, s. 9; 7 & 8 W. III., c. 28, s. 1; and 9 W. III., c. 40.

9 and 10 William III., c. 33.—An Act for erecting Hospitals and Workhouses within the City and County of the City of Exon, for the better employing and maintaining the poor there. —Private Act.

12 William III., c. 4.—An Act for appointing Wardens and Assay-Masters for assaying Wrought Plate in the Cities of York, Exeter, Bristol, Chester, and Norwich.—Public Act.

ACTS OF PARLIAMENT. 271

1 Anne, c. 29.—An Act to enable the Dean and Chapter of the Cathedral Church of St. Peter in Exeter, and their farmers and tenants to make leases of and in the Manor of Culmstock, in the County of Devon.—Private Act.

3 and 4 Anne, c. 51.—An Act for sale of several lands and chattel estates in the County of Devon, and City and County of Exon, of Joseph Price, for payment of his debts and legacies, charged upon his estate, and for a provision for himself, his wife, and family.—Private Act.

9 Anne, c. 19.—An Act to enable Her Majesty to grant the site of the Castle of Exon (parcel of the Duchy of Cornwall), for 99 years, for the use and benefit of the County of Devon.—Public Act.

9 Anne, c. 4.—An Act for ratifying several purchases lately made with the Public Stock of the County of Devon, and for making further purchases for the use of the said County with the Public Stock thereof; and also for regulating and better employment of the Public Stock of the said County.—Private Act.

26 George II., c. 8.—An Act for opening the port of Exeter for the importation of wool and woollen yarn from Ireland.—Public Act.

26 George II., c. 57.—An Act for raising a sum of money by a County Rate, for purchasing a proper prison for Debtors, in the County of Devon.—Public Act.

26 George II., c. 74.—An Act for amending several Roads leading from the City of Exeter.—Public Act.

29 George II., c. 55.—An Act to amend and render more effectual an Act passed in the twenty-sixth year of the reign of his present Majesty, for amending several Roads leading from the City of Exeter.—Public Act.

31 George II., c. 53.—An Act to explain, amend, and render more effectual an Act passed in the ninth and tenth years of the reign of his late Majesty King William III., intituled "An Act for erecting Hospitals and Workhouses within the City and County of the City of Exon, for the better employing and maintaining the poor there.—Public Act."

1 Geo. III., c. 28.—An Act for enlightening the streets within the City of Exeter and suburbs thereof.—Public Act.

8 and 9 George III. (Second Session), c. 93.—An Act to continue and render more effectual two Acts for amending several Roads leading from the City of Exeter, and for repairing and widening several other Roads therein mentioned; and for rebuilding or repairing Exe Bridge, and making the avenues leading thereto more commodious; and for building a Bridge over the

272   HISTORY OF EXETER.

river Exe at or near Countess Wear, in the County of Devon.—
Public Act.

10 Geo. III., c. 73.—An Act to empower the Justices of the Peace
for the County of Devon to apply a sum of money out of the
County Stock for the opening, making, and maintaining a
convenient and commodious highway from the High-street,
in the City of Exeter, to the Castle of Exeter.—Public Act.

13 Geo. III., c. 16.—An Act for taking down the Shire House of
the County of Devon, and for building a new Shire Hall in a
more commodious manner.—Public Act.

13 Geo. III., c. 27.—An Act for the more easy and speedy recovery
of small Debts within the City and County of the City of
Exeter.—Public Act.

13 Geo. III., c. 109.—An Act for more effectually amending several
Roads leading from the City of Exeter, and for rebuilding or
repairing Exe Bridge, and making the avenues leading thereto
more commodious, and for building a Bridge over the river
Exe at or near Countess Wear, and for amending several other
roads therein mentioned.—Public Act.

14 Geo. III., c. 61.—An Act to explain and amend two several Acts
of Parliament for erecting Hospitals and Workhouses within
the City and County of the City of Exon, for the better
employing and maintaining the poor there; and to raise further
sums of money for the more effectually carrying the purposes
of the said Acts into execution.—Public Act.

15 Geo. III., c. 33.—An Act for vesting several Messuages, Lands,
and Hereditaments in the County of Devon and City of Exeter,
late the estate of Robert Stone, gentleman, deceased, in
Trustees, to enable them to convey the same to the purchasers
thereof; and to apply the money arising by such sale in payment of the debts of the said Robert Stone, pursuant to a decree
of the Court of Chancery.—Private Act.

23 Geo. III., c. 20.—An Act to dissolve the marriage of John
Williams, of the City of Exeter, gentleman, with Elizabeth,
his now wife, and to enable him to marry again, and for other
purposes therein mentioned.—Private Act.

25 Geo. III., c. 21.—An Act to render more effectual several Acts
of Parliament for erecting Hospitals and Workhouses within
the City and County of the City of Exon, for the better employing and maintaining the poor there, and to raise further
sums of money for the better carrying the purposes of the said
Acts into execution.—Public Act.

27 Geo. III., c. 59.—An Act for making and declaring the Gaol
of the County of Devon, called the High Gaol, a public and
common Gaol, and for discharging Denys Rolle and John Rolle,
Esquires, and their respective heirs and assigns, from the office

ACTS OF PARLIAMENT. 273

of keeper of the said Gaol; and for improving and enlarging the same, or building a new one; and also for taking down the Chapel in the Castle of Exeter; and for other purposes therein mentioned.—Public Act.

28 Geo. III., c. 76.—An Act for raising further sums of money, for the better relief of the Poor of the City and County of the City of Exon, and to explain and amend an Act passed in the twenty-fifth year of the reign of his present Majesty, for rendering more effectual several Acts of Parliament for erecting Hospitals and Workhouses within the said City and County, for the better employing and maintaining the poor there.— Public Act.

36 Geo. III., c. 46.—An Act for making a navigable Canal from the river Exe, near the town of Topsham, in the county of Devon, to the river Tone, near the town of Taunton, in the county of Somerset, for cleansing and making navigable a certain part of the said river Tone, and for making certain cuts from the said Canal.—Public Act.

41 Geo. III., c. 61.—An Act for improving and extending the navigation of the river Exe, from the public quay at Exeter, to the public road adjoining Four Mills, near Crediton, in the county of Devon, by making a navigable Canal, or cuts, and deepening and widening such parts of the rivers Exe and Creedy as shall be necessary for that purpose.—Local and personal.

43 Geo. III., c. 122.—An Act for more effectually repairing and improving the several Roads leading to and from the City of Exeter, and for keeping in repair Exeter Bridge and Countess Wear Bridge.—Local and personal.

46 Geo. III., c. 39.—An Act for better repairing the Streets, Lanes, and Passages within the City of Exeter, and County of the said City, and for amending an Act passed in the first year of his present Majesty, intituled, " An Act for enlightening the streets within the City of Exeter, and suburbs thereof," and for the better regulation of the Watch within the said city and county, and for otherwise improving the same.—Local and personal.

50 George III., c. 85.—An Act to explain and amend an Act of the twenty-seventh year of his present Majesty, for making and declaring the Gaol for the County of Devon a public and common Gaol; and for other purposes in the said Act mentioned.—Local and personal.

50 Geo. III., c. 165.—An Act for better and more effectually Paving, Lighting, Cleansing, Watching, and otherwise improving the Streets, Ways, and other public Passages and Places in the City and County of the City of Exeter.—Local and personal.

T

HISTORY OF EXETER.

51 Geo. III., c. 166.—An Act to vary and alter the line of a cut, authorized to be made by an Act of the thirty sixth year of his present Majesty, for making a Canal from the river Exe, near Topsham, in the County of Devon, to the river Tone, near Taunton, in the County of Somerset; and to amend the said Act.—Local and personal.

52 Geo. III., c. 109.—An Act for repairing the Parish Church of St. Sidwell, in the City and County of the City of Exeter.—Local and personal.

54 Geo. III., c. 10.—An Act to enable the West of England Fire and Life Insurance Company to sue and be sued in the name of their Secretary.—Local and personal.

54 Geo. III., c. 110.—An Act for enlarging the powers of an Act of his present Majesty, for repairing the Church of St. Sidwell, in the City of Exeter.—Local and personal.

55 Geo. III., c. 12.—An Act for repairing and improving the Roads leading to and from the City of Exeter, and for keeping in repair Exe Bridge and Countess Wear Bridge.—Local and personal.

56 Geo. III., c. 10.—An Act for lighting with Gas the City and County of the City of Exeter.—Local and personal.

58 Geo. III., c. 51.—An Act for building a new Gaol and House of Correction for the City and County of the City of Exeter.—Local and personal.

1 Geo. IV., c. 78.—An Act for removing the Markets held within the City of Exeter, and for providing another Market-place or other Market-places in lieu thereof.—Local and personal.

1 and 2 Geo. IV., c. 37.—An Act for enlarging the powers of an Act of his late Majesty for repairing the Roads leading to and from the City of Exeter, and for making a new branch of Road to communicate therewith.—Local and personal.

7 Geo. IV., c. 25.—An Act for repairing, widening, and improving the several Roads leading to and from the City of Exeter, and for making certain new lines of Road to communicate with the same, and for keeping in repair Exe Bridge and Countess Wear Bridge.—Local and personal.

7 and 8 Geo. IV., c. 10.—An Act for vesting in the Dean and Chapter of the Cathedral Church of Saint Peter in Exeter certain Messuages and Lands, situate within the Close of the said Cathedral Church, belonging to the Archdeaconries o_ Totnes, Barnstaple, and Cornwall, founded in the said Cathedral Church in consideration of certain perpetual yearly sums to be

ACTS OF PARLIAMENT. 275

payable to the said several Archdeacons and their successors; and for enabling the said Dean and Chapter to grant Leases of the same premises.—Local and personal.

10 Geo. IV., c. 47.—An Act for altering, extending, and improving the Exeter Canal.—Local and personal.

1 and 2 Will. IV., c. 62.—An Act to amend an Act of his late Majesty King George the Fourth for repairing the several Roads leading to and from the City of Exeter, and for making certain new lines of Road to communicate with the same; and for keeping in repair Exe Bridge and Countess Wear Bridge; and to make and maintain other Roads communicating with the said Roads.—Local and personal.

1 and 2 Will. IV., c. 11.—An Act for enabling the Mayor, Bailiffs, and Commonalty of the City of Exeter to Sell two Houses in the parish of Saint Stephen's, Exeter, vested in them, and to Purchase other Estates for the performance of the charitable purposes of the Will of Joan Tuckfield.—Local and personal.

2 and 3 Will. IV., c. 93.—An Act for making and maintaining a Railway from the basin of the Exeter Canal, in the parish of Saint Thomas the Apostle, in the County of Devon, to the Four Mills in the parish of Crediton, in the said county.—Local and personal.

2 and 3 Will. IV., c. 106.—An Act for better Paving, Lighting, Watching, Cleansing, and otherwise improving the City of Exeter and County of the same City.—Local and personal.

3 and 4 Will. IV., c. 31.—An Act for better supplying with Water the City and County of the City of Exeter, and such part of the parish of Saint David as is situated in the County of Devon.—Local and personal.

3 and 4 Will. IV., c. 32.—An Act for more effectually supplying with Water the City and County of the City of Exeter, and places adjacent thereto.—Local and personal.

4 and 5 Will. IV., c. 8.—An Act for removing the Markets held in the High and Fore Streets, and other places within the City of Exeter, and for providing other Markets in lieu thereof.— Local and personal.

4 and 5 Will. IV., c. 37.—An Act to amend an Act of the fifty-fourth year of King George the Third, for enabling the West of England Fire and Life Insurance Company to sue and be sued in the name of their Secretary; and to give further Powers to the said Company.—Local and personal.

5 and 6 Will. IV., c. 29.—An Act for building a Bridge over the river Exe from the Shilhay at the City of Exeter, and for

T 2

276   HISTORY OF EXETER.

making approaches thereto ; and for removing the present Ferry across the said River, and establishing another Ferry or a Footbridge in lieu thereof.—Local and personal.

5 and 6 Will. IV., c. 98.—An Act to amend an Act of the third year of his present Majesty for more effectually supplying with Water the City and County of the City of Exeter, and places adjacent thereto.—Local and personal.

6 and 7 Will. IV., c. 4.—An Act to establish a Company for more effectually lighting with Gas the City and County of the City of Exeter, and certain parishes and places in the County of Devon.—Local and personal.

6 and 7 Will. IV., c. 27.—An Act to alter, amend, and enlarge the powers of an Act for lighting with Gas the City and County of the City of Exeter, and for lighting with Gas the several parishes of Alphington, Heavitree, Saint Leonard, Saint Thomas the Apostle, and Topsham, in the County of Devon.—Local and personal.

1 and 2 Vict., c. 51.—An Act to enable the Exeter Commercial Gas Light and Coke Company to raise a further sum of money.—Local and personal.

3 and 4 Vict., c. 58.—An Act to amend the Acts for supplying with Water the City and County of the City of Exeter, and places adjacent thereto.—Local and personal.

3 and 4 Vict., c. 74.—An Act for equalizing, defining, and regulating the Petty Customs, and for facilitating the Collection thereof and of the Quay Dues payable to the Mayor, Aldermen, and Burgesses of the City and Borough of Exeter, and for preserving the Navigation of the river Exe.—Local and personal.

3 and 4 Vict., c. 81.—An Act to amend the provisions of the Acts relating to the Turnpike Roads leading to and from the City of Exeter, and for making a new Branch Road to communicate therewith.—Local and personal.

3 and 4 Vict., c. 122.—An Act to alter, amend, and enlarge the powers and provisions of an Act for removing the Markets held in the High and Fore Streets, and other places within the City of Exeter, and for providing other Markets in lieu thereof.—Local and personal.

4 and 5 Vict., c. 73.—An Act for the more easy and speedy Recovery of Small Debts within the City and County of the City of Exeter.—Local and personal.

15 and 16 Vict., c. 154.—An Act to repeal the Acts relating to the Exeter and the Countess Wear Turnpike Roads, and to make other provisions in lieu thereof; and to authorize the Construction of certain new Roads.—Local and personal.

DATES OF COMMENCEMENT OF REGISTERS. 277

No. II.

A TABLE SHEWING THE DATE OF COMMENCEMENT OF THE CATHEDRAL AND PAROCHIAL REGISTERS OF EXETER AND ITS SUBURBS.

	BAPTISMS.	MARRIAGES.	BURIALS.
The Cathedral	Dec. 26, 1594	Oct. 24, 1597	Mar. 13, 1593
Allhallows, Goldsmith Street.	Feb. 6, 1566	Jan. 28, 1561	Aug. 8, 1561
Allhallows on the Walls . .	Oct. 17, 1694	July 29, 1694	April 5, 1694
St. David	Oct. 8, 1559	Feb. 8, 1559	Jan. 3, 1559
St. Edmund, on the Bridge .	Jan. 11, 1571	July 15, 1572	Dec. 24, 1571
St. George	Jan. 12, 1681	Jan. 29, 1681	Feb. 14, 1681
St. John	Sept. 17, 1682	May 16, 1683	Sept. 9, 1682
St. Kerrian	Feb. 5, 1558	Jan. 13, 1558	May 2, 1558
St. Lawrence	July 21, 1604	Aug. 20, 1604	June 30, 1604
St. Martin	May 28, 1572	July 26, 1572	May 21, 1572
St. Mary Arches	Nov. 10, 1538	Oct. 27, 1538	Dec. 12, 1538
St. Mary Major	Dec. 25, 1561	Jan. 18, 1561	Jan. 2, 1561
St. Mary Steps	Jan. 28, 1654	Dec. 17, 1655	Mar. 28, 1655
St. Olave	Mar. 5, 1601	Dec. 6, 1601	Nov. 27, 1601
St. Pancras	July 15, 1664	May 29, 1670	Dec. 28, 1672
St. Paul [1]	April 8, 1562	May 8, 1562	June 5, 1562
St. Petrock	Jan. 11, 1538	Oct. 13, 1538	Jan. 17, 1538
St. Sidwell	April 4, 1569	May 10, 1569	Mar. 28, 1569
St. Stephen	Jan. 11, 1668	June 12, 1668	July 24, 1668
Trinity	Aug. 19, 1563	Aug. 20, 1539	Sept. 9, 1563
Heavitree	Oct. 20, 1653	Feb. 24, 1653	Nov. 3, 1653
St. Leonard	Mar. 1, 1704	Sept. 12, 1708	Oct. 19, 1710
St. Thomas	Nov. 13, 1541	Mar. 23, 1576	April 4, 1554

[1] *This Register is deposited with the Cathedral Register; the Register deposited in the Parish Chest commences*

Aug. 8, 1705	Sept. 3, 1705	July 5, 1705

278   HISTORY OF EXETER.

No. III.

CHRONOLOGICAL TABLE OF CHARTERS OF THE CITY OF EXETER.

The following are selected from a MS. volume of charters, in the office of the Town Clerk, purporting to be transcripts from the originals. Most of them appear to have been examined copies. With the exception of the governing charter, given at the end of this Table, the instruments are not here copied in extenso, but are only abstracted and described. Some have been erroneously described in the above volume, and are here corrected.

Doctor Oliver has referred (p. 46, ante) to a charter of Henry I., granted to the city, which has been also noticed by Lysons in his Devonshire (p. 192), and by Izacke in his Memorials. It is believed that no such charter will be found among the records of the city, nor is any such charter recited in the Inspeximus Charters of later date, though they mention the *fact* that Exeter enjoyed privileges and exemptions in the reign of Henry I., and was then possessed of the customs of London. We know from other sources (6 Dugdale's Monast., p. 150, et seq. last ed.), that the queen of Henry I. had a grant of the fee-farm of the city for her life, of which she assigned two-thirds, being the yearly sum of 25*l.*, to the priory of the Holy Trinity in London, and that this last grant was confirmed to the priory by the king, her husband; but at present I have no knowledge of any charter of his reign granted to the citizens of Exeter.

It must not be supposed that all the franchises of this city originated in the charters hereafter specified, or that its corporate character is wholly derived from them. It has always been claimed and pleaded as a corporation existing from time immemorial; and no other city in the realm can show a better title to that claim. I am even willing to accede to the opinion of an eminent historian and antiquary, whom we have lately lost, that Exeter "probably enjoyed franchises and liberties before any one of our Anglo-Saxon kings had a crown upon his head or a sceptre in his hand." See Palgrave's History of England, Anglo-Saxon period, p. 205, and his larger work on the Rise and Progress of the Commonwealth, Part 1., p. 410, where that most learned writer is disposed to think that the city was a free republic before the final reduction of the British inhabitants of West Devon, paying only its "gafol" to the Saxon kings, but in other respects as loosely subject to their authority as the ancient free cities of Germany or Italy. If their claim to all the franchises of London was recognized as early as the 12th century, we are not likely to find any earlier charter expressed in terms other than those of a general confirmation of undefined, pre-existing, freedom.

Dr. Oliver has said little or nothing of those subordinate fraternities or companies, of which we know the existence from other

TABLE OF CHARTERS.

quarters. He has not even referred to those remarkable Saxon gilds in connexion with Exeter with which Dr. Hickes has made us acquainted in his celebrated Dissertatio Epistolaris. It would have been desirable to learn more about the origin and constitution of those affiliated trade-gilds of Exeter, which are common to the municipal polity of all our old cities. The records of the city must surely contain ample information respecting them, for the MS. collections of Hoker often refer to them. Companies of this kind form no part of the dominant corporation ; but if my acquaintance with these, however imperfect, has not deceived me, the ruling body at Exeter claimed to establish them without resort to the royal prerogative for that purpose, though I find proof that, at a later period, a more correct view of the law prevailed and seems to have suggested the expediency, or the necessity, of obtaining letters patent from the Crown.

It appears to me that the city authorities relied upon their undisputed power to make ordinances for the good government of the city as necessarily including in itself the right to associate the different trades of the city into separate bodies, and as inconsistent with any independent right of those trades to seek elsewhere the means of self-government. Accordingly we find a complaint of the mayor and bailiffs of Exeter by petition in Parliament, 22nd Edward IV., that this right had been infringed by letters-patent in the 6th year of his reign, purporting to erect the craft of tailors into a gild or fraternity, under which the tailors had presumed to have a master and wardens, and to act in prejudice of the civic government. It is remarkable that this petition was successful, and the letters patent were annulled by Parliament (Rot. Parl., vol. vi. p. 219, and vol. v. p. 390).

That the law relating to the power to form gilds, without the direct authority of the Crown, was even in much later times in an unsettled state, will be seen from the reported cases collected in Viner's Abridgment, vol. vi. p. 259, and Blackstone's Commentaries, vol. i. p. 474. The power to dispense with a resort to the Crown probably depends on the corporate attributes and compulsory powers which the association proposes to assume or to exercise.—E. S.

(1.) HENRY II.—Henricus Rex Angliæ et Dux Normannie et Aquitanæ et Comes Andegaviæ Episcopo Exon' et Baronibus et fidelibus suis Franciæ et Angliæ, Salutem. Sciatis me concessisse civibus meis Exoniæ omnes rectas consuetudines quas habuerunt in tempore Regis Henrici, avi mei, remotis omnibus pravis consuetudinibus post avum meum ibi elevatis. Et sciatis eos habere consuetudines London', et ita testati coram me ipsi mei barones London', ita liberè honorificè et justè sicut unquam melius habuerent tempore avi mei. Teste Arn. Ep. Lexov., Reg. Com. Cornub., et Toma Cancell. Apud London.

(2.), (3.), (4.) These three documents are treated in the volume of transcripts as independent charters of Henry I. They are,

HISTORY OF EXETER.

in fact, writs or precepts of Henry II., notifying to all that the citizens of Exeter were exempt from certain tolls. They all run, with slight variations, in the following form, and are attested by the same witnesses as the above charter:—

HENRY, King of England, Duke of Normandy and Aquitaine, Earl of Anjou, &c., to all justices, sheriffs, and ministers. "Precipio vobis," that all my citizens of Exeter and their merchandise are quit of toll, lastage, and passage, and all other customs on land or water, or elsewhere—penalty 10*l.* for disturbing them. In witness, Reginald [Earl of Cornwall], Arn. Bishop of Lisieux, and Thomas, Chancellor, and the citizens of London.

(5.) RICHARD I.—Confirms to the "burgesses of Exeter" freedom from toll, passage, and *pontage,* in all lands, waters, fairs, and markets, and from all secular service and customs, "citra et ultra mare." Testibus, &c. Dat. 29 March, anno regni 1ᵃ, at Rouen.

(6.) RICHARD I.—Confirms to the "citizens" of Exeter freedom from toll, passage, and lastage. (No date or place.)

(7.) JOHN "Com. Morit." (Earl of Mortain, afterwards king) grants to "his citizens" of Exeter all right customs which they had in the time of his great grandfather (Henrici avi patris mei), and recites that they had the customs of London. Teste, &c., apud Craneburne. (No date.)

(8.) JOHN, King of England, Lord of Ireland, Duke, &c., grants to his citizens of Exeter all right customs, &c. (as in his last charter), and confirms the charter of his father, and of his brother Richard (supra, No. 5). He further grants to them freedom from lastage and *stallage* over all his land, "quantum ad nos pertinet." Test., &c. Dat. apud Salm' (Saumur?), 15 June, aº reg. 2ᵈᵒ.

(9.) HENRY III.—Inspects the charter of John next preceding, and confirms that and other charters in general terms. Dat. Westm., 24 March, aº reg. 21ᵐᵒ.

(10.) RICHARD, King of the Romans, grants to the citizens of Exeter and "their heirs," to have and hold the city of Exeter, with the appurtanances at fee-farm, as they have been before accustomed to hold it, with all liberties and free customs as fully as in past times, before Walter Galun, our bailiff, took the city into our hands, rendering to us and our heirs the old fee-farm as they have heretofore done to us and our ancestors, lords of Exeter, saving to us reasonable talliages when the king shall tally his cities of England, &c. Sealed with our royal seal. Testibus Philip Basset and others. Dat. apud Mere., 25 May, aº gratiæ, 1259, aº regni nostri 3ᵗⁱᵒ.

(11.) RICHARD, King of the Romans, grants to the mayors, bailiffs, and citizens of Exeter, and their heirs, to hold the city at the old fee-farm, videlicet, 13*l.* 9*s.* yearly, payable at Easter and Michaelmas, saving to us and our heirs the right to tally the city whenever the king tallies his cities and boroughs. Sealed with "our royal

TABLE OF CHARTERS.

281

seal." Testibus, Master Arnold de Holland our prothonotary, Philip de Eya our treasurer, Philip de Oya our steward, Roger de Sancto Constant', Michael de Northampton, our clerks; Henry Tracy, Reginald de Boterell, Guido de Nonant, milites; Stephen Heyne [or Heym] our steward of Cornwall, and others. Dat. apud London, 7 Novemb., anno regni nostri 3$^{tio.}$ [1]

(12.) HENRY III.—Inspeximus of the charter of his brother Richard, King of Aleman' (namely, the last charter, No. 11), and confirmation of it. Dat. Westminster, 6 Nov$^{r.}$, a° reg. 44$^{to.}$

(13.) EDWARD I.—Letters patent addressed to the mayor, bailiffs, and "probi homines" of the city of Exeter, authorising them to take the following tolls on saleable articles arriving within the city, for three years from the date thereof, in aid of the paving of the city, viz. :—

For every load of corn	1 ob.
Every horse, mare, ox, or cow	1 ob.
Every hide, undressed or tanned, of the same beasts [2]	1 qr.
For five bacons	1 ob.
Every salmon, fresh or salt [3]	1 qr.
Every ten goats or pigs	1 qr.
Every ten fleeces	1 qr.
Every hundredweight of woolfels, goatskins, and deerskins . .	1 ob.
Every hundredweight of skins of lambs, kids, hares, calves, foxes, cats, and squirrels	1 ob.
Every load of cloths [4]	1 ob.
Every entire cloth	1 ob.

The remaining articles enumerated are linen cloths, silk, cloth worked with gold and samite, diaspre, and baudekin, or without gold, &c., ships with saleable cargoes, wine, beer, honey, sacs of wool, iron, goods sold by weight [averio de pondere], tallow, &c., wode, alum, coperose, argoil, and "vertegrece," copes [coparum?], herrings, seafish, boards, millstones, salt, butter, and cheese, nails, horse-shoes, and cart-clouts, tan, trussels of merchandise, tin, brass, and copper; vinegar, hemp, oil, and all other unspecified goods worth 5s. Dat. apud Gulford, 10 March, a° reg. 3$^{tio.}$ [5]

(14.) EDMUND, Earl of Cornwall, son of Richard, king of Aleman', inspects and confirms the charter of his father, No. 10, supra. Dat. apud Berkham (Berkhampsted), 18 June, a° reg. 14 Edward I.

(15.) EDMUND, Earl, &c. (ut supra).—A general remission of the earl's wrath and indignation against the mayor and citizens of

---

[1] Richard Earl of Cornwall, brother of Henry III., was elected King of the Romans A.D. 1257. Crowned 17 May, 1257. The above two charters were therefore made respectively in the 43rd and 44th years of the reign of Henry.

[2] The words in the old office copy before me are, "pro quolibet corio frisco salvo aut tannato:" but "salvo" ought perhaps to be read "salso" or "salito."

[3] "Frisco vel salvo"—probably "salso."

[4] "Sumagio pannorum."

[5] There is a similar grant of the same reign in aid of the repair of London Bridge in which the articles charged nearly correspond with this Exeter tariff. See Hearne Lib. Nig., p. 479, vol. i.

282   HISTORY OF EXETER.

Exeter, by reason of certain trespasses committed before the Sunday next after the octaves of Trinity last past. The earl further respites a debt of 50 marks, part of a debt of 250 marks due from the city on bond, " quamdiu se benè et fidelitèr gesserint erga nos," with a power to reclaim the respited debt on the legal conviction of the obligors of any future trespass against the earl. Dated at Berkhampsted, Monday after the feast of the Nativity of St. John Baptist, a° 14 Edward I.⁶

(16.) EDWARD I.—This is not a charter of franchises, but a grant to the mayor of Exeter of the custody, at will, of the king's seal for sealing recognizances of debts acknowledged before him by force of the statutes 11 Ed. I. and of 13 Ed. I., stat iii. cap. 1. It is dated 22 August, a° reg. 20$^{mo.}$

(17.) EDWARD I.—This inspects and confirms the previous charters, supra, of Henry II., John (No. 7), and Henry III. (No. 9), and further grants exemption from *murage* and *pavage* throughout the realm, and confirms such liberties under former grants as may have been otherwise lost by disuse. Dated Easton, near Stamford, 4 May, a° reg. 28$^{ro.}$ [7]

(18.) EDWARD II.—Recites and confirms the previous charters, and further grants exclusive jurisdiction to the mayor and bailiffs of Exeter of all pleas of land and tenements, trespasses and contracts, arising within the city or suburbs, except pleas relating to the crown, or its ministers, or the commonalty of the city ; exemption from service on assizes, juries, and inquests out of the city ; and also freedom from murage, pavage, pickage, anchorage, strandage, and " segiagio,"⁸ on the goods of the citizens. Dat. Westm., 12 November, a° reg. 14$^{to.}$ [9]

(19.) EDWARD III.—Inspeximus and general confirmation of the principal preceding charters, including those of Edward I. and II. Dated apud Eltham, 1 March, a° reg. 3$^{tio.}$

(20.) EDWARD III.—Letters patent reciting that the mayor and citizens of Exeter had been called upon, in the Court of Exchequer,

---

⁶ This is the document noticed in the text, ante pp. 62, 63. The first part is a simple remission of anger and ill-will ; a form of ideal pardon not uncommon in the early patent-rolls. What may have been its legal effect is not very apparent. The conditional respite of part of the debt was a more decided benefit to the obligors. The precise transaction referred to in the charter is not explained by Dr. Oliver. It must have occurred in the summer of 1286, and the daughters of the king must have been in some way mixed up with it ; for their intercession is stated in the pardon as the moving cause of the charter.

⁷ This seems to be the charter referred to in the text, supra p. 63. It is printed in Hearne's Liber Niger, vol. ii. p. 812.

⁸ If this word be correctly read, it must mean the berth or place of mooring of a ship in the waters of the city.

⁹ Under this charter cognizance was claimed and allowed in an action of trespass *quare clausum*, &c., of White v. Bruerton, in the Court of Queen's Bench, East. Term, 17 Eliz., Rot. 411, in the record exemplified on behalf of the mayor, bailiffs, and commonalty, 22 June, same year.

TABLE OF CHARTERS. 283

to show by what title they claimed to hold the city at the fee-farm of 12*l.* 19*s.* per annum, and had exhibited a charter of Richard, king of the Romans, with confirmation by certain of the kings of England, including that of the present king; but that it had been ascertained, on inspection of the rolls of the Exchequer, that the city had, in the time of King Henry and of other of the king's progenitors, been an ancient demesne of the Crown, and as such been used to be answered at the Exchequer by the sheriff of Devon, as part of the farm of the "corpus" of the said county; and that the said Richard had no estate in fee in the said city, nor any other interest in it except a farm or rent of 12*l.* 19*s.*, granted to him in aid by assignment of King Henry [the Third] at will; and that thereupon the city had been seized into the king's hands by the Court of Exchequer. And thereupon the king grants and confirms the city to the mayor and citizens to hold for ever in fee-farm at the rent of 20*l.*, payable at the Exchequer at Easter and Michaelmas. Dated at Eltham Saint Cross, 6 Feb., a° reg. 6*to.* "Per ipsum regem et consilium et pro fine 50 marcarum." [1]

(21.) EDWARD III.—This is not a charter, but a writ to the mayor, bailiffs, and "probi homines" of Exeter, notifying the grant of the fee-farm rent of 20*l.* to Edward, Duke of Cornwall, to whom they are to be afterwards attendant and respondent for such rent. Dated Westm., 24 July, a° reg. 11*mo.* "Per ipsum regem et totum consilium in Parliamento." [2]

(22.) EDWARD III.—A commission under the Great Seal, dated Westminster, 20 Aug., a° reg. 18*ro.*, to the mayor and bailiffs of Exeter. It recites robberies and breaches of the peace in the city; and authorises and enjoins them to keep the peace in the city and suburbs, and to arrest, try by inquest, and punish the malefactors. It professes to be grounded on the statutes of Winchester, 13 Edw. I., and of Northampton, 2 Edw. III. [ch. 6 and 7]. [3]

(23.) EDWARD III.—A writ or precept, addressed to the "bailiffs, probi homines, and commonalty of the city and vills of Exeter, Topsham, and Kenton;" recites an order of council at Westminster, for providing 120 great ships to accompany the king in his expedition to France, and for defence and protection of the realm, of which sixty were to be raised by the admiral of the west. It then requires three ships to be supplied by the three towns above-named,

---

[1] This instrument seems to be founded on the alleged nullity of the different royal confirmations of the charter of Earl Richard, because the kings, when they confirmed it, had been ignorant of the earl's defective title. This ground of nullity is one recognized of old by the law in the case of crown grants. Viner, Abridgment, vol. xvii. pp. 98, 104, *et seq.*

[2] These words were held to show a statutable authority in the "*Prince's*

Case." Coke's Report, Part 8.

[3] Izacke calls this a special commission of oyer and terminer. It is not in the later form of a permanent commission of the peace. The Statute of Winton gave no power to try or to punish offenders; but this was given by the Statute of Northampton, chap. 6. General commissions of the peace first became a permanent statutable institution in this reign. See Statute 1 Edw. III. Chap. 16; 18 Edw. III. Chap. 2.

284   HISTORY OF EXETER.

each with sixty well-armed mariners, and twenty archers, to repair to Sandwich on Easter Monday following.   Teste Lionel, the king's son, Custos of England.   At Reading, 25 March, aº reg. 21ᵐᵒ· " Per ipsum regem et totum consilium." [4]

(24.) EDWARD III.—Exemplification under the Great Seal, at the instance of the mayor, bailiffs, and commonalty of the city of Exeter, of the certificate of the Court of Exchequer of the entry in Domesday touching Exeter, and of a like certificate of the record of a quo warranto against the city executed before the justices in Eyre at Exeter, on the utas of St. Martin, 9 and 10 Edward I., wherein the inquest found the fee-farm of the city to be 39l. 18s. 0d., whereof 25l. 12s. 5d. was paid to the prior of Trinity, London, and the rest to the Earl of Cornwall, by charter of Henry brother of Earl Richard ; that such payment to the prior of Trinity had been made from the time of Henry I. [sic]; that the burgesses claimed return of writs, estreats, fines, placita de vetito namio, gallows, pillory, tumbrel, amends of assize of ale, waif, forefeng, and a coroner of their own ; a fair at the Gule of August for four days, and a market for three days in the week, viz., Monday, Wednesday, and Friday ; and all these franchises were claimed from the time of the Conquest. The date of their exemplification is 3rd February, aº reg. 39ᵃ·

(25.) RICHARD II.—A general confirmation of the preceding royal charters.   Date Westminster, 5th December, aº reg. 2ᵈᵒ·

(26.) HENRY IV.—No charter of this reign is recorded in the above list of corporation charters.   The only two documents referred to under this head are exemplifications under the Great Seal of certain certificates of the Court of Exchequer touching the manor and fee of St. Sidwell, of which no entry is there stated to be found in Domesday ; and of certain records of process there in 21 Edward III., touching the fee-farm of the city, and of the lastage and stallage of fairs there, and of houses at Wyke and Alricheston, villa or members of the manor of Lydford.   The exemplifications are of the dates respectively of 11th December, anno regni 8ᵛᵒ·, and 1 December, anno 14ᵗᵒ· That there was a charter of confirmation by Henry IV. appears by the next document.

(27.) HENRY V.—This is a constat or exemplification of an enrolment in the chancery rolls of a charter of Henry IV., which is set forth therein and is in fact a charter dated Westminster, 14 December, anno reg. (Henry IV.) 2ᵈᵒ· inspecting and confirming the charter of Richard II., cited, supra, No. 25.   The constat professes only to be a copy, and not a confirmation.

(28.) HENRY VI.—This is a charter of confirmation, dated 14th July,

---

[4] Other writs of this kind will be found in Rymer's Fœdera of about the same date.   They constitute some of the earliest precedents for the impressment of ships and seamen, and are accordingly familiar in the treatises on that subject.

TABLE OF CHARTERS.

285

anno reg. 16ᵃ, and recites the authority of the Parliament held in the first year of the king's reign for such ratification.

There was an Act of 15 Henry VI. for ascertaining and settling the boundaries of the fee of St. Sidwell and the rights of the contending claimants, viz. the Chapter and the City. This was exemplified by letters patent of Henry in the same year, and was afterwards inspected and *ratified*[5] by his successor Edward IV. in the first year of his reign. The letters patent are set forth in Dr. Oliver's History of Exeter, ed. 1821, in the Appendix.

(29.) EDWARD IV.—Grants to the mayor, bailiffs, and commonalty certain franchises, viz., " bona et catalla, vocata manuopera, capienda cum aliquâ personâ ubicunque infra jurisdictionem civitatis per eandem personam deadvocata; catalla felonum, fugitivorum, utlegatorum, attinctorum, necnon qualitercunque damnatorum seu convictorum, felonum de se, escapia felonum et fines, &c., in quibuscunque curiis nostris tam coram nobis quam aliis justiciariis," &c., with power to the mayor and bailiffs, to seize and take them *by themselves or their ministers*, with all fines, amercements, issues, forfeitures of residents, &c.;[6] also to hold a fair once a year on the vigil of St. Magdalen for two days successively at Exeter, with a proviso excluding the mayor, &c., from any franchise or jurisdiction within the fee of the bishop, commonly called St. Stephen's fee, the cathedral, cemetery, close, palace, &c. Dated Westminster, 1st July, aº reg. 3ᵗⁱᵒ·

(30.) HENRY VII.—A general inspeximus and confirmation of previous charters from Henry II. to Edward IV. Dated Westminster, 12th October, aº reg. 2ᵈᵒ·

(31.) HENRY VII.—There is a copy, under the first year of this reign, 10th June, of an ordinance under the King's privy seal establishing an order, with the assent of the common council of the city and others, for the election of mayors and other officers in future. The document is inserted in Izacke's Memorials (p. 99, ed. 1681), but is there dated 10th *July* in the *thirteenth* year of this reign. The difficulty can only be removed by inspection of the original.

(32.) HENRY VIII.—A charter inspecting and confirming the charter of Henry VII., and, with it, all the preceding charters. 26th February, aº reg. 1º·

(33.) HENRY VIII.—A charter granting to the mayor, bailiffs, and commonalty of the city and their successors, that the mayor and

---

[5] The ratification of an act of parliament by the letters patent of a successor is somewhat anomalous ; but as Edward IV. disputed the authority of Henry VI., such a confirmation was, at least, a prudent precaution.

[6] The object of this is to enable the mayor or his officers to claim and take such fines and forfeitures in person, and directly, without waiting to claim them at the exchequer on the sheriff's account there, as the general and regular practice was upon such grants of profits which belong *primâ facie* to the Crown.

286　　　　　　　HISTORY OF EXETER.

recorder for the time being, as well as ex-mayors as long as they remain aldermen, shall be keepers of the peace and justices to enquire, hear, and determine felonies, trespasses, and misdemeanours committed within the city and liberties thereof. It also grants all fines, assessments, and issues incidental to such commission, saving the fee-farm of the city. Dated Westminster, 16th February, a° reg. 26to. (A.D. 1535).

(34.) HENRY VIII.—The charter confirms all previous charters, and liberties in general terms, and further grants that the city shall thenceforth be one entire county corporate *per se, re et nomine*, distinct and wholly separate from the county of Devon, and that twenty-four of the council of the city, or the major part of them, shall on every succeeding Monday next after the feast of St. Michael elect one of themselves to be sheriff of the said county of the city, to whom all powers and jurisdictions incident to that office in other counties is given, to the exclusion of the sheriff of Devon. It also provides for the election of *nine* aldermen in the manner there specified, of whom the recorder is to be one. The aldermen to have the same powers within liberties and without as aldermen of London. It provides who shall be thenceforth justices of the peace for the city, and that the mayor, recorder, and aldermen, or three of them, of whom the mayor and recorder shall be two, are to be justices of gaol delivery for the city ; and gives power to erect and keep a gaol within the city, and a gibbet within the liberties. The charter gives various other powers, profits, and franchises, including cognizance of pleas, real, personal or mixed, pending in other courts of the King, of lands and tenements within the city, and of contracts and trespasses arising there.[7] Dated Westminster, 23rd August, a° reg. 29°. (A.D. 1537).

(35.) EDWARD VI.—A charter, inspecting and confirming the last charter in extenso. Dated Westminster, 24th February, a° reg. 3tio. (A.D. 1549).

(36.) EDWARD VI.—These letters patent contain a recital of the loyalty and sufferings of the corporation and citizens during the late rebellion in the West, and the siege of the city (referred to in p. 97 ante), and as a mark of the king's special favour confirm the ancient liberties of the city, and confer on the mayor, bailiffs, and commonalty the demesne and manor of Exeland, with the appurtenants in the county or city, late the property of Henry Marquis of Exeter, attainted of treason, and situate in the parishes of St. Thomas, St. Edmund's on Exebridge, and St. Mary de Gradibus, to hold of the Crown as of the manor of Sidmouth in the county of

---

[7] The limits and bounds of the county of Exeter were afterwards defined by an act 1 & 2 Ed. VI., the tenor of which was certified by writ of certiorari and exemplified, at the request of the corporation, by letters patent, 18 March, 3 Ed. VI. Those limits are intended to exclude the precinct of the cathedral as well as of the castle, which continue part of the County of Devon ; but they include St. Sidwell's parish, and extend to St. David's and other places beyond the gates.

TABLE OF CHARTERS.

287

Devon, in as ample manner as the late marquis held it, paying 5s. annually to the castle of Exeter, with sufficient wood and underwood from Cotley and Pirage woods, in the county of Devon, for amending Calebear and Hooper's wears in the water of Exe, and a power to acquire further land not exceeding 100l. in value in mortmain. Dated at Westminster, 22nd December, a° reg. 4$^{to.}$ (A.D. 1550).

(37.) ELIZABETH.—Letters patent confirming in general terms former grants. They also constitute the mayor to be escheator of the queen and her successors within the city without intromission of any other escheator; and provide that the sheriff of the city shall hold two Tourns with view of frank pledge every year as in other counties, and appoint an undersheriff in like manner as in London and Bristol; that the corporation shall have power to make ordinances for the government of the city not at variance with the laws of the realm; that there shall be a chamberlain of the city, to be elected in the Guildhall by the mayor and common council of twenty-four or major part of them, being a freeman of the city, who shall have a seal of office, and exercise the same powers as the chamberlain of London, and plead in that name in all our courts in all matters touching the city or orphans, and receive and safely keep the revenues of the city to the use of the corporation, and annually account for them. The duties of the chamberlain as to orphans and children of citizens and their property are specified, and are expressly assimilated to those of the chamberlain of London. Dated Westminster, 21st February, anno reg. 3$^{tio.}$ (1561). These letters were confirmed by Act of Parliament, 5 Elizabeth, of which the tenor was certified and exemplified by letters patent on 3rd May following.

(38.) ELIZABETH.—The queen transfers to the mayor and aldermen of Exeter the appointment of the almsmen of the Bonville Charity and of the Hospital of St. John Baptist, theretofore appointed by the Crown. Dated Westminster, 8th November, a° reg. 4$^{to.}$

(39) CHARLES I.—This is now the governing charter of the city. It recites generally, and not by inspeximus or particular reference, the grants of former kings, and the fidelity of the city in the time of Henry VII. and Edward VI., and the existence of ambiguities in former charters.

It ordains that there shall be a common council for life of twenty-four citizens and inhabitants, removable only for cause.

Vacancies to be filled by election of the rest or the major part of them.

It constitutes the first mayor under this charter and the first common council.

It prescribes the mode and time of election of mayors.

Four bailiffs are to be chosen by the common council, one to be receiver: also three serjeants-at-mace.

There is to be a recorder and town clerk.

A fourth serjeant is to be chosen by the mayor.

Power is given to fine persons refusing to take office.

HISTORY OF EXETER.

If any custom heretofore in use in the city be difficult or defective, the council or major part, including the mayor, is to have power to amend or make new ordinances not repugnant to the king's prerogative or the law and statutes of the realm.

.It recites the charter 29 Henry VIII. (supra No. 34) and makes some variations in the execution of the office of justices of the peace and of gaol delivery for the city.

It grants fines and forfeitures, &c., to the mayor, bailiffs, and commonalty, and the power to take recognizances under the statutes of Acton Burnell and de Mercatoribus.

It contains a general confirmation of all liberties or franchises formerly enjoyed. Dated Westminster, 17th December, a° reg. 3ᵗⁱᵒ·[8]

[See this Charter given *in extenso* at the close of this Chronological Table.]

(40.) GEORGE III.—This is the latest charter. It bears date 25th April, a° reg. 10ᵐᵒ· (1770).

It recites the charters of Henry VIII. (No. 34), and of Charles I., and that inconveniences had arisen in holding the sessions and gaol delivery, so few justices being of the quorum. It then grants to the mayor, bailiffs, and commonalty of Exeter and their successors, that the mayor, recorder, and all the aldermen of the city for the time being, or any three or more of them, of whom some of the mayor, recorder, and seven senior aldermen for the time being should be two, may hold and keep the sessions of the peace for the city of Exeter and county of the same; and appoints the mayor, recorder, and aldermen of the said city for the time being or any three or more of them, of whom some of the mayor, recorder, and seven senior aldermen should be two, to be the justices to hold the sessions of the peace of the city of Exeter and county of the same city. It also grants to the said mayor, bailiffs, and commonalty of the city of Exeter and their successors, that the mayor, recorder, and all the aldermen of the said city for the time being, or any three or more of them, of whom the mayor or some one of the seven senior aldermen and the said recorder shall be two, shall be justices to deliver the gaol, and appoints the said mayor, recorder, and aldermen of the said city of Exeter for the time being, or any three or more of them, of whom the said mayor or some one of the seven senior aldermen and the said recorder should be two, to be justices to deliver the gaol; and directs that the sheriff or coroner of the said city for the time being shall from time to time make returns of all juries, inquisitions, panels, attachments and indentures by them taken before the said mayor, recorder, and aldermen of the said city for the time being, or any three or more

---

[8] It will be seen that the above is a very abbreviated abstract of this charter. Many of its provisions are of little importance, and others seem to include grants of powers which the corporation possessed before. The provision for self-election conferred on the common council is an important one, but it is not clear what the previous usage was. The mode of election resembles that which was prescribed by the ordinance under the privy seal of Henry VII., noticed under No. 31 supra, and recited in Izacke's Memorials.

CHARTER OF KING CHARLES I. 289

of them, of whom the mayor or some one of the seven senior aldermen of the city for the time being and the said recorder should be two, when and as often as they should be willing to deliver the gaol, and that the sheriff and coroner should be attendant on the said mayor, recorder, and aldermen in all things touching the delivery of the gaol, and from time to time to execute the precepts of the said mayor, recorder, and aldermen of the city aforesaid for the time being, or any three or more of them, of whom the mayor, or some one of the seven senior aldermen of the said city for the time being, and the said recorder should be two.

CHARTER OF KING CHARLES I. TO THE CITY OF EXETER.

The following is a full copy of the Charter of King Charles I., of which an abstract is given in the preceding List of Charters, No. 39. This must be still regarded as the governing Charter, subject nevertheless to the provisions of the late ' Municipal Reform Act.'

CAROLUS Dei gratia Angliæ Scotiæ Franciæ et Hiberniæ Rex Fidei Defensor &c., Omnibus ad quos præsentes literæ pervenerint, Salutem.

CUM diversi præclarissimorum progenitorum vel antecessorum nostrorum nuper Regum et Reginarum Angliæ, ex eorum gratiâ speciali et munificentiâ regiâ erga dilectos subditos suos Majorem Ballivos et Communitatem Civitatis Exoniensis ac bonum publicum ejusdem Civitatis exhibitâ; NEC NON in consideratione approbatæ fidelitatis et fidelis servitii, quæ ipsi præfati Major Ballivi et Communitas dictis Regibus et Reginis et Coronæ Angliæ de tempore in tempus præstiterunt, et præcipuè tempore regni Domini HENRICI nuper Regis Angliæ Septimi progenitoris nostri, nec non tempore regni EDWARDI nuper Regis Angliæ Sexti, tempore commotionis, insurrectionis, et rebellionis ingratorum et infidelium subditorum suorum, in diversis partibus hujus regni, præsertim in occidentalibus partibus regni Angliæ, in Comitatibus Devoniæ et Cornubiæ, dicto nuper Regi fidelissime adhærendo, et eisdem rebellionibus viriliter resistendo, ac civitatem Exoniensem prædictam cameramque Regis ejusdem defendendo adversus ferocissimos eorum insultus et obsidiones, per tempus diutinum, modo guerrino cum magno populi numero, continuo insidiantes et circumdantes; non solum maximis custagiis, expensis, et oneribus prædictorum Majoris Ballivorum et Communitatis Civitatis prædictæ, verum etiam cum magnâ periclitatione et amissione vitæ eorum et penuriâ ob defectus victualium, antequam dictus nuper Rex armis et hostilibus copiis suis in eos armatis, obsidionem prædictam dissolvere potuisset;—diversas libertates, consuetudines, privilegia, franchesia, jurisdictiones et alia, per seperales chartas sive literas patentes concesserint et confirmaverint :

U

290

HISTORY OF EXETER.

Cumque Nos informamur quod quidam defectus et ambiguitates in prædictis chartis et literis patentibus existunt, ratione quòd nonnulla in eisdem contenta non plane expressa nec verbis satis aptis et idoneis concessa fuerunt pro bono regimine gubernatione et commodo civitatis nostræ Exoniensis prædictæ, et comitatûs ejusdem civitatis; et superinde iidem Major Ballivi et Communitas Civitatis prædictæ nobis humillimè supplicaverint, quatenus Nos eisdem Majori, Ballivis et Communitati Civitatis prædictæ et successoribus suis, gratiam, et munificentiam nostram Regiam in hac parte exhibere et extendere velimus, pro eisdem defectibus ambiguitatibus et dubiis prædictarum chartarum et literarum patentium explicandis et in certitudinem redigendis, cum additione quarumdam libertatum franchesiorum et privilegiorum, prout Nobis melius fieri et fore videbitur ;

Nos igitur præmissa, nec non fidem, obedientiam, et fidele servitium Majoris Ballivorum et Communitatis Civitatis prædictæ de tempore in tempus Coronæ Angliæ continuatam perpendentes, de gratiâ nostrâ speciali ac ex certâ scientiâ et mero motu nostris, Volumus ordinavimus concessimus et constituimus, ac per præsentes pro Nobis heredibus et successoribus nostris volumus ordinamus concedimus et constituimus, quod Civitas nostra Exoniensis prædicta, ac Comitatus ejusdem Civitatis, ac circuitus, jurisdictio, et præcincta eorundem, de cætero sint et se extendant et protendant, ac extendere et protendere valeant et possint, tam in longitudine et latitudine, quam in circuitu et præcinctu, ad tales et consimiles et hujusmodi bundas, metas, et limites, ad quas et quales ac prout prædicta civitas Exoniensis, et Comitatus ejusdem, ac circuitus et præcincta ac jurisdictio eorundem aliquo tempore ante datum præsentium se extenderent aut protenderent.

Et ulterius, ut omnes et singulæ quæstiones, inconvenientiæ et lites, in aut circa electionem Majoris, quatuor Ballivorum, viginti quatuor de Communi Consilio, et quatuor servientium ad clavam Civitatis prædictæ de cætero penitus tollantur, ac tumultus evitetur popularis, et pro pacificâ et quietâ electione in eâ parte fiendâ, de uberiori gratiâ nostrâ speciali, ac ex certâ scientiâ et mero motu nostris Volumus ordinavimus concessimus constituimus et stabilivimus, ac per præsentes pro Nobis heredibus et successoribus nostris volumus ordinamus concedimus constituimus et stabilimus, quod de cætero in perpetuum sint et erunt Viginti Quatuor de discretioribus et valentioribus civibus et inhabitantibus Civitatis prædictæ de Communi Concilio ejusdem Civitatis pro termino vitarum suarum ; et quod nullus eorum amovebitur, nisi sit pro paupertate ægritudine senectute aut aliâ causâ rationabili, quæ causæ adjudicabuntur et determinabuntur per residuos dictorum viginti quatuor de Communi Concilio Civitatis prædictæ, sive eorum majorem partem ; in quibus casibus, ob causas illas sic allocandas, aliquem vel aliquos prædictorum viginti quatuor de Communi Concilio prædicto, per residuos eorundem, vel majorem partem eorum, de tempore in tempus amobilem et amobiles esse volumus et declaramus per præsentes : Et quod post decessum sivo amotionem alicujus vel

CHARTER OF KING CHARLES I. 291

aliquorum hujusmodi viginti quatuor de Communi Concilio Civitatis prædictæ in formâ prædictâ, residui dictorum viginti quatuor, vel major pars eorum præmunitorum et interessentium, infra tempus conveniens post hujusmodi mortem vel amotionem eligent et præficient unum alium vel plures alios de valentioribus et discretioribus civibus et liberis hominibus Civitatis prædictæ ad supplendum prædictum numerum viginti quatuor de Communi Concilio dictæ Civitatis secundum consuetudinem in Civitate nostrâ Londoni pro Electione viginti quatuor Aldermannorum ibidem usitatam.

Et ULTERIUS pro meliori executione voluntatis et concessionis nostræ in hac parte Assignavimus nominavimus constituimus et fecimus ac per presentes pro Nobis heredibus et successoribus nostris Assignamus nominamus constituimus et facimus dilectum et fidelem nostrum Johannem Acland, armigerum, modernum Majorem Civitatis nostræ Exoniensis prædictæ, ac dilectos nobis Thomam Walker, Walterum Borough, Ignatium Jurdain, Johannem Mcdyford, Thomam Crossing et Johannem Tailler Aldermannos ejusdem Civitatis, ac Georgium Pyle, Johannem Lynne, Johannem Jurdain, Nicholaum Spycer, Thomam Fflaye, Nicholaum Martin, Johannem Hakewill, Gilbertum Sweete, Johannem Crocker, Georgium Passemere, Franciscum Crossing, Adamum Bennett, Rogerum Mallack, Jacobum Tucker, Johannem Hayne, Johannem Pennye, et Ricardum Saunders, mercatores et liberos homines Civitatis prædictæ, fore et esse primos et modernos viginti quatuor de communi Concilio Civitatis prædictæ continuandos in officio sive loco illo durantibus vitis suis naturalibus, nisi interim pro aliquâ causâ, ut præfertur, amovebuntur, aut eorum aliquis amovebitur.

Et ULTERIUS volumus, ac per præsentes pro Nobis heredibus et successoribus nostris concedimus præfatis Majori Ballivis et Communitati et successoribus suis, quod bene liceat et licebit Majori Civitatis nostræ Exoniensis pro tempore existenti, cum fratribus suis et cæteris de Communitate ejusdem Civitatis existentibus liberis hominibus dictæ Civitatis annuatim quolibet Die Lunæ proximo ante festum Sancti Michaelis Archangeli convenire et seipsos in guihalda Civitatis prædictæ assemblare, ac tunc et ibidem prædicti viginti quatuor de Communi Concilio sive major pars eorum interessentium super sacramenta sua per eorum scrutinia privatim et singulatim per Recordatorem et Communem Clericum dictæ Civitatis pro tempore existentes vel eorum deputatos capienda, et super sacramenta sua colligenda et computanda, seponere et nominare valeant et possint duos de melioribus et valentioribus civibus dictorum viginti quatuor de Communi Concilio, ex eis (videlicet) qui in officiis Majoris vel Receptoris Civitatis prædictæ antea approbati fuerint (Majore pro tempore existente excepto), ex quibus duobus alter eorum in Majorem dictæ Civitatis pro anno tunc proximo sequente eligendus fuerit. Quodque prædicti viginti quatuor, aut eorum interessentium major pars eodem tempore eligere valeant et possint quatuor BALLIVOS Civitatis prædictæ pro anno tunc proximo sequente, quorum unus sit et erit RECEPTOR dictæ Civitatis tam de prædictis viginti quatuor quam de aliis melioribus et valentioribus civibus et inhabitantibus infra Civitatem nostram prædictam liberis

u 2

292   HISTORY OF EXETER.

hominibus ejusdem Civitatis, ac boni nominis et famæ existentibus. Quodque dicti viginti quatuor aut eorum interessentium major pars eodem die eligere valeant secundum discretionem suam tres servientes ad clavas de liberis hominibus dictæ Civitatis, qui officium illud melius exequi et attendere possint, et post hujusmodi scrutinium nominationem et electionem sic per prædictos viginti quatuor aut eorum interessentium majorem partem factam et habitam, Recordator et Communis Clericus Civitatis prædictæ pro tempore existentes nomina illorum duorum, qui per majorem partem suffragiorum dictorum viginti quatuor in scrutiniis prædictis pro officio Majoris Civitatis prædictæ pro anno tunc sequente nominati fuerint, Communitati Civitatis prædictæ, existentibus liberis hominibus ejusdem Civitatis, indicabunt et publicabunt, seu eorum alter indicabit et publicabit : Et quod dicta Communitas unum dictorum duorum fore Majorem Civitatis prædictæ pro uno anno tunc proximo sequente eliget ; et quod ille qui majorem partem suffragiorum liberorum hominum Civitatis prædictæ habebit, in officium Majoris dictæ Civitatis præfectus et admissus erit. Er post hoc factum prædicti Recordator et Communis ´Clericus ostendent et præsentabunt, vel eorum alter ostendet et præsentabit, Communitati ejusdem Civitatis, in presentia dictorum viginti quatuor de Communi Concilio Civitatis prædictæ interessentium, nomina omnium aliorum officiariorum pro anno subsequente electorum. Er quod annuatim et quolibet anno in perpetuum Die Lunæ proximo post hujusmodi assemblationem electionem et publicationem sequente prædictus Civis sic in Majorem electus, ac omnes alii officiarii prædicti modo et formâ prædictis electi, in Guihalda Civitatis prædictæ ad Curiam ibidem tenendam coram judicibus ejusdem Curiæ pro tempore existentibus sacramenta sua corporalia super sancta Dei Evangelia ad officia sua respectivè benè et fideliter exequenda præstabunt, et eorum quilibet præstabit, secundum antiquum Usum et laudabilem consuetudinem Civitatis nostræ Exoniensis prædictæ ; quodque iidem sic in officia illa respectivè electi præfecti et jurati in officiis illis pro uno anno integro tunc pr ximo sequente secundum Usum et consuetudinem prædictam respectivè continuabunt : Er quod dictus Major, postquam sacramentum suum in formâ prædictâ præstitit, nominabit et eliget unum habilem civem et liberum hominem Civitatis prædictæ fore et esse quartum servientem ad clavam dictæ Civitatis secundum antiquam consuetudinem in eâdem Civitate usitatam : Et quod in casu mortis vel amotionis Majoris Ballivorum vel Servientium ad Clavam aut eorum aliquorum vel alicujus, alius vel alii in locum sive loca ipsius vel ipsorum sic mori vel amoveri contingentium eligentur modo et formâ prædictis, infra tempus conveniens post hujusmodi mortem vel amotionem, continuandi in Officiis illis respectivè durante residuo anni tunc inexpirato, nec non præstabunt sacramentum prout superius appunctuatur.

Et ULTERIUS volumus ac per præsentes pro Nobis heredibus et successoribus nostris concedimus præfatis Majori Ballivis et Communitati Civitatis prædictæ et successoribus suis, nec non statuimus et ordinamus, quod nominatio, electio, et juratio Recordatoris et

CHARTER OF KING CHARLES I. 293

Communis Clerici ac omnium aliorum officiariorum Civitatis prædictæ dehinc in perpetuum sint erunt et fiant eisdem diebus locis et temporibus, ac hujusmodi modo et formâ prout ex antiquâ consuetudine in eâdem Civitate antehac legitimo modo usitatum et approbatum fuit.

Er insuper volumus ac per præsentes pro Nobis heredibus et successoribus nostris concedimus præfato Majori Ballivis et Communitati Civitatis Exoniensis prædictæ et successoribus suis, quod si aliquis vel aliqui de Communi Concilio vel aliis de civibus et liberis hominibus dictæ Civitatis, licet sint residentes seu commorantes, vel eorum aliquis sit residens vel commorans, infra Civitatem prædictam, vel comitatum ejusdem Civitatis, libertates vel præcincta eorumdem, vel extra, qui in posterum ad officium Majoris, vel Ballivorum, vel in prædictum numerum viginti quatuor de Communi Concilio, vel ad officium Vicecomitis Coronatoris vel Constabularii, sive aliud officium sive locum inferiorem Civitatis prædictæ sive ad eorum aliquod vel aliqua (excepto officio Recordatoris et Communis Clerici Civitatis prædictæ) electi vel nominati fuerint, aut electus vel nominatus fuerit, et habens vel habentes notitiam et cognitionem de electione et nominatione illa, recusabunt vel renuent recusabit vel renuet officium illud vel officia illa ad quod vel quæ ipse vel ipsi sic recusantes vel renuentes electi et nominati fuerint vel fuerit, quod tunc et toties bene liceat et licebit prædictis viginti quatuor de Communi Concilio Civitatis prædictæ pro tempore existentibus vel majori parti eorum, ipsum vel ipsos sic recusantem vel renuentem recusantes vel renuentes exercere officium illud vel officia illa ad quod vel quæ ipse vel ipsi sic electus vel nominatus fuerit electi vel nominati fuerint, committere gaolæ Civitatis prædictæ, ibidem remansuros quousque officium illud vel officia illa exercere velit vel velint; et fines et amerciamenta super hujusmodi recusantem vel recusantes taxare et imponere, prout eisdem viginti quatuor de Communi Concilio pro tempore existentibus vel eorum majori parti rationabiliter videbitur expedire; ac quod ipsum vel ipsos sic recusantem vel recusantes ac gaolæ Civitatis prædictæ pro tempore existenti commissum vel commissos ibidem retinere possint et valeant, quousque fines vel amerciamenta illorum ad publicum usum Civitatis prædictæ plenariè solvat seu solvi faciat; solvant seu solvi faciant. Ac, si dictis viginti quatuor de Communi Concilio Civitatis prædictæ pro tempore existente vel majori parti eorum expedire videbitur, ipsum vel ipsos a libertate et franchesio Civitatis prædictæ discommunicare expellere et amovere.

Nec non pro Nobis heredibus et successoribus nostris constituimus et ordinamus per præsentes quod tam quælibet persona sic ut præfertur renuens vel recusans officium suum in formâ prædictâ suscipere, quam quælibet alia persona quæ has ordinationes nostras concernentes electiones prædictas officiariorum aut eorum aliquorum vel alicujus contra tenorem præsentium disturbet impediet aut opponet, aut in eisdem electionibus faciendis verbis aut factis aliquam insolentiam aut pacis perturbationem aut fractionem perpetraverit, incurrent pœnam indignationis nostræ hæredum et successorum nostrorum.

294 HISTORY OF EXETER.

CONCESSIMUS ULTERIUS ac per præsentes pro Nobis heredibus et successoribus nostris concedimus præfatis Majori Ballivis et Communitati Civitatis prædictæ et successoribus suis in perpetuum, quod si aliquæ consuetudines in Civitate prædictâ hactenus obtentæ et usitatæ in aliquâ parte difficiles seu defectivæ existent, aut in aliquo in eâdem Civitate de novo emergente, ubi remedium prius non fuit ordinatum, emendatione indigebunt, tunc prædicti viginti quatuor de Communi Concilio Civitatis prædictæ pro tempore existentes sive major pars eorum (quorum Majorem dictæ Civitatis pro tempore existentem unum esse volumus) de communi assensu suo remedium congruum bonæ fidei et rationi consentaneum pro communi utilitate et regimine civium et inhabitantium ejusdem Civitatis et aliorum fidelium nostrorum ad eamdem confluentium apponere possint et ordinare, quoties et quando eis melius videbitur expedire; dum tamen ordinationes hujusmodi nobis et populo nostro utiles et bonæ fidei et rationi sint consonantes, sicut prædictum est, et quod non sint repugnantes prærogativæ nostræ regiæ heredum et successorum nostrorum, nec contrariæ statutis et legibus regni nostri Angliæ tunc in vigore existentibus.

CUMQUE DOMINUS HENRICUS nuper Rex Angliæ Octavus per litteras suas patentes magno sigillo Angliæ sigillatas gerentes datum apud Westmonasterium vicesimo tertio die Augusti anno regni sui vicesimo nono concesserit (inter alia) pro se heredibus et successoribus suis Majori Ballivis et Communitati Comitatûs Civitatis prædictæ et successoribus suis, quod Major et Recordator Comitatûs Civitatis illius et singuli alii octo Aldermannorum, qui onus Majoratus Civitatis prædictæ gesserat supportaverat et sustentaverat, aut tunc deinceps gereret aut supportaret, et successores sui quamdiu aldermanni ejusdem Civitatis existerent, essent Justiciarii et custodes pacis dicti nuper Regis heredum et successorum suorum ubilibet infrà comitatum Civitatis prædictæ et præcinctorum et libertatum ejusdem tam infrà libertates quam extrà ubicunque infrà fines et limites Comitatûs Civitatis prædictæ. Et quod ipsi Major Recordator et octo alii Aldermanni dicti Comitatus Civitatis Exoniensis aut tres eorum (quorum Major et Recordator pro tempore existentes omnino essent duo) extunc imperpetuum essent Justiciarii dicti nuper Regis heredum et successorum suorum ad omnia et singula talia et similia felonias transgressiones et alia malefacta infrà eundem Comitatum Civitatis Exoniensis et libertates ejusdem tam infrà libertates quam extra emergentia tunc deinceps committenda et perpetranda ibidem inquirenda audienda et terminanda, qualiter et prout justiciarii dicti nuper Regis ad pacem in Comitatu Devoniæ conservandam assignati virtute commissionis dicti Regis eis directæ et virtute et authoritate legum hujus regni Angliæ inquirere audire et terminare possent aut valerent. Et quod iidem Major Recordator et Aldermanni aut tres eorum (quorum dicti Major et Recordator pro tempore existentes omnino essent duo eorum) essent Justiciarii dicti nuper Regis heredum et successorum suorum ad gaolam dicti Comitatus Civitatis Exoniensis prædictæ de tempore in tempus quotiens opus esset secundum legem et consuetudinem regni Angliæ de prisonariis in ea tunc existentibus et essendis deliberandam ac ad diversa alia facienda et exequenda pro custodia pacis dicti nuper Regis heredum

CHARTER OF KING CHARLES I. 295

et successorum suorum infrà Comitatum Civitatis prædictæ ac libertates ejusdem tam infrà libertates quam extra, prout in eisdem literis patentibus plenius et specialiter specificatur; ita quod nec Justiciarii et Custodes pacis dicti nuper Regis heredum et successorum suorum aut [aliqui] Justiciariorum heredum et successorum suorum ad diversas felonias transgressiones et alia malefacta inquirenda audienda et terminanda assignati vel assignandi nec Vicecomes Coronator Escaetor nec aliquis alius Justiciarius dicti nuper Regis heredum vel successorum suorum dicti Comitatûs Devoniæ tunc deinceps pro aliquibus rebus causis querelis materiis defectibus et articulis, Justiciariis dicti nuper Regis heredum et successorum suorum ad Pacem, sive Justiciariis dicti nuper Regis heredum et successorum suorum ad diversas felonias transgressiones et alia malefacta inquirenda audienda et terminanda assignatis aut assignandis pertinentia sive spectantia infrà Comitatum Civitatis prædictæ et libertates ejusdem non ingrederentur nec se inde ibidem in aliquo intromitterent nec eorum aliquis ullo modo intromitteret, prout per easdem litteras patentes particulariter et plenius apparet.

Cumque etiam accidere posset quod Major et Recordator Civitatis prædictæ (qui soli Justiciarii de le Quorum per easdem litteras patentes constituuntur) ex ægritudine vel infirmitate aut alia causa inevitabili impediti necessaria negotia dictæ Civitatis intendere non possint aut eorum alter non possit, ita quod reliqui Justiciariorum qui in sessionibus pro Civitate illâ et Comitatu ejusdem tenendis ad servitia publica ibidem prosequenda in absentiâ predictorum Majoris et Recordatoris vel eorum alterius procedere nequeant, ad justitiæ retardationem aut delinquentium impunitatem, Nos remedium in hac parte adhiberi volentes, et ut pax nostra ibidem melius conservetur, cæteraque facta justitiæ ibidem perpetuis futuris temporibus debitè et tempestivè præstentur ac condita et stabilita remaneant, de gratiâ nostrâ speciali ac ex certâ scientiâ et mero motu nostris Concessimus ac per præsentes pro nobis heredibus et successoribus nostris Concedimus præfatis Majori Ballivis et Communitati Civitatis prædictæ et successoribus suis, quod Major Recordator et Aldermanni Civitatis prædictæ pro tempore existentes perpetuis futuris temporibus sint et erunt Justiciarii nostri, et quilibet eorum sit et erit Justiciarius noster heredum et successorum nostrorum ad Pacem nostram heredum et successorum nostrorum infrà Civitatem nostram Exoniensem ac Comitatum Civitatis Exoniensis ac infrà limites libertates et præcincta dictæ Civitatis et Comitatus ejusdem tam infrà Libertates quam extrà conservandam et custodiendam ac conservari et custodiri faciendam, nec non ad Statuta de artificibus et laboratoribus ponderibus et mensuris infrà Civitatem prædictam ac Comitatum ejusdem Civitatis ac infrà libertates limites et præcincta prædicta corrigendis, conservandis et custodiendis et corrigi faciendis, et ad omnia alia ibidem facienda quæ ad officium Justiciarii ad pacem conservandam assignati pertinent facienda, vel facienda pertinebunt in futurum. Et quod dicti Major Recordator et Aldermanni sic ut præfertur in officio Justiciariorum ad pacem virtute præsentium confecti et conficiendi, constituti et constituendi, aut aliqui tres sive plures eorum (quo-

296　HISTORY OF EXETER.

rum aliquos præfatorum Majoris et Recordatoris et duorum prim-
ariorum et per electionem seniorum Aldermannorum Civitatis
prædictæ pro tempore existentium duos esse volumus) sessiones
pacis appunctuare servare et tenere possint et valeant eisdem modo
et formâ prout aliqui alii Justiciarii ad pacem conservandam vel'ad
malefacta aut transgressiones perpetratas audiendas et terminandas
assignati vel assignandi in aliquibus comitatibus Angliæ possint et
valeant aut valere poterunt in futurum, Quodque plenam habeant
potestatem et authoritatem ad inquirendum de quibuscunque
offensionibus delictis defaltis et articulis infrà Civitatem prædictam
et Comitatum ejusdem Civitatis ac infrà libertates limites et
præcincta eorum vel eorum alterius factis motis sive perpetratis aut
in posterum movendis fiendis sive perpetrandis, ac ad omnia alia
ibidem facienda et exequenda quæ.custodes et Justiciarii pacis in
aliquo Comitatu regni nostri Angliæ per leges et statuta ejusdem
regni Angliæ, ut Justiciarii pacis, seu Justiciarii ad felonias transgressiones et alia malefacta perpetrata audienda et terminanda
assignati seu assignandi infrà aliquem Comitatum vel aliquam
civitatem villam seu burgum incorporatum infrà hoc regnum Angliæ
inquirere facere aut exequi possint et valeant poterunt seu valebunt:
ITA QUOD nullus alius Justiciarius nec aliqui alii Justiciarii ad
pacem nostram heredum et successorum nostrorum conservandam
assignati vel assignandi virtute vel prætextu alicujus commissionis
vel alicujus associationis vel aliter quovismodo ad aliquod vel
aliqua infrà Civitatem prædictam vel Comitatum ejusdem Civitatis
vel infrà libertates limites vel præcincta ejusdem facienda agenda
vel præcipienda quod vel quæ ad Justiciarium pacis aut ad pacem
conservandam assignatum ibidem spectant vel pertinent seu spec-
tabunt vel pertinebunt, aliqualiter se intromittat vel intromittant.

VOLUMUS etiam, ac per præsentes pro Nobis heredibus et successoribus nostris concedimus præfatis Majori Ballivis et Communitati
Civitatis prædictæ et successoribus suis, quod Major Recordator et
Aldermanni Civitatis prædictæ pro tempore existentes aut tres vel
plures eorum (quorum Majorem et Recordatorem Civitatis prædictæ pro tempore existentes duos esse volumus) de tempore in
tempus in perpetuum sint Justiciarii nostri heredum et successorum nostrorum ad Gaolam nostram Civitatis nostræ Exoniensis
prædictæ et Comitatûs Civitatis prædictæ de prisonariis in eâ existentibus de tempore in tempus secundum leges consuetudines et
statuta regni nostri Angliæ deliberandam, et quod Vicecomes et
Coronator Comitatus Civitatis prædictæ pro tempore existentes
omnia jurata inquisitiones panella attachiamenta et indenturas
per ipsos captas et in posterum capiendas coram præfatis Majore
Recordatore et Aldermannis Civitatis prædictæ pro tempore existentibus vel aliquibus tribus vel pluribus eorum (quorum Majorem
et Recordatorem Civitatis prædictæ pro tempore existentes in formâ
prædictâ duos esse volumus) quando et quoties gaolam illam de
prisonariis in eadem gaolâ existentibus deliberare voluerint, de
tempore in tempus faciont retornum, ac eis in omnibus Delibera-
tionem Gaolæ prædictæ tangentibus sint attendentes, et præcepta
eorum Majoris Recordatoris et Aldermannorum Civitatis prædiotæ

CHARTER OF KING CHARLES I. 297

pro tempore existentium vel aliquorum talium trium vel plurium eorum ut præfertur exequantur de tempore in tempus eisdem modo et formâ prout aliqui Vicecomites vel Coronatores infrà regnum nostrum Angliæ coram Justiciariis ad gaolam in aliquibus aliis comitatibus dicti regni nostri heredum vel successorum nostrorum deliberandum assignatis vel assignandis facere retornare intendere vel exequi quovismodo per leges et statuta hujus regni nostri Angliæ consueverunt et debuerunt. Quodque iidem Major Recordator et Aldermanni Civitatis prædictæ pro tempore existentes aut eorum aliqui quoscunque murdratores homicidas felones latrones et alios malefactores infrà civitatem prædictam suburbia libertates et præcincta ejusdem ac infrà Comitatum Civitatis prædictæ inventos vel inveniendos per se vel per ministros aut deputatos suos capere et arrestare et eos ad gaolam Comitatus Civitatis prædictæ committere possint vel causabunt aut eorum aliquis committere possit et causabit ibidem salvo custodiendos quousque per debitum legis processum deliberentur, aliquâ aliâ ordinatione decreto ordine seu consuetudine in aliquo nonobstante: ITA tamen quod ad determinationem alicujus proditionis aut misprisionis proditionis infrà Civitatem prædictam libertates aut præcincta ejusdem vel infrà Comitatum ejusdem Civitatis absque speciali mandato nostro heredum vel successorum nostrorum quoquomodo in posterum non procedant nec eorum aliqui vel aliquis procedant vel procedat.

ET PRÆTEREA de uberiori gratiâ nostrâ ac in supportationem et meliorationem Civitatis nostræ Exon' prædictæ Concessimus ac per præsentes pro Nobis heredibus et successoribus nostris Concedimus præfatis Majori Ballivis et Communitati Civitatis prædictæ, quod ipsi et successores sui ex nunc in perpetuum habeant omnes et omnimodos fines, forisfacta et forisfacienda, redemptiones, exitus, et forisfacturas tam reales quam non reales, recognitiones forisfactas et forisfaciendas, et forisfacturas et amerciamenta quæcunque (licet Nos heredes vel successores nostri fuerimus aut fuerint pars) pro transgressionibus oppressionibus extortionibus deceptionibus conspirationibus concelamentis regratariis forstallariis manutenentibus ambidextris falsitatibus escapiis negligentiis feloniis misprisionibus et aliis delictis et malefactis quibuscunque, et omnes fines pro licentiâ concordandi; nec non omnia et omnimoda amerciamenta redemptiones fines exitus forisfacta realia et non realia, catalla felonum de se, fugitivorum et in exigendo positorum, deodanda thesauros inventos forisfacta et omnia et omnimoda forisfacta tam per brevia præcepta billas et mandata nostra heredum vel successorum nostrorum quæcunque et omnia quæ ad nos vel hæredes nostros pertinere possint vel deberent de murdris escapiis negligentiis contingen felonum raptionibus mulierum et felonum quibuscunque, ac pro quâcunque aliâ causâ per leges sive per statuta hujus regni Angliæ ad sectam nostram heredum vel successorum nostrorum vel ad sectam alterius pro scipso vel ad sectam alterius qui tam pro Nobis heredibus vel successoribus nostris quam pro se emergente sive imposterum emergenda infrà Comitatum Civitatis prædictæ, ac de omnibus et singulis subditis nostris heredum vel successorum nostrorum infrà Comitatum Civitatis prædictæ pro tempore existen-

298   HISTORY OF EXETER.

tibus morantibus seu residentibus accidente emergente sive con-
tingente in quibuscunque curiis nostris heredum vel successorum
nostrorum aut in quacunque curiâ nostrâ heredum vel successorum
nostrorum aut coram Nobis heredibus vel successoribus nostris
ubicunque fuerimus aut fuerint in Anglia aut coram Nobis heredibus vel successoribus nostris in Cancellariâ nostrâ heredum vel
successorum nostrorum aut coram Thesaurario et Baronibus de
Scaccario nostro heredum vel successorum nostrorum, seu coram
Baronibus de Scaccario nostro heredum vel successorum nostrorum,
aut coram Justiciariis nostris heredum vel successorum nostrorum ad
placita coram Nobis heredibus aut successoribus nostris tenenda, vel
coram Justiciariis nostris heredum aut successorum nostrorum de
Communi banco vel coram Senescallo et Marescallo hospitii nostri
heredum vel successorum nostrorum, seu coram Coronatore Hospitii
nostri heredum aut successorum nostrorum vel Clerico Mercati
nostri heredum vel successorum nostrorum qui pro tempore fuerit,
vel coram Justiciariis nostris heredum aut successorum nostrorum
itinerantibus ad communia placita Coronæ nostræ audienda et terminanda assignatis aut coram Justiciariis nostris heredum et successorum nostrorum ad felonias proditiones murdra transgressiones
oppressiones excessus et alia gravamina ac alia malefacta tam ad
sectam nostram et hæredum nostrorum quam aliorum quorumcunque
vel alterius cujuscunque audienda et terminanda assignatis vel
assignandis, Justiciariis nostris ad assisas jurata certificata et quascumque alias inquisitiones capiendas vel ad gaolam deliberandam
assignatis vel assignandis, Justiciariis sive custodibus pacis nostræ
heredum vel successorum nostrorum ad statuta et ordinationes de
artificibus laboratoribus servientibus operariis vitellariis forstallariis ac de ponderibus et mensuris conservandis assignatis vel
assignandis, quam coram quibuscunque aliis Justiciariis officiariis
et ministris nostris heredum vel successorum nostrorum tam in
præsentiâ nostrâ heredum vel successorum nostrorum quam in
absentia nostra vel absentia heredum vel successorum nostrorum
ubi ipsos subditos nostros heredum vel successorum nostrorum aut
eorum aliquem infra dictum Comitatum Civitatis nostræ Exon' prædictæ aut successores suos aut eorum aliquem fines facere, amerciari
exitus forisfacere, recognitiones forisfacere, escapia negligent contingen felon murdr vel al felon forisfact adjudicari contigerit, licet
Nos ipsi heredes vel successores nostri fuerimus inde pars vel
nostrorum aliquis fuerit pars, ac licet aliquis alius vel aliqui alii
tam pro seipso vel seipsis secutus fuerit vel secuti fuerint, quæ
quidem fines exitus amerciamenta recognitiones escapia felon
murdr' felon' forisfact' nobis hæredibus vel successoribus nostris
pertinere debeant seu deberent si ea præfatis Majori Ballivis et
Communitati Civitatis prædictæ et successoribus suis per præsentes
concessa non fuissent. Et quod bene licebit eisdem Majori Ballivis
et Communitati Civitatis prædictæ et successoribus suis in perpetuum
omnia prædicta fines amerciamenta redemptiones exitus recognitiones forisfactas forisfacturas et omnia quæ ad nos heredes et successores nostros de dictis murdr' felon' escapiis et ceteris præmissis
pertinere possint seu poterunt per ipsos Ballivos Vicecomitem seu

CHARTER OF KING CHARLES I. 299

ministros suos quoscumque levare colligere percipere et habere et seipsos in seisinam inde ponere ad opus et usum ipsorum Majoris Ballivorum et Communitatis Civitatis nostræ Exon' prædictæ et successorum suorum absque calumniâ impetitione vel impedimento nostri heredum vel successorum nostrorum Justiciariorum officciariorum seu ministrorum nostrorum heredum vel successorum nostrorum quorumcunque aut aliorum Justiciariorum Escaetorum Vicecomitum Coronatorum Majorum Ballivorum Constabulariorum seu ministrorum nostrorum heredum vel successorum nostrorum quorumcunque; licet prædicti subditi nostri heredum vel successorum nostrorum aut alicujus eorum plegii manucaptores aut fidejussores seu eorum alicujus de nobis heredibus vel successoribus nostris vel de aliquâ aliâ personâ vel de aliquibus aliis personis infrà dictum Comitatum Civitatis nostræ Exon' prædictæ vel alibi tenuerint vel eorum aliquis tenuerit, licet insuper prædicti subditi nostri heredum et successorum nostrorum Ballivi Officiarii seu Ministri nostri heredum vel successorum nostrorum aut dictorum Majoris Ballivorum et Communitatis et successorum suorum aut alicujus alius personæ existant seu eorum aliquis existat; licet etiam dicti plegii manucaptores sive fidejussores infrà dictum Comitatum Civitatis Exon' prædictæ aut extra eundem Comitatum moraverint seu habitaverint aut eorum aliquis moraverit seu habitaverit.

ET INSUPER Concessimus et per præsentes pro Nobis heredibus et successoribus nostris Concedimus præfatis Majori Ballivis et Communitati Civitatis prædictæ et successoribus suis in perpetuum, quod nec Thesaurarius Cancellarius aut Barones de Scaccario nostro heredum vel successorum nostrorum nec eorum aliqui vel aliquis de cetero faciant seu faciat aliquem processum versus aliquos Justiciarios nostros pacis aut Justiciarios pacis heredum et successorum nostrorum dicti Comitatus Civitatis nostræ Exon' seu versus aliquos Justiciarios nostros heredum vel successorum nostrorum ad diversa felonias transgressiones et alia malefacta infra eundem Comitatum ejusdem Civitatis Exon' et libertates ejusdem perpetrata et perpetranda audienda et terminanda assignatos vel assignandos aut versus eorum aliquos vel aliquem pro aliquibus extractis de sessionibus suis ibidem factis sive imposterum fiendis in Scaccarium nostrum heredum vel successorum nostrorum mittendis seu liberandis; sed volumus et concedimus per præsentes pro nobis heredibus et successoribus nostris quod omnes et singuli hujusmodi Justiciarii nostri heredum et successorum nostrorum pro et de liberatione et liberationibus hujusmodi extractis de sessionibus suis prædictis imposterum, ut præmittitur, fiendis erga nos heredes et successores nostros exonerentur et eorum quilibet in perpetuum exoneretur per præsentes.

CUMQUE in Civitate nostrâ Exon' prædictâ et Comitatu ejusdem Civitatis et in partibus adjacentibus quam plurimi mercatores et pannifices commorantur, ex quorum quotidianis ibidem commerciis et negotiationibus in bonum publicum dictæ Civitatis et meliorem expeditionem subditorum nostrorum in partibus illis degentium et ibidem confluentium in contractibus mercaturis et conventionibus suis multum conduceret quod Major Ballivi et Communitas Civitatis

300 HISTORY OF EXETER.

prædictæ et successores sui haberent potestatem recipiendi quascunque recognitiones inter mercatorem et mercatorem et executiones superinde faciendi juxta statuta Mercatorum ac statuta apud Acton Burnell nuper edita prout in aliis civitatibus burgis et villis incorporatis minoris eminentiæ jamdudum concessum et stabilitum sit, Nos communi utilitate Civitatis nostræ Exon' prædictæ et publico subditorum nostrorum in partibus illis commodo et beneficio gratiose annuentes, Volumus ac per præsentes pro Nobis heredibus et successoribus nostris de uberiori gratiâ nostrâ speciali certâ scientiâ et mero motu nostris concedimus Majori Ballivis et Communitati Civitatis nostræ Exon' prædictæ et successoribus suis quod Major ejusdem Civitatis pro tempore existens et Clericus ad recognitiones debitorum secundum formam Statuti de Mercatoribus et Statuti apud Acton Burnell nuper editi accipiendas assignandus modo et formâ postea in his præsentibus expressis aut mentionatis appunctuandus habeant in perpetuum plenam potestatem et auctoritatem capiendi et recipiendi quascumque recognitiones et executiones inde faciendi juxta formam Statuti de Mercatoribus et Statuti apud Acton Burnell nuper editi, nec non omnia alia faciendi et exequendi infra Civitatem prædictam et Comitatum ejusdem Civitatis quæ vigore eorundem statutorum seu eorum alicujus ad aliquem Majorem Vicecomitem Ballivum vel alium Officiarium et ad aliquem Clericum in aliqua Civitate sive Burgo incorporato infra hoc regnum nostrum Angliæ ad recognitiones debitorum secundum formam Statutorum prædictorum vel eorum alterius appunctuatum vel eorum aliquem pertinent vel pertinere possint vel debeant. Et quod iidem Major et Clericus pro tempore existentes habeant et habebunt et vigore præsentium conficient assument et applicabunt unum Sigillum de duabus peciis, cujus una pars erit major pars et altera pars ejusdem erit minor pars, ad recognitiones prædictas coram eis imposterum cognoscendas sigillandas juxta formam Statuti prædicti de Mercatoribus et Statuti apud Acton Burnell nuper editi; quod quidem Sigillum erit et appellabitur deinceps in perpetuum Sigillum Regis ad recognitiones prædictas infrà civitatem nostram Exon' prædictam capiendas sigillandas; cujus quidem Sigilli major pars remanebit semper in custodiâ Majoris ejusdem civitatis pro tempore existentis, et altera pars ejusdem Sigilli erit et remanebit in perpetuum in manibus et custodiâ Clerici pro tempore existentis deputati vel appunctuati ad recognitiones prædictas scribendas et irrotulandas secundum intentionem harum literarum nostrarum patentium. Quodque Communis Clericus Civitatis prædictæ pro tempore existens, quamdiu in eodem Officio remanebit, sit et erit Clericus noster heredum et successorum nostrorum ad recognitiones debitorum secundum formam Statutorum prædictorum aut eorum alterius infrà civitatem prædictam ac Comitatum Civitatis prædictæ et libertates limites ac præcincta eorum accipiendas scribendas et irrotulandas, et ad rotulum memorandorum et recordorum inde servandum et custodiendum, ac ad minorem peciam Sigilli prædicti custodiendam, et ad omnia alia facienda et exequenda quæ ad aliquem Clericum recognitionum debitorum secundum formam Statutorum prædictorum vel eorum alterius appunctuatum

CHARTER OF KING CHARLES I.   301

pertinent facienda et exequenda; dictumque Communem Clericum
Civitatis prædictæ Clericum nostrum heredum et successorum nostrorum ad recognitiones debitorum infrà Civitatem prædictam secundum formam Statutorum prædictorum et eorum alterius accipiendas
scribendas et irrotulandas, et ad minorem peciam Sigilli prædicti
custodiendam, et ulterius ad omnia alia facienda et exequenda quæ
ad aliquem Clericum ad recognitiones debitorum secundum formam Statutorum prædictorum et eorum alterius appunctuatum
pertinent facienda vel exequenda, pro Nobis heredibus et successoribus nostris facimus ordinamus et constituimus per præsentes
absque aliquo breve proinde impetrando, et absque aliquâ aliâ
electione fiendâ.

CUMQUE etiam diversa terræ tenementa et hereditamenta, ad
seperales bonos et pios usus infrà Civitatem prædictam et Comitatum ejusdem Civitatis perimplendos ante hæc tempora quibusdam
feoffatis et fidei commissariis data et concessa fuerint, quiquidem
feoffati eadem terras tenementa et hæreditamenta in manus præfatorum Majoris Ballivorum et Communitatis Civitatis nostræ Exon'
prædictæ ponere desiderant pro majore eorundem, terrarum tene-
mentorum et hæreditamentorum, securitate et meliore inde dis-
positione et gubernatione secundum intentionem laudabilem pri-
morum et originalium inde donatorum, Nos hujusmodi bonum
desiderium gratiosê approbantes, de gratiâ nostrâ speciali, ac ex
certâ scientiâ et mero motu nostris DEDIMUS et CONCESSIMUS ac per
præsentes pro Nobis heredibus et successoribus nostris Damus et
concedimus præfatis Majori Ballivis et Communitati Civitatis prædictæ et successoribus suis, quod bene liceat et licebit omnibus et
singulis hujusmodi feoffatis de aliquibus maneriis terris tenementis
decimis redditis vel hæreditamentis ad bonos vel pios usus infrà
Civitatem prædictam vel Comitatum ejusdem Civitatis perimplendos
de statu hæreditario seisitis existentibus, eadem maneria terras
tenementa et cætera præmissa præfatis Majori Ballivis et Communitati Civitatis prædictæ et successoribus suis dare concedere et
alienare; quodque etiam bene liceat et licebit eisdem Majori
Ballivis et Communitati Civitatis prædictæ eadem maneria terras
tenementa decimas reddita vel hæreditamenta de præfatis feoffatis
et eorum superviventibus habere perquirere et recipere sibi et
successoribus suis imperpetuum, statuto de terris et tenementis ad
manum mortuam non ponendis aut aliquo alio statuto aut provisione legis restrictione vel consuetudine in contrarium inde non
obstante; PROVISO semper quod prædicti Major Ballivi et Communitas
Civitatis prædictæ et successores sui omnia et singula dicta maneria
terras tenementa et hereditamenta virtute præsentium illis sic ut
præferter concedenda, necnon exitus redditus et proficua inde de
tempore in tempus provenientia ad tales et eosdem usus pios et
publicos convertere et disponere teneantur ad quos et quales eadem
maneria terræ tenementa et hæreditamenta respectivè primum et
originaliter data et concessa fuerunt, secundum voluntatem et veram
intentionem donatorum eorundem maneriorum terrarum tenemen-
torum et hæreditamentorum per chartas suas respectivè declaratam
ac juxta formam Statutorum hujus regni nostri Angliæ in hac parte

302   HISTORY OF EXETER.

editorum et provisorum seu in posterum edendorum et providendorum aliquo in præsentibus in contrarium inde non obstante.

ET ULTERIUS sciatis quod Nos eâ intentione ut Major Ballivi et Communitas Civitatis prædictæ de tempore in tempus publica onera et expensa ejusdem Civitatis melius sustinere et supportare possint et valeant, de gratiâ nostrâ speciali ac ex certâ scientiâ et mero motu nostris DEDIMUS et CONCESSIMUS ac per præsentes pro Nobis heredibus et successoribus nostris Damus et concedimus præfatis Majori Ballivis et Communitati Civitatis prædictæ et successoribus suis licentiam specialem liberamque et licitam potestatem facultatem et authoritatem habendi perquirendi et recipiendi, eis et successoribus suis imperpetuum, tam de Nobis heredibus et successoribus nostris quam de quibuscunque subditis et ligeis nostris heredum et successorum nostrorum, aut de aliis personis quibuscunque, maneria messuagia terras tenementa rectorias decimas redditus reventiones servitia et alias possessiones et hæreditamenta quæcunque quæ de Nobis hæredibus et successoribus nostris non tenentur in capite nec per servitium militare, nec de aliquo alio sive aliquibus aliis non consentientibus per servitium militare, non excedentia in toto annualem valorem centum librarum, ultra omnia onera et reprisas et ultra omnia maneria terras tenementa et hæreditamenta per aliquem vel aliquos progenitorum vel antecessorum nostrorum nuper Regum vel Reginarum Angliæ eisdem Majori Ballivis et Communitati vel prædecessoribus suis antehac concessa, et ultra omnia alia, terras tenementa et hereditamenta, quæ ipsi aut prædecessores sui antehac perquisiti sunt, aut ipsi vel successores sui imposterum perquirere possint aut debeant virtute vigore vel prætextu aliquarum aliarum chartarum vel literarum patentium per aliquem progenitorum vel antecessorum nostrorum prædictorum, statuto de terris et tenementis ad manum mortuam non ponendis, aut aliquo alio statuto actu provisione lege restrictione vel consuetudine in contrarium inde in aliquo non obstante.

QUARE VOLUMUS ac per præsentes pro Nobis heredibus et successoribus nostris DAMUS et CONCEDIMUS cuicunque subdito nostro et quibuscunque subditis nostris heredum et successorum nostrorum, quod ipsi aut eorum aliquis vel aliqui aliqua maneria messuagia terras tenementa rectorias decimas reddita reventiones servitia et alias possessiones et hereditamenta quæcunque, quæ non tenentur de Nobis heredibus et successoribus nostris in capite vel per servitium militare aut de aliquo alio sive aliquibus aliis non consentientibus per servitium militare, præfatis Majori Ballivis et Communitati Civitatis prædictæ et successoribus suis dare concedere vendere legare seu alienare possint et valeant ; ita tamen quod maneria messuagia terræ tenementa et cetera hæreditamenta sic danda concedenda leganda vel alienanda non excedant in toto clarum annualem valorem centum librarum ultra omnia onera et reprisas et ultra prædicta maneria terras tenementa et hæreditamenta sic ut præfertur concessa perquisita aut perquirenda, prædicto Statuto de terris et tenementis ad manum mortuam non ponendis aut aliquo alio statuto actu ordinatione lege provisione seu consuetudine in contrarium inde in aliquo non obstante.

CHARTER OF KING CHARLES I. 303

ET ULTERIUS VOLUMUS ac per præsentes pro Nobis heredibus et successoribus nostris concedimus præfatis Majori Ballivis et Communitati Civitatis nostræ Exon' prædictæ et successoribus suis, quod Major Ballivi et Communitas Civitatis prædictæ et successores sui de cætero imperpetuum habeant et teneant omnes et omnimodas libertates authoritates exemptiones maneria terras tenementa fines forisfacturas redemptiones exitus et alia hæreditamenta privilegia quietancias jurisdictiones et franchesia quæcumque quæ per aliquas literas patentes aliquorum progenitorum vel antecessorum nostrorum Majori Ballivis et Communitati Comitatus Civitatis Exon' mentionantur fuisse concessa, vel quæ prædictis Majori Ballivis et Communitati Civitatis prædictæ per quodcunque nomen vel per quamcunque incorporationem vel prætextu cujuscunque incorporationis unquam antehac concessa fuerunt vel quæ prædicti Major Ballivi et Communitas Civitatis Exon' prædictæ modo habent vel tenent vel quibus usi vel gavisi fuerunt aut habere tenere uti vel gaudere debuerunt de statu hereditario ratione vel prætextu aliquarum chartarum aut literarum patentium per aliquem progenitorum aut antecessorum nostrorum Regum vel Reginarum Angliæ quoquomodo antehâc facta concessa, seu confirmata seu quocunque alio legali modo jure titulo consuetudine usu sive prescriptione antehac legitime usitata habita seu consueta, licet eisdem aut eorum aliquo vel aliquibus antehac usi non fuerunt vel fuit, aut abusi vel male usi vel discontinuati fuerunt aut fuit, ac licet eadem vel eorum aliquod aut aliqua forisfacta aut deperdita sunt aut fuerunt, HABENDA, tenenda et gaudenda præfatis Majori Ballivis et Communitati Civitatis prædictæ et successoribus suis imperpetuum, reddendo et solvendo inde Nobis heredibus et successoribus nostris annuatim tot tanta talia eadem et hujusmodi redditus servitia denariorum summas et demanda quæcunque quot quanta qualia et quæ Nobis antehâc pro eisdem reddi seu solvi consueverunt seu reddere seu solvere debuerunt. QUARE volumus, ac per præsentes pro Nobis heredibus et successoribus nostris firmiter injungendo præcipimus, quod præfati Major Ballivi et Communitas Civitatis nostræ Exon' prædictæ et successores sui habeant teneant utantur et gaudeant ac plene et integre habere tenere uti et gaudere valeant et possint imperpetuum omnes libertates liberas consuetudines authoritates jurisdictiones quietancias prædictas et alia præmissa secundum tenorem et effectum harum literarum nostrarum patentium sine occasione vel impedimento nostro heredum et successorum nostrorum quorumcunque: NOLENTES quod iidem Major Ballivi et Communitas Civitatis prædictæ et successores sui vel eorum aliquis vel aliqui ratione præmissorum vel eorum alicujus per Nos vel per hæredes vel successores nostros Justiciarios Vicecomites Escaetores aut alios Ballivos sive Ministros nostros heredum vel successorum nostrorum quorumcunque inde occasionentur molestentur vexentur seu graventur occasionetur molestetur vexetur seu gravetur seu in aliquo perturbetur; VOLENTES et per præsentes pro Nobis heredibus et successoribus nostris mandantes et præcipientes tam Thesaurario Cancellario et Baronibus Scaccarii nostri heredum et successorum nostrorum

304 HISTORY OF EXETER.

quam Attornato nostro Generali pro tempore existenti et eorum cuilibet et omnibus aliis officiariis et ministris nostris heredum et successorum nostrorum quibuscunque, quod nec ipsi nec eorum aliquis vel aliqui aliquod breve vel summonitionem de Quo Warranto sive aliquod aliud breve vel processum nostrum quemcunque versus Majorem Ballivos et Communitatem Civitatis prædictæ vel eorum aliquem vel aliquos pro aliquibus causis rebus vel materiis offensis clameis aut usurpationibus aut eorum aliquo per ipsos aut eorum aliquos debitis clamatis attemptis usitatis habitis seu usurpatis ante diem confectionis præsentium prosequantur aut continuent aut prosequi aut continuari facient aut causabunt seu eorum aliquis faciet et causabit; VOLENTES etiam quod Major Ballivi et Communitas Civitatis prædictæ vel eorum aliquis per aliquem vel aliquos justiciarios officiarios aut ministros prædictos in aut pro debito usu clamea usurpatione vel abusu aliquarum aliarum libertatum franchesiorum aut jurisdictionum ante diem confectionis harum literarum nostrarum patentium minime molestentur aut impediantur aut ad ea vel eorum aliquod respondere compellantur, EO QUOD expressa mentio de vero valore annuo vel de certitudine præmissorum sive eorum alicujus, aut de aliis donis sive concessionibus per Nos seu per aliquem progenitorum sive predecessorum nostrorum præfatis Majori Ballivis et Communitati ante hæc tempora factis in præsentibus minimè facta existit, aut aliquo statuto actu ordinatione provisione proclamatione sive restrictione in contrarium inde antehâc habito facto edito ordinato sive proviso aut aliquâ aliâ re causâ vel materiâ quâcumque in aliquo non obstante.

In cujus rei testimonium has literas nostras fieri fecimus patentes. TESTE ME IPSO apud Westmonasterium decimo septimo die Decembris anno regni nostri tertio.

WOLSELEY.

Per breve de privato Sigillo.

No. IV.

COURT ROLLS, AND ACCOUNT ROLLS, OF EXETER.

THE enrolled records of the City of Exeter form a very remarkable series, beginning in the reign of Edward the First. They consist not only of rolls of the courts which the chief officers of the city have been used to hold for the purposes of contentious jurisdiction, civil and criminal, but also of many of the general proceedings of the corporate body and freemen in their administrative character; and they preserve a minute record of the annual revenue of the city belonging to it in its corporate capacity. Such a series is sufficiently rare to deserve some notice in a History of Exeter; a more careful and extended examination of them than the writer can profess to have made, would supply materials for municipal, and even for general local, history of which no author has yet availed himself in any but a very limited extent.

The present introductory notice of this class of documents will necessarily be short and imperfect, but it may serve to engage the attention and excite the curiosity of those whose leisure and facilities of access may enable them to make further inquiries, and to turn them to a useful account. It has been thought desirable to present an abridged copy of one of the court rolls of the reign of Edward III., which is a favourable specimen of the series, and a full abstract of a contemporaneous " compotus," or account, rendered by the Receiver of the city. The originals are, of course, in Latin, until they come down to a period when that language was superseded, and books were substituted for rolls; which however were not generally contemporaneous events in the practice of our public records.

It will be seen, on inspection of the originals, that the entries on the prepared side of the parchment generally consist of the records of pleadings, process, continuances, adjournments, and judgments in suits, or pleas of land, or personal actions in the " curia civitatis; " or of proceedings of a criminal nature. On the back, commonly called the " dorse," or " pars nigra," of the parchment, are entered proceedings not of a litigious character, but which relate to the election of the governing body and other officers of the city; of notes and memoranda of corporate transactions, such as leases, &c.; of the probates of wills of land and other property in the city; of customary process for obtaining possession of land or houses from insolvent tenants; of recognizance of debt, or adjudications on the statute of labourers on the complaint of masters; of the assise of bread and beer; of private conveyances, assurances, &c., enrolled (as it seems) for security and better proof; of fines of land on examination of married women; of prosecutions for breach of bye laws; seisure of waifs, estrays, and felons' goods; admissions to the freedom " per successionem," or by purchase, or " ex gratia," or " ad instantiam " of some third person; of apprentice deeds; of caption

X

306   HISTORY OF EXETER.

of bail or security to keep the peace; inquests ex officio by the mayor; and a variety of other miscellaneous matters.

On these court rolls are also occasionally recorded the holding of the "turnus," tourn, or court-leet, of the mayor, for each of the four quarters of the city, corresponding with the four great gates, East, West, North, and South. This tourn seems to have been held once in each year for each quarter, but the occasional omission of them or some of them from the roll of the curia civitatis would lead us to infer that they were either not regularly entered, or sometimes entered on other separate rolls, or in some cases confounded under the common head of the city court; for it is evident on some of the rolls that presentments of nuisances and misdemeanors, great and small, are often intermixed with civil plaints and pleadings.

At these tourns or leets we find the aldremanni, or aldermen, formerly elected;[1] a class of officer not mentioned in the charters till late in the series, when the office and character of a city alderman had apparently assumed, as elsewhere, a rank of higher dignity than it possessed at first, when his duties related chiefly to the orderly keeping of the streets and the denunciation of public nuisances and infractions of civic ordinances.

As far as a partial knowledge of these documents will enable us to decide, the earliest elections seem to have been conducted by the sworn freemen of the city, who chose the mayor and four seneschalli, naming one of the latter as receiver. The number of electors present was generally from 30 to 36. In later times this body of electors has been supposed to be the same as the common council of the city, afterwards reduced by charter to twenty-four (see Hoker's 'Offices, &c., of the City of Excester,' p. 168, ed. 1584, reprinted). But the roll of 26-27 Edw. III., abridged hereafter, shows that the select body of twelve elected "ad auxiliandum et consulendum majorem," &c., was another and different body; and even this author, himself a chamberlain of Exeter in the reign of Elizabeth, speaks of the duty of every freeman " to come yearly to the election of a mayor and officers, and then and there to give his voice." See also Izacke's Mem. A.D. 1544. And this general summons to attend and vote was, I am informed, the constant practice.

With respect to the "seneschalli," so called in the reign of Edward I., they are reputed to be synonymous with the "ballivi," and to be therefore included in the general style of "mayor, bailiffs and commonalty," which was eventually the corporate name used in all legal documents. The earlier charters and precepts of the Crown were by no means exact or precise in adhering to a particular name of incorporation. "Our citizens," "our burgesses," and even "our men" of Exeter, were designations of the city in the twelfth century. Earl Richard calls them "our mayor, bailiffs, and citizens of Exeter." Edward I. calls them the "mayor, bailiffs, and probi homines" of the city of Exeter; Edward II. styles them " majores et ballivi;" Edward III. calls them, in his commission,

---

[1] See Cur. Civitat. 17-18 Ed. III., Rot. 5, 6, 7; 45-46 Ed. III., Rot. 1. See also Izacke's Memorials, &c. p. 26 (1st ed.), citing Rot. 11 of 16 Ed. I.

COURT ROLLS AND ACCOUNT ROLLS. 307

a° reg. 18, "our mayor and bailiffs," and also addresses his press-warrant to the "bailiffs, probi homines, and commune" of the city, and another writ to his "beloved mayor, bailiffs, and probi homines" of his city of Exeter; and again he grants the fee-farm to the "mayor and citizens of our city of Exeter," and in another instrument calls them by their latest name of "mayor, bailiffs, and commonalty." As many of these instruments are contemporaneous with the court rolls, on which the election of officers is recorded, we know that these variations of style indicate no like variation in the component members of the body corporate.[2]

It is remarkable that the court rolls are currently known by the name of the Provost Rolls, and the court has, in late times, been called the Provost Court. Hoker says that the bailiffs were originally called "prepositi," or provosts, and that "curia civitatis" means the court of the mayor and stewards (or bailiffs), when sitting on Monday, and the provost court when sitting (by adjournment) before the stewards on the other days of the week (Hoker's Office of Stewards, p. 164). It is certain that the court, which always opened on Monday, was continued on other days in the week. All the rolls show this, and some occasionally introduce the marginal term "Provostria" over against the adjourned sittings. This occurs for example in membrane 32 of the roll 26-27 Edward III. described hereafter. In roll 33-34 Edward III. occur the words "adhuc de curiâ prepositi," or "curia prevostri," and also in membrane 44, ibid., we have, under "curia civitatis," the memorandum, "nulla curia fuit in provostr' istâ septimanâ propter sessionem justic' assisarum:"—i.e. "No provost court was held this week, because of the sitting of the justices of assize." This supports the statement of Hoker.

With regard to the subjects of litigation, we are struck both with the enormous amount of it disclosed in these rolls of the 13th and 14th centuries, and the wide scope of it. Not only all pleas real and personal are included in it, but crown proceedings of a character unknown to local courts of more recent times and long before the grant of a standing commission of gaol delivery, such as Exeter and Bristol lately had, are recorded among the "placita Coronæ Civitatis." Thus in the roll of 25 Edward I. we find two men and three women captured at the suit ("ad sectam") of Walter Wymound, on a charge of burglary in his house, and of binding him and carrying off his goods. The male prisoners acknowledge the felony, and turn approvers. The three women, Agnes, Rosamond, and Mariet, plead not guilty, are convicted by the jury, and are all sentenced to be hanged, and are executed accordingly after a respite of Rosamond during her pregnancy in prison.

At the same sitting three others are tried for burglary—one turns approver, the two others are hanged.

---

[2] Izacke, probably copying Hoker's unpublished collections, professes to give the names of mayors and bailiffs in the reigns of John and Henry III. These must have been ascertained from documents and records other than the court rolls.

x 2

308   HISTORY OF EXETER.

It might be surmised that the proceedings under some special commission had found their way into the city rolls; but there is no caption or heading to indicate the presence of the king's justices; and it must not be forgotten that the original common-law jurisdiction of a court leet (which the curia civitatis evidently exercised) extended not only to inquiry, but to determination and judgment; that this immense power unaccountably survived the 17th chapter of Magna Charta, and was hardly extinguished until the statute 1 Edward III., which was held to direct and require the transmission of such inquests to the king's justices of oyer and terminer.

Nor are the civil proceedings on the rolls without some interest. We find, for example, the old process of trial by law-wager—*i.e.* by the oath of the party defendant—in full activity; and resorted to on issues where such trial was held by all lawyers to be inapplicable long before the formal abolition of it in our own recollection. The plea on which its existence was long upheld was founded on the supposed secrecy of the litigated transaction, which might be supposed to be known only to the two parties; or (as Lord Chief Justice Holt thought) on the right of the plaintiff to a discovery upon oath; reasons which would hardly justify it on such occasions as the following :—

On the court rolls 18-19 Edward I., rot. 22, we find the defendant waging his law (*i.e.* offering to bar the plaintiff by his decisory oath) that " he did not, on the feast of St. Gregory last, call Matilda B—— a false 'meretrix,' and say that she had picked Walter's pocket."

In rot. 25, the defendant wages his law that " he did not call plaintiff a false thief or traitor, and tear his coat, and push him into a ditch." In rot. 18 of the roll of Edward III., hereafter abstracted (p. 315), another anomalous case of law-wager, in the case of a distress, occurs.

In truth the trials "per legem" seem to be as numerous as those "per inquisitionem." Some, however, are expressed to be by consent, and in others a marginal sceptic has expressed his doubts thus, "*Qu. si jacet ?* " I have some suspicion that the compurgators, whose office it was to swear "de credulitate," were orally interrogated by the court, and that the defendant was not always admitted to wage his law as of course, and without previous inquiry.

The court was no doubt a good deal occupied by trifling causes. Indeed, where a fine or amercement of some sort accompanied almost every act done in court, and the city reaped a handsome revenue from its cause-list and calendar, it is not to be expected that the mayor or other city officers would be hard upon suitors in small or frivolous causes. Hence we have such an entry as the following in Cur. Civitatis 18 and 19 Edward I., rot. 20 :—John de Whitemarestail is amerced for saying "Quod vellet quod omnes dentes Stephani de London extraherentur a capite, et quod mansio esset in profundo inferni; et hoc in præsentiâ ballivorum," &c. What had been the meritorious cause of this malediction of John does not appear. He had perhaps lost the verdict and his temper, and stood committed for contempt of court.

COURT ROLLS AND ACCOUNT ROLLS. 309

Inquisitions *ex officio* before the mayor are not uncommon. They probably refer to his office of coroner or escheator; but other subjects of official inquiry may also be suggested.

The interference of other courts, lay or secular, was jealously excluded; and instances of amercement for suing in the Court Christian, or even in the superior courts of law, are numerous. The city courts seem indeed to have had, in some causes, a sort of concurrent jurisdiction with the former tribunal; as we have already found them taking cognizance of oral imputations upon chastity.

With regard to the local customs of the city in connexion with tenure, the transmission of property inter vivos, or by will, the descent of land and other matters, it would not be difficult to compile a complete custumal from the rolls of the city court. To some extent this has already been done by Hoker, from whom Izacke has largely borrowed the materials of his careless work. Such a custumal appears to have been formerly in the hands of the corporation; and we hear of the Black Book or Lieger of the City, or the Black Roll, said to have been delivered to Sir Wm. Cecil in the reign of Edward VI., and never returned (Izacke, Mem. 95, sub anno 1489). If this be so, the precious volume may be still at Hatfield, where the cartulary of St. Michael's Mount once was. It should seem, however, that Hoker, in a subsequent reign, had, if not in his possession, at least access to, a certain "general lieger of the city;" a "great lieger book;" a "black lieger;" or a "black book," in which the customs and duties of the city officers were described fully. Perhaps this may still be forthcoming.[3]

Of the customary process constantly recurring on the rolls, that of proceeding *per glebam* is the most frequent. The production of a turf, stone, or other fragment of the house or land of the defaulting tenant is produced before the court on seven successive quarters. This is entered as a "tulit glebam." If the rent is then unpaid, the court awards seisin to the lord for a year and a day, called "seisina propter gavellac," or "gavelake." On further default at the end of that time his seisin becomes absolute, and there is judgment of "shortford,"—"adjudicatum est ei sortfort." (See Cur. Civit. 18 and 19 Edward I., rot. 48.) This process resembles (with some differences) that of Gavelet described, and perhaps extended to a different class of lords, in the statute so called, 10 Edward II., but certainly not then first established; for it had before prevailed in London and Kent, as well as Exeter, and was equivalent to the older remedy called *cessavit per biennium*. That statute calls the judgment of *shortford* by the name of "*forseelet*" in the common Latin text, and *forschoke* in the translation of the common edition. In the copy in the Liber Albus (Riley's Monum. Gildhallæ, &c., vol. i., p. 469) the word *forseelet* is altered to "*forshot.*"[4] It is probable that all these technical terms are corrupt forms of the originals. The words Gavelet and

---

[3] Mr. Gidley informs me that the book, or roll, has been searched for in vain; and there is reason to think that no such MS. exists at Hatfield.

[4] In the Register of St. John's Hospital at Exeter, the final award is called "*Schotford*, quod gallicè dicitur *forclot.*"

310   HISTORY OF EXETER.

Gavelac, or Gavelake (sometimes Gavelock), seem to be the same word, and have an Anglo-Saxon aspect. Possibly the words Short-ford, Sortfort, Forshot, Forseelet, and Forschoke, may all be different forms of the same word, and may be equivalent to foreclosure. The old term *foriscelatus*, from which the term " forceller" or " for-cheler" is derived, may supply a plausible etymon to the last. "Forchele dicitur, qui statuto die censum domino non solvit," is one of the illustrations of this expression furnished by Ducange from the cartularies of France. I am inclined to think that Gavel-lac is " privatio gabuli." But the explanation must still be regarded as an open question.

Before we close this notice of the court and account rolls of Exeter, it is worth while to remark on three other words which, or some of which, occur in both sets of documents, and are incidentally mentioned in other records, viz. the terms " baggavel," " bethugavel," and " chippingavel." See Izacke in his Memorials, Proem. p. 20, and in the subsequent part of the book, pp. 13, 19 (ed. 1). These payments are by him (and therefore probably by Hoker also) called a yearly tribute paid for all wares sold, or brought to be sold, within the city towards paving the streets, repairing the walls, and better support, &c., of the city; and they are by him referred to a grant by Edward I., dated 10th March, in the 3rd year of his reign. This explanation is copied by Cowell and Blount, and repeated by subsequent glossographers, down to Halliwell's Archaic Dictionary.

Now this grant of Edward I. is extant, and will be found under the Table of Charters, No. III., supra p. 281. It is simply a grant of a pavage-toll on certain specified articles for three years only. It does not contain any one of the above three " gavels " by name, nor can it possibly serve to explain them, for obvious reasons.

Earlier mention of the payments is made in a record of a composition before the Justices in Eyre at Lanceston in 33 Henry III. The record is described incorrectly by Izacke, sub hoc anno; more correctly by Hoker in his MS. collections; and in an earlier, and probably verbatim copy (in the 15th century) in the Register of St. John's Hospital (cited *ante*, note '). In this last they are called " consuetudines quæ dicuntur *Balgavel, Bra[or Bru]gavel, Schepgavel*," and are there represented as collected from the tenants of the Dean and Chapter in the city and suburbs. The original has not been found among the records of that Eyre in the Public Record Office, and the spelling in the original is therefore unknown.

It is probable that these payments were of very early, perhaps of Saxon, date; and like many other immemorial payments in cities, boroughs, and manors, they have become unintelligible. Even in the 13th and 14th centuries the words were very likely unintelligible, and therefore variously spelt. But the *things* meant by them must have been then well understood; for we find these duties annually let to farm, like other tolls, by persons who gave security for payment. In the Account rolls they come under the " issues of the city," and not under " rents of assize," and the receipts varied in amount; they were, therefore, casual profits and not quit rents. The patent roll 1 Edward IV., recites a statute 15 Henry

COURT ROLLS AND ACCOUNT ROLLS. 311

VI. for settling some controverted questions respecting St. Sidwell's. One of these was the question of "certain profites and customes called *baggavell*, *chepgavell*, and *brithyngavell* of all and everye tenant receyant and inhabitant withinne the soill and freehold of the said Dene and Chapitre withinne the citee forsaide."[5] The Act then goes on to declare these profits to belong wholly to the city. Hence we may safely conclude that elsewhere, as well as in the manors or fee of the Dean and Chapter, the three customs, or some of them at least, were claimed from resident inhabitants within the city, whether tenants of the corporation or of other freeholders. This conclusion, of course, does not show *on what* the above payments or dues were levied. The three must be presumed to be several and separate. That of "chepgavell" is not mentioned so often as the other two. The earliest spelling of the other two in the city rolls is *bagabulum* and *burgabulum*, sometimes spelt also, and on the same roll, *brugabulum*. In some rolls (as rot. 27 of court roll 9-10 Edward III.) the names given are *bridgabil'* and *batchgabil'*. In court roll 41-42 Edward III., the words are written *baggabulum* and *brythengabulum*. In court roll 45-46 Edward III., *baggabulum* and *breugabulum* is the spelling. *Balgavel* is the spelling in the copy of the record 33 Hen. III. *Bethugavel*, as written in later documents, seems to have taken the place of the original Burgavel.

Our forefathers (especially collectors of town dues) cared very little about etymology or orthography; yet it is only through the latter that we can make a reasonable guess at the former, especially after we have long lost sight of the dues themselves which are the subject of inquiry. At present no such items appear in the city accounts.

It is worth mention that a payment, called chepping-gavel, designated a payment formerly made at Maldon on the alienation of a tenement in a borough (MS. penes editorem); and that brugable and burgable are terms of frequent occurrence in old surveys and accounts; as in the Liber Winton; in the records of the Soke manor of the Bishop of Winchester; and at Shaftesbury (Hutchins' Dorset, vol. i., p. 86), &c., but in most cases with very uncertain and disputable import.[6]

Without further and earlier documentary illustration, there seems little hope of ascertaining the origin of these words. But, whatever their import, their antiquity and aspect incline me to include them among the "consuetudines" which belonged to the

---

[5] The very words on the original roll are here used. They differ from the printed copies. Under the composition 33 Hen. III., cited *supra*, the dues were equally divided between the Chapter and City.

[6] Mr. Gidley, who took much pains to ascertain the nature of these ancient dues when he first entered on his official duties, informs me that he failed to obtain any satisfactory account of their nature, but thought he detected a market-toll in the "chepping-gavel." It had long been the practice to include these dues nominally in the lease of other tolls, leaving the lessee to find out what they were. This practice shows that the mere nominal appearance of such items in an old compotus is not very cogent evidence that the meaning of the term was then well understood, or that any payment was actually made in respect of it.

HISTORY OF EXETER.

King at Exeter at the compilation of Domesday, and passed to the city with their tenure in fee-farm (Exon. Domesday, fo. 82);[7] or even among the "consuetudines" which belonged to the city before the Conquest. These will be noticed hereafter under No. V. *post.*

E. S.

ABSTRACT OF THE ROLL OF THE CURIA CIVITATIS 26, 27 Ed. III.

Rot. 1. Curia civitatis Exon. ibid. tent. die Lunæ prox. post. fest. Sci. Michis. anno regni regis Edwardi tertii a conq. Angl. 26.

Entries in pleas of land and personal actions.

On the dorse are the following entries:—

"Electio majoris et seneschallorum civitatis predictæ facta apud Exon. die et anno ut infra."

Then follow 36 names of persons.

"Qui per eorum sacramentum elegerunt Robertum de Brideport in majorem, Ricardum Oliver in seneschallum et receptorem," and three others "in seneschallos."

Alexander Leche gives for having the petty customs (minutæ custumæ) this year, 26s. 8d.

Robert Brown gives 5s. for the pasture between the south gate extra muros as far as the castle for this year.

Somaster gives 20d. for the pasture this year between the north gate and Windesore extra muros.

Three others give 10l. for the custom of bakers and butchers this year, and each makes a separate payment for his own part.

The "custuma ollarum" is sold or farmed this year at 2s.

The "custuma farinæ" is sold for 7s.

Spicer and another give 43s. 4d. pro "bagabulo et burgabulo" this year on the security of each other—"per mutuam plevinam."

The custom of bread is taken at 3s.

The custom of woad at 3s.

There is an entry of the appraised value of certain goods seized by process on certain specified suits, perhaps on process of attachment, the proceeds of which would accrue to the corporation under their charters.

The names of the twelve, elected "ad auxiliandum et consulendum majorem et reliquos officiarios in omnibus arduis negotiis communitatem tangentibus, are here entered.

Entries of the process of bringing a "glebe" into court for recovering arrears of rent, and praying seisin for a year and a day in the name of "gavelak."

Rot. 2.—Curia civitatis (as before) on Monday next before St. Dionysius.

Entries of pleas as above.

---

[7] There was a "collecta de gep'-gabulum," or "scepgabulum" (the reading is not clear), which belonged to William I., as appears by the St. John's Cartulary, fo. 36.

COURT ROLLS AND ACCOUNT ROLLS. 313

On the dorse are the following casual profits entered :—

A mazer bowl, mounted with silver, waived by a thief.

Proceedings before the mayor or his locum tenens under the Statutes of Labourers, 23 Edw. III. and 25 of the same reign.

Rot. 3.—Curia civitatis, &c. on Monday next before St. Luke Evang.

Pleas, &c., as before.

On the dorse are the following :—

Proof of a will of tenements in the city before the mayor, and precept to the under-bailiffs to deliver seisin to the executors.

A fine of land in the city levied before the mayor and seneschalli. The wife of one of the parties is examined as to coercion of her husband, and a precept issued to under-bailiffs to deliver seisin.

List of names of under-bailiffs (as it seems).

Assisa panis made on Thursday in this week—of wastell, simenel, cocket, boxlof, wigg, and panis siliginis.

The bread of each baker (in all eleven) is examined, and deficiencies in weight punished by amercements amounting on the whole to 10*d.* which are estreated.

Rot. 4.—Curia civitatis, &c., on Monday next after St. Luke.

Pleas as before.

On the dorse are the following[1] :—

" Turnus Quarterii Orientalis tent' apud Exon. die Jovis " next before the feast of St. Simon and Jude (28 November).

14 jurors sworn. Numerous defaulters amerced for selling wine, beer, cider, and meth' (mead) per parvas mensuras sigillo regis non consignatas ; as also for buying corn by like measures.

Forestallers of food coming to the Exeter market are also presented and amerced.

Amercements for nuisances by swine and pigs in the public street (regia stratâ) against the orders of the city.

One woman is presented for putting " burle and teseltou " (teaseltow ?) " in griseo."

Several are charged with putting " floccum in candelis parisiensibus, in deceptionem populi. Ideo attachiatur."

Two leprous persons are presented as secreting themselves out of the place appointed for them.

Rot. 5.—Curia civitatis, &c., Monday next after St. Simon and Jude.

Common pleas, and " placita inter Dominum Regem querentem et W. L." and others for trespasses, occur on both sides of the skin.

Rot. 6.—Curia civitatis, &c., on Monday next before All Saints.

Pleas of land in the suburbs of Exeter and some personal plaints occupy both sides of the skin.

---

[1] There is no entry in the rolls of the Curia Civitatis of this year recording the holding of a Tourn for the other quarters of the city. Whether any were held for those quarters in this year does not appear, at least by these rolls. They may have been recorded elsewhere.

314 HISTORY OF EXETER.

Also an application on the Statute of Labourers for desertion of a servant.

Rot. 7.—Curia civitatis, &c., on Monday after St. Martin.
Long pleadings in a writ of assize of disseisin between Nicholas Pynne and others, plaintiffs, and Isabella at-Scarpe and others, defendants, relating to freehold land in the suburb left by will of an ancestor of one of the parties, which was proved in this court—an assise was eventually summoned.
Other common pleas are entered, but theıe is nothing on the dorse of the roll.

Rot. 8.—Curia civitatis, &c., Monday next before St. Clement.
Entry of the delivery of the king's writ of right patent in a suit for the recovery of land in Exeter claimed to be held of the King by free service. It is addressed to the mayor and bailiffs, and is in the form given in the common Registrum Brevium.
Among other ordinary suits there is an entry of an inquest or jury summoned in a suit between the king as plaintiff and Walter Lorymer defendant, in trespass for suing one J. B. in the Court Christian. It went off for defect of jurors.
Some entries of suits, &c., are continued on the dorse, where there is also a grant of probate of a will of lands in the city.

Rot. 9.—(slightly defective) curia civitatis, &c., Monday next after the feast of St. Katherine, virgin.
Entries of common pleas and inquisitions.
On the dorse there is an assise of bread.

Rot. 10.—Curia civitatis, &c., on Monday next after St. Andreas, apost.
Pleas of land and common plaints, continued on the dorse, on which a fine of a rent-charge on a shop in the city is also recorded.

Rot. 11.—Curia civitatis, &c., Monday before St. Nicholas.
Pleas of land, &c., as above.
On the dorse are recorded the issues or profits of the fair of St. Nicholas, 48s.

Rot. 12.—Curia civitatis, &c., Monday after the feast of St. Lucie, virgin.
Pleas, &c., as above.
On the dorse is the entry of the goods of a Spanish felon pledged by him to an innkeeper in the city for a loan of 4s. : the appraised value was 20s., and the Receiver of the city is debited for the amount.

Rot. 13.—Curia civitatis, &c., Monday after St. Thomas.
The sum total of the fines and amercements of the past quarter is entered at 4l. 17s. 11d., with 20s. for goods waived ; 48s. from the fair of St. Nicholas, and a cup of the prior of St. Nicholas not yet appraised.

Rot. 14.—Curia civitatis, &c., Monday next before the Circumcision.
Pleas of land and other pleas adjourned " propter solemnitatem festi."

COURT ROLLS AND ACCOUNT ROLLS. 315

These and the previous pleadings in a writ of right between Durneford and his wife against Bayoun and his wife incidentally show the customary descent of freeholds in the city to be among males equally. They also show that records could not be certified under the seal of the corporation in the interval between Christmas Day and the Monday after Epiphany, "propter solemnitatem festi."

Rot. 15.—Curia civitatis, &c., Monday after Epiphany.

Pleas and inquisitions in plaints; among others an action at detinue by Juliana, Prioress of Polslo.[2]

On the dorse is a testamentary probate; a recognisance of debt before the mayor; and an assise of bread, in which no deficiency is found except that wastell is minus 7*d.*, but good as to weight, though ill-fermented. Also the following admission to freedom :—"John Molyns ingressus est libertatem dando de fine 20*s.* et juratus est ut decet," and finds sureties for payment.

Rot. 16.—Curia civitatis, &c., Monday after St. Hilary.

Entry of a writ of right patent and of other pleas real and personal.

Indorsed are a probate, several seisures in execution, and proceedings under the Statute of Labourers.

Rot. 17.—Curia civitatis, &c., Monday after the feast of Fabian and Sebastian.

Pleas real and personal.

On the dorse are proceedings on the Statute of Labourers.

Rot. 18.—Curia civitatis, &c., Monday after the Conversion of St. Paul—27 Ed. III.

Pleas, &c. as before.

In a plea for taking the plaintiff's cattle the defendant justifies taking them damage feasant, and the trial is " per legem," in which the defendant failed—" defecit de lege."[3]

Rot. 19.—Curia civitatis, &c., Monday after the Purification.

The indorsements on this roll relate to the Statute of Labourers, recognizances of debt before the mayor and sureties of the peace.

Rot. 20.—Curia civitatis, &c., Monday after St. Scolastica.

Pleas real and personal only.

Rot. 21.—Curia civitatis, &c., Monday next before St. Peter in Cathedra.

Pleas real and personal.

On the dorse like proceedings as on the dorse of roll 19 ante.

Rot. 22.—Curia civitatis, &c., Monday next after St. Peter in Cathedra.

Pleas real and personal.

---

[2] Juliana de Bruton, mentioned in Dr. Oliver's 'Monasticon,' p. 163, was prioress at this time. The names of other heads of religious houses, in or near Exeter, frequently occur in the pleadings, — such as Cowick, St. Nicholas, St. James, Plympton, &c. &c.

[3] Allowing law-wager in a suit founded on an alleged trespass—such as a distress of cattle—is contrary to the general principle of that ancient mode of trial. See the observations which precede this abstract.

HISTORY OF EXETER.

On the dorse a recognizance of debt, and an entry of one Richard of London, cordwainer, into the freedom, paying 20s. by two instalments.

Rot. 23.—This court roll has only entries of pleas and process.

Rot. 24.—Curia civitatis, &c., Monday next before the feast of St. Gregory, pope.
Pleas real and personal, including some for suing in the Court Christian instead of the City Court: such suits are instituted in the Curia Civitatis in the King's name.
Indorsed are assises of bread on two different occasions.

Rot. 25.—Curia civitatis, &c., next after the feast of St. Gregory. Pleas as before.
At the foot is a memorandum of the sum total of fines and amercements for the last quarter, viz. 3l. 19s. 5d., besides admission of freeman, 2l.

Rot. 26.—Contains only pleas.

Rot. 27.—Curia civitatis, &c., Monday next after the Annunciation. Pleas real and personal.
Proceedings on the Statute of Labourers are indorsed.[4]

Rot. 28.—Contains only entries of pleas.

Rot. 29.—Curia civitatis, &c., Monday after the feast of St. Leo, pope.
Pleas real and personal.
On the dorse is proof of the will of Dionysius de Bruges, a goldsmith, apparently of considerable landed property in the city, in South Street, at St. Leonard's Mount, and near Magdalen Street, very fully described in the will.
A number of citizens pay fines for their customary works (" pro custum' operū ") for the year down to Michaelmas ; probably they compounded in money for some personal services to which they were liable.

Rot. 30.—Curia civitatis, &c., Monday before St. Mark.
Pleas real and personal.
On the dorse is a conveyance in fee to Agnes, the devisee of the lands of Dionysius de Bruges mentioned in the last roll, to John Dyrkyn ; witnesses, the mayor and seneschalli of the city and many others, &c.   This is followed by a like enrolment of a conveyance by J. Dyrkin to the same Agnes, of a " solarium " and " camera " under it, lately occupied by D. de Bruges in one of the tenements conveyed by Agnes by the last deed.

Rot. 31.—Only contains entries of pleas.

Rot. 32.—Curia civitatis, &c., Monday after the Invention of the Cross.

---

[4] The proceedings on this statute seem to have become numerous about this time, as the rolls testify. It is probable that the pestilence and other causes had reduced the number of labourers, and enabled them to demand higher wages. The statutes of 23 and of 25 Ed. III. are particularly severe, and even unjust. They are the subject of interesting comments by Barrington in his 'Observations on the Ancient Statutes,' p. 264, 5th ed.

COURT ROLLS AND ACCOUNT ROLLS. 317

Pleas real and personal and fines for customary works.

On the dorse are entries of executions, and also certain pleas under the of head *Sabbati de Provostr'*.[5]

Rot. 33.—Contains only pleadings and inquiries in suits.

Rot. 34.—Only pleas as usual.

There is among them a proceeding in the nature of an indictment against various persons for undermining the highway at Croldych and carrying away the soil. A venire is awarded to the under-bailiff to cause a jury of 18 to come "ad inquirendum."

On the dorse is a recognizance of a debt taken by one of the seneschalli of the city.

Rot. 35.—Pleadings in the curia civitatis as usual.

On the dorse is a recognizance of debt taken before the mayor, with an agreement that on default to pay the obligee, the amount is to be levied by the bailiffs of the city to the use of the obligee.

Rot. 36.—Contains only pleas, and personal and other process in the curia civitatis.

Rot. 37.—Contains only pleas and process of execution in the same court.

Rot. 38.—Pleas and proceedings in the same court.

On the dorse are entered executions, and complaints on the Statute of Labourers.

Rot. 39.—Pleas and proceedings in suits in the same court.

On the dorse, process of execution.

Rot. 40.—Like pleas and proceedings.

Rot. 41.—Like pleas and proceedings.

On the dorse is an assise of bread made on Tuesday next after the Translation of St. Thomas (3 July).

Rot. 42.—Pleadings and proceedings in suits in the same court. On the margin of some entries of amercements " pro non prose-quendo," the words " in pixide" occur.[6]

On the dorse is a payment for admittance into the freedom 20s., and several complaints on the Statute of Labourers.

Rot. 43.—Pleadings and proceedings in suits in the same court.

Rot. 44.—A writ of right patent was addressed to the mayor and bailiffs—other entries in suits follow.

Complaints on Statute of Labourers on the dorse.

---

[5] It is not clear whether the entries headed " Sabbati de Provostr'" are proceedings in the Curia Civitatis, as on the other side of the roll; but they probably are so, as there is no separate caption or heading descriptive of the court. The court was, perhaps, held on Saturday by adjournment (as elsewhere seems to have been the case), and the word *Provostria* added to denote that the entry related to that court, though not on the usual side of the roll. See the observations preceding this abstract.

[6] The old account rolls of the receivers of the city sometimes contain an entry of the sums accounted for in the *pizis*, or corporation box. It seems that some small miscellaneous payments were usually deposited in such a box ; and these are examples of such deposits.

HISTORY OF EXETER.

Rot. 45.—Entries of proceedings in suits in the same court. On the dorse complaints on the Statute of Labourers.

Rot. 46.—Entries of suits, &c., as above. Process "ad emend' viam regalem apud Crolledych," against persons convicted of a nuisance on it, "ad nocumentum totius communitatis" (*i.e.* commonalty) "et patriæ." [7]
A complaint on Statute of Labourers is indorsed.

Rot. 47.—Entries of suits, &c., as above. Several amercements are entered as paid into the "pixis."
On the dorse, among other entries of suits, &c., in the same court, is a curious one of an action by Willm. Dene against Will. Servyngton for assaulting and beating him in the High Street, near "Fishfold" Gate. The defendant pleaded that plaintiff was his "*nativus*" of his manor of Ayshe, and denied that he was bound to answer. The plaintiff replied that he was not the defendant's nativus, and offered to verify the fact and prayed an inquiry; and thereupon the defendant prayed judgment (*i.e.* it should seem, demurred in law) for that the plaintiff had taken issue on a plea of personal exception, which could not be tried on this plaint nor in the court, "propter debilitatem curiæ." The court took time to consider. [8]

Rot. 48.—Only pleadings and proceedings in suits, as above.

Rot. 49.—Only pleadings, &c., as above.

Rot. 50.—Same as above.
On the dorse are proceedings on the Statute of Labourers against apprentices deserting during their term of service. In the case of a fuller's apprentice for 3 years, the apprentice was to have 4*d.* a week for the first year, 5*d.* for the second, and 6*d.* for the third, and was to pay 10*s.* before the end of his term for his teaching. Besides the weekly wages, he was to have "legumina et alias curialitates." Whether the "curialities" were of a comestible sort, or perquisites of another kind, does not appear.

Rot. 51.—Only pleadings, &c. as above.

Rot. 52.—Curia civitatis as before, on Monday next after St. Matthew, apostle.
Pleas real and personal on both sides of the roll. Among the entries is the case of Dene against Servyngton, already noticed in

---

[7] This is the proceeding at the suit of the Crown for a public nuisance, mentioned in the roll 34 *ante.*
[8] The defendant, or lord of the villain, seems to have thought that the exception of villenage could not properly come in issue in this suit, nor be tried by an inferior court like that of the court of the city. It is certain that in the superior courts such an issue was triable by jury (Coke on Littleton, f. 124) ; and that a verdict for the villein would have made him, conclusively, a freeman. But whether this issue could have been tried in a local court is another question, on which the mayor and stewards might well enter a *curia advisare vult.* There is, in the next Monday's roll, an entry of further consideration, "quia curia nondum plenè inde consulta est," and a like entry in rolls 49, 50, and 51.—The judgment for defendant is on the dorse of roll 52. See *post.*

COURT ROLLS AND ACCOUNT ROLLS. 319

Roll 47, supra, and note *ib.* The entry is overlined by the words "dimittitur quia non potest terminari," which appears to be meant for a judgment for the defendant on the ground of want of jurisdiction.

On the dorse are also proceedings on the Statute of Labourers.

ABSTRACT OF THE COMPOTUS CIVITATIS, 42, 43 Ed. III.

Compotus Reymondi Gos senescall' et receptoris bonorum commun' civitatis prædictæ a festo Sti. Michaelis anno regni Regis Edwardi tertii a conquestu quadragesimo secundo usque ad idem festum anno revoluto.

Arreragia.

Idem respondet de 35*l.* 3*s.* 0¼*d* de arreragiis compoti sui de Duryerd. Summa 35*l.* 3*s.* 0¼*d.*

Redditus assis'.

Et de 8*l.* 12*s.* 4*d.* de redditu civitatis prædictæ et in suburbio ejusdem civitatis cum redditu de Pratteshide.

Summa 8*l.* 12*s.* 4*d.*

Exitus civitatis.

Et de 11*l.* recept' de custum' pistorum hoc anno.

22*s.* de custuma carnis.

33*s.* 4*d.* de minutis custumis.

12*d.* de custuma waid.

40*s.* de baggabulo et burgabulo.

13*d.* de custum' panis.

2*s.* de custum' ollarum.

7*s.* de custum' farinæ.

61*s.* 7*d.* de nundinis St. Nicholai.

5*s.* 6*d.* de pasturâ vendit' apud Crolledych.

3*s.* de pasturâ vendit' extra partem borialem.

20*d.* de pasturâ vendit' infra muros civitatis inter portam australem et Crikelepytte.

9*l.* 16*s.* 4½*d.* de custum' vinorum.

4*l.* 9*s.* 3½*d.* de custum' ferri et aliorum mercimoniorum.

50*s.* de stallis, ubi carnés venduntur.

41*s.* 8*d.* de exitu pixidis hoc anno.

16*s.* 11*d.* recep' de muragio. Summa 39*l.* 12*s.* 5*d.*

Perquisita curiarum.

Et de 18*l.* 15*s.* 10*d.* de amerciamentis curiarum hoc anno ut patet per extractas ballivorum.

19*l.* 13*s.* 4*d.* de ingredientibus in libertatem.

46*s.* 6*d.* de amerciamentis pistorum.

24*s.* 2*d.* de diversis finibus factis.

21*l.* 3*s.* 7*d.* de Turno Majoris.

17*s.* 6½*d.* de catallis forisfactis.

18*s.* 4*d.* recept' de diversis extrauris. Summa 64*l.* 19*s.* 3½*d.*

Summa totius receptûs 148*l.* 7*s.* 0¼*d.*

HISTORY OF EXETER.

Defectus redditûs.

In defectu redditûs tenementi Vyke in Maudelynestrete, 20d: De tenemento nuper Johannis Hopere infra portam orientalem, 12d. De domo nuper Gilberti Harpour infra portam borialem, 12d. De decremento redditûs apud Pratteshide, 2s. 2d. De domo nuper Walteri Plente extra portam borialem, 12d. De portâ nuper Will. Bykelegh nunc in manibus Fratrum Prædicatorum, 6d. De 2 placeis quas Will. Pontingdone tenuit propinquis tenemento Archdiaconi Totton', 16d. De exitu in posteriori parte tenementi Arch. Totton', 2s. De quâdam placeâ supra portam borialem, 6d. De tenemento nuper Joh' Roke in aurifabriâ, 10s. De placeâ quam Will. Cogan tenuit infra muros civitatis, 1d. De shopâ juxta Giald' quam Henricus Cotillere tenuit, 5s. De quâdam placeâ quam Johannes Uphaven tenuit juxta introitum messuagii sui, 1d. De quâdam placeâ quam Walterus Giffard cancellarius tenuit juxta introitum suum, 6d. De tenemento nuper Joh. Dollyng extra portam australem, 3s. De placeâ quam idem Joh. tenuit juxta ten. suum, 12d. De ten. nuper Ricardi Giffard infra portam borialem, 2s. 8d. De priore de l'Iympton pro quodam gradu figendo in regia stratâ juxta portam episcopi, 4d. De redditû circa pilloriam, 5s. De portâ quam Henricus Ballok, archidiaconus Cornubiæ, tenuit, 2s. De passagio de Pratteshide, quia caret batillo, 20s. De quodam trabe Rogeri Sture, 4d. De quodam trabe Joh. Colleford, 4d. Et de 6d. de muro juxta Giald' nuper Joh. Spycere. Summa 62s.

Resolut' redditus.

Item computat solvisse domino Joh' de Sully, milite, de redditu firmæ civitatis prædictæ sibi concessæ per Dominum Principem Walliæ ad terminum vitæ suæ, 20l., ut patet per 2 acquietancias. Item Prior Sanctæ Trinitatis, London', pro firmâ civitatis prædictæ, 25l. 12s. 6d., ut patet per 2 acquietan'. Item rectoribus parochiarum civitatis prædictæ, 4s. 8d.

Feoda soluta.

These fees are as follows:—To Roger Plente, mayor, for the year, 100s. Three senescalli, 60s. Receiver, 40s. For his clerk, 10s. Will. Wyke, recordor of the city, 60s. Will. Gerveys, 40s., and his robe, 15s. Four bailiffs for 4 robes, 48s. For their fees, 40s. 4d. Four janitors of the gates, 12s. In bread and wine sent to the mayor, Jno. Gist, Nicholas Tavernere, and other officers against the feast of the Nativity of the Lord, 21s. 9d. In wine given to the baker, 2½d. In bread and wine sent to them against Easter, 23s. Wine for the baker, 3d. Payment to Thomas Wayte for his fee, 26s. 8d. Summa 24l. 17s. 2½d.

Pensiones solutæ.

To Joh. Dabernoun, for his yearly pension, 40s. Joh. Kary, 20s. Nicholas Wytyng, 20s. Robert Wreye, 20s. Jno. Bosoun, attorney of the commonalty " in banco communi," 13s. 4d. Summa 113s. 4d.

Dona et exhennia.

Two gallons and 1 pottel of red wine, and 1 pottel of white wine sent to the king's justices in Lent, 19d.

COURT ROLLS AND ACCOUNT ROLLS. 321

Given to a courtier of the king on Tuesday next after the feast of St. Barnabas, 12*d.* One tunic given to Will Wyke, 9*s.* Also to Robert Hille ½ a mark.   Summa 18*s.* 3*d.* (*sic*).

Expensa necessaria.
The following is a summary of this head:—Parchment for rolls of court, 10*s.* 4*d.* Incaustum (ink), 8*d.* Man and horse for 6 days for carriage of stones from the North Gate to the Gildhall, 2*s.* 7*d.* 7 quarters and 4lb. lime, 6*s.* 10½*d.* Sand and the carriage of it, 2*s.* 2*d.* Hire of mason (pro latomo locato) for 2 weeks and 3 days to make a wall in the cellar under the Gildhall, 6*s.* 3*d.* Another mason for the like time, 5*s.* Hire of a servant (labourer?) for the like time, 4*s.* 2*d.* Nonsch'⁹ for the said workmen, 3*d.* Candles for making the wall, 4*d.* Collecting stones for one day, 4*d.* Cleansing the cellar, 3*d.* Spykes bought for mending the benches " in provostria," 3*d.* Hire of a carpenter for the same, 2*d.* For cleaning the " herbarium " against the feast of St. Nicholas, 8*d.* For carriage of gravel ("in gravello inde portando ") 2*d.* A man hired " pro sectâ faciendâ pro muragio habendo ad consilium domini principis," 15*s.* Item Henrico Percehay pro eodem, 20*s.* Horse-hire for the said man riding to London, 5*s.* " Item soluto pro muragio habend', 40*s.* ¹ Purchase of timber for the east gate, 14*s.* Hire of 3 carpenters for 6 days, 6*s.* 10*d.* ; 2 sawyers for do., 4*s.* 6*d.* ; nonsch'² for the said workmen, 6*d.* Iron for the same purpose with the making (facturâ), 18*d.* Hire of a man " pro spinis falcandis " (for cutting thorns or trimming the hedges ?) between Westgate and Eastgate, 15*d.* Tables and tressels bought for " le Freysfolde," 8*s.* A quarter of lime for covering the Gildhall (pro giald' cooperiend') 12*d.* Tiles for the same purpose, 21*d.* Sand for the same, 1½*d.* Cleaning the conduit near Crikelepytte, 6*d.* Lime bought of Rob. Gatepath by order of the mayor, 20*s.*³ Hire of two masons for 4 weeks for facing the strone (" pro petris doliandis "), 22*s.* Beer for them, 8*d.* Two pair of panniers bought, 6*d.*   Summa 7*l.* 3*s.* 7*d.*

Expensa forinseca.
As follow :—Rector of St. Pancras, 2*s.* Wine for the taxers⁴ of the court, and the Tourn of the mayor, and bakers, 2*s.* 10*d.* John Hille for expenses of the knight (of the shire) at the parliament at the feast of St. John Bap., 13*s.* 4*d.* In " piris "⁵ at the election of the mayor, 12*d.* Four flagons [or gallons? (lagenis)] of wine on same day, 2*s.* 8*d.* Two flagons [or gallons ?] of wine sent to Roger Plente,

---

⁹ Nunch or luncheon.
¹ The last item is struck out, with the words " quia respectuatur sub pede compoti " interlined above. The purport of the last four items is, that the Corporation had sent special messengers to wait on the Prince's Council in London to obtain the king's grant of murage, such grants being the subject of temporary taxation like the

pavage toll of 3 Ed. I., already noticed under the last head of this Appendix. It will doubtless be found on the patent rolls of the year.
² See note⁹, *supra.*
³ This last item is struck out.
⁴ That is, the assessors, or persons chosen to assess the amercements, &c.
⁵ *i.e.* " pyris," bonfires.

Y

322   HISTORY OF EXETER.

and two to Martin Gatteshille on same day, 2s. 8d. In rushes (cirpis) for the Gildhall and the solar for the year, 6d. Payment to the minstrels on Wednesday in Pentecoste when the men of the city shew their arms ("armas") before the Earl of Devon, 10s. For the same on Saturday next before St. Augustin's day for the same, 12d. Making a wall " ad taxh'"* next the house of John Grote for putting the bakers' tables upon, 4s. "In par' gymys⁷ emp'" 15d. Wax bought for the indictments and for other necessaries, 3d. To the Earl of Devon for a third part of the customs of wine accruing to him, 65s. 5½d. To Willm. Wyke pro uno breve impetrando at the feast of St. Martin, half a mark. Paid to the same for business of the city at Epiphany, 40d. To the same "in loco libertatis eidem concessæ per communitatem," 20d.* To Willm. Gerveys pro consilio, 20s. To Wytelegh for riding to meet the justices to invite them to dinner, ½ a mark. Also for expenses of the justices at assise in Lent, 8l. 7s. 3½d.

Summa 18l. 7s. 7d.

Amerciamenta condonata per Majorem et Communitatem.
   A long list of small amercements remitted by the mayor and commonalty.   Summa 74s. 1d.
   Amercements remitted by the mayor.   Summa 7d.
   Do. remitted by the receiver.   Summa 6d.
   Amercements remitted by Adam Scot.   Summa 7d.
   Do. by Walter Leche.   Summa 6d.

Feoda St. Nicholai.
   The names and sums, ten in number, all struck out.

Feoda St. Stephani.
   Struck out as above.⁹
          Sum (of the two last heads) 4s. 9d. *not* struck out.

Amerciamenta quæ non possunt levari.
   The names and sums in part struck out.   Summa 6s. 11d.

Allocationes.
   The accountant prays for certain deductions to be allowed for various items, *e.g.* strays stolen at Duryard; for certain amercements, because imposed at the mayor's Tourn; for certain forfeitures delivered to the Dean and Chapter by order of the Mayor and Commonalty; for a stray horse still remaining (impounded?) at Duryard.   Summa 2s. 6d.

---

⁶ *Taxhm*, with a sign of the letter *a* over the *m*; *i.e.* "ad taxham," by *task-work*, not *by the day.*
   ⁷ A pair of handcuffs? [J. Gidley.]
   ⁸ Wyke was Recorder, and probably sued out the necessary writs for passing the accounts of the bailiffs of the Liberty of the City, and for appearing by attorney at the Exchequer.
   ⁹ The Priory of St. Nicholas at Exeter, and the Bishop, in respect of his fee of St. Stephen, were entitled to the amercements of their own tenants. Hence the city received and paid them over to the prior and bishop. This appears in the rental of St. Nicholas, under the head "De Ballivo Civitatis super compotum ut in pede compoti" (Mon. Exon. 126).

EXTRACTS FROM THE DOMESDAY. 323

After this comes the " pes compoti " or foot of the accounts, viz. : Sum of all expenses and allowances, 111*l*. 9*s*. 6½*d*. Balance or " debet," 36*l*. 17*s*. 6½*d*. Out of this balance 40*s*. is respited, said to have been paid for the expenses of murage ultrà, &c., " as appears in the account suprà ;" also the several amercements in respect of the fees of St. Nicholas and St. Stephen, struck out as appears suprà ; and other condoned or illeviable amercements, &c. Total allowance is 10*s*. 3*d*., and so the debt is reduced to 36*l*. 7*s*. 3½*d*. At the end the balance is paid or accounted for, and a quietus entered.

No. V.

EXTRACTS FROM THE EXETER DOMESDAY RELATING TO THE CITY.

Fol.

88. In civitate Essecestre habet Rex CCC domus, XV minus, quæ reddunt consuetudinem. Haec reddit XVIII lib. per annum. De his habet B[alduinus] Vicecomes VI lib. ad pensum et ad arsuram, et Colvinus habet inde XII lib. in ministeriis Reginæ Eddide ad numerum. Hæc civitas non reddidit gildum tempore Regis Edwardi nisi quando Londonia reddebat, et Eburacum, et Wintonia, et hoc erat dimidia argenti ad solidarios. Et quando expeditio ibat per terram aut per mare serviebat ista civitas quantum V hidæ terræ. Et Totoneis et Lideforda et Barnestabla serviebant quantum et prædicta civitas. In hâc vero sunt XLVIII domus vastatæ postquam Willelmus Rex habuit Angliam. Et supradicti burgenses habent terram XII carrucatū extra civitatem quæ non reddit ullam consuetudinem nisi ad ipsam civitatem.[1]

106. *Episcopus* [*Essecestrensis*] habet IX domos in burgo Essecestre qui reddunt per annum III solidos.

120. b. *Episcopus* (ut suprà) habet I ecclesiam in Essecestrâ que reddit per annum I marcam argenti et XLVI domos,[2] et de his . . . . domibus reddunt X ex illis X solidos et X denarios de consuetudine et II sunt vastatæ per ignem et II agros et dimidium terræ qui jacent cum terrâ burgensium qui pertinent ad ecclesiam.

---

[1] There is at folio 94 b an interlined entry of five houses at Essecestra belonging to the king ; whether included in the above does not appear. " Dimidia argenti ad solidarios " is entered thus—"dimid' marka argenti ad opus milit'," in the Exchequer Domesday.

[2] The number 46 is corrected by interlineation to 47, which corresponds with the Exchequer copy.

Y 2

324　　HISTORY OF EXETER.

Fol.

163. *Episcopus* [*Constantiensis*] habet in Essecestrâ III domus et I vastatam, quæ fuerunt in dominio Edwardi Regis eâ die quâ ipse fuit vivus et mortuus, et reddiderunt consuetudinem.

Episcopus habet VI domos in Essecestrâ quas tenet Drogo de eo, et IIII ex his erant quietæ de consuetudine tempore Regis Edwardi, et II reddiderunt consuetudinem et hanc Drogo retinet. Hoc est XVI denarios.

180 b. *Abbas* [*Tavestochensis Ecclesiæ*] habet in Essecestrâ I domum quam habuit in vadimonio de uno burgense, quæ solebat reddere consuetudinem regis. Hoc est VIII denarios.

196. *Abbas Batailliæ* habet in Essecestrâ I ecclesiam de Sancto Oilafo ["Olavo"] et VII domos quæ reddebant consuetudinem et I quæ non reddebat. Hoc est IIII solidos et VIII denarios per annum.

222 b, 223. *Comes de Moritonio* habet in Essecestrâ I ecclesiam, et I domum et I virgultum, quæ fuerunt in dominicatu Regis Eduardi eâ die quâ ipse fuit vivus et mortuus.

297. *Balduinus* [*Vicecomes*] habet I mansionem quæ vocatur Chent . . . Hæc mansio valet X lib. . . . Huic mansioni adjacent XI burgenses, qui manent in Exoniâ, et reddunt IIII solidos et V denarios. Isti sunt in supradicto pretio.

315. *Balduinus* habet in Essecestrâ XII domos quæ pertinuerunt ad suam mansionem quæ vocatur Chent eâ die quâ Rex Edwardus fuit vivus et mortuus, et habet ibi VII alias domos de dono Regis Willelmi quæ fuerunt in dominio Regis Edwardi eâ die quâ ipse fuit vivus et mortuus.[3]

334 b. *Juhellus* habet I. domum in Essecestrâ quæ reddit consuetudinem tempore Edwardi Regis. Hoc est VIII denarios per annum.

344. *Radulfus de Pomariâ* habet in Essecestrâ VI domos unde habet consuetudinem Regis retentam. Hoc est III solidos et IIII denarios.

349 b. *Walscinus* [*de Duaco*][4] habet in Essecestrâ X domos quas tenuit Ansgerus eâ die quâ Rex Eduardus fuit vivus et mortuus, et habet aliam domum in vadimonio de uno burgense, unde consuetudo est retenta.

406. *Willelmus* [*Capra*] habet in Essecestrâ II domos quæ reddebant tempore Edwardi Regis XVI denarios per annum de consuetudine.

---

[3] These two entries are in part repetitions of the same. The Exchequer copy shows that there were 12 houses in the city appurtenant to the manor of Kenn. The first of the above entries makes the number 11, and the houses "burgenses." The manorial annexation of these tenements to Kenn is similar to that of the Bradninch precinct, near the Castle, to the manor of Bradninch to this day.

[4] Called "Walterius de Dowai" in the Exchequer copy, and also "Walscinus," as appears under the same head.

EXTRACTS FROM THE DOMESDAY. 325

Fol.

410 b. *Tetbaldus* [*filius Bernerii*] habet I domum in Essecestrâ quæ reddebat tempore Edwardi Regis VIII denarios per annum de consuetudine.

460. *Radulfus Paganus* [one of the " franci milites"] habet . . . . I domus (*sic*) in Essecestrâ qui (*sic*) reddit X solidos.

462 b. *Osbernus de Salcet* [or, *Salceio*] habet I domum in Essecestrâ quæ reddebat VIII denarios per annum de consuetudine tempore Edwardi Regis, et Osbernus hanc detinet.

473. *Godeboldus* [*Arbalestarius*] habet II domos in Essecestrâ quæ fuerunt in consuetudine Edwardi Regis eâ die quâ fuit vivus et mortuus, reddentes XVI denarios per annum.

505 b, 506. Under the head of " Terræ occupatæ in Devonescirâ," some of the above names and tenures are repeated with no substantial variation. Under the same head the following are entries not found in previous notices of property at Exeter :—

Aluredus Brito habet I domum in Exoniâ quæ reddidit tempore Regis Edwardi VIII denarios de consuetudine quos per annum ipse detinuit postquam eam habuit.

Rualdus Adobatus habet I domum in Exoniâ quæ reddidit de consuetudine VIII denarios tempore Regis Edwardi quos Rex Willelmus nunquam habuit.

Ricardus filius Turulfi habet I domum in Exoniâ de quâ ipse retinet cousuetudinem Regis. Hoc est VIII denarios per annum.

OBSERVATIONS.

It has been thought proper to insert in this Appendix the above extracts from Domesday, to show the state of the city in or about the year 1085, when the Domesday was compiled by King William.

The first extract is, alone, sufficient to prove the corporate character of the city before and at the date of the document. The king is not there said to have the city itself, but only 285 houses in it which rendered custom; the city itself rendering 18*l*. a-year, of which Baldwin, the sheriff, has 6*l*. by weight and by the test of fire, and Colvin 12*l*. by tale, as an officer of the dowager Queen Edith. The city is taxed only when London, York, and Winchester are taxed, and then at a fixed amount, for the pay of soldiers. It is also liable to contribute to the expense of military expeditions by sea or land, and is, for that purpose, charged as five hides of land. 48 houses are said to have been destroyed since the Conquest. It has been supposed that this destruction was occasioned by the siege of the city in the year 1066 ; but it is not clear how a siege of a few days'

---

[5] Called Radulfus Pagenel in the Exchequer copy.

[6] Called Ricardus filius Turoldi in the Exchequer copy.

326 HISTORY OF EXETER.

duration, without effective artillery, about 20 years before, in which the city had yielded voluntarily before capture and on favourable terms, can be confidently stated to be the cause of 48 dilapidated houses. The suburban property of the city is also referred to, and estimated at 12 carrucates ; but this is said to pay no customs to the king, but only *to the city itself.*

The king is not stated to have " the city" as in the case of Lidford or Barnstaple, where the record says, " Rex habet burgum Lideford "—" burgum Barnstaple, &c.," nor is the above statement entered in the Exchequer Survey, under head of " Terra Regis," which is the usual test, and indeed the sole evidence, of ancient demesne. I am, however, aware that the city is so designated in some early records. [See Charter 6 Edward III., *ante* pp. 282-3.]

The city is treated as a body politic, capable of possessing land and of claiming customs issuing out of municipal property—" non reddit consuetudinem *nisi ad ipsam.*"

It seems that in the time of the Confessor, the same franchises were then enjoyed by the citizens, and that his queen was then in the receipt of a sum of 12*l.*, parcel of the fixed payment of 18*l.* due to the Crown. Whether this sum was a strict fee-farm rent in respect of a prior grant of the city by the Crown, or was in the nature of a tax unconnected with any property in the city as a whole, does by no means appear. The conduct of the citizens at the siege, already referred to (*ante* pp. 32, 180), would imply that it was considered to be a tax or charge similar to the war-taxes also specified on the record. Their language, as reported by Ordericus, is very significant : " Neque sacramentum Regi faciemus neque in urbem eum intromittemus : sed tributum ei ex consuetudine pristinâ reddemus." The words " puberes et senatus," and the "majores" of the city, used by Ordericus in describing the population of it, point strongly to an internal municipal organization. These passages have attracted the notice of Maseres, who edited this part of Ordericus. " It seems," he says, that " *puberes* " may have been inserted here by mistake instead of *plebes.*" " The sense will then be that " both the common people and the magistrates, or town council " were violent enemies of the French nation." . . . " The answer " of the people of Exeter is a proof of the great degree of liberty or " independency they had enjoyed under the former kings of England of the Saxon line, and that they had obeyed those kings only " as far as they had chosen to do :—' Angliæ regi nisi ad libitum " ' suum famulari . . . olim despexerat.' "—Historiæ Anglicanæ Selecta Monumenta, a F. Maseres, London, p. 210, ed. 1807.

The Survey further shows that many other large landed proprietors were the owners of houses or land in Exeter. The bishop was one of the most considerable, and among them is mentioned his " church," *i. e.*, the temporalities of his See at Exeter. It is apparent that one of these tenements was, and others may have been, portions of extramural, and even distant, lordships or manors with their own franchises and territorial liberties, the fertile causes of endless disputes and litigation, down to a late period of the middle ages, and everywhere coming in conflict with the chartered claims of the

OBSERVATIONS ON EXTRACTS.

Commonalty. The See, the Chapter, the Castle, and the Courtenays, supplied the never-failing materials for altercation with the burger authorities of the city.

The Survey suggests observations on some passages in Dr. Oliver's History which are open to exception.

He states, p. 181, *ante*, that the Castle is not mentioned in it, and that it was perhaps not completed till the following reign. The selection of the site for one, and the immediate instructions given to Baldwin to erect it 20 years before, are so distinctly stated in Ordericus, and the necessity was so obvious and urgent, that so long a delay is not probable; nor can I find in Henry of Knyghton's work any ground for the author's doubt. The mere absence of any notice of one is of little value as evidence. Sir H. Ellis says that no notice of it can be expected, "Exeter having been designedly omitted." I cannot quite appreciate this reason; for the city is certainly mentioned repeatedly; but I can understand why a castle in the immediate custody of the Crown, or its castellan, was not considered the subject of public taxation, or the source of any pecuniary profit. The castles of Dover, Nottingham, and Durham, and the Tower of London itself, all originally built by William, are also unnoticed in Domesday. How many houses were destroyed at Exeter to clear the site is not mentioned, as it is at Winchester, Gloucester, Wallingford, Cambridge, Warwick, Lincoln, Stamford, &c., where they are mentioned, not as objects of hydage, but to show why the sites had become unproductive. Perhaps in the case of Exeter some of the 48 ruined houses may have supplied the site; and, if the ruin was caused by the siege, this is the quarter of the town where the siege-works would probably have been most vigorously prosecuted. •

Dr. Oliver speaks, as some of our earlier writers are apt to do, of the "revolting inquisitorial survey called Domesday," and the "broken spirit" of a population who could be "so completely overawed as to swear evidence against their own interests" (p. 33). The worthy writer, no doubt, relied upon the absurd complaints of the compilers of the Saxon Chronicle (anno 1085), that "not even an oxe, cow, or pig, was omitted in the census," and the dishonest avowals of the apocryphal monk Ingulphus, who plainly tells us that the jurors "benevoli et amantes penes nostrum monasterium" had cheated the king's commissioners by purposely underrating the possessions of his abbey. Such is the tone in which some of our annalists have spoken of this Survey.

Those who have given to it a better consideration, and brought to bear upon it a clearer judgment, have pronounced a more favourable opinion both on the political necessity of that great work, and on the general fairness with which it appears to have been executed. That the commissioners relied mainly upon the legal and popular instruments of inquiry is certain; that they only did well what had been before done ill and inadequately by the compilers of the Saxon landbocs, is probable. No one, who has examined the volume which now contains the abstract of the numerous inquests on which it is based, can have failed to observe the fairness of its general tone, so

HISTORY OF EXETER.

far, at least, as details so succinctly expressed, can disclose the animus of its authors. Instances are mentioned by Sir H. Ellis (Introduction to Domesday, vol. i. p. 31); and the general character and objects of the book have been well described by Lappenberg in his English History, Norman Period, and in Pearson's Early and Middle Ages of England, chap. 23. It need hardly be remarked that the cows and pigs so feelingly described as objects of taxation by the Saxon Chronicler, are specified only for the same reason as the number of ploughs kept by the landowner, —as one of the reasonable tests of his rateable ability. Such tests have been employed in all times and in all countries, especially in cases where mere superficial measurement can be no test at all. The main burden of the tax must have fallen on the great Norman feudatories of William himself.   E. S.

LIST OF SUBSCRIBERS.

ABRAHAM, R. T., Esq., Heavitree.
Acland, Sir T. D., Bart., Killerton (6 copies).
Acland, T. D., Esq., Sprydoncote, Broadclyst.
Acland, Rev. P. L. D., the Vicarage, Broadclyst.
Acland, Dr., Oxford.
Addington, Hon. W. W., Up-Ottery.
Angel, A., Esq., the Close, Exeter.
Arden, C., Esq., Exeter.
Arnold, T. O., Esq., Park, Iddesleigh.
Arnold, Mr. G., jun., Dolton.
Atcherley, Miss Caroline, Exeter (3 copies).

Baigent, F. J., Esq., Winchester.
Baker, Mrs., Heavitree.
Balkwill, Mr. Robert, Exeter.
Banfield, Mr. W., Awliscombe.
Barnes, Ralph, Esq., Exeter (2 copies).
Barnes, Rev. Reginald H., St. Marychurch.
Barnes, W., Esq., Exeter.
Barry, Mr. John, Barnstaple.
Barter, Rev. Charles, Sarsden, Chipping-Norton.
Bartholomew, Venerable, the Archdeacon, Morchard-Bishop(2 copies).
Bartrum, Mr., Bystock Terrace, Exeter.
Bayley, R. W., Esq., Cotford, Sidbury.
Bedford, His Grace the Duke of, Endsleigh.
Beer, Mr. Alfred, Exeter.
Benison, W. M., Esq., Exeter.
Bent, Major, St. Leonards, Exeter.
Bere, Montague, Esq., Morebath.
Bere, Rev. C. S., Uplowman.
Besly, Rev. Dr., Long Benton.
Bethune, Rev. G. C., Chulmleigh.
Bewes, Rev. T. A., Beaumont, Plymouth.
Biggs, Dr., County Asylum, Surrey.
Bishop, W. R., Esq., Exeter.
Blackall, Dr., Exeter.
Blencowe, Miss C., Dawlish.
Blencowe, R. W., Esq., the Hooke, Lewes.
Bockett, Rev. J., Baring Crescent, Heavitree.
Boger, Deeble, Esq., Stonehouse.
Boles, Rev. J. T., Exmouth (2 copies).
Bond, Rev. J. Hamilton, Romansleigh.
Borlase, Rev. W., Zennor, St. Ives.

LIST OF SUBSCRIBERS.

Bowring, Sir J., Larkbeare, Exeter.
Braund, G., Esq., Exeter.
Braund, M. K., Esq., Furnival's Inn, London,
Bremridge, T. J., Esq., Exeter.
Brent, Dr., Woodbury.
Brickdale, J. Fortescue, Esq., Newland, Gloucestershire.
Bridges, Miss, Mount Radford, Exeter.
Brock, Mrs. W., Exeter.
Brown, Rev. Wilse, Whitestone.
Browne, Rev. Canon, Exeter.
Buckingham, Rev. J., Doddiscombsleigh.
Buckingham, W., Esq., Exeter.
Buller, J. W., Esq., M.P., Downes, Crediton.
Burch, Arthur, Esq., Exeter.
Burne, Rev. C., Tedburn St. Mary.

Cann, W., Esq., Exeter.
Carew, J., Esq., Exeter (6 copies).
Carew, W. H. Pole, Esq., Antony, Devonport.
Carew, T., Esq., Collepriest, Tiverton.
Carew, Rev. R. P. Rattery, Totnes.
Carnarvon, Right Hon. the Earl of, Highclere, Newbury.
Carne, Rev. J., Marley, Totnes.
Carnsew, Rev. T., Flexbury, Poughill, Bude.
Carwithen, Rev. J. C., Challacombe.
Cary, S. E., Esq., Follaton, Totnes.
Champernowne, Rev. R., Dartington.
Chanter, Rev. J. M., Ilfracombe.
Chave, Rev. Dr., Cullompton.
Chichester, Charles. Esq., Hall, Barnstaple.
Chichester, Rev. J. H., Arlington.
Christophers, Rev. S. W., 1 Hayley Terrace, Birmingham.
Churchill, Miss, Drayton, Torquay.
Churchill, Miss F., St. Leonards, Exeter.
Churston, Right. Hon. Lord, Lupton, Brixham.
Clarke, R., Esq., Bridwell, Cullompton.
Clatworthy, Mr., Exeter.
Clifford, Right Hon. Lord, Ugbrooke, Chudleigh (6 copies).
Clifford, Mr., *Bookseller*, Exeter (6 copies).
Clinton, Right Hon. Lord, Heanton Satchville.
Coffin, Sir E. Pine, Bath.
Colborne, Hon. and Rev. Grahame, Dittisham.
Coldridge, Rev. S. P., Budleigh.
Cole, Robert, Esq., 52, Bolsover Street, London.
Cole, W. Cole, Esq., Highfield, Exmouth.
Coleridge, Right Hon. Sir. J. T., Ottery St. Mary.
Coleridge, Rev. F., Eton College.
Coleridge, F. J., Esq., Ottery St. Mary.
Coleridge, Rev. F. J., Cadbury (2 copies).
Coleridge, J. D., Esq., Q.C., Temple, London.
Collins-Splatt, H., Esq., Brixton, Plympton St. Mary.

LIST OF SUBSCRIBERS. 331

Cooper, Mr. G., Exeter (2 copies).
Cope, Rev. Sir W. H., Bramhill, Hartfordbridge.
Copelston, Rev. W. J., Crumhall, Gloucestershire.
Corfe, Rev. J., Exeter.
Cornish, R. S., Esq., Exeter.
Cornish, Rev. Dr., Ottery St. Mary.
Cornish, James, Esq., Blackhall, Totnes.
Cornish, Rev. R. K., Coleridge.
Cornish, Mr., *Bookseller*, Barnstaple (2 copies).
Cotton, W., Esq., Highland House, Ivybridge.
Cotton, R. W., Esq., Barnstaple.
Courtenay, Hon. and Rev. C. L., Bovey Tracey.
Crabbe, W. R., Esq., Heavitree.
Cuming, C. T., Esq., Bradninch.
Curry, W., Esq., Barnstaple.

Damerel, Mr. Exeter.
Danby, W., Esq., Park House, Mount Radford, Exeter.
Daniel, T., Esq., Stoodleigh.
D'Arcy, W. F., Esq., Newton Abbott.
Davidson, Jas., Esq., Secktor, Axminster.
Davie, Sir H. F., Bart., M.P., Creedy, Crediton.
Davies, Robt., Esq., F.S.A., the Mount, York.
Davy, D. B., Esq., Topsham.
Davy, Francis, Esq., Topsham.
Davy, Mrs. Charles, Exeter.
Daw, J., Esq. Exeter.
Dawson, W., Esq., Exeter.
Deane, W. A., Esq., Webbery, Bideford.
De la Garde, P. C., Esq., Exeter.
De la Garde, J. L., Esq., Exeter.
Dene, Rev. Arthur, Horwood.
Devon and Exeter Institution, Exeter.
Devon, the Right Hon. the Earl of, Powderham Castle.
Dinham, Mr. J., Exeter.
Divett, E., Esq., M.P., Bystock, Exmouth.
Divett, J., Esq., Bovey Tracey.
Doe, G., Esq., Torrington.
Downall, Ven. Archdeacon, Okehampton.
Drake, Sir Trayton, Bart., Nutwell Court, Lympston.
Drake, T. E., Esq., Exeter.
Drake, Dr., Exeter.
Drayton, Messrs., *Booksellers*, Exeter (6 copies).
Drew, H., Esq., Peamore, Exeter.
Drew, Mr. W., Bradninch.
Drewe, E. S., Esq., the Grange, Honiton.
Duckworth, Sir J. T. B., Bart., Weir, Exeter.
Durant, R., Esq., Sharpham, Totnes.
Dymond, R., Esq., Exeter.

Eales, C., Esq., Bristol.

332 LIST OF SUBSCRIBERS.

Egremont, Right Hon. the Countess of, Silverton Park (3 copies).
Ellacombe, Rev. H. T., Clyst St. George.
Ellis, H., Esq., Grovelands, Exeter.
Elton, Sir E. M., Bart., Widworthy Court.
Elton, Rev. Dr., Exeter.
Exeter, Right Rev. the Lord Bishop of, Bishopstowe.
Exeter, the Venerable the Dean and Chapter of, Exeter.

Follett, J., Esq., Topsham.
Follett, R. B., Esq., 25, Norfolk Crescent, London.
Ford, Rev. Prebendary, Torquay.
Ford, H., Esq., Exeter.
Fortescue, Right Hon. the Earl, Castle Hill.
Fortescue, Hon. and Rev. J., Poltimore.
Fortescue, Hon. G. M., Boconnoc, Cornwall.
Fortescue, Rev. J. F. C., Burlington Hotel, London.
Fortescue, Rev. R. H., Stockleigh Pomeroy.
Foweraker, Mr. E. T., Cathedral School, Exeter (2 copies).
Franklin, F., Esq., Exeter.
Franklin, H., Esq., Exeter.
Freeman, Rev. Philip, Thorverton.
Friend, Walter, Esq., Exeter.
Froude, W., Esq., Paignton.
Fursdon, Rev. E., Dawlish.

Galton, Rev. J. L., Exeter.
Gard, R. S., Esq., M.P., Exeter (2 copies).
Garratt, J., Esq., Bishop's Court.
Geale, Hamilton, Esq., Temple, London.
Geare, John, Esq., Exeter.
Geaves, J. L., Esq., Heavitree.
Gee, Rev. W., Exeter.
Gibbs, W., Esq., Tyntesford, Bristol (3 copies),
Gibbs, H. H., Esq., St. Dunstan's, Regent's Park, London (2 copies).
Gidley, J., Esq., Exeter.
Gill, Rev. W., Venn, Tavistock.
Godwin, Mr. J., 8, Walton Street, Oxford.
Gould, J., Esq., Highouse, Kenton.
Gould, Daniel, Esq., Honiton.
Gould, Mr. J. B., Exeter.
Granger, Dr., Exeter.
Greenfield, B. W., Esq., Shirley, Southampton.

Haggerston, Lady, Teignmouth.
Hale, the Venerable Archdeacon, London.
Hall, Dr. W., Exeter.
Halliday, Rev. W. J., Glenthorne, Lynton.
Harding, Lt.-Col., Exeter.
Harting, Vincent, Esq., 24, Lincoln's Inn Fields, London (2 copies).
Harding, Rev. J. L., Littleham.
Hare, Miss M. J., Durnford Street, Stonehouse.

LIST OF SUBSCRIBERS.

Harington, Rev. Chancellor, Exeter.
Harris, Rev. Dr., Tor, Torquay.
Harris, C. A., Esq., Hayne, Lifton.
Hartnoll, T. W., Esq., Exeter.
Hawker, Rev. R. S., Morwinstow.
Hayward, J., Esq., Exeter.
Head, R. T., Esq., Exeter.
Heberden, Rev. W., Broadhembury.
Hedgeland, Rev. Philip, Penzance.
Hingeston, Rev. F. C., Ringmore, Ivybridge.
. Hodge, Mr., *Stationer*, Exeter (2 copies).
Hogg, T. D., Esq., Newton Tracey.
Holden, Mr., *Bookseller*, Liverpool (6 copies).
Hole, Rev. N., Broadwoodkelly.
Holmes, G. K., Esq., Budleigh Salterton.
Holroyd, G. C., Esq., Exeter.
Hooper, H., Esq., Exeter.
Howell, Rev. Hinds, Drayton Rectory, Norwich.
Hugo, Rev. J. P., Exminster.
Hugo, Rev. T., 5, Finsbury Circus, London.
Husband, Rev. J. E. Colvile, Bath.
Husband, Mr. M., Exeter.
Hutchinson, Rev. Æneas B., Devonport.
Huyshe, Rev. J., Clysthydon.

Jackson, Rev. W., Weston-super-Mare.
Jackson, Mr. Thomas, Exeter.
Jagoe, R. S., Esq., Crescent, Plymouth.
James, J. H., Esq., Exeter.
James, H. M., Esq., Exeter.
Jesse, J., Esq., Llanbedr Hall, Ruthin.
Jones, Winslow, Esq., Exeter.
Joslin, Mr. J. P., Exeter.

Karslake, Rev. W. H., Meshaw.
Karslake, Rev. J. W., Culmstock.
Karslake, E., Esq., Lincoln's Inn, London.
Karslake, J., Esq., 8, Fig Court, Temple, London.
Kell, W., Esq., F.S.A., Newcastle.
Kelly, Admiral, Saltford House, Bath.
Kelly, Mrs., Filleigh, Chudleigh.
Kekewich, S. T., Esq., M.P., Peamore, Exeter.
Kempe, Rev. J. C., Merton.
Kempe, Arthur, Esq., Exeter.
Kendall, W., Esq., Exeter.
Kennaway, Sir J., Bart., Escot, Ottery St. Mary.
Kennaway, G., Esq., Exeter.
Kennaway, Mark, Esq., Exeter.
Kennaway, W., Esq., the Shrubbery, Exeter.
Kerslake, Mr., *Bookseller*, Bristol.
King, R. J., Esq., Fordton, Crediton.

334 LIST OF SUBSCRIBERS.

Kingdon, Kent, Esq., Exeter.
Kitson, Rev. T., Shiphay.
Kitson, W., Esq., Torquay.
Knight, Rev. T. H., Stoke Canon.
Knight, J. A., Esq., Axminster.

Laidman, C. J., Esq., Exeter.
Latimer, T., Esq., Exeter.
Lawrence, N. H. P., Esq., Ipplepen.
Lee, Rev. Prebendary, Exeter.
Lee, Col., Pennsylvania, Exeter.
Ley, J. P., Esq., Teignmouth.
Ley, Rev. T. H., Rame, Devonport.
Ley, W., Esq., Woodlands, Kenn (2 copies).
Lightfoot, Rev. J. P., Exeter College, Oxford.
Limpenny, Mr., Exeter.
Littleton, Thomas, Esq., M.B., Saltash.
Lloyd, Mr. Horace, Exeter (2 copies).
Luke, H., Esq., Exeter.
Luscombe, J., Esq., Coombe-Royal, Kingsbridge.
Luxmoore, Rev. Charles, Eton College.
Luxton, Rev. J., Bondleigh.
Lyne, Rev. Prebendary, Tywardreath.

Mackay, Lieut.-Col., Fairhill, Exeter.
Maclaine, J., Esq., War Office, Pall Mall, London.
Manley, Mr. W. H., Exeter.
Matthews, H., Esq., Bradninch.
Matthews, Capt., R.N., the Lodge, Sidmouth.
Mayne, Mr., *Bookseller*, Exeter.
Mears, Mr., Exeter (2 copies).
Merivale, Hermann, Esq., Barton Place, Exeter.
Miles, W., Esq., Exeter (6 copies).
Milford, J., Esq., Coaver, Exeter.
Milford, F., Esq., Exeter.
Miller, Dr., the Grove, Exeter.
Moore, W., Denis, Esq., Exeter.
Moore, Mr. W., Exeter.
Mortimer, Mrs., Exeter.
Mountford, J., Esq., Exeter.
Mowbray, Right Hon. J. R., M.P., London.
Mules, H. P., Esq., Honiton.
Munk, W., Esq., M.D., 26, Finsbury Place, London.
Munk, Mr. E., Exeter.

Nagle, Lady H. Chichester, Calverleigh Court, Tiverton.
Ness, Rev. J. D., Morthoe.
Newcastle Literary and Philosophical Society.
Newman, T., Esq., Mamhead.
Newport, Rev. H., Exeter.
Norris, T. G., Esq., Exeter.

LIST OF SUBSCRIBERS. 335

Northcote, Sir Stafford H., Bart., M.P., Pynes, Exeter.
Northcote, Rev. Mowbray, Monkokehampton.
Northmore, J., Esq., Cleeve, Exeter.
Norton, Mr., jun., Exeter.

Ormerod, G. W., Esq., Chagford.

Padley, Rev. C., Bedwell Hall, Nottingham.
Palk, Rev. W. H., Ashcombe.
Palk, Rev. H., Shillingford.
Palmer, Mr., Exeter.
Parker, Mrs., Whiteway, Chudleigh.
Parker, Messrs., *Booksellers*, Oxford.
Pascoe, Rev. T., St. Hilary Vicarage, Marazion.
Pasmore, Mr., Exeter.
Pearse, P., Esq., Penlee, Devonport.
Phillips, W., Esq., Mount Radford, Exeter.
Pigott, Rev. J. T., Fremington.
Pinckney, Rev. R., Cullompton.
Pitman, Rev. W. P., Aveton Gifford.
Podmore, Rev. R. H., St. Columb.
Pollard, Mr. W., Exeter.
Ponsford, Rev. W., Drewsteignton.
Porter, Rev. Reginald, Kenn.
Powley, Mr., St. David's, Exeter.
Prideaux, Sir E. S., Bart., Netherton Hall, Honiton.
Prideaux, G., Esq., Mill Lane, Plymouth.
Prince, Mr., 14, Gray's Place, Brompton, London.
Prior, Rev. John, Lynby Rectory, Nottingham.
Pyke, Rev. J., Parracombe.

Radford, Rev. W. T. A., Down St. Mary.
Rayer, Rev. W., Tiverton.
Roberts, Mr. W., *Bookseller*, Broadgate, Exeter (6 copies).
Roberts, Mr. W. T., *Bookseller*, Exeter.
Rogers, Mrs. Canon, Dix Field, Exeter.
Rolle, Right Hon. Lady, Bicton (4 copies).
Rolle, Hon. Mark, Stevenstone, Torrington.
Roper, Rev. C. R., Mount Radford, Exeter.
Row, W. N., Esq., Cove, Tiverton.
Rowe, Sir Joshua, C.B., 10, Queen Ann Street, Cavendish Square,
  London.
Rowe, Rev, J. J., Mont-le-Grand, Exeter.
Rowe, Mr. Mark, Exeter.
Rowlatt, Rev. J. C., Exeter.

St. Aubyn, J. P., Esq., 35, St. John Street, Bedford Row, London.
Sanders, Rev. Lloyd, Whimple.
Sanders, Rev. H., Sowton.
Sanders, Ralph, Esq., Exeter.
Sanders, F., Esq., Exeter.

336 LIST OF SUBSCRIBERS.

Sanders, E. A., Esq., Exeter.
Saville, Rev. F. A., North Huish.
Scully, Miss, Torquay.
Shaw, Mr., Exeter.
Sheffield, T., Esq., Exeter.
Sheppard, J., Esq., Cowley House, Exeter.
Shapter, Dr., Exeter.
Smirke, E., Esq., *Vice- Warden of the Stannaries*, Cheltenham (2 copies).
Smith, Montague, Esq., M.P., London.
Smyth,Mrs.,4,Cumberland Terrace, Regent's Park, London(2 copies).
Snow, T., Esq., Franklyn, Exeter
Snow, T. M., Esq., Wear Cliff, Exeter.
Southcomb, Rev. Hamilton, Rose Ash.
Spinck, Rev. Marshall, Saltash.
Stevens, J. C. Moore, Esq., Winscott, Torrington.
Stowey, A., Esq., Kenbury, Kenn.
Stucley, Sir G. S., Bart., Hartland Abbey.
Studd, Major General, Oxton House, Kenton.
Sweetland, Miss, Spurbarn, Exeter.
Sydenham, Rev. J. P., Cullompton.

Talbot, Reginald, Esq., Rhode Hill, Lyme.
Tanner, Rev. T., Burlescombe.
Tatham, Rev. Prebendary, Broadoak, Lostwithiel.
Thomas, Rev. C. A. Neville, Chudleigh.
Thomas, Mr. J. L., Exeter.
Tiverton Decanal Library.
Tombs, W., Esq., Exeter.
Toms, Rev. W. H., Combmartin.
Tonar, Mrs., Exeter.
Tonkin, Sir Warwick H., Teignmouth.
Tordiff, J. P., Esq., Hawktor.
Treble, Mr., Exwick, Exeter.
Treby, H. H., Esq., Goodamoor, Plympton.
Trefusis, Hon. Charles, M.P., Heanton Satchville.
Trevelyan, Sir Walter, Bart., Nettlecombe, Taunton.
Tucker, C., Esq., Marlands, Exeter.
Tucker, Capt., Norfolk Villa, Budleigh Salterton.
Tucker, Mr., *Bookseller*, Southmolton.
Tuckett, J., Esq., 66, Great Russell Street, London.
Turner, Mrs., Larkby, Exeter.
Turner, Rev. C. C., Exeter.
Turner, C. H., Esq., Dawlish.
Turquand, Rev. A. P., Ottery St. Mary.
Tyrrell, J., Esq., Newcourt, Exeter.

Vickary, Mr., Exeter.
Vowler, J. N., Esq., Leawood, Bridestowe.

Walker, F. J., Esq., Little Matford, Exeter.
Walkey, Rev. C. E., Clyst St. Lawrence.

LIST OF SUBSCRIBERS. 337

Walkey, J. E. C., Esq., Ide, Exeter.
Walrond, Bethell, Esq., Dulford House, Cullompton.
Warren, F. H., Esq., Exeter.
Warren, Mr., 54, High Street, Exeter.
Way, Albert, Esq., 26, Suffolk Street, Pall Mall (2 copies).
Webb, C. K., Esq., Exeter (2 copies).
Welman, C. Noel, Esq., Norton Manor, Taunton.
Were, J., Esq., Broadclyst.
Wescomb, C., Esq., Exeter.
Wheaton and Co., Messrs., *Booksellers*, Exeter (6 copies).
Whiteway, J. H., Esq., Fishwick House, Teignbridge.
Wilcocks, J. M., Esq., Bartholomew Yard, Exeter.
Wilcocks, J. M., Esq., Spurbarn, Exeter.
Wilkinson, Thos., Esq., 5, Torrington Place, Plymouth.
Williams, Rev. Philip, Rewe.
Williams, J., Esq., Chudleigh.
Wills, Rev. W., Holcombe-Rogus.
Wilmot, Paul, Esq., Clift House, Northam.
Wippell, Mr. C. J., 231, High Street, Exeter.
Wolston, Rev. Christopher, Tor, Newton.
Wood, J., Esq., Courtlands, Lympston.
Woolmer, Mrs., Exeter.
Wrey, Sir Bourchier P., Bart., Tawstock.
Wrey, Mrs., Robert, Wear Cliff, Lyme Regis.

Yarde, T., Esq., Culver House, Chudleigh.
Yonge, J. B., Esq., Puslinch, Yealmpton.
Yule, Rev. J. C. D., Bradford.

CPSIA information can be obtained
at www.ICGtesting.com
Printed in the USA
BVHW041340270622
640732BV00001B/91